GREAT BRITISH SHORT STORIES

Rudolf Stone is a freelance writer and literary enthusiast with a passion for storytelling. He has been writing for over three decades, and his work has appeared in various publications, including literary magazines, blogs and newspapers.

GREAT BRITISH SHORT STORIES

Compiled by **RUDOLF STONE**

RUPA

First published by
Rupa Publications India Pvt. Ltd 2023
7/16, Ansari Road, Daryaganj
New Delhi 110002

Sales Centres:
Bengaluru Chennai
Hyderabad Jaipur Kathmandu
Kolkata Mumbai Prayagraj

P-ISBN: 978-93-5702-655-0
E-ISBN: 978-93-5702-915-5

First impression 2023

10 9 8 7 6 5 4 3 2 1

Printed in India

CONTENTS

THE OLD NURSE'S STORY

Elizabeth Gaskell

You know, my dears, that your mother was an orphan, and an only child; and I dare say you have heard that your grandfather was a clergyman up in Westmoreland, where I come from. I was just a girl in the village school, when, one day, your grandmother came in to ask the mistress if there was any scholar there who would do for a nurse-maid; and mighty proud I was, I can tell ye, when the mistress called me up, and spoke to my being a good girl at my needle, and a steady, honest girl, and one whose parents were very respectable, though they might be poor. I thought I should like nothing better than to serve the pretty young lady, who was blushing as deep as I was, as she spoke of the coming baby, and what I should have to do with it. However, I see you don't care so much for this part of my story, as for what you think is to come, so I'll tell you at once. I was engaged and settled at the parsonage before Miss Rosamond (that was the baby, who is now your mother) was born. To be sure, I had little enough to do with her when she came, for she was never out of her mother's arms, and slept by her all night long; and proud enough was I sometimes when missis trusted her to me. There never was such a baby before or since, though you've all of you been fine enough in your turns; but for sweet, winning ways, you've none of you come up to your mother. She took after her mother, who was a real lady born; a Miss Furnivall, a grand-daughter of Lord Furnivall's, in Northumberland. I believe she had neither brother nor sister, and had been brought up in my lord's family till she had married your grandfather, who was just a curate, son to a shopkeeper in Carlisle—but a clever, fine gentleman as ever was—and one who was a right-down hard worker in his parish, which was very wide, and scattered all abroad over the Westmoreland Fells. When your mother, little Miss Rosamond, was about four or five years old, both her parents died in a fortnight—one after the other. Ah! that was a sad time. My pretty young mistress and me was looking for another baby, when my master came home from one of his long rides, wet and tired, and took the fever he died of; and then she never held up her head again, but just lived to see her dead baby, and have it laid on her breast, before she sighed away her life. My mistress had asked me, on her death-bed, never to leave Miss Rosamond; but if she had never spoken a word, I would have gone with the little child to the end of the world.

The next thing, and before we had well stilled our sobs, the executors and guardians came to settle the affairs. They were my poor young mistress's own cousin, Lord Furnivall, and Mr Esthwaite, my master's brother, a shopkeeper in Manchester; not so well-to-do then as he was afterwards, and with a large family rising about him. Well! I don't know if it were their settling, or because of a letter my mistress wrote on her death-bed to her cousin, my lord; but somehow it was settled that Miss Rosamond and me were to go to Furnivall Manor House, in Northumberland; and my lord spoke as if it had been her mother's wish that she should live with his family, and as if he had no objections, for that one or two more or less could make no difference in so grand a household. So, though that was not the way in which I should have wished the coming of my bright and pretty pet to have been looked at—who was like a sunbeam in any family, be it never so grand—I was well pleased that all the folks in the Dale should stare and admire, when they heard I was going to be young lady's maid at my Lord Furnivall's at Furnivall Manor.

But I made a mistake in thinking we were to go and live where my lord did. It turned out that the family had left Furnivall Manor House fifty years or more. I could not hear that my poor young mistress had ever been there, though she had been brought up in the family; and I was sorry for that, for I should have liked Miss Rosamond's youth to have passed where her mother's had been.

My lord's gentleman, from whom I asked as many questions as I durst, said that the Manor House was at the foot of the Cumberland Fells, and a very grand place; that an old Miss Furnivall, a great-aunt of my lord's, lived there, with only a few servants; but that it was a very healthy place, and my lord had thought that it would suit Miss Rosamond very well for a few years, and that her being there might perhaps amuse his old aunt.

I was bidden by my lord to have Miss Rosamond's things ready by a certain day. He was a stern, proud man, as they say all the Lords Furnivall were; and he never spoke a word more than was necessary. Folk did say he had loved my young mistress; but that, because she knew that his father would object, she would never listen to him, and married Mr Esthwaite; but I don't know. He never married, at any rate. But he never took much notice of Miss Rosamond; which I thought he might have done if he had cared for her dead mother. He sent his gentleman with us to the Manor House, telling him to join him at Newcastle that same evening; so there was no great length of time for him to make us known to all the strangers before he, too, shook us off; and we were left, two lonely young things (I was not eighteen) in the great old Manor House. It seems like yesterday that we drove there. We had left our own dear parsonage very early, and we had both cried as if our hearts would break, though we were travelling in my lord's carriage, which I thought so much of once. And now it was long past noon on a September day, and we stopped to change horses for the last time at a little smoky town, all full of colliers and miners. Miss Rosamond had fallen asleep, but Mr Henry told me to waken her, that she might see the park and the Manor House as we drove up. I thought it rather a pity; but I did what he bade me, for fear he should complain of me to my lord. We had left all signs of a town, or even a village, and were then inside the gates of a large wild park—not like the parks here in the south, but with rocks, and the noise of running water, and gnarled thorn-trees, and old oaks, all white and peeled with age.

The road went up about two miles, and then we saw a great and stately house, with many trees close around it, so close that in some places their branches dragged against the walls when the wind blew, and some hung broken down; for no one seemed to take much charge of the place;—to lop the wood, or to keep the moss-covered carriage-way in order. Only in front of the house all was clear. The great oval drive was without a weed; and neither tree nor creeper was allowed to grow over the long, many-windowed front; at both sides of which a wing projected, which were each the ends of other side fronts; for the house, although it was so desolate, was even grander than I expected. Behind it rose the Fells, which seemed unenclosed and bare enough; and on the left hand of the house, as you stood facing it, was a little, old-fashioned flower-garden, as I found out afterwards. A door opened out upon it from the west front; it had been scooped out of the thick, dark wood for some old Lady Furnivall; but the branches of the great forest-trees had grown and overshadowed it again, and there were very few flowers that would live there at that time.

When we drove up to the great front entrance, and went into the hall, I thought we should be lost—it was so large, and vast, and grand. There was a chandelier all of bronze, hung down from the middle of the ceiling; and I had never seen one before, and looked at it all in amaze. Then, at one end of the hall, was a great fireplace, as large as the sides of the houses in my country, with massy andirons and dogs to hold the wood; and by it were heavy, old-fashioned sofas. At the opposite end of the hall, to the left as you went in—on the western side—was an organ built into the wall, and so large that it filled up the best part of that end. Beyond it, on the same side, was a door; and opposite, on each side of the fireplace, were also doors leading to the east front; but those I never went through as long as I stayed in the house, so I can't tell you what lay beyond.

The afternoon was closing in, and the hall, which had no fire lighted in it, looked dark and gloomy; but we did not stay there a moment. The old servant, who had opened the door for us, bowed to Mr Henry, and took us in through the door at the further side of the great organ, and led us through several smaller halls and passages into the west drawing-room, where he said that Miss Furnivall was sitting. Poor little Miss Rosamond held very tight to me, as if she were scared and lost in that great place; and as for myself, I was not much better. The west drawing-room was very cheerful-looking, with a warm fire in it, and plenty of good, comfortable furniture about. Miss Furnivall was an old lady not far from eighty, I should think, but I do not know. She was thin and tall, and had a face as full of fine wrinkles as if they had been drawn all over it with a needle's point. Her eyes were very watchful, to make up, I suppose, for her being so deaf as to be obliged to use a trumpet. Sitting with her, working at the same great piece of tapestry, was Mrs Stark, her maid and companion, and almost as old as she was. She had lived with Miss Furnivall ever since they both were young, and now she seemed more like a friend than a servant; she looked so cold, and grey, and stony, as if she had never loved or cared for any one; and I don't suppose she did care for any one, except her mistress; and, owing to the great deafness of the latter, Mrs Stark treated her very much as if she were a child. Mr Henry gave some message from my lord, and then he bowed goodbye to us all—taking no notice of my sweet little Miss Rosamond's outstretched hand—and left us standing there, being looked at by the two old ladies through their spectacles.

I was right glad when they rung for the old footman who had shown us in at first, and told him to take us to our rooms. So we went out of that great drawing-room, and into another sitting-room, and out of that, and then up a great flight of stairs, and along a broad gallery—which was something like a library, having books all down one side, and windows and writing-tables all down the other—till we came to our rooms, which I was not sorry to hear were just over the kitchens; for I began to think I should be lost in that wilderness of a house. There was an old nursery, that had been used for all the little lords and ladies long ago, with a pleasant fire burning in the grate, and the kettle boiling on the hob, and tea-things spread out on the table; and out of that room was the night-nursery, with a little crib for Miss Rosamond close to my bed. And old James called up Dorothy, his wife, to bid us welcome; and both he and she were so hospitable and kind, that by-and-by Miss Rosamond and me felt quite at home; and by the time tea was over, she was sitting on Dorothy's knee, and chattering away as fast as her little tongue could go. I soon found out that Dorothy was from Westmoreland, and that bound her and me together, as it were; and I would never wish to meet with kinder people than were old James and his wife. James had lived pretty nearly all his life in my lord's family, and thought there was no one so grand as they. He even looked down a little on his wife; because, till he had married her, she had never lived in any but a farmer's household. But he was very fond of her, as well he might be. They had one servant under them, to do all the rough work. Agnes they called her; and she and me, and James and Dorothy, with Miss Furnivall and Mrs Stark, made up the family; always remembering my sweet little Miss Rosamond! I used to wonder what they had done before she came, they thought so much of her now. Kitchen and drawing-room, it was all the same. The hard, sad Miss Furnivall, and the cold Mrs Stark, looked pleased when she came fluttering in like a bird, playing and pranking hither and thither, with a continual murmur, and pretty prattle of gladness. I am sure, they were sorry many a time when she flitted away into the kitchen, though they were too proud to ask her to stay with them, and were a little surprised at her taste; though to be sure, as Mrs Stark said, it was not to be wondered at, remembering what stock her father had come of. The great, old rambling house was a famous place for little Miss Rosamond. She made expeditions all over it, with me at her heels: all, except the east wing, which was never opened, and whither we never thought of going. But in the western and northern part was many a pleasant room; full of things that were curiosities to us, though they might not have been to people who had seen more. The windows were darkened by the sweeping boughs of the trees, and the ivy which had overgrown them; but, in the green gloom, we could manage to see old china jars and carved ivory boxes, and great heavy books, and, above all, the old pictures!

Once, I remember, my darling would have Dorothy go with us to tell us who they all were; for they were all portraits of some of my lord's family, though Dorothy could not tell us the names of every one. We had gone through most of the rooms, when we came to the old state drawing-room over the hall, and there was a picture of Miss Furnivall; or, as she was called in those days, Miss Grace, for she was the younger sister. Such a beauty she must have been! but with such a set, proud look, and such scorn looking out of her handsome eyes, with her eyebrows just a little raised, as if she wondered how any one could have the impertinence to look at her, and her lip curled at us, as we stood there gazing. She had a dress on, the like of which I had never seen before, but it was all the fashion when she was young: a hat of some soft white stuff like beaver, pulled a little over her brows, and a beautiful plume of feathers sweeping round it on one side; and her gown of blue satin was open in front to a quilted white stomacher.

'Well, to be sure!' said I, when I had gazed my fill. 'Flesh is grass, they do say; but who would have thought that Miss Furnivall had been such an out-and-out beauty, to see her now?'

'Yes,' said Dorothy. 'Folks change sadly. But if what my master's father used to say was true, Miss Furnivall, the elder sister, was handsomer than Miss Grace. Her picture is here somewhere; but, if I show it you, you must never let on, even to James, that you have seen it. Can the little lady hold her tongue, think you?' asked she.

I was not so sure, for she was such a little sweet, bold, open-spoken child, so I set her to hide herself; and then I helped Dorothy to turn a great picture, that leaned with its face towards the wall, and was not hung up as the others were. To be sure, it beat Miss Grace for beauty; and I think, for scornful pride, too, though in that matter it might be hard to choose. I could have looked at it an hour but Dorothy seemed half frightened at having shown it to me, and hurried it back again, and bade me run and find Miss Rosamond, for that there were some ugly places about the house, where she should like ill for the child to go. I was a brave, high-spirited girl, and thought little of what the old woman said, for I liked hide-and-seek as well as any child in the parish; so off I ran to find my little one.

As winter drew on, and the days grew shorter, I was sometimes almost certain that I heard a noise as if some one was playing on the great organ in the hall. I did not hear it every evening; but, certainly, I did very often, usually when I was sitting with Miss Rosamond, after I had put her to bed, and keeping quite still and silent in the bedroom. Then I used to hear it booming and swelling away in the distance. The first night, when I went down to my supper, I asked Dorothy who had been playing music, and James said very shortly that I was a gowk to take the wind soughing among the trees for music; but I saw Dorothy look at him very fearfully, and Bessy, the kitchen-maid, said something beneath her breath, and went quite white. I saw they did not like my question, so I held my peace till I was with Dorothy alone, when I knew I could get a good deal out of her. So, the next day, I watched my time, and I coaxed and asked her who it was that played the organ; for I knew that it was the organ and not the wind well enough, for all I had kept silence before James. But Dorothy had had her lesson, I'll warrant, and never a word could I get from her. So then I tried Bessy, though I had always held my head rather above her, as I was evened to James and Dorothy, and she was little better than their servant. So she said I must never, never tell; and if ever told, I was never to say she had told me; but it was a very strange noise, and she had heard it many a time, but most of all on winter nights, and before storms; and folks did say it was the old lord playing on the great organ in the hall, just as he used to do when he was alive; but who the old lord was, or why he played, and why he played on stormy winter evenings in particular, she either could not or would not tell me. Well! I told you I had a brave heart; and I thought it was rather pleasant to have that grand music rolling about the house, let who would be the player; for now it rose above the great gusts of wind, and wailed and triumphed just like a living creature, and then it fell to a softness most complete, only it was always music, and tunes, so it was nonsense to call it the wind. I thought at first, that it might be Miss Furnivall who played, unknown to Bessy; but one day, when I was in the hall by myself, I opened the organ and peeped all about it and around it, as I had done to the organ in Crosthwaite Church once before, and I saw it was all broken and destroyed inside, though it looked so brave and fine; and then, though it was noon-day, my flesh began to creep a little, and I shut it up, and run away pretty quickly to my own bright nursery; and I did not like hearing the music for some time after that, any more than James and Dorothy did. All this time Miss Rosamond was making herself more and more beloved. The old ladies liked her to dine with them at their early dinner James stood behind Miss Furnivall's chair, and I behind Miss Rosamond's all in state; and, after dinner, she would play about in a corner of the great drawing-room as still as any mouse, while Miss Furnivall slept, and I had my dinner in the kitchen. But she was glad enough to come to me in the nursery afterwards; for, as she said Miss Furnivall was so sad, and Mrs Stark so dull; but she and I were merry enough; and, by-and-by, I got not to care for that weird rolling music, which did one no harm, if we did not know where it came from.

That winter was very cold. In the middle of October the frosts began, and lasted many, many weeks. I remember one day, at dinner, Miss Furnivall lifted up her sad, heavy eyes, and said to Mrs Stark, 'I am afraid we shall have a terrible winter,' in a strange kind of meaning way. But Mrs Stark pretended not to hear, and talked very loud of something else. My little lady and I did not care for the frost; not we! As long as it was dry, we climbed up the steep brows behind the house, and went up on the Fells which were bleak and bare enough, and there we ran races in the fresh, sharp air; and once we came down by a new path, that took us past the two old gnarled holly-trees, which grew about half-way down by the east side of the house. But the days grew shorter and shorter, and the old lord, if it was he, played away, more and more stormily and sadly, on the great organ. One Sunday afternoon—it must have been towards the end of November—I asked Dorothy to take charge of little missy when she came out of the drawing-room, after Miss Furnivall had had her nap; for it was too cold to take her with me to church, and yet I wanted to go, And Dorothy was glad enough to promise and was so fond of the child, that all seemed well; and Bessy and I set off very briskly, though the sky hung heavy and black over the white earth, as if the night had never fully gone away, and the air, though still, was very biting.

'We shall have a fall of snow,' said Bessy to me. And sure enough, even while we were in church, it came down thick, in great large flakes—so thick, it almost darkened the windows. It had stopped snowing before we came out, but it lay soft, thick, and deep beneath our feet, as we tramped home. Before we got to the hall, the moon rose, and I think it was lighter then—what with the moon, and what with the white dazzling snow—than it had been when we went to church, between two and three o'clock. I have not told you that Miss Furnivall and Mrs Stark never went to church; they used to read the prayers together, in their quiet, gloomy way; they seemed to feel the Sunday very long without their tapestry-work to be busy at. So when I went to Dorothy in the kitchen, to fetch Miss Rosamond and take her upstairs with me, I did not much wonder when the old woman told me that the ladies had kept the child with them, and that she had never come to the kitchen, as I had bidden her, when she was tired of behaving pretty in the drawing-room. So I took off my things and went to find her, and bring her to her supper in the nursery. But when I went into the best drawing-room, there sat the two old ladies, very still and quiet, dropping out a word now and then, but looking as if nothing so bright and merry as Miss Rosamond had ever been near them. Still I thought she might be hiding from me; it was one of her pretty ways,—and that she had persuaded them to look as if they knew nothing about her; so I went softly peeping under this sofa and behind that chair, making believe I was sadly frightened at not finding her.

'What's the matter, Hester?' said Mrs Stark sharply. I don't know if Miss Furnivall had seen me for, as I told you, she was very deaf, and she sat quite still, idly staring into the fire, with her hopeless face. 'I'm only looking for my little Rosy Posy,' replied I, still thinking that the child was there, and near me, though I could not see her.

'Miss Rosamond is not here,' said Mrs Stark. 'She went away, more than an hour ago, to find Dorothy.' And she, too, turned and went on looking into the fire.

My heart sank at this, and I began to wish I had never left my darling. I went back to Dorothy and told her. James was gone out for the day, but she, and me, and Bessy took lights, and went up into the nursery first; and then we roamed over the great, large house, calling and entreating Miss Rosamond to come out of her hiding-place, and not frighten us to death in that way. But there was no answer; no sound.

'Oh!' said I, at last, 'can she have got into the east wing and hidden there?'

But Dorothy said it was not possible, for that she herself had never been in there; that the doors were always locked, and my lord's steward had the keys, she believed; at any rate, neither she nor James had ever seen them: so I said I would go back, and see if, after all, she was not hidden in the drawing-room, unknown to the old ladies; and if I found her there, I said, I would whip her well for the fright she had given me; but I never meant to do it. Well, I went back to the west drawing-room, and I told Mrs Stark we could not find her anywhere, and asked for leave to look all about the furniture there, for I thought now that she might have fallen asleep in some warm, hidden corner; but no! we looked—Miss Furnivall got up and looked, trembling all over—and she was nowhere there; then we set off again, every one in the house, and looked in all the places we had searched before, but we could not find her. Miss Furnivall shivered and shook so much, that Mrs Stark took her back into the warm drawing-room; but not before they had made me promise to bring her to them when she was found. Well-a-day! I began to think she never would be found, when I bethought me to look into the great front court, all covered with snow. I was upstairs when I looked out; but, it was such clear moonlight, I could see, quite plain, two little footprints, which might be traced from the hall-door and round the corner of the east wing. I don't know how I got down, but I tugged open the great stiff hall-door, and, throwing the skirt of my gown over my head for a cloak, I ran out. I turned the east corner, and there a black shadow fell on the snow but when I came again into the moonlight, there were the little foot-marks going up—up to the Fells. It was bitter cold; so cold, that the air almost took the skin off my face as I ran; but I ran on, crying to think how my poor little darling must be perished and frightened.

I was within sight of the holly-trees, when I saw a shepherd coming down the hill, bearing something in his arms wrapped in his maud. He shouted to me, and asked me if I had lost a bairn; and, when I could not speak for crying, he bore towards me, and I saw my wee bairnie, lying still, and white, and stiff in his arms, as if she had been dead. He told me he had been up the Fells to gather in his sheep, before the deep cold of night came on, and that under the holly-trees (black marks on the hill-side, where no other bush was for miles around) he had found my little lady—my lamb—my queen—my darling—stiff and cold in the terrible sleep which is frost-begotten. Oh! the joy and the tears of having her in my arms once again I for I would not let him carry her; but took her, maud and all, into my own arms, and held her near my own warm neck and heart, and felt the life stealing slowly back again into her little gentle limbs. But she was still insensible when we reached the hall, and I had no breath for speech. We went in by the kitchen-door.

'Bring the warming-pan,' said I; and I carried her upstairs, and began undressing her by the nursery fire, which Bessy had kept up. I called my little lammie all the sweet and playful names I could think of,—even while my eyes were blinded by my tears; and at last, oh! at length she opened her large blue eyes. Then I put her into her warm bed, and sent Dorothy down to tell Miss Furnivall that all was well; and I made up my mind to sit by my darling's bedside the live-long night. She fell away into a soft sleep as soon as her pretty head had touched the pillow, and I watched by her till morning light; when she wakened up bright and clear—or so I thought at first—and, my dears, so I think now.

She said, that she had fancied that she should like to go to Dorothy, for that both the old ladies were asleep, and it was very dull in the drawing-room; and that, as she was going through the west lobby, she saw the snow through the high window falling—falling—soft and steady; but she wanted to see it lying pretty and white on the ground; so she made her way into the great hall: and then, going to the window, she saw it bright and soft upon the drive; but while she stood there, she saw a little girl, not so old as she was, 'but so pretty,' said my darling; 'and this little girl beckoned to me to come out; and oh, she was so pretty and so sweet, I could not choose but go.' And then this other little girl had taken her by the hand, and side by side the two had gone round the east corner.

'Now you are a naughty little girl, and telling stories,' said I. 'What would your good mamma, that is in heaven, and never told a story in her life, say to her little Rosamond, if she heard her—and I dare say she does—telling stories!'

'Indeed, Hester,' sobbed out my child, 'I'm telling you true. Indeed I am.'

'Don't tell me!' said I, very stern. 'I tracked you by your foot-marks through the snow; there were only yours to be seen: and if you had had a little girl to go hand-in-hand with you up the hill, don't you think the footprints would have gone along with yours?'

'I can't help it, dear, dear Hester,' said she, crying, 'if they did not; I never looked at her feet, but she held my hand fast and tight in her little one, and it was very, very cold. She took me up the Fell-path, up to the holly-trees; and there I saw a lady weeping and crying; but when she saw me, she hushed her weeping, and smiled very proud and grand, and took me on her knee, and began to lull me to sleep, and that's all, Hester—but that is true; and my dear mamma knows it is,' said she, crying. So I thought the child was in a fever, and pretended to believe her, as she went over her story—over and over again, and always the same. At last Dorothy knocked at the door with Miss Rosamond's breakfast; and she told me the old ladies were down in the eating parlour, and that they wanted to speak to me. They had both been into the night-nursery the evening before, but it was after Miss Rosamond was asleep; so they had only looked at her—not asked me any questions.

'I shall catch it,' thought I to myself, as I went along the north gallery. 'And yet,' I thought, taking courage, 'it was in their charge I left her; and it's they that's to blame for letting her steal away unknown and unwatched.' So I went in boldly, and told my story. I told it all to Miss Furnivall, shouting it close to her ear; but when I came to the mention of the other little girl out in the snow, coaxing and tempting her out, and wiling her up to the grand and beautiful lady by the holly-tree, she threw her arms up—her old and withered arms—and cried aloud, 'Oh! Heaven forgive! Have mercy!'

Mrs Stark took hold of her; roughly enough, I thought; but she was past Mrs Stark's management, and spoke to me, in a kind of wild warning and authority.

'Hester! keep her from that child! It will lure her to her death! That evil child! Tell her it is a wicked, naughty child.' Then, Mrs Stark hurried me out of the room; where, indeed, I was glad enough to go; but Miss Furnivall kept shrieking out, 'Oh, have mercy! Wilt Thou never forgive! It is many a long year ago—'

I was very uneasy in my mind after that. I durst never leave Miss Rosamond, night or day, for fear lest she might slip off again, after some fancy or other; and all the more, because I thought I could make out that Miss Furnivall was crazy, from their odd ways about her; and I was afraid lest something of the same kind (which might be in the family, you know) hung over my darling. And the great frost never ceased all this time; and, whenever it was a more stormy night than usual, between the gusts, and through the wind we heard the old lord playing on the great organ. But, old lord, or not, wherever Miss Rosamond went, there I followed; for my love for her, pretty, helpless orphan, was stronger than my fear for the grand and terrible sound. Besides, it rested with me to keep her cheerful and merry, as beseemed her age. So we played together, and wandered together, here and there, and everywhere; for I never dared to lose sight of her again in that large and rambling house. And so it happened, that one afternoon, not long before Christmas-day, we were playing together on the billiard-table in the great hall (not that we knew the right way of playing, but she liked to roll the smooth ivory balls with her pretty hands, and I liked to do whatever she did); and, by-and-by, without our noticing it, it grew dusk indoors, though it was still light in the open air, and I was thinking of taking her back into the nursery, when, all of a sudden, she cried out—

'Look, Hester! Look! there is my poor little girl out in the snow!'

I turned towards the long narrow windows, and there, sure enough, I saw a little girl, less than my Miss Rosamond—dressed all unfit to be out-of-doors such a bitter night—crying, and beating against the window panes, as if she wanted to be let in. She seemed to sob and wail, till Miss Rosamond could bear it no longer, and was flying to the door to open it, when, all of a sudden, and close upon us, the great organ pealed out so loud and thundering, it fairly made me tremble; and all the more, when I remembered me that, even in the stillness of that dead-cold weather, I had heard no sound of little battering hands upon the window-glass, although the phantom child had seemed to put forth all its force; and, although I had seen it wail and cry, no faintest touch of sound had fallen upon my ears. Whether I remembered all this at the very moment, I do not know; the great organ sound had so stunned me into terror; but this I know, I caught up Miss Rosamond before she got the hall-door opened, and clutched her, and carried her away, kicking and screaming, into the large, bright kitchen, where Dorothy and Agnes were busy with their mince-pies.

'What is the matter with my sweet one?' cried Dorothy, as I bore in Miss Rosamond, who was sobbing as if her heart would break.

'She won't let me open the door for my little girl to come in; and she'll die if she is out on the Fells all night. Cruel, naughty Hester,' she said, slapping me; but she might have struck harder, for I had seen a look of ghastly terror on Dorothy's face, which made my very blood run cold.

'Shut the back-kitchen door fast, and bolt it well,' said she to Agnes. She said no more; she gave me raisins and almonds to quiet Miss Rosamond; but she sobbed about the little girl in the snow, and would not touch any of the good things. I was thankful when she cried herself to sleep in bed. Then I stole down to the kitchen, and told Dorothy I had made up my mind. I would carry my darling back to my father's house in Applethwaite; where, if we lived humbly, we lived at peace. I said I had been frightened enough with the old lord's organ-playing; but now that I had seen for myself this little moaning child, all decked out as no child in the neighbourhood could be, beating and battering to get in, yet always without any sound or noise—with the dark wound on its right shoulder; and that Miss Rosamond had known it again for the phantom that had nearly lured her to death (which Dorothy knew was true); I would stand it no longer.

I saw Dorothy change colour once or twice. When I had done, she told me she did not think I could take Miss Rosamond with me, for that she was my lord's ward, and I had no right over her; and she asked me would I leave the child that I was so fond of just for sounds and sights that could do me no harm; and that they had all had to get used to in their turns? I was all in a hot, trembling passion; and I said it was very well for her to talk, that knew what these sights and noises betokened, and that had, perhaps, had something to do with the spectre child while it was alive. And I taunted her so, that she told me all she knew at last; and then I wished I had never been told, for it only made me more afraid than ever.

She said she had heard the tale from old neighbours that were alive when she was first married; when folks used to come to the hall sometimes, before it had got such a bad name on the country side: it might not be true, or it might, what she had been told.

The old lord was Miss Furnivall's father—Miss Grace, as Dorothy called her, for Miss Maude was the elder, and Miss Furnivall by lights. The old lord was eaten up with pride. Such a proud man was never seen or heard of; and his daughters were like him. No one was good enough to wed them, although they had choice enough; for they were the great beauties of their day, as I had seen by their portraits, where they hung in the state drawing-room. But, as the old saying is, 'Pride will have a fall;' and these two haughty beauties fell in love with the same man, and he no better than a foreign musician, whom their father had down from London to play music with him at the Manor House. For, above all things, next to his pride, the old lord loved music. He could play on nearly every instrument that ever was heard of; and it was a strange thing it did not soften him; but he was a fierce, dour old man, and had broken his poor wife's heart with his cruelty, they said. He was mad after music, and would pay any money for it. So he got this foreigner to come; who made such beautiful music, that they said the very birds on the trees stopped their singing to listen. And, by degrees, this foreign gentleman got such a hold over the old lord, that nothing would serve him but that he must come every year; and it was he that had the great organ brought from Holland, and built up in the hall, where it stood now. He taught the old lord to play on it; but many and many a time, when Lord Furnivall was thinking of nothing but his fine organ, and his finer music, the dark foreigner was walking abroad in the woods, with one of the young ladies: now Miss Maude, and then Miss Grace.

Miss Maude won the day and carried off the prize, such as it was; and he and she were married, all unknown to any one; and, before he made his next yearly visit, she had been confined of a little girl at a farm-house on the Moors, while her father and Miss Grace thought she was away at Doncaster Races. But though she was a wife and a mother, she was not a bit softened, but as haughty and as passionate as ever; and perhaps more so, for she was jealous of Miss Grace, to whom her foreign husband paid a deal of court—by way of blinding her—as he told his wife. But Miss Grace triumphed over Miss Maude, and Miss Maude grew fiercer and fiercer, both with her husband and with her sister; and the former—who could easily shake off what was disagreeable, and hide himself in foreign countries—went away a month before his usual time that summer, and half-threatened that he would never come back again. Meanwhile, the little girl was left at the farm-house, and her mother used to have her horse saddled and gallop wildly over the hills to see her once every week, at the very least; for where she loved she loved, and where she hated she hated. And the old lord went on playing—playing on his organ; and the servants thought the sweet music he made had soothed down his awful temper, of which (Dorothy said) some terrible tales could be told. He grew infirm too, and had to walk with a crutch; and his son—that was the present Lord Furnivall's father—was with the army in America, and the other son at sea; so Miss Maude had it pretty much her own way, and she and Miss Grace grew colder and bitterer to each other every day; till at last they hardly ever spoke, except when the old lord was by. The foreign musician came again the next summer, but it was for the last time; for they led him such a life with their jealousy and their passions, that he grew weary, and went away, and never was heard of again. And Miss Maude, who had always meant to have her marriage acknowledged when her father should be dead, was left now a deserted wife, whom nobody knew to have been married, with a child that she dared not own, although she loved it to distraction; living with a father whom she feared, and a sister whom she hated. When the next summer passed over, and the dark foreigner never came, both Miss Maude and Miss Grace grew gloomy and sad; they had a haggard look about them, though they looked handsome as ever. But, by-and-by, Miss Maude brightened; for her father grew more and more infirm, and more than ever carried away by his music, and she and Miss Grace lived almost entirely apart, having separate rooms, the one on the west side, Miss Maude on the east—those very rooms which were now shut up. So she thought she might have her little girl with her, and no one need ever know except those who dared not speak about it, and were bound to believe that it was, as she said, a cottager's child she had taken a fancy to. All this, Dorothy said, was pretty well known; but what came afterwards no one knew, except Miss Grace and Mrs Stark, who was even then her maid, and much more of a friend to her than ever her sister had been. But the servants supposed, from words that were dropped, that Miss Maude had triumphed over Miss Grace, and told her that all the time the dark foreigner had been mocking her with pretended love—he was her own husband. The colour left Miss Grace's cheek and lips that very day for ever, and she was heard to say many a time that sooner or later she would have her revenge; and Mrs Stark was for ever spying about the east rooms.

One fearful night, just after the New Year had come in, when the snow was lying thick and deep; and the flakes were still falling—fast enough to blind any one who might be out and abroad—there was a great and violent noise heard, and the old lord's voice above all, cursing and swearing awfully, and the cries of a little child, and the proud defiance of a fierce woman, and the sound of a blow, and a dead stillness, and moans and wailings, dying away on the hill-side! Then the old lord summoned all his servants, and told them, with terrible oaths, and words more terrible, that his daughter had disgraced herself, and that he had turned her out of doors—her, and her child—and that if ever they gave her help, or food, or shelter, he prayed that they might never enter heaven. And, all the while, Miss Grace stood by him, white and still as any stone; and, when he had ended, she heaved a great sigh, as much as to say her work was done, and her end was accomplished. But the old lord never touched his organ again, and died within the year; and no wonder I for, on the morrow of that wild and fearful night, the shepherds, coming down the Fell side, found Miss Maude sitting, all crazy and smiling, under the holly-trees, nursing a dead child, with a terrible mark on its right shoulder. 'But that was not what killed it,' said Dorothy: 'it was the frost and the cold. Every wild creature was in its hole, and every beast in its fold, while the child and its mother were turned out to wander on the Fells! And now you know all! and I wonder if you are less frightened now?'

I was more frightened than ever; but I said I was not. I wished Miss Rosamond and myself well out of that dreadful house for ever; but I would not leave her, and I dared not take her away. But oh, how I watched her, and guarded her! We bolted the doors, and shut the window-shutters fast, an hour or more before dark, rather than leave them open five minutes too late. But my little lady still heard the weird child crying and mourning; and not all we could do or say could keep her from wanting to go to her, and let her in from the cruel wind and snow. All this time I kept away from Miss Furnivall and Mrs Stark, as much as ever I could; for I feared them—I knew no good could be about them, with their grey, hard faces, and their dreamy eyes, looking back into the ghastly years that were gone. But, even in my fear, I had a kind of pity for Miss Furnivall, at least. Those gone down to the pit can hardly have a more hopeless look than that which was ever on her face. At last I even got so sorry for her—who never said a word but what was quite forced from her—that I prayed for her; and I taught Miss Rosamond to pray for one who had done a deadly sin; but often, when she came to those words, she would listen, and start up from her knees, and say, 'I hear my little girl plaining and crying, very sad,—oh, let her in, or she will die!'

One night—just after New Year's Day had come at last, and the long winter had taken a turn, as I hoped—I heard the west drawing-room bell ring three times, which was the signal for me. I would not leave Miss Rosamond alone, for all she was asleep—for the old lord had been playing wilder than ever—and I feared lest my darling should waken to hear the spectre child; see her I knew she could not. I had fastened the windows too well for that. So I took her out of her bed, and wrapped her up in such outer clothes as were most handy, and carried her down to the drawing-room, where the old ladies sat at their tapestry-work as usual. They looked up when I came in, and Mrs Stark asked, quite astounded, 'Why did I bring Miss Rosamond there, out of her warm bed?' I had begun to whisper, 'Because I was afraid of her being tempted out while I was away, by the wild child in the snow,' when she stopped me short (with a glance at Miss Furnivall), and said Miss Furnivall wanted me to undo some work she had done wrong, and which neither of them could see to unpick. So I laid my pretty dear on the sofa, and sat down on a stool by them, and hardened my heart against them, as I heard the wind rising and howling.

Miss Rosamond slept on sound, for all the wind blew so; and Miss Furnivall said never a word, nor looked round when the gusts shook the windows. All at once she started up to her full height, and put up one hand, as if to bid us listen.

'I hear voices!' said she. 'I hear terrible screams—I hear my father's voice!'

Just at that moment my darling wakened with a sudden start: 'My little girl is crying, oh, how she is crying!' and she tried to get up and go to her, but she got her feet entangled in the blanket, and I caught her up; for my flesh had begun to creep at these noises, which they heard while we could catch no sound. In a minute or two the noises came, and gathered fast, and filled our ears; we, too, heard voices and screams, and no longer heard the winter's wind that raged abroad. Mrs Stark looked at me, and I at her, but we dared not speak. Suddenly Miss Furnivall, went towards the door, out into the ante-room, through the west lobby, and opened the door into the great hall. Mrs Stark followed, and I durst not be left, though my heart almost stopped beating for fear. I wrapped my darling tight in my arms, and went out with them. In the hall the screams were louder than ever; they seemed to come from the east wing—nearer and nearer—close on the other side of the locked-up doors—close behind them. Then I noticed that the great bronze chandelier seemed all alight, though the hall was dim, and that a fire was blazing in the vast hearth-place, though it gave no heat; and I shuddered up with terror, and folded my darling closer to me. But as I did so the east door shook, and she, suddenly struggling to get free from me, cried, 'Hester! I must go. My little girl is there I hear her; she is coming! Hester, I must go!'

I held her tight with all my strength; with a set will, I held her. If I had died, my hands would have grasped her still, I was so resolved in my mind. Miss Furnivall stood listening, and paid no regard to my darling, who had got down to the ground, and whom I, upon my knees now, was holding with both my arms clasped round her neck; she still striving and crying to get free.

All at once, the east door gave way with a thundering crash, as if torn open in a violent passion, and there came into that broad and mysterious light, the figure of a tall old man, with grey hair and gleaming eyes. He drove before him, with many a relentless gesture of abhorrence, a stern and beautiful woman, with a little child clinging to her dress.

'O Hester! Hester!' cried Miss Rosamond; 'it's the lady! the lady below the holly-trees; and my little girl is with her. Hester! Hester! let me go to her; they are drawing me to them. I feel them—I feel them. I must go!'

Again she was almost convulsed by her efforts to get away; but I held her tighter and tighter, till I feared I should do her a hurt; but rather that than let her go towards those terrible phantoms. They passed along towards the great hall-door, where the winds howled and ravened for their prey; but before they reached that, the lady turned; and I could see that she defied the old man with a fierce and proud defiance; but then she quailed—and then she threw up her arms wildly and piteously to save her child—her little child—from a blow from his uplifted crutch.

And Miss Rosamond was torn as by a power stronger than mine, and writhed in my arms, and sobbed (for by this time the poor darling was growing faint).

'They want me to go with them on to the Fells—they are drawing me to them. Oh, my little girl! I would come, but cruel, wicked Hester holds me very tight.' But when she saw the uplifted crutch, she swooned away, and I thanked God for it. Just at this moment—when the tall old man, his hair streaming as in the blast of a furnace, was going to strike the little shrinking child—Miss Furnivall, the old woman by my side, cried out, 'O father! father! spare the little innocent child!' But just then I saw—we all saw—another phantom shape itself, and grow clear out of the blue and misty light that filled the hall; we had not seen her till now, for it was another lady who stood by the old man, with a look of relentless hate and triumphant scorn. That figure was very beautiful to look upon, with a soft, white hat drawn down over the proud brows, and a red and curling lip. It was dressed in an open robe of blue satin. I had seen that figure before. It was the likeness of Miss Furnivall in her youth; and the terrible phantoms moved on, regardless of old Miss Furnivall's wild entreaty,—and the uplifted crutch fell on the right shoulder of the little child, and the younger sister looked on, stony, and deadly serene. But at that moment, the dim lights, and the fire that gave no heat, went out of themselves, and Miss Furnivall lay at our feet stricken down by the palsy—death-stricken.

Yes! she was carried to her bed that night never to rise again. She lay with her face to the wall, muttering low, but muttering always: 'alas! Alas! what is done in youth can never be undone in age! What is done in youth can never be undone in age!'

MRS BADGERY

Wilkie Collins

Is there any law in England which will protect me from Mrs Badgery?

I am a bachelor, and Mrs Badgery is a widow. Let nobody rashly imagine that I am about to relate a common-place grievance, because I have suffered that first sentence to escape my pen. My objection to Mrs Badgery is, not that she is too fond of me, but that she is too fond of the memory of her late husband. She has not attempted to marry me; she would not think of marrying me, even if I asked her. Understand, therefore, if you please, at the outset, that my grievance in relation to this widow lady is a grievance of an entirely new kind.

Let me begin again. I am a bachelor of a certain age. I have a large circle of acquaintance; but I solemnly declare that the late Mr Badgery was never numbered on the list of my friends. I never heard of him in my life; I never knew that he had left a relict; I never set eyes on Mrs Badgery until one fatal morning when I went to see if the fixtures were all right in my new house.

My new house is in the suburbs of London. I looked at it, liked it, took it.

Three times I visited it before I sent my furniture in. Once with a friend, once with a surveyor, once by myself, to throw a sharp eye, as I have already intimated, over the fixtures. The third visit marked the fatal occasion on which I first saw Mrs Badgery. A deep interest attaches to this event, and I shall go into details in describing it.

I rang at the bell of the garden-door. The old woman appointed to keep the house answered it. I directly saw something strange and confused in her face and manner. Some men would have pondered a little and questioned her. I am by nature impetuous and a rusher at conclusions. 'Drunk,' I said to myself, and walked on into the house perfectly satisfied.

I looked into the front parlour. Grate all right, curtain-pole all right, gas chandelier all right. I looked into the back parlour—ditto, ditto, ditto, as we men of business say. I mounted the stairs. Blind on back window right? Yes; blind on back window right. I opened the door of the front drawing-room—and there, sitting in the middle of the bare floor, was a large woman on a little camp-stool! She was dressed in the deepest mourning; her face was hidden by the thickest crape veil I ever saw; and she was groaning softly to herself in the desolate solitude of my new unfurnished house.

What did I do? Do! I bounced back into the landing as if I had been shot, uttering the national exclamation of terror and astonishment, 'Hullo!' (And here I particularly beg, in parenthesis, that the printer will follow my spelling of the word, and not put Hillo or Halloa instead, both of which are senseless compromises which represent no sound that ever yet issued from an Englishman's lips.) I said, 'Hullo!' and then I turned round fiercely upon the old woman who kept the house, and said 'Hullo!' again.

She understood the irresistible appeal that I had made to her feelings, and curtseyed, and looked towards the drawing-room, and humbly hoped that I was not startled or put out. I asked who the crape-covered woman on the camp-stool was, and what she wanted there. Before the old woman could answer, the soft groaning in the drawing-room ceased, and a muffled voice, speaking from behind the crape veil, addressed me reproachfully, and said:

'I am the widow of the late Mr Badgery.'

What did I say in answer? Exactly the words which, I flatter myself, any other sensible man in my situation would have said. And what words were they? These two:

'Oh, indeed?'

'Mr Badgery and myself were the last tenants who inhabited this house,' continued the muffled voice. 'Mr Badgery died here.' The voice ceased, and the soft groans began again.

It was perhaps not necessary to answer this; but I did answer it. How? In one word:

'Ha!'

'Our house has been long empty,' resumed the voice, choked by sobs. 'Our establishment has been broken up. Being left in reduced circumstances, I now live in a cottage near; but it is not home to me. This is home. However long I live, wherever I go, whatever changes may happen to this beloved house, nothing can ever prevent me from looking on it as *my* home. I came here, sir, with Mr Badgery after our honey-moon. All the brief happiness of my life was once contained within these four walls. Every dear remembrance that I fondly cherish is shut up in these sacred rooms.'

Again the voice ceased, and again the soft groans echoed round my empty walls, and oozed out past me down my uncarpeted staircase.

I reflected. Mrs Badgery's brief happiness and dear remembrances were not included in the list of fixtures. Why could she not take them away with her? Why should she leave them littered about in the way of my furniture? I was just thinking how I could put this view of the case strongly to Mrs Badgery, when she suddenly left off groaning and addressed me once more.

'While this house has been empty,' she said, 'I have been in the habit of looking in from time to time, and renewing my tender associations with the place. I have lived, as it were, in the sacred memories of Mr Badgery and of the past, which these dear, these priceless rooms call up, dismantled and dusty as they are at the present moment. It has been my practice to give a remuneration to the attendant for any slight trouble that I might occasion—'

'Only sixpence, sir,' whispered the old woman, close at my ear. 'And to ask nothing in return,' continued Mrs Badgery, 'but the permission to bring my camp-stool with me, and to meditate on Mr Badgery in the empty rooms, with every one of which some happy thought, or eloquent word, or tender action of his, is so sweetly associated. I came here on my usual errand to-day. I am discovered, I presume, by the new proprietor of the house—discovered, I am quite ready to admit, as an intruder. I am willing to go, if you wish it after hearing my explanation. My heart is full, sir; I am quite incapable of contending with you. You would hardly think it, but I am sitting on the spot once occupied by our ottoman. I am looking towards the window in which my flower-stand once stood. In this very place Mr Badgery first sat down and clasped me to his heart, when we came back from our honey-moon trip. "Matilda," he said, "your drawing-room has been expensively papered, carpeted, and furnished for a month; but it has only been adorned, love, since you entered it." If you have no sympathy, sir, for such remembrances as these; if you see nothing pitiable in my position, taken in connection with my presence here; if you cannot enter into my feelings, and thoroughly understand that this is not a house, but a Shrine—you have only to say so, and I am quite willing to go.'

She spoke with the air of a martyr—a martyr to my insensibility. If she had been the proprietor and I had been the intruder, she could not have been more mournfully magnanimous. All this time, too, she never raised her veil—she never has raised it, in my presence, from that time to this. I have no idea whether she is young or old, dark or fair, handsome or ugly: my impression is, that she is in every respect a finished and perfect Gorgon; but I have no basis of fact on which I can support that dismal idea. A moving mass of crape and a muffled voice—that, if you drive me to it, is all I know, in a personal point of view, of Mrs Badgery.

'Ever since my irreparable loss, this has been the shrine of my pilgrimage, and the altar of my worship,' proceeded the voice. 'One man may call himself a landlord, and say that he will let it; another man may call himself a tenant, and say that he will take it. I don't blame either of those two men; I don't wish to intrude on either of those two men; I only tell them that this is my home; that my heart is still in possession, and that no mortal laws, landlords, or tenants can ever turn it out. If you don't understand this, sir; if the holiest feelings that do honour to our common nature have no particular sanctity in your estimation, pray do not scruple to say so; pray tell me to go.'

'I don't wish to do anything uncivil, ma'am,' said I. 'But I am a single man, and I am not sentimental.' (Mrs Badgery groaned.) 'Nobody told me I was coming into a Shrine when I took this house; nobody warned me, when I first went over it, that there was a Heart in possession. I regret to have disturbed your meditations, and I am sorry to hear that Mr Badgery is dead. That is all I have to say about it; and, now, with your kind permission, I will do myself the honour of wishing you good morning, and will go up-stairs to look after the fixtures on the second floor.'

Could I have given a gentler hint than this? Could I have spoken more compassionately to a woman whom I sincerely believe to be old and ugly? Where is the man to be found who can lay his hand on his heart and honestly say that he ever really pitied the sorrows of a Gorgon? Search through the whole surface of the globe, and you will discover human phenomena of all sorts; but you will not find that man.

To resume. I made her a bow, and left her on the camp-stool in the middle of the drawing-room floor, exactly as I had found her. I ascended to the second floor, walked into the back room first, and inspected the grate. It appeared to be a little out of repair, so I stooped down to look at it closer. While I was kneeling over the bars, I was violently startled by the fall of one large drop of warm water, from a great height, exactly in the middle of a bald place, which has been widening a great deal of late years on the top of my head. I turned on my knees, and looked round. Heaven and earth! the crape-covered woman had followed me up-stairs—the source from which the drop of warm water had fallen was no other than Mrs Badgery's eye!

'I wish you could contrive not to cry over the top of my head, ma'am,' said I. My patience was becoming exhausted, and I spoke with considerable asperity. The curly-headed youth of the present age may not be able to sympathize with my feelings on this occasion; but my bald brethren know as well as I do that the most unpardonable of all liberties is a liberty taken with the unguarded top of the human head.

Mrs Badgery did not seem to hear me. When she had dropped the tear, she was standing exactly over me, looking down at the grate; and she never stirred an inch after I had spoken. 'Don't cry over my head, ma'am,' I repeated, more irritably than before.

'This was his dressing-room,' said Mrs Badgery, indulging in muffled soliloquy. 'He was singularly particular about his shaving-water. He always liked to have it in a little tin pot, and he invariably desired that it might be placed on this hob.' She groaned again, and tapped one side of the grate with the leg of her camp-stool.

If I had been a woman, or if Mrs Badgery had been a man, I should now have proceeded to extremities, and should have vindicated my right to my own house by an appeal to physical force. Under existing circumstances, all that I could do was to express my indignation by a glance. The glance produced not the slightest result—and no wonder. Who can look at a woman with any effect through a crape veil?

I retreated into the second-floor front room, and instantly shut the door after me. The next moment I heard the rustling of the crape garments outside, and the muffled voice of Mrs Badgery poured lamentably through the keyhole. 'Do you mean to make that your bedroom?' asked the voice on the other side of the door. 'Oh, don't, don't make that your bedroom! I am going away directly—but, oh pray, pray let that one room be sacred! Don't sleep there! If you can possibly help it, don't sleep there!'

I opened the window, and looked up and down the road. If I had seen a policeman within hail I should certainly have called him in. No such person was visible. I shut the window again, and warned Mrs Badgery, through the door, in my sternest tones, not to interfere with my domestic arrangements. 'I mean to have my bedstead put up here,' I said. 'And what is more, I mean to sleep here. And what is more, I mean to snore here!' Severe, I think, that last sentence? It completely crushed Mrs Badgery for the moment. I heard the crape garments rustling away from the door; I heard the muffled groans going slowly and solemnly down the stairs again.

In due course of time I also descended to the ground-floor. Had Mrs Badgery really left the premises? I looked into the front parlour—empty. Back parlour—empty. Any other room on the ground-floor? Yes; a long room at the end of the passage. The door was closed. I opened it cautiously, and peeped in. A faint scream, and a smack of two distractedly-clasped hands saluted my appearance. There she was, again on the camp-stool, again sitting exactly in the middle of the floor.

'Don't, don't look in, in that way!' cried Mrs Badgery, wringing her hands. 'I could bear it in any other room, but I can't bear it in this. Every Monday morning I looked out the things for the wash in this room. He was difficult to please about his linen; the washerwoman never put starch enough into his collars to satisfy him. Oh, how often and often has he popped his head in here, as you popped yours just now; and said, in his amusing way, "More starch!" Oh, how droll he always was—how very, very droll in this dear little back room!'

I said nothing. The situation had now got beyond words. I stood with the door in my hand, looking down the passage towards the garden, and waiting doggedly for Mrs Badgery to go out. My plan succeeded. She rose, sighed, shut up the camp-stool, stalked along the passage, paused on the hall mat, said to herself, 'Sweet, sweet spot!' descended the steps, groaned along the gravel-walk, and disappeared from view at last through the garden-door.

'Let her in again at your peril!' said I to the woman who kept the house. She curtseyed and trembled. I left the premises, satisfied with my own conduct under very trying circumstances; delusively convinced also that I had done with Mrs Badgery.

The next day I sent in the furniture. The most unprotected object on the face of this earth is a house when the furniture is going in. The doors must be kept open; and employ as many servants as you may, nobody can be depended on as a domestic sentry so long as the van is at the gate. The confusion of 'moving in' demoralizes the steadiest disposition, and there is no such thing as a properly-guarded post from the top of the house to the bottom. How the invasion was managed, how the surprise was effected, I know not; but it is certainly the fact that, when my furniture went in, the inevitable Mrs Badgery went in along with it.

I have some very choice engravings, after the old masters; and I was first awakened to a consciousness of Mrs Badgery's presence in the house while I was hanging up my proof impression of Titian's Venus over the front- parlour fireplace. 'Not there!' cried the muffled voice, imploringly. '*His* portrait used to hang there. Oh, what a print—what a dreadful, dreadful print to put where *his* dear portrait used to be!' I turned round in a fury. There she was, still muffled up in crape, still carrying her abominable camp-stool. Before I could say a word in remonstrance, six men in green baize aprons staggered in with my sideboard, and Mrs Badgery suddenly disappeared. Had they trampled her under foot, or crushed her in the doorway? Though not an inhuman man by nature, I asked myself those questions quite composedly. No very long time elapsed before they were practically answered in the negative by the re-appearance of Mrs Badgery herself, in a perfectly unruffled condition of chronic grief. In the course of the day I had my toes trodden on, I was knocked about by my own furniture, the six men in baize aprons dropped all sorts of small articles over me in going up and down stairs; but Mrs Badgery escaped unscathed. Every time I thought she had been turned out of the house she proved, on the contrary, to be groaning close behind me. She wept over Mr Badgery's memory in every room, perfectly undisturbed to the last by the chaotic confusion of moving in. I am not sure, but I think she brought a tin box of sandwiches with her, and celebrated a tearful pic-nic of her own in the groves of my front garden. I say I am not sure of this; but I am positively certain that I never entirely got rid of her all day; and I know to my cost that she insisted on making me as well acquainted with Mr Badgery's favourite notions and habits as I am with my own. It may interest the reader if I report that my taste in carpets is not equal to Mr Badgery's; that my ideas on the subject of servants' wages are not so generous as Mr Badgery's; and that I ignorantly persisted in placing a sofa in the position which Mr Badgery, in his time, considered to be particularly fitted for an arm-chair. I could go nowhere, look nowhere, do nothing, say nothing, all that day, without bringing the widowed incubus in the crape garments down upon me immediately. I tried civil remonstrances, I tried rude speeches, I tried sulky silence—nothing had the least effect on her. The memory of Mr Badgery was the shield of proof with which she warded off my fiercest attacks. Not till the last article of furniture had been moved in did I lose sight of her; and even then she had not really left the house. One of my six men in green baize aprons routed her out of the back-garden area, where she was telling my servants, with floods of tears, of Mr Badgery's virtuous strictness with his housemaid in the matter of followers. My admirable man in green baize courageously saw her out, and shut the garden-door after her. I gave him half-a-crown on the spot; and if anything happens to him, I am ready to make the future prosperity of his fatherless family my own peculiar care.

The next day was Sunday, and I attended morning service at my new parish church. A popular preacher had been announced, and the building was crowded. I advanced a little way up the nave, and looked to my right, and saw no room. Before I could look to my left, I felt a hand laid persuasively on my arm. I turned round—and there was Mrs Badgery, with her pew-door open, solemnly beckoning me in. The crowd had closed up behind me; the eyes of a dozen members of the congregation, at least, were fixed on me. I had no choice but to save appearances, and accept the dreadful invitation. There was a vacant place next to the door of the pew. I tried to drop into it, but Mrs Badgery stopped me. '*His* seat,' she whispered, and signed to me to place myself on the other side of her. It is unnecessary to say that I had to climb over a hassock, and that I knocked down all Mrs Badgery's devotional books before I succeeded in passing between her and the front of the pew. She cried uninterruptedly through the service; composed herself when it was over; and began to tell me what Mr Badgery's opinions had been on points of abstract theology. Fortunately there was great confusion and crowding at the door of the church; and I escaped, at the hazard of my life, by running round the back of the carriages. I passed the interval between the services alone in the fields, being deterred from going home by the fear that Mrs Badgery might have got there before me.

Monday came. I positively ordered my servants to let no lady in deep mourning pass inside the garden-door without first consulting me. After that, feeling tolerably secure, I occupied myself in arranging my books and prints. I had not pursued this employment much more than an hour, when one of the servants burst excitably into the room, and informed me that a lady in deep mourning had been taken faint, just outside my door, and had requested leave to come in and sit down for a few moments. I ran down the garden-path to bolt the door, and arrived just in time to see it violently pushed open by an officious and sympathizing crowd. They drew away on either side as they saw me. There she was, leaning on the grocer's shoulder, with the butcher's boy in attendance, carrying her camp-stool! Leaving my servants to do what they liked with her, I ran back and locked myself up in my bedroom. When she evacuated the premises, some hours afterwards, I received a message of apology, informing me that this particular Monday was the sad anniversary of her wedding-day, and that she had been taken faint, in consequence, at the sight of her lost husband's house.

Tuesday forenoon passed away happily, without any new invasion. After lunch I thought I would go out and take a walk. My garden-door has a sort of peep-hole in it, covered with a wire grating. As I got close to this grating, I thought I saw something mysteriously dark on the outer side of it. I bent my head down to look through, and instantly found myself face to face with the crape veil. 'Sweet, sweet spot!' said the muffled voice, speaking straight into my eyes through the grating. The usual groans followed, and the name of Mr Badgery was plaintively pronounced before I could recover myself sufficiently to retreat to the house.

Wednesday is the day on which I am writing this narrative. It is not twelve o'clock yet, and there is every probability that some new form of sentimental persecution is in store for me before the evening. Thus far, these lines contain a perfectly true statement of Mrs Badgery's conduct towards me since I entered on the possession of *my* house and *her* shrine. What am I to do?—that is the point I wish to insist on—what am I to do? How am I to get away from the memory of Mr Badgery, and the unappeasable grief of his disconsolate widow? Any other species of invasion it is possible to resist; but how is a man placed in my unhappy and unparalleled circumstances to defend himself? I can't keep a dog ready to fly at Mrs Badgery. I can't charge her at a police-court with being oppressively fond of the house in which her husband died. I can't set man-traps for a woman, or prosecute a weeping widow as a trespasser and a nuisance. I am helplessly involved in the unrelaxing folds of Mrs Badgery's crape veil. Surely there was no exaggeration in my language when I said that I was a sufferer under a perfectly new grievance! Can anybody advise me? Has anybody had even the faintest and remotest experience of the peculiar form of persecution under which I am now suffering? If nobody has, is there any legal gentleman in the United Kingdom who can answer the all-important question which appears at the head of this narrative? I began by asking that question because it was uppermost in my mind. It is uppermost in my mind still, and I therefore beg leave to conclude appropriately by asking it again:

Is there any law in England which will protect me from Mrs Badgery?

THE SIGNAL-MAN

Charles Dickens

'Halloa! Below there!'

When he heard a voice thus calling to him, he was standing at the door of his box, with a flag in his hand, furled round its short pole. One would have thought, considering the nature of the ground, that he could not have doubted from what quarter the voice came; but instead of looking up to where I stood on the top of the steep cutting nearly over his head, he turned himself about, and looked down the Line. There was something remarkable in his manner of doing so, though I could not have said for my life what. But I know it was remarkable enough to attract my notice, even though his figure was foreshortened and shadowed, down in the deep trench, and mine was high above him, so steeped in the glow of an angry sunset, that I had shaded my eyes with my hand before I saw him at all.

'Halloa! Below!'

From looking down the Line, he turned himself about again, and, raising his eyes, saw my figure high above him.

'Is there any path by which I can come down and speak to you?'

He looked up at me without replying, and I looked down at him without pressing him too soon with a repetition of my idle question. Just then there came a vague vibration in the earth and air, quickly changing into a violent pulsation, and an oncoming rush that caused me to start back, as though it had force to draw me down. When such vapour as rose to my height from this rapid train had passed me, and was skimming away over the landscape, I looked down again, and saw him refurling the flag he had shown while the train went by.

I repeated my inquiry. After a pause, during which he seemed to regard me with fixed attention, he motioned with his rolled-up flag towards a point on my level, some two or three hundred yards distant. I called down to him, 'All right!' and made for that point. There, by dint of looking closely about me, I found a rough zigzag descending path notched out, which I followed.

The cutting was extremely deep, and unusually precipitate. It was made through a clammy stone, that became oozier and wetter as I went down. For these reasons, I found the way long enough to give me time to recall a singular air of reluctance or compulsion with which he had pointed out the path.

When I came down low enough upon the zigzag descent to see him again, I saw that he was standing between the rails on the way by which the train had lately passed, in an attitude as if he were waiting for me to appear. He had his left hand at his chin, and that left elbow rested on his right hand, crossed over his breast. His attitude was one of such expectation and watchfulness that I stopped a moment, wondering at it.

I resumed my downward way, and stepping out upon the level of the railroad, and drawing nearer to him, saw that he was a dark, sallow man, with a dark beard and rather heavy eyebrows. His post was in as solitary and dismal a place as ever I saw. On either side, a dripping-wet wall of jagged stone, excluding all view but a strip of sky; the perspective one way only a crooked prolongation of this great dungeon; the shorter perspective in the other direction terminating in a gloomy red light, and the gloomier entrance to a black tunnel, in whose massive architecture there was a barbarous, depressing, and forbidding air. So little sunlight ever found its way to this spot, that it had an earthy, deadly smell; and so much cold wind rushed through it, that it struck chill to me, as if I had left the natural world.

Before he stirred, I was near enough to him to have touched him. Not even then removing his eyes from mine, he stepped back one step, and lifted his hand.

This was a lonesome post to occupy (I said), and it had riveted my attention when I looked down from up yonder. A visitor was a rarity, I should suppose; not an unwelcome rarity, I hoped? In me, he merely saw a man who had been shut up within narrow limits all his life, and who, being at last set free, had a newly-awakened interest in these great works. To such purpose I spoke to him; but I am far from sure of the terms I used; for, besides that I am not happy in opening any conversation, there was something in the man that daunted me.

He directed a most curious look towards the red light near the tunnel's mouth, and looked all about it, as if something were missing from it, and then looked at me.

That light was part of his charge? Was it not?

He answered in a low voice,—'Don't you know it is?'

The monstrous thought came into my mind, as I perused the fixed eyes and the saturnine face, that this was a spirit, not a man. I have speculated since, whether there may have been infection in his mind.

In my turn, I stepped back. But in making the action, I detected in his eyes some latent fear of me. This put the monstrous thought to flight.

'You look at me,' I said, forcing a smile, 'as if you had a dread of me.'

'I was doubtful,' he returned, 'whether I had seen you before.'

'Where?'

He pointed to the red light he had looked at.

'There?' I said.

Intently watchful of me, he replied (but without sound), 'Yes.'

'My good fellow, what should I do there? However, be that as it may, I never was there, you may swear.'

'I think I may,' he rejoined. 'Yes; I am sure I may.'

His manner cleared, like my own. He replied to my remarks with readiness, and in well-chosen words. Had he much to do there? Yes; that was to say, he had enough responsibility to bear; but exactness and watchfulness were what was required of him, and of actual work—manual labour—he had next to none. To change that signal, to trim those lights, and to turn this iron handle now and then, was all he had to do under that head. Regarding those many long and lonely hours of which I seemed to make so much, he could only say that the routine of his life had shaped itself into that form, and he had grown used to it. He had taught himself a language down here,—if only to know it by sight, and to have formed his own crude ideIs of its pronunciation, could be called learning it. He had also worked at fractions and decimals, and tried a little algebra; but he was, and had been as a boy, a poor hand at figures. Was it necessary for him when on duty always to remain in that channel of damp air, and could he never rise into the sunshine from between those high stone walls? Why, that depended upon times and circumstances. Under some conditions there would be less upon the Line than under others, and the same held good as to certain hours of the day and night. In bright weather, he did choose occasions for getting a little above these lower shadows; but, being at all times liable to be called by his electric bell, and at such times listening for it with redoubled anxiety, the relief was less than I would suppose.

He took me into his box, where there was a fire, a desk for an official book in which he had to make certain entries, a telegraphic instrument with its dial, face, and needles, and the little bell of which he had spoken. On my trusting that he would excuse the remark that he had been well educated, and (I hoped I might say without offence) perhaps educated above that station, he observed that instances of slight incongruity in such wise would rarely be found wanting among large bodies of men; that he had heard it was so in workhouses, in the police force, even in that last desperate resource, the army; and that he knew it was so, more or less, in any great railway staff. He had been, when young (if I could believe it, sitting in that hut,—he scarcely could), a student of natural philosophy, and had attended lectures; but he had run wild, misused his opportunities, gone down, and never risen again. He had no complaint to offer about that. He had made his bed, and he lay upon it. It was far too late to make another.

All that I have here condensed he said in a quiet manner, with his grave, dark regards divided between me and the fire. He threw in the word, 'Sir,' from time to time, and especially when he referred to his youth,—as though to request me to understand that he claimed to be nothing but what I found him. He was several times interrupted by the little bell, and had to read off messages, and send replies. Once he had to stand without the door, and display a flag as a train passed, and make some verbal communication to the driver. In the discharge of his duties, I observed him to be remarkably exact and vigilant, breaking off his discourse at a syllable, and remaining silent until what he had to do was done.

In a word, I should have set this man down as one of the safest of men to be employed in that capacity, but for the circumstance that while he was speaking to me he twice broke off with a fallen colour, turned his face towards the little bell when it did NOT ring, opened the door of the hut (which was kept shut to exclude the unhealthy damp), and looked out towards the red light near the mouth of the tunnel. On both of those occasions, he came back to the fire with the inexplicable air upon him which I had remarked, without being able to define, when we were so far asunder.

Said I, when I rose to leave him, 'You almost make me think that I have met with a contented man.'

(I am afraid I must acknowledge that I said it to lead him on.)

'I believe I used to be so,' he rejoined, in the low voice in which he had first spoken; 'but I am troubled, sir, I am troubled.'

He would have recalled the words if he could. He had said them, however, and I took them up quickly.

'With what? What is your trouble?'

'It is very difficult to impart, sir. It is very, very difficult to speak of. If ever you make me another visit, I will try to tell you.'

'But I expressly intend to make you another visit. Say, when shall it be?'

'I go off early in the morning, and I shall be on again at ten to-morrow night, sir.'

'I will come at eleven.'

He thanked me, and went out at the door with me. 'I'll show my white light, sir,' he said, in his peculiar low voice, 'till you have found the way up. When you have found it, don't call out! And when you are at the top, don't call out!'

His manner seemed to make the place strike colder to me, but I said no more than, 'Very well.'

'And when you come down to-morrow night, don't call out! Let me ask you a parting question. What made you cry, "Halloa! Below there!" to-night?'

'Heaven knows,' said I. 'I cried something to that effect—'

'Not to that effect, sir. Those were the very words. I know them well.'

'Admit those were the very words. I said them, no doubt, because I saw you below.'

'For no other reason?'

'What other reason could I possibly have?'

'You had no feeling that they were conveyed to you in any supernatural way?'

'No.'

He wished me good-night, and held up his light. I walked by the side of the down Line of rails (with a very disagreeable sensation of a train coming behind me) until I found the path. It was easier to mount than to descend, and I got back to my inn without any adventure.

Punctual to my appointment, I placed my foot on the first notch of the zigzag next night, as the distant clocks were striking eleven. He was waiting for me at the bottom, with his white light on. 'I have not called out,' I said, when we came close together; 'may I speak now?' 'By all means, sir.' 'Good-night, then, and here's my hand.' 'Good-night, sir, and here's mine.' With that we walked side by side to his box, entered it, closed the door, and sat down by the fire.

'I have made up my mind, sir,' he began, bending forward as soon as we were seated, and speaking in a tone but a little above a whisper, 'that you shall not have to ask me twice what troubles me. I took you for some one else yesterday evening. That troubles me.'

'That mistake?'

'No. That some one else.'

'Who is it?'

'I don't know.'

'Like me?'

'I don't know. I never saw the face. The left arm is across the face, and the right arm is waved,—violently waved. This way.'

I followed his action with my eyes, and it was the action of an arm gesticulating, with the utmost passion and vehemence, 'For God's sake, clear the way!'

'One moonlight night,' said the man, 'I was sitting here, when I heard a voice cry, "Halloa! Below there!" I started up, looked from that door, and saw this Some one else standing by the red light near the tunnel, waving as I just now showed you. The voice seemed hoarse with shouting, and it cried, "Look out! Look out!" And then again, "Halloa! Below there! Look out!" I caught up my lamp, turned it on red, and ran towards the figure, calling, "What's wrong? What has happened? Where?" It stood just outside the blackness of the tunnel. I advanced so close upon it that I wondered at its keeping the sleeve across its eyes. I ran right up at it, and had my hand stretched out to pull the sleeve away, when it was gone.'

'Into the tunnel?' said I.

'No. I ran on into the tunnel, five hundred yards. I stopped, and held my lamp above my head, and saw the figures of the measured distance, and saw the wet stains stealing down the walls and trickling through the arch. I ran out again faster than I had run in (for I had a mortal abhorrence of the place upon me), and I looked all round the red light with my own red light, and I went up the iron ladder to the gallery atop of it, and I came down again, and ran back here. I telegraphed both ways, "An alarm has been given. Is anything wrong?" The answer came back, both ways, "All well."'

Resisting the slow touch of a frozen finger tracing out my spine, I showed him how that this figure must be a deception of his sense of sight; and how that figures, originating in disease of the delicate nerves that minister to the functions of the eye, were known to have often troubled patients, some of whom had become conscious of the nature of their affliction, and had even proved it by experiments upon themselves. 'As to an imaginary cry,' said I, 'do but listen for a moment to the wind in this unnatural valley while we speak so low, and to the wild harp it makes of the telegraph wires.'

That was all very well, he returned, after we had sat listening for a while, and he ought to know something of the wind and the wires,—he who so often passed long winter nights there, alone and watching. But he would beg to remark that he had not finished.

I asked his pardon, and he slowly added these words, touching my arm,—

'Within six hours after the Appearance, the memorable accident on this Line happened, and within ten hours the dead and wounded were brought along through the tunnel over the spot where the figure had stood.'

A disagreeable shudder crept over me, but I did my best against it. It was not to be denied, I rejoined, that this was a remarkable coincidence, calculated deeply to impress his mind. But it was unquestionable that remarkable coincidences did continually occur, and they must be taken into account in dealing with such a subject. Though to be sure I must admit, I added (for I thought I saw that he was going to bring the objection to bear upon me), men of common sense did not allow much for coincidences in making the ordinary calculations of life.

He again begged to remark that he had not finished.

I again begged his pardon for being betrayed into interruptions.

'This,' he said, again laying his hand upon my arm, and glancing over his shoulder with hollow eyes, 'was just a year ago. Six or seven months passed, and I had recovered from the surprise and shock, when one morning, as the day was breaking, I, standing at the door, looked towards the red light, and saw the spectre again.' He stopped, with a fixed look at me.

'Did it cry out?'

'No. It was silent.'

'Did it wave its arm?'

'No. It leaned against the shaft of the light, with both hands before the face. Like this.'

Once more I followed his action with my eyes. It was an action of mourning. I have seen such an attitude in stone figures on tombs.

'Did you go up to it?'

'I came in and sat down, partly to collect my thoughts, partly because it had turned me faint. When I went to the door again, daylight was above me, and the ghost was gone.'

'But nothing followed? Nothing came of this?'

He touched me on the arm with his forefinger twice or thrice giving a ghastly nod each time:—

'That very day, as a train came out of the tunnel, I noticed, at a carriage window on my side, what looked like a confusion of hands and heads, and something waved. I saw it just in time to signal the driver, Stop! He shut off, and put his brake on, but the train drifted past here a hundred and fifty yards or more. I ran after it, and, as I went along, heard terrible screams and cries. A beautiful young lady had died instantaneously in one of the compartments, and was brought in here, and laid down on this floor between us.'

Involuntarily I pushed my chair back, as I looked from the boards at which he pointed to himself.

'True, sir. True. Precisely as it happened, so I tell it you.'

I could think of nothing to say, to any purpose, and my mouth was very dry. The wind and the wires took up the story with a long lamenting wail.

He resumed. 'Now, sir, mark this, and judge how my mind is troubled. The spectre came back a week ago. Ever since, it has been there, now and again, by fits and starts.'

'At the light?'

'At the Danger-light.'

'What does it seem to do?'

He repeated, if possible with increased passion and vehemence, that former gesticulation of, 'For God's sake, clear the way!'

Then he went on. 'I have no peace or rest for it. It calls to me, for many minutes together, in an agonized manner, "Below there! Look out! Look out!" It stands waving to me. It rings my little bell—'

I caught at that. 'Did it ring your bell yesterday evening when I was here, and you went to the door?'

'Twice.'

'Why, see,' said I, 'how your imagination misleads you. My eyes were on the bell, and my ears were open to the bell, and if I am a living man, it did NOT ring at those times. No, nor at any other time, except when it was rung in the natural course of physical things by the station communicating with you.'

He shook his head. 'I have never made a mistake as to that yet, sir. I have never confused the spectre's ring with the man's. The ghost's ring is a strange vibration in the bell that it derives from nothing else, and I have not asserted that the bell stirs to the eye. I don't wonder that you failed to hear it. But I heard it.'

'And did the spectre seem to be there, when you looked out?'

'It *was* there.'

'Both times?'

He repeated firmly: 'Both times.'

'Will you come to the door with me, and look for it now?'

He bit his under lip as though he were somewhat unwilling, but arose. I opened the door, and stood on the step, while he stood in the doorway. There was the Danger-light. There was the dismal mouth of the tunnel. There were the high, wet stone walls of the cutting. There were the stars above them.

'Do you see it?' I asked him, taking particular note of his face. His eyes were prominent and strained, but not very much more so, perhaps, than my own had been when I had directed them earnestly towards the same spot.

'No,' he answered. 'It is not there.'

'Agreed,' said I.

We went in again, shut the door, and resumed our seats. I was thinking how best to improve this advantage, if it might be called one, when he took up the conversation in such a matter-of-course way, so assuming that there could be no serious question of fact between us, that I felt myself placed in the weakest of positions.

'By this time you will fully understand, sir,' he said, 'that what troubles me so dreadfully is the question, What does the spectre mean?'

I was not sure, I told him, that I did fully understand.

'What is its warning against?' he said, ruminating, with his eyes on the fire, and only by times turning them on me. 'What is the danger? Where is the danger? There is danger overhanging somewhere on the Line. Some dreadful calamity will happen. It is not to be doubted this third time, after what has gone before. But surely this is a cruel haunting of me. What can I do?'

He pulled out his handkerchief, and wiped the drops from his heated forehead.

'If I telegraph Danger, on either side of me, or on both, I can give no reason for it,' he went on, wiping the palms of his hands. 'I should get into trouble, and do no good. They would think I was mad. This is the way it would work,—Message: "Danger! Take care!" Answer: "What Danger? Where?" Message: "Don't know. But, for God's sake, take care!" They would displace me. What else could they do?'

His pain of mind was most pitiable to see. It was the mental torture of a conscientious man, oppressed beyond endurance by an unintelligible responsibility involving life.

'When it first stood under the Danger-light,' he went on, putting his dark hair back from his head, and drawing his hands outward across and across his temples in an extremity of feverish distress, 'why not tell me where that accident was to happen,—if it must happen? Why not tell me how it could be averted,—if it could have been averted? When on its second coming it hid its face, why not tell me, instead, "She is going to die. Let them keep her at home"? If it came, on those two occasions, only to show me that its warnings were true, and so to prepare me for the third, why not warn me plainly now? And I, Lord help me! A mere poor signal-man on this solitary station! Why not go to somebody with credit to be believed, and power to act?'

When I saw him in this state, I saw that for the poor man's sake, as well as for the public safety, what I had to do for the time was to compose his mind. Therefore, setting aside all question of reality or unreality between us, I represented to him that whoever thoroughly discharged his duty must do well, and that at least it was his comfort that he understood his duty, though he did not understand these confounding Appearances. In this effort I succeeded far better than in the attempt to reason him out of his conviction. He became calm; the occupations incidental to his post as the night advanced began to make larger demands on his attention: and I left him at two in the morning. I had offered to stay through the night, but he would not hear of it.

That I more than once looked back at the red light as I ascended the pathway, that I did not like the red light, and that I should have slept but poorly if my bed had been under it, I see no reason to conceal. Nor did I like the two sequences of the accident and the dead girl. I see no reason to conceal that either.

But what ran most in my thoughts was the consideration how ought I to act, having become the recipient of this disclosure? I had proved the man to be intelligent, vigilant, painstaking, and exact; but how long might he remain so, in his state of mind? Though in a subordinate position, still he held a most important trust, and would I (for instance) like to stake my own life on the chances of his continuing to execute it with precision?

Unable to overcome a feeling that there would be something treacherous in my communicating what he had told me to his superiors in the Company, without first being plain with himself and proposing a middle course to him, I ultimately resolved to offer to accompany him (otherwise keeping his secret for the present) to the wisest medical practitioner we could hear of in those parts, and to take his opinion. A change in his time of duty would come round next night, he had apprised me, and he would be off an hour or two after sunrise, and on again soon after sunset. I had appointed to return accordingly.

Next evening was a lovely evening, and I walked out early to enjoy it. The sun was not yet quite down when I traversed the field-path near the top of the deep cutting. I would extend my walk for an hour, I said to myself, half an hour on and half an hour back, and it would then be time to go to my signal-man's box.

Before pursuing my stroll, I stepped to the brink, and mechanically looked down, from the point from which I had first seen him. I cannot describe the thrill that seized upon me, when, close at the mouth of the tunnel, I saw the appearance of a man, with his left sleeve across his eyes, passionately waving his right arm.

The nameless horror that oppressed me passed in a moment, for in a moment I saw that this appearance of a man was a man indeed, and that there was a little group of other men, standing at a short distance, to whom he seemed to be rehearsing the gesture he made. The Danger-light was not yet lighted. Against its shaft, a little low hut, entirely new to me, had been made of some wooden supports and tarpaulin. It looked no bigger than a bed.

With an irresistible sense that something was wrong,—with a flashing self-reproachful fear that fatal mischief had come of my leaving the man there, and causing no one to be sent to overlook or correct what he did,—I descended the notched path with all the speed I could make.

'What is the matter?' I asked the men.

'Signal-man killed this morning, sir.'

'Not the man belonging to that box?'

'Yes, sir.'

'Not the man I know?'

'You will recognize him, sir, if you knew him,' said the man who spoke for the others, solemnly uncovering his own head, and raising an end of the tarpaulin, 'for his face is quite composed.'

'O, how did this happen, how did this happen?' I asked, turning from one to another as the hut closed in again.

'He was cut down by an engine, sir. No man in England knew his work better. But somehow he was not clear of the outer rail. It was just at broad day. He had struck the light, and had the lamp in his hand. As the engine came out of the tunnel, his back was towards her, and she cut him down. That man drove her, and was showing how it happened. Show the gentleman, Tom.'

The man, who wore a rough dark dress, stepped back to his former place at the mouth of the tunnel.

'Coming round the curve in the tunnel, sir,' he said, 'I saw him at the end, like as if I saw him down a perspective-glass. There was no time to check speed, and I knew him to be very careful. As he didn't seem to take heed of the whistle, I shut it off when we were running down upon him, and called to him as loud as I could call.'

'What did you say?'

'I said, "Below there! Look out! Look out! For God's sake, clear the way!"'

I started.

'Ah! it was a dreadful time, sir. I never left off calling to him. I put this arm before my eyes not to see, and I waved this arm to the last; but it was no use.'

Without prolonging the narrative to dwell on any one of its curious circumstances more than on any other, I may, in closing it, point out the coincidence that the warning of the engine-driver included, not only the words which the unfortunate signal-man had repeated to me as haunting him, but also the words which I myself—not he—had attached, and that only in my own mind, to the gesticulation he had imitated.

THE BREAD OF DISCONTENT

Mary De Morgan

Once there was a baker who had a very bad, violent temper, and whenever a batch of bread was spoiled he flew into such a rage, that his wife and daughters dared not go near him. One day it happened that all his bread was burnt, and on this he stamped and raved with anger. He threw the loaves all about the floor, when one, burnt blacker than the rest, broke in half, and out of it crept a tiny thin black man, no thicker than an eel, with long arms and legs.

'What are you making all this fuss about, Master Baker?' said he. 'If you will give me a home in your oven I will see to the baking of your bread, and will answer for it that you shall never have so much as a loaf spoiled.'

'And pray what sort of bread would it be, if you were in the oven, and helped to bake it?' said the baker; 'I think my customers might not like to eat it.'

'On the contrary,' said the imp, 'they would like it exceedingly. It is true that it would make them rather unhappy, but that will not hurt you, as you need not eat it yourself.'

'Why should it make them unhappy?' said the baker. 'If it is good bread it won't do any one harm, and if it is bad they won't buy it.'

'It will taste very good,' replied the imp, 'but it will make all who eat it discontented, and they will think themselves very unfortunate whether they are so or no; but this will not do you any harm, and I promise you that you shall sell as much as you wish.'

'Agreed!' said the baker. So the little imp crept into the oven and curled himself into the darkness behind, and the baker saw no more of him.

But next day he made a great batch of bread, and though he took no heed of the time when he put it in, and drew it out, just as he wanted it, it was done quite right—neither too dark nor too light—and the baker was in high good humour.

The first person who tasted the bread was the chief justice. He came down to breakfast in high spirits, for he had just heard that an old aunt was dead, and had left him a great deal of money. So he kissed his wife and chucked his daughters under the chin, and told them that he had good news for them. His old aunt had left him twenty thousand pounds in her will. On this his wife clapped her hands for joy, and his daughters ran to him and kissed him, and begged him to let them have some of it. So they all sat down to breakfast in great glee, but no sooner had the justice tasted the bread than his face fell.

'This is excellent bread,' he said, taking a large slice; 'I wish everything else were as good;' and he heaved a deep sigh.

'Why?' cried his wife, who had not yet begun to eat. 'This morning, I am sure, there is nothing for you to complain of.'

'Nay!' said the mayor; 'it is very nice to have twenty thousand pounds, but think how much nicer it would have been if it had been thirty. How much more one could have done with that! Or even if it had been twenty-five thousand pounds, or even twenty-one. Twenty-one thousand pounds is a very nice sum of money, but twenty thousand pounds is no good at all. I am not sure that it would not be better not to have had any.'

'Nonsense!' cried his wife, who was now eating her breakfast also; 'you are very wicked to be so discontented; but one thing I do say. It would have been much nicer if we had had it when we were young and better able to enjoy it. Money is very little use to people at our time of life. It would have been really nice if we had had it fifteen years ago. As it is, I can't say I care much for it, and it makes me sad to think we did not get it before.'

'Nay,' cried the daughters; 'in that case how much better it would have been for us to have it instead of you; we are young, and able to enjoy ourselves, and we could have given you a little of it if you'd liked, but we could have been very happy with the rest; as it is, it is no pleasure to us.'

So they fell to quarrelling about the money, and by the time breakfast was done, they all had tears in their eyes, and felt discontented and unhappy.

The next person to eat the bread was the village doctor. All night long he had been sitting up with a man who had broken his leg, and he had feared lest he should die, but as morning came he saw he would live, so he returned home to his wife in very good spirits, although he was sadly tired. The wife had already had her breakfast, but she had made all ready for her husband, with a loaf of the baker's new bread.

'See, dear husband,' she said, 'here is your breakfast, and some nice bread quite new, because I know you like it. How glad we ought to be, that this poor man is likely to live.'

'Yes, indeed,' said the doctor; 'being up all night is tiring work, but I don't grudge it when I know that it does some good,' and then he began to eat. 'I am not sure, after all, that I have done such a good thing in curing this man. It is true that his broken leg hurt him very much, but perhaps when he is well again, he may break his back, and that would be much worse. Perhaps I had better have left him to die. I daresay when he is quite well, all kinds of misfortunes will befall him; I had much better have let him alone.'

'Why,' cried his wife in surprise, 'what are you saying, husband? Are you not a doctor, and is it not your business to cure people? And when you succeed ought you not to be glad?'

'I wish I were not a doctor,' said the husband, sighing. 'It would be much better if there were no doctors at all;' and he sat and lamented, and nothing his wife could say, could cheer him.

In a pretty little cottage near the doctor's house lived a young couple, who were newly married, and were as happy as the day was long. Their cottage was covered with roses, and filled with pretty things, and they had everything their hearts could desire. This morning they both came down smiling and happy, and the young wife kissed her husband, and sang for joy. So they sat down to breakfast, chattering like two birds in a nest; but no sooner had the husband tasted the bread than his face fell, and he was silent for a time; then he said,

'It is a very terrible thing to think how happy we are, for it cannot last. Something melancholy is sure to happen to us, and till it comes we shall live in dread of it; for we know happiness never lasts, and this is a thought that makes me very sad.'

The wife had now also taken some bread.

'What is this you are saying?' she said. 'How can you think such dreadful things? I do not like you when you talk like that; and I think it is very hard for me to be married to a man who wants to be unhappy.'

'The best thing we can hope for,' said the husband, sighing, 'is for some great misfortune to befall us; then we should be all right, for we should know then, that we knew the worst that could come. As it is we shall live in suspense all our days.'

'Now,' cried his wife, 'I am indeed unfortunate. What could be worse than to have a husband who does not like being happy? I wish I had married some one else; or indeed had no husband at all.'

So both began to grumble, and at last to quarrel, and finally both were crying with anger.

Not far out of the village was a large pleasant farmhouse, standing amongst fields, and the farmer was a hale, bright man, with a good wife and pretty children. He was very busy just now getting in the corn, for it was autumn, and he stood among his men, directing them as they worked in the fields. He had not had time to have a proper breakfast before going to work, but his wife sent some out to him with some of the baker's new bread, and he sat down under a tree to eat it. As he did so he looked up at the farmhouse, and thought, with pride, that it was the largest farm in all the country round, and that it had belonged to his father, and his grandfather, and his great-grandfather, before him.

''Tis a fine old house, for sure,' thought he, as he took a large piece of bread, ''Tis so well built and strong;' but no sooner had he swallowed a mouthful than his thoughts changed.

'What should I do if it were to fall down and crush me some day,' he said to himself. 'After all, 'tis only built of brick, and might tumble any day. How much stronger it would have been if it had been built of stone. Then it would not have been nearly so likely to give way. Really when my great-grandfather built it he should have thought of this. How selfish all men are;' and he became quite unhappy lest his house should fall, and lamented while he ate.

In the kitchen the farmer's wife was very busy cooking and cleaning, and scarcely stopped to eat till near mid-day. Then she took up a piece of bread and cheese, and leant against the window as she ate it, that she might watch for her eldest girl and boy, Janey and Jimmy, who would now be returning from school.

'Our baker really bakes very decent bread,' said she; ''tis almost as good as my own;' and she went on eating till she saw her two children coming through the fields together.

'Here they come,' said she; 'How bonny they look. Really I ought to be very proud of them. I don't know which is the prettier, Janey or Jimmy, but 'tis a pity, for sure, that Janey is the eldest. It would be much better if Jimmy were older than she. 'Tis a bad thing for the sister to be older than the brother. Now, if he were her age, and she were his, that would be really nice, for then he could take care of her and see after her; but, as it is, she will try to direct him, and boys never like to obey their sisters; I really almost think I had better not have had any children at all,' and the tears filled her eyes, and when her girl and boy ran in to her, her face was very sad, and she seemed to be scarcely glad to see them.

So things went on all over the village. Each one as he tasted the bread grew discontented and angry, till at last all the people went about grumbling and complaining, or else shedding tears outright. Only the baker himself was cheerful and merry, and sang as he kneaded his dough, and sold it to his customers with a light heart, for his trade had never been so good. Every atom of bread he made was sold at once, so he cared not one whit for the trouble of the other people, and laughed to himself when he heard them complaining, and thought of the words of the dark little elf.

One day as he stood kneading at the door and whistling to himself, the doctor walked past and looked angrily at him.

'What on earth are you making that whistling for?' he asked. 'I declare one would think that you were as happy as a man could be.'

'And so I am,' said the baker, 'And so I should think were you too, for you have nothing to trouble you.'

'Nothing to trouble me, forsooth!' cried the doctor in a rage. 'How dare you insult me in this way? I tell you what it is, my fine fellow, I think you are very impertinent, and if I have any more of your impudence I will take my stick and thrash you soundly. It really is not to be borne, that one man should be allowed to tell another that he has nothing to complain of.'

'Nay, you can have as much to complain of as you like, so long as I have not,' cried the baker, and he laughed loudly. This only made the doctor angrier still, and he was just going to seize the baker when up came the farmer.

'Was there ever such a village as this?' he cried. 'It is not fit for any one to live in, there is always such fighting and quarrelling going on. What is the matter here?'

'Matter enough,' cried the doctor. 'Here is a fellow dares to tell me I have nothing to complain of, nor he either.'

'This is monstrous!' said the farmer; 'he deserves to be hung. How dares he say such a thing on such a wretched day as this, with such a blue sky and such a bright sun?'

'Why, Master Farmer,' cried the baker, 'yesterday you grumbled because it was raining, and now you grumble because it is fine.'

'And I tell you that it is enough to make one grumble,' said the farmer. 'It should have been fair yesterday, and should have rained to-day. You ought to be ashamed of such talk, Master Baker, and I think it would serve you justly right if we took you before the Justice and let us see what he thinks of your conduct.'

'Nay!' cried the baker, beginning to be frightened, 'what have I done that I am to be taken before the Justice?'

'What have you done, indeed!' said the doctor. 'We will see if the Justice cannot find that out pretty quickly.' So they seized the baker and dragged him away in spite of himself, and as they pulled him through the village the people thronged about them, and followed till there was quite a large crowd.

The Justice sat at his door smoking a pipe, with tears in his eyes.

'Now what is all this uproar for?' cried he. 'Am I never to be left in peace? How hard is the life of a Justice!' but he got up and came out on the steps to meet them.

'See here,' cried the doctor; 'here is a man who says he has nothing to complain of, and we have brought him to you, to know if he is to be punished, or to be allowed to go on talking like this.'

'Certainly not,' cried the Justice, 'or we shall soon have the whole village in an uproar. Let him be taken to the market-place, and I will order that he be publicly flogged by the soldiers.'

At this the poor baker burst out crying, and entreated to be let off, saying that now indeed he had plenty to complain of, but at this the justice was angrier still. 'Then,' said he, 'you certainly deserve to be flogged for having told an untruth before, when you said you had not. Take him away, and do as I bid.'

So they dragged the baker off to the market-place, and made a ring round him, so that he could not escape, and then there came down two or three soldiers with ropes in their hands, and they seized him, and began to beat him before all the crowd.

But by this time all the people were so enraged against him, that a number of them cried, 'Let us go to his house and pull it down.' So off they ran to the baker's house, and broke the windows and knocked about the furniture, and then some of them fell on the oven, and wrenched off the door, and others seized the pokers and tongs, and smashed in its sides, and in the hurry and scuffle, the little dark man crept out of the oven and scuttled away unseen by any one. But no sooner had he gone than a great change came across the people.

The soldiers on the green stopped beating the baker, and looked at each other aghast, and the Justice called out,

'Stop! What is all this uproar about? And what has this man done that you are beating him without my orders?' and the people in the crowd whispered to each other; 'It is true,—what has he done?' and they slunk away, looking ashamed.

The Justice also at first looked somewhat ashamed of himself, but he drew himself up, and looking very important, said,

'There, my man, you are forgiven for this once, and now go your way, and see that you behave better in future;' and then he walked away with much dignity.

So the baker was left alone in the market-place, and he cried for rage and pain.

'This all comes of the oven imp,' cried he, as he limped home. 'Directly I get home I will drive him out of my oven, and away from my house. Better to have a hundred batches of bread spoiled than to be flogged for saying one is happy.' But when he reached his house the little dark man was nowhere to be found; there was nought but the broken oven with its sides battered in.

The baker mended the oven, and from that time forth his bread was just like other people's; but for all that he had learnt to be quite contented, for now he knew that there were worse things than having his loaves burnt black, and he was only too well pleased to take his chance with other people, without the help of fairy folk. As for the little black imp, he was never heard of more, and the people in the village soon recovered their good humour, and were just as happy and contented as they had been before they tasted the bread of discontent.

THE THREE STRANGERS

Thomas Hardy

Among the few features of agricultural England which retain an appearance but little modified by the lapse of centuries, may be reckoned the high, grassy, and furzy downs, coombs, or ewe-leases, as they are indifferently called, that fill a large area of certain counties in the south and southwest. If any mark of human occupation is met with hereon, it usually takes the form of the solitary cottage of some shepherd.

Fifty years ago such a lonely cottage stood on such a down, and may possibly be standing there now. In spite of its loneliness, however, the spot, by actual measurement, was not more than five miles from a county-town. Yet that affected it little. Five miles of irregular upland, during the long inimical seasons, with their sleets, snows, rains, and mists, afford withdrawing space enough to isolate a Timon or a Nebuchadnezzar; much less, in fair weather, to please that less repellent tribe, the poets, philosophers, artists, and others who 'conceive and meditate of pleasant things'.

Some old earthen camp or barrow, some clump of trees, at least some starved fragment of ancient hedge, is usually taken advantage of in the erection of these forlorn dwellings. But, in the present case, such a kind of shelter had been disregarded. Higher Crowstairs, as the house was called, stood quite detached and undefended. The only reason for its precise situation seemed to be the crossing of two footpaths at right angles hard by, which may have crossed there and thus for a good five hundred years. Hence the house was exposed to the elements on all sides. But, though the wind up here blew unmistakably when it did blow, and the rain hit hard whenever it fell, the various weathers of the winter season were not quite so formidable on the coomb as they were imagined to be by dwellers on low ground. The raw rimes were not so pernicious as in the hollows, and the frosts were scarcely so severe. When the shepherd and his family who tenanted the house were pitied for their sufferings from the exposure, they said that upon the whole they were less inconvenienced by 'wuzzes and flames' (hoarses and phlegms) than when they had lived by the stream of a snug neighbouring valley.

The night of March 28, 182–, was precisely one of the nights that were wont to call forth these expressions of commiseration. The level rainstorm smote walls, slopes, and hedges like the clothyard shafts of Senlac and Crecy. Such sheep and outdoor animals as had no shelter stood with their buttocks to the winds; while the tails of little birds trying to roost on some scraggy thorn were blown inside-out like umbrellas. The gable-end of the cottage was stained with wet, and the eavesdroppings flapped against the wall. Yet never was commiseration for the shepherd more misplaced. For that cheerful rustic was entertaining a large party in glorification of the christening of his second girl.

The guests had arrived before the rain began to fall, and they were all now assembled in the chief or living room of the dwelling. A glance into the apartment at eight o'clock on this eventful evening would have resulted in the opinion that it was as cosy and comfortable a nook as could be wished for in boisterous weather. The calling of its inhabitant was proclaimed by a number of highly-polished sheep-crooks without stems that were hung ornamentally over the fireplace, the curl of each shining crook varying from the antiquated type engraved in the patriarchal pictures of old family Bibles to the most approved fashion of the last local sheep-fair. The room was lighted by half a dozen candles, having wicks only a trifle smaller than the grease which enveloped them, in candlesticks that were never used but at high-days, holy-days, and family feasts. The lights were scattered about the room, two of them standing on the chimney-piece. This position of candles was in itself significant. Candles on the chimney-piece always meant a party.

On the hearth, in front of a back-brand to give substance, blazed a fire of thorns, that crackled 'like the laughter of the fool'.

Nineteen persons were gathered here. Of these, five women, wearing gowns of various bright hues, sat in chairs along the wall; girls shy and not shy filled the window-bench; four men, including Charley Jake the hedge-carpenter, Elijah New the parish-clerk, and

John Pitcher, a neighbouring dairyman, the shepherd's father-in-law, lolled in the settle; a young man and maid, who were blushing over tentative *pourparlers* on a life-companionship, sat beneath the corner-cupboard; and an elderly engaged man of fifty or upward moved restlessly about from spots where his betrothed was not to the spot where she was. Enjoyment was pretty general, and so much the more prevailed in being unhampered by conventional restrictions. Absolute confidence in each other's good opinion begat perfect ease, while the finishing stroke of manner, amounting to a truly princely serenity, was lent to the majority by the absence of any expression or trait denoting that they wished to get on in the world, enlarge their minds, or do any eclipsing thing whatever—which nowadays so generally nips the bloom and *bonhomie* of all except the two extremes of the social scale.

Shepherd Fennel had married well, his wife being a dairyman's daughter from the valley below, who brought fifty guineas in her pocket—and kept them there, till they should be required for ministering to the needs of a coming family. This frugal woman had been somewhat exercised as to the character that should be given to the gathering. A sit-still party had its advantages; but an undisturbed position of ease in chairs and settles was apt to lead on the men to such an unconscionable deal of toping that they would sometimes fairly drink the house dry. A dancing-party was the alternative; but this, while avoiding the foregoing objection on the score of good drink, had a counterbalancing disadvantage in the matter of good victuals, the ravenous appetites engendered by the exercise causing immense havoc in the buttery. Shepherdess Fennel fell back upon the intermediate plan of mingling short dances with short periods of talk and singing, so as to hinder any ungovernable rage in either. But this scheme was entirely confined to her own gentle mind: the shepherd himself was in the mood to exhibit the most reckless phases of hospitality.

The fiddler was a boy of those parts, about twelve years of age, who had a wonderful dexterity in jigs and reels, though his fingers were so small and short as to necessitate a constant shifting for the high notes, from which he scrambled back to the first position with sounds not of unmixed purity of tone. At seven the shrill tweedle-dee of this youngster had begun, accompanied by a booming ground-bass from Elijah New, the parish-clerk, who had thoughtfully brought with him his favourite musical instrument, the serpent. Dancing was instantaneous, Mrs Fennel privately enjoining the players on no account to let the dance exceed the length of a quarter of an hour.

But Elijah and the boy, in the excitement of their position, quite forgot the injunction. Moreover, Oliver Giles, a man of seventeen, one of the dancers, who was enamoured of his partner, a fair girl of thirty-three rolling years, had recklessly handed a new crown-piece to the musicians, as a bribe to keep going as long as they had muscle and wind. Mrs Fennel, seeing the steam begin to generate on the countenances of her guests, crossed over and touched the fiddler's elbow and put her hand on the serpent's mouth. But they took no notice, and fearing she might lose her character of genial hostess if she were to interfere too markedly, she retired and sat down helpless. And so the dance whizzed on with cumulative fury, the performers moving in their planet-like courses, direct and retrograde, from apogee to perigee, till the hand of the well-kicked clock at the bottom of the room had travelled over the circumference of an hour.

While these cheerful events were in course of enactment within Fennel's pastoral dwelling, an incident having considerable bearing on the party had occurred in the gloomy night without. Mrs Fennel's concern about the growing fierceness of the dance corresponded in point of time with the ascent of a human figure to the solitary hill of Higher Crowstairs from the direction of the distant town. This personage strode on through the rain without a pause, following the little-worn path which, farther on in its course, skirted the shepherd's cottage.

It was nearly the time of full moon, and on this account, though the sky was lined with a uniform sheet of dripping cloud, ordinary objects out of doors were readily visible. The sad wan light revealed the lonely pedestrian to be a man of supple frame; his gait suggested that he had somewhat passed the period of perfect and instinctive agility, though not so far as to be otherwise than rapid of motion when occasion required. In point of fact, he might have been about forty years of age. He appeared tall, but a recruiting sergeant, or other person accustomed to the judging of men's heights by the eye, would have discerned that this was chiefly owing to his gauntness, and that he was not more than five-feet-eight or nine.

Notwithstanding the regularity of his tread, there was caution in it, as in that of one who mentally feels his way; and despite the fact that it was not a black coat nor a dark garment of any sort that he wore, there was something about him which suggested that he naturally belonged to the black-coated tribes of men. His clothes were of fustian, and his boots hobnailed, yet in his progress he showed not the mud-accustomed bearing of hobnailed and fustianed peasantry.

By the time that he had arrived abreast of the shepherd's premises the rain came down, or rather came along, with yet more determined violence. The outskirts of the little settlement partially broke the force of wind and rain, and this induced him to stand still. The most salient of the shepherd's domestic erections was an empty sty at the forward corner of his hedgeless garden, for in these latitudes the principle of masking the homelier features of your establishment by a conventional frontage was unknown. The traveller's eye was attracted to this small building by the pallid shine of the wet slates that covered it. He turned aside, and, finding it empty, stood under the pent-roof for shelter.

While he stood, the boom of the serpent within the adjacent house, and the lesser strains of the fiddler, reached the spot as an accompaniment to the surging hiss of the flying rain on the sod, its louder beating on the cabbage-leaves of the garden, on the eight or ten beehives just discernible by the path, and its dripping from the eaves into a row of buckets and pans that had been placed under the walls of the cottage. For at Higher Crowstairs, as at all such elevated domiciles, the grand difficulty of housekeeping was an insufficiency of water; and a casual rainfall was utilized by turning out, as catchers, every utensil that the house contained. Some queer stories might be told of the contrivances for economy in suds and dish-waters that are absolutely necessitated in upland habitations during the droughts of summer. But at this season there were no such exigencies: a mere acceptance of what the skies bestowed was sufficient for an abundant store.

At last the notes of the serpent ceased and the house was silent. This cessation of activity aroused the solitary pedestrian from the reverie into which he had lapsed, and, emerging from the shed, with an apparently new intention, he walked up the path to the house-door. Arrived here, his first act was to kneel down on a large stone beside the row of vessels, and to drink a copious draught from one of them. Having quenched his thirst he rose and lifted his hand to knock, but paused with his eye upon the panel. Since the dark surface of the wood revealed absolutely nothing, it was evident that he must be mentally looking through the door, as if he wished to measure thereby all the possibilities that a house of this sort might include, and how they might bear upon the question of his entry.

In his indecision he turned and surveyed the scene around. Not a soul was anywhere visible. The garden-path stretched downward from his feet, gleaming like the track of a snail; the roof of the little well (mostly dry), the well cover, the top rail of the garden-gate, were varnished with the same dull liquid glaze; while, far away in the vale, a faint whiteness of more than usual extent showed that the rivers were high in the meads. Beyond all this winked a few bleared lamplights through the beating drops, lights that denoted the situation of the county-town from which he had appeared to come. The absence of all notes of life in that direction seemed to clinch his intentions, and he knocked at the door.

Within, a desultory chat had taken the place of movement and musical sound. The hedge-carpenter was suggesting a song to the company, which nobody just then was inclined to undertake, so that the knock afforded a not unwelcome diversion.

'Walk in!' said the shepherd promptly.

The latch clicked upward, and out of the night our pedestrian appeared upon the door-mat. The shepherd arose, snuffed two of the nearest candles, and turned to look at him.

Their light disclosed that the stranger was dark in complexion and not unprepossessing as to feature. His hat, which for a moment he did not remove, hung low over his eyes, without concealing that they were large, open, and determined, moving with a flash rather than a glance round the room. He seemed pleased with the survey, and, baring his shaggy head, said, in a rich deep voice, 'The rain is so heavy, friends, that I ask leave to come in and rest awhile.'

'To be sure, stranger,' said the shepherd. 'And faith, you've been lucky in choosing your time, for we are having a bit of a fling for a glad cause—though, to be sure, a man could hardly wish that glad cause to happen more than once a year.'

'Nor less,' spoke up a woman. 'For 'tis best to get your family over and done with, as soon as you can, so as to be all the earlier out of the fag o't.'

'And what may be this glad cause?' asked the stranger.

'A birth and christening,' said the shepherd.

The stranger hoped his host might not be made unhappy either by too many or too few of such episodes, and being invited by a gesture to a pull at the mug, he readily acquiesced. His manner, which, before entering, had been so dubious, was now altogether that of a careless and candid man.

'Late to be traipsing athwart this coomb—hey?' said the engaged man of fifty.

'Late it is, master, as you say.—I'll take a seat in the chimney-corner, if you have nothing to urge against it, ma'am; for I am a little moist on the side that was next the rain.'

Mrs Shepherd Fennel assented, and made room for the self-invited comer, who, having got completely inside the chimney-corner, stretched out his legs and his arms with the expansiveness of a person quite at home.

'Yes, I am rather thin in the vamp,' he said freely, seeing that the eyes of the shepherd's wife fell upon his boots, 'and I am not well fitted either. I have had some rough times lately, and have been forced to pick up what I can get in the way of wearing, but I must find a suit better fit for working-days when I reach home.'

'One of hereabouts?' she inquired.

'Not quite that—farther up the country.'

'I thought so. And so am I; and by your tongue you come from my neighbourhood.'

'But you would hardly have heard of me,' he said quickly. 'My time would be long before yours, ma'am, you see.'

This testimony to the youthfulness of his hostess had the effect of stopping her cross-examination.

'There is only one thing more wanted to make me happy,' continued the new-comer. 'And that is a little baccy, which I am sorry to say I am out of.'

'I'll fill your pipe,' said the shepherd.

'I must ask you to lend me a pipe likewise.'

'A smoker, and no pipe about ye?'

'I have dropped it somewhere on the road.'

The shepherd filled and handed him a new clay pipe, saying, as he did so, 'Hand me your baccy-box—I'll fill that too, now I am about it.'

The man went through the movement of searching his pockets.

'Lost that too?' said his entertainer, with some surprise.

'I am afraid so,' said the man with some confusion. 'Give it to me in a screw of paper.' Lighting his pipe at the candle with a suction that drew the whole flame into the bowl, he resettled himself in the corner, and bent his looks upon the faint steam from his damp legs, as if he wished to say no more.

Meanwhile the general body of guests had been taking little notice of this visitor by reason of an absorbing discussion in which they were engaged with the band about a tune for the next dance. The matter being settled, they were about to stand up, when an interruption came in the shape of another knock at the door.

At sound of the same the man in the chimney-corner took up the poker and began stirring the fire as if doing it thoroughly were the one aim of his existence; and a second time the shepherd said 'Walk in!' In a moment another man stood upon the straw-woven door-mat. He too was a stranger.

This individual was one of a type radically different from the first. There was more of the commonplace in his manner, and a certain jovial cosmopolitanism sat upon his features. He was several years older than the first arrival, his hair being slightly frosted, his eyebrows bristly, and his whiskers cut back from his cheeks. His face was rather full and flabby, and yet it was not altogether a face without power. A few grog-blossoms marked the neighbourhood of his nose. He flung back his long drab greatcoat, revealing that beneath it he wore a suit of cinder-grey shade throughout, large heavy seals, of some metal or other that would take a polish, dangling from his fob as his only personal ornament. Shaking the water-drops from his low-crowned glazed hat, he said, 'I must ask for a few minutes' shelter, comrades, or I shall be wetted to my skin before I get to Casterbridge.'

'Make yourself at home, master,' said the shepherd, perhaps a trifle less heartily than on the first occasion. Not that Fennel had the least tinge of niggardliness in his composition; but the room was far from large, spare chairs were not numerous, and damp companions were not altogether desirable at close quarters for the women and girls in their bright-coloured gowns.

However, the second comer, after taking off his greatcoat, and hanging his hat on a nail in one of the ceiling-beams as if he had been specially invited to put it there, advanced and sat down at the table. This had been pushed so closely into the chimney-corner, to give all available room to the dancers, that its inner edge grazed the elbow of the man who had ensconced himself by the fire; and thus the two strangers were brought into close companionship. They nodded to each other by way of breaking the ice of unacquaintance, and the first stranger handed his neighbour the family mug—a huge vessel of brown ware, having its upper edge worn away like a threshold by the rub of whole generations of thirsty lips that had gone the way of all flesh, and bearing the following inscription burnt upon its rotund side in yellow letters:—

THERE IS NO FUN
UNTiLL i CUM.

The other man, nothing loth, raised the mug to his lips, and drank on, and on, and on—till a curious blueness overspread the countenance of the shepherd's wife, who had regarded with no little surprise the first stranger's free offer to the second of what did not belong to him to dispense.

'I knew it!' said the toper to the shepherd with much satisfaction. 'When I walked up your garden before coming in, and saw the hives all of a row, I said to myself, "Where there's bees there's honey, and where there's honey there's mead." But mead of such a truly comfortable sort as this I really didn't expect to meet in my older days.' He took yet another pull at the mug, till it assumed an ominous elevation.

'Glad you enjoy it!' said the shepherd warmly.

'It is goodish mead,' assented Mrs Fennel with an absence of enthusiasm, which seemed to say that it was possible to buy praise for one's cellar at too heavy a price. 'It is trouble enough to make—and really I hardly think we shall make any more. For honey sells well, and we ourselves can make shift with a drop o' small mead and metheglin for common use from the comb-washings.'

'Oh, but you'll never have the heart!' reproachfully cried the stranger in cinder-grey, after taking up the mug a third time and setting it down empty. 'I love mead, when 'tis old like this, as I love to go to church o' Sundays, or to relieve the needy any day of the week.'

'Ha, ha, ha!' said the man in the chimney-corner, who, in spite of the taciturnity induced by the pipe of tobacco, could not or would not refrain from this slight testimony to his comrade's humour.

Now the old mead of those days, brewed of the purest first-year or maiden honey, four pounds to the gallon—with its due complement of white of eggs, cinnamon, ginger, cloves, mace, rosemary, yeast, and processes of working, bottling, and cellaring—tasted remarkably strong, but it did not taste so strong as it actually was. Hence, presently, the stranger in cinder-grey at the table, moved by its creeping influence, unbuttoned his waistcoat, threw himself back in his chair, spread his legs, and made his presence felt in various ways.

'Well, well, as I say,' he resumed, 'I am going to Casterbridge, and to Casterbridge I must go. I should have been almost there by this time; but the rain drove me into your dwelling, and I'm not sorry for it.'

'You don't live in Casterbridge?' said the shepherd.

'Not as yet; though I shortly mean to move there.'

'Going to set up in trade, perhaps?'

'No, no,' said the shepherd's wife. 'It is easy to see that the gentleman is rich, and don't want to work at anything.'

The cinder-grey stranger paused, as if to consider whether he would accept that definition of himself. He presently rejected it by answering, 'Rich is not quite the word for me, dame. I do work, and I must work. And even if I only get to Casterbridge by midnight I must begin work there at eight tomorrow morning. Yes, het or wet, blow or snow, famine or sword, my day's work tomorrow must be done.'

'Poor man! Then, in spite o' seeming, you be worse off than we?' replied the shepherd's wife.

''Tis the nature of my trade, men and maidens. 'Tis the nature of my trade more than my poverty… But really and truly I must up and off, or I shan't get a lodging in the town.' However, the speaker did not move, and directly added, 'There's time for one more draught of friendship before I go; and I'd perform it at once if the mug were not dry.'

'Here's a mug o' small,' said Mrs Fennel. 'Small, we call it, though to be sure 'tis only the first wash o' the combs.'

'No,' said the stranger disdainfully. 'I won't spoil your first kindness by partaking o' your second.'

'Certainly not,' broke in Fennel. 'We don't increase and multiply every day, and I'll fill the mug again.' He went away to the dark place under the stairs where the barrel stood. The shepherdess followed him.

'Why should you do this?' she said reproachfully, as soon as they were alone. 'He's emptied it once, though it held enough for ten people; and now he's not contented wi' the small, but must needs call for more o' the strong! And a stranger unbeknown to any of us. For my part, I don't like the look o' the man at all.'

'But he's in the house, my honey; and 'tis a wet night, and a christening. Daze it, what's a cup of mead more or less? there'll be plenty more next bee-burning.'

'Very well—this time, then,' she answered, looking wistfully at the barrel. 'But what is the man's calling, and where is he one of, that he should come in and join us like this?'

'I don't know. I'll ask him again.'

The catastrophe of having the mug drained dry at one pull by the stranger in cinder-grey was effectually guarded against this time by Mrs Fennel. She poured out his allowance in a small cup, keeping the large one at a discreet distance from him. When he had tossed off his portion the shepherd renewed his inquiry about the stranger's occupation.

The latter did not immediately reply, and the man in the chimney-corner, with sudden demonstrativeness, said, 'Anybody may know my trade—I'm a wheelwright.'

'A very good trade for these parts,' said the shepherd.

'And anybody may know mine—if they've the sense to find it out,' said the stranger in cinder-grey.

'You may generally tell what a man is by his claws,' observed the hedge-carpenter, looking at his own hands. 'My fingers be as full of thorns as an old pin-cushion is of pins.'

The hands of the man in the chimney-corner instinctively sought the shade, and he gazed into the fire as he resumed his pipe. The man at the table took up the hedge-carpenter's remark, and added smartly, 'True; but the oddity of my trade is that, instead of setting a mark upon me, it sets a mark upon my customers.'

No observation being offered by anybody in elucidation of this enigma, the shepherd's wife once more called for a song. The same obstacles presented themselves as at the former time—one had no voice, another had forgotten the first verse. The stranger at the table, whose soul had now risen to a good working temperature, relieved the difficulty by exclaiming that, to start the company, he would sing himself. Thrusting one thumb into the arm-hole of his waistcoat, he waved the other hand in the air, and, with an extemporizing gaze at the shining sheep-crooks above the mantelpiece, began:—

> 'Oh my trade it is the rarest one,
> Simple shepherds all—
> My trade is a sight to see;
> For my customers I tie, and take them up on high,
> And waft 'em to a far countree!'

The room was silent when he had finished the verse—with one exception, that of the man in the chimney-corner, who, at the singer's word, 'Chorus!' joined him in a deep bass voice of musical relish—

> 'And waft 'em to a far countree!'

Oliver Giles, John Pitcher the dairyman, the parish-clerk, the engaged man of fifty, the row of young women against the wall, seemed lost in thought not of the gayest kind. The shepherd looked meditatively on the ground, the shepherdess gazed keenly at the singer, and with some suspicion; she was doubting whether this stranger were merely singing an old song from recollection, or was composing one there and then for the occasion. All were as perplexed at the obscure revelation as the guests at Belshazzar's Feast, except the man in the chimney-corner, who quietly said, 'Second verse, stranger,' and smoked on.

The singer thoroughly moistened himself from his lips inwards, and went on with the next stanza as requested:—

> 'My tools are but common ones,
> Simple shepherds all,
> My tools are no sight to see:
> A little hempen string, and a post whereon to swing,
> Are implements enough for me!'

Shepherd Fennel glanced round. There was no longer any doubt that the stranger was answering his question rhythmically. The guests one and all started back with suppressed exclamations. The young woman engaged to the man of fifty fainted half-way, and would have proceeded, but finding him wanting in alacrity for catching her she sat down trembling.

'Oh, he's the—!' whispered the people in the background, mentioning the name of an ominous public officer. 'He's come to do it. 'Tis to be at Casterbridge jail tomorrow—the man for sheep-stealing—the poor clock-maker we heard of, who used to live away at Shottsford and had no work to do—Timothy Sommers, whose family were a-starving, and so he went out of Shottsford by the high-road, and took a sheep in open daylight, defying the farmer and the farmer's wife and the farmer's lad, and every man jack among 'em. He' (and they nodded towards the stranger of the deadly trade) 'is come from up the country to do it because there's not enough to do in his own country-town, and he's got the place here now our own county man's dead; he's going to live in the same cottage under the prison wall.'

The stranger in cinder-grey took no notice of this whispered string of observations, but again wetted his lips. Seeing that his friend in the chimney-corner was the only one who reciprocated his joviality in any way, he held out his cup towards that appreciative comrade, who also held out his own. They clinked together, the eyes of the rest of the room hanging upon the singer's actions. He parted his lips for the third verse; but at that moment another knock was audible upon the door. This time the knock was faint and hesitating.

The company seemed scared; the shepherd looked with consternation towards the entrance, and it was with some effort that he resisted his alarmed wife's deprecatory glance, and uttered for the third time the welcoming words, 'Walk in!'

The door was gently opened, and another man stood upon the mat. He, like those who had preceded him, was a stranger. This time it was a short, small personage, of fair complexion, and dressed in a decent suit of dark clothes.

'Can you tell me the way to—?' he began; when, gazing round the room to observe the nature of the company amongst whom he had fallen, his eyes lighted on the stranger in cinder-grey. It was just at the instant when the latter, who had thrown his mind into his song with such a will that he scarcely heeded the interruption, silenced all whispers and inquiries by bursting into his third verse:—

'Tomorrow is my working day,
  Simple shepherds all—
Tomorrow is a working day for me:

For the farmer's sheep is slain, and the lad who did it ta'en,
And on his soul may God ha' merc-y!'

The stranger in the chimney-corner, waving cups with the singer so heartily that his mead splashed over on the hearth, repeated in his bass voice as before:—

'And on his soul may God ha' merc-y!'

All this time the third stranger had been standing in the doorway. Finding now that he did not come forward or go on speaking, the guests particularly regarded him. They noticed to their surprise that he stood before them the picture of abject terror—his knees trembling, his hand shaking so violently that the door-latch by which he supported himself rattled audibly; his white lips were parted, and his eyes fixed on the merry officer of justice in the middle of the room. A moment more and he had turned, closed the door, and fled.

'What a man can it be?' said the shepherd.

The rest, between the awfulness of their late discovery and the odd conduct of this third visitor, looked as if they knew not what to think, and said nothing. Instinctively they withdrew farther and farther from the grim gentleman in their midst, whom some of them seemed to take for the Prince of Darkness himself, till they formed a remote circle, an empty space of floor being left between them and him—

'...circulus, cujus centrum diabolus.'

The room was so silent—though there were more than twenty people in it—that nothing could be heard but the patter of the rain against the window-shutters, accompanied by the occasional hiss of a stray drop that fell down the chimney into the fire, and the steady puffing of the man in the corner, who had now resumed his pipe of long clay.

The stillness was unexpectedly broken. The distant sound of a gun reverberated through the air—apparently from the direction of the county-town.

'Be jiggered!' cried the stranger who had sung the song, jumping up.

'What does that mean?' asked several.

'A prisoner escaped from the jail—that's what it means.'

All listened. The sound was repeated, and none of them spoke but the man in the chimney-corner, who said quietly, 'I've often been told that in this county they fire a gun at such times; but I never heard it till now.'

'I wonder if it is *my* man?' murmured the personage in cinder-gray.

'Surely it is!' said the shepherd involuntarily. 'And surely we've seen him! That little man who looked in at the door by now, and quivered like a leaf when he seed ye and heard your song!'

'His teeth chattered, and the breath went out of his body,' said the dairyman.

'And his heart seemed to sink within him like a stone,' said Oliver Giles.

'And he bolted as if he'd been shot at,' said the hedge-carpenter.

'True—his teeth chattered, and his heart seemed to sink; and he bolted as if he's been shot at,' slowly summed up the man in the chimney-corner.

'I didn't notice it,' remarked the hangman.

'We were all a-wondering what made him run off in such a fright,' faltered one of the women against the wall, 'and now 'tis explained.'

The firing of the alarm-gun went on at intervals, low and sullenly, and their suspicions became a certainty. The sinister gentleman in cinder-grey roused himself. 'Is there a constable here?' he asked in thick tones. 'If so, let him step forward.'

The engaged man of fifty stepped quavering out of the corner, his betrothed beginning to sob on the back of the chair.

'You are a sworn constable?'

'I be, sir.'

'Then pursue the criminal at once, with assistance, and bring him back here. He can't have gone far.'

'I will, sir, I will—when I've got my staff. I'll go home and get it, and come sharp here, and start in a body.'

'Staff!—never mind your staff; the man'll be gone!'

'But I can't do nothing without my staff—can I, William, and John, and Charles Jake? No; for there's the king's royal crown a painted on en in yaller and gold, and the lion and the unicorn, so as when I raise en up and hit my prisoner, 'tis made a lawful blow thereby. I wouldn't 'tempt to take up a man without my staff—no, not I. If I hadn't the law to gie me courage, why, instead o' my taking up him he might take up me!'

'Now, I'm a king's man myself, and can give you authority enough for this,' said the formidable officer in grey. 'Now then, all of ye, be ready. Have ye any lanterns?'

'Yes—have ye any lanterns?—I demand it!' said the constable.

'And the rest of you able-bodied—'

'Able-bodied men—yes—the rest of ye!' said the constable.

'Have you some good stout staves and pitchforks—'

'Staves and pitchforks—in the name o' the law! And take 'em in yer hands and go in quest, and do as we in authority tell ye!'

Thus aroused, the men prepared to give chase. The evidence was, indeed, though circumstantial, so convincing, that but little argument was needed to show the shepherd's guests that after what they had seen it would look very much like connivance if they did not instantly pursue the unhappy third stranger, who could not as yet have gone more than a few hundred yards over such uneven country.

A shepherd is always well provided with lanterns; and, lighting these hastily, and with hurdle-staves in their hands, they poured out of the door, taking a direction along the crest of the hill, away from the town, the rain having fortunately a little abated.

Disturbed by the noise, or possibly by unpleasant dreams of her baptism, the child who had been christened began to cry heart-brokenly in the room overhead. These notes of grief came down through the chinks of the floor to the ears of the women below, who jumped up one by one, and seemed glad of the excuse to ascend and comfort the baby, for the incidents of the last half-hour greatly oppressed them. Thus in the space of two or three minutes the room on the ground-floor was deserted quite.

But it was not for long. Hardly had the sound of footsteps died away when a man returned round the corner of the house from the direction the pursuers had taken. Peeping in at the door, and seeing nobody there, he entered leisurely. It was the stranger of the chimney-corner, who had gone out with the rest. The motive of his return was shown by his helping himself to a cut piece of skimmer-cake that lay on a ledge beside where he had sat, and which he had apparently forgotten to take with him. He also poured out half a cup more mead from the quantity that remained, ravenously eating and drinking these as he stood. He had not finished when another figure came in just as quietly—his friend in cinder-grey.

'Oh—you here?' said the latter, smiling. 'I thought you had gone to help in the capture.' And this speaker also revealed the object of his return by looking solicitously round for the fascinating mug of old mead.

'And I thought you had gone,' said the other, continuing his skimmer-cake with some effort.

'Well, on second thoughts, I felt there were enough without me,' said the first confidentially, 'and such a night as it is, too. Besides, 'tis the business o' the Government to take care of its criminals—not mine.'

'True; so it is. And I felt as you did, that there were enough without me.'

'I don't want to break my limbs running over the humps and hollows of this wild country.'

'Nor I neither, between you and me.'

'These shepherd-people are used to it—simple-minded souls, you know, stirred up to anything in a moment. They'll have him ready for me before the morning, and no trouble to me at all.'

'They'll have him, and we shall have saved ourselves all labour in the matter.'

'True, true. Well, my way is to Casterbridge; and 'tis as much as my legs will do to take me that far. Going the same way?'

'No, I am sorry to say! I have to get home over there' (he nodded indefinitely to the right), 'and I feel as you do, that it is quite enough for my legs to do before bedtime.'

The other had by this time finished the mead in the mug, after which, shaking hands heartily at the door, and wishing each other well, they went their several ways.

In the meantime the company of pursuers had reached the end of the hog's-back elevation which dominated this part of the coomb. They had decided on no particular plan of action; and, finding that the man of the baleful trade was no longer in their company, they seemed quite unable to form any such plan now. They descended in all directions down the hill, and straightway several of the party fell into the snare set by Nature for all misguided midnight ramblers over this part of the cretaceous formation. The 'lynchets', or flint slopes, which belted the escarpment at intervals of a dozen yards, took the less cautious ones unawares, and losing their footing on the rubbly steep they slid sharply downwards, the lanterns rolling from their hands to the bottom, and there lying on their sides till the horn was scorched through.

When they had again gathered themselves together, the shepherd, as the man who knew the country best, took the lead, and guided them round these treacherous inclines. The lanterns, which seemed rather to dazzle their eyes and warn the fugitive than to assist them in the exploration, were extinguished, due silence was observed; and in this more rational order they plunged into the vale. It was a grassy, briery, moist defile, affording some shelter to any person who had sought it; but the party perambulated it in vain, and ascended on the other side. Here they wandered apart, and after an interval closed together again to report progress. At the second time of closing in they found themselves near a lonely ash, the single tree on this part of the upland, probably sown there by a passing bird some fifty years before. And here, standing a little to one side of the trunk, as motionless as the trunk itself, appeared the man they were in quest of, his outline being well defined against the sky beyond. The band noiselessly drew up and faced him.

'Your money or your life!' said the constable sternly to the still figure.

'No, no,' whispered John Pitcher. ''Tisn't our side ought to say that. That's the doctrine of vagabonds like him, and we be on the side of the law.'

'Well, well,' replied the constable impatiently; 'I must say something, mustn't I? and if you had all the weight o' this undertaking upon your mind, perhaps you'd say the wrong thing too!—Prisoner at the bar, surrender, in the name of the Father—the Crown, I mane!'

The man under the tree seemed now to notice them for the first time, and, giving them no opportunity whatever for exhibiting their courage, he strolled slowly towards them. He was, indeed, the little man, the third stranger; but his trepidation had in a great measure gone.

'Well, travellers,' he said, 'did I hear ye speak to me?'

'You did: you've got to come and be our prisoner at once,' said the constable. 'We arrest ye on the charge of not biding in Casterbridge jail in a decent proper manner to be hung tomorrow morning. Neighbours, do your duty, and seize the culpet!'

On hearing the charge, the man seemed enlightened, and, saying not another word, resigned himself with preternatural civility to the search-party, who, with their staves in their hands, surrounded him on all sides, and marched him back towards the shepherd's cottage.

It was eleven o'clock by the time they arrived. The light shining from the open door, a sound of men's voices within, proclaimed to them as they approached the house that some new events had arisen in their absence. On entering they discovered the shepherd's living-room to be invaded by two officers from Casterbridge jail, and a well-known magistrate who lived at the nearest country-seat, intelligence of the escape having become generally circulated.

'Gentlemen,' said the constable, 'I have brought back your man—not without risk and danger; but every one must do his duty! He is inside this circle of able-bodied persons, who have lent me useful aid, considering their ignorance of Crown work. Men, bring forward your prisoner!' And the third stranger was led to the light.

'Who is this?' said one of the officials.

'The man,' said the constable.

'Certainly not,' said the turnkey; and the first corroborated his statement.

'But how can it be otherwise?' asked the constable. 'Or why was he so terrified at sight o' the singing instrument of the law who sat there?' Here he related the strange behaviour of the third stranger on entering the house during the hangman's song.

'Can't understand it,' said the officer coolly. 'All I know is that it is not the condemned man. He's quite a different character from this one; a gauntish fellow, with dark hair and eyes, rather good-looking, and with a musical bass voice that if you heard it once you'd never mistake as long as you lived.'

'Why, souls—'twas the man in the chimney-corner!'

'Hey—what?' said the magistrate, coming forward after inquiring particulars from the shepherd in the background. 'Haven't you got the man after all?'

'Well, sir,' said the constable, 'he's the man we were in search of, that's true; and yet he's not the man we were in search of. For the man we were in search of was not the man we wanted, sir, if you understand my everyday way; for 'twas the man in the chimney-corner!'

'A pretty kettle of fish altogether!' said the magistrate. 'You had better start for the other man at once.'

The prisoner now spoke for the first time. The mention of the man in the chimney-corner seemed to have moved him as nothing else could do. 'Sir,' he said, stepping forward to the magistrate, 'take no more trouble about me. The time is come when I may as well speak. I have done nothing; my crime is that the condemned man is my brother. Early this afternoon I left home at Shottsford to tramp it all the way to Casterbridge jail to bid him farewell. I was benighted, and called here to rest and ask the way. When I opened the door I saw before me the very man, my brother, that I thought to see in the condemned cell at Casterbridge. He was in this chimney-corner; and jammed close to him, so that he could not have got out if he had tried, was the executioner who'd come to take his life, singing a song about it and not knowing that it was his victim who was close by, joining in to save appearances. My brother looked a glance of agony at me, and I knew he meant, "Don't reveal what you see; my life depends on it." I was so terror-struck that I could hardly stand, and, not knowing what I did, I turned and hurried away.'

The narrator's manner and tone had the stamp of truth, and his story made a great impression on all around. 'And do you know where your brother is at the present time?' asked the magistrate.

'I do not. I have never seen him since I closed this door.'

'I can testify to that, for we've been between ye ever since,' said the constable.

'Where does he think to fly to?—what is his occupation?'

'He's a watch-and-clock-maker, sir.'

''A said 'a was a wheelwright—a wicked rogue,' said the constable.

'The wheels of clocks and watches he meant, no doubt,' said Shepherd Fennel. 'I thought his hands were palish for's trade.'

'Well, it appears to me that nothing can be gained by retaining this poor man in custody,' said the magistrate; 'your business lies with the other, unquestionably.'

And so the little man was released off-hand; but he looked nothing the less sad on that account, it being beyond the power of magistrate or constable to raze out the written troubles in his brain, for they concerned another whom he regarded with more solicitude than himself. When this was done, and the man had gone his way, the night was found to be so far advanced that it was deemed useless to renew the search before the next morning.

Next day, accordingly, the quest for the clever sheep-stealer became general and keen, to all appearance at least. But the intended punishment was cruelly disproportioned to the transgression, and the sympathy of a great many country-folk in that district was strongly on the side of the fugitive. Moreover, his marvellous coolness and daring in hob-and-nobbing with the hangman, under the unprecedented circumstances of the shepherd's party, won their admiration. So that it may be questioned if all those who ostensibly made themselves so busy in exploring woods and fields and lanes were quite so thorough when it came to the private examination of their own lofts and outhouses. Stories were afloat of a mysterious figure being occasionally seen in some old overgrown trackway or other, remote from turnpike-roads; but when a search was instituted in any of these suspected quarters nobody was found. Thus the days and weeks passed without tidings.

In brief, the bass-voiced man of the chimney-corner was never recaptured. Some said that he went across the sea, others that he did not, but buried himself in the depths of a populous city. At any rate, the gentleman in cinder-grey never did his morning's work at Casterbridge, nor met anywhere at all, for business purposes, the genial comrade with whom he had passed an hour of relaxation in the lonely house on the coomb.

The grass has long been green on the graves of Shepherd Fennel and his frugal wife; the guests who made up the christening party have mainly followed their entertainers to the tomb; the baby in whose honour they all had met is a matron in the sere and yellow leaf. But the arrival of the three strangers at the shepherd's that night, and the details connected therewith, is a story as well known as ever in the country about Higher Crowstairs.

THE ADVENTURE OF THE SPECKLED BAND

Arthur Conan Doyle

On glancing over my notes of the seventy odd cases in which I have during the last eight years studied the methods of my friend Sherlock Holmes, I find many tragic, some comic, a large number merely strange, but none commonplace; for, working as he did rather for the love of his art than for the acquirement of wealth, he refused to associate himself with any investigation which did not tend towards the unusual, and even the fantastic. Of all these varied cases, however, I cannot recall any which presented more singular features than that which was associated with the well-known Surrey family of the Roylotts of Stoke Moran. The events in question occurred in the early days of my association with Holmes, when we were sharing rooms as bachelors in Baker Street. It is possible that I might have placed them upon record before, but a promise of secrecy was made at the time, from which I have only been freed during the last month by the untimely death of the lady to whom the pledge was given. It is perhaps as well that the facts should now come to light, for I have reasons to know that there are widespread rumours as to the death of Dr Grimesby Roylott which tend to make the matter even more terrible than the truth.

It was early in April in the year '83 that I woke one morning to find Sherlock Holmes standing, fully dressed, by the side of my bed. He was a late riser, as a rule, and as the clock on the mantelpiece showed me that it was only a quarter-past seven, I blinked up at him in some surprise, and perhaps just a little resentment, for I was myself regular in my habits.

'Very sorry to knock you up, Watson,' said he, 'but it's the common lot this morning. Mrs Hudson has been knocked up, she retorted upon me, and I on you.'

'What is it, then—a fire?'

'No; a client. It seems that a young lady has arrived in a considerable state of excitement, who insists upon seeing me. She is waiting now in the sitting-room. Now, when young ladies wander about the metropolis at this hour of the morning, and knock sleepy people up out of their beds, I presume that it is something very pressing which they have to communicate. Should it prove to be an interesting case, you would, I am sure, wish to follow it from the outset. I thought, at any rate, that I should call you and give you the chance.'

'My dear fellow, I would not miss it for anything.'

I had no keener pleasure than in following Holmes in his professional investigations, and in admiring the rapid deductions, as swift as intuitions, and yet always founded on a logical basis with which he unravelled the problems which were submitted to him. I rapidly threw on my clothes and was ready in a few minutes to accompany my friend down to the sitting-room. A lady dressed in black and heavily veiled, who had been sitting in the window, rose as we entered.

'Good-morning, madam,' said Holmes cheerily. 'My name is Sherlock Holmes. This is my intimate friend and associate, Dr Watson, before whom you can speak as freely as before myself. Ha! I am glad to see that Mrs Hudson has had the good sense to light the fire. Pray draw up to it, and I shall order you a cup of hot coffee, for I observe that you are shivering.'

'It is not cold which makes me shiver,' said the woman in a low voice, changing her seat as requested.

'What, then?'

'It is fear, Mr Holmes. It is terror.' She raised her veil as she spoke, and we could see that she was indeed in a pitiable state of agitation, her face all drawn and grey, with restless frightened eyes, like those of some hunted animal. Her features and figure were those of a woman of thirty, but her hair was shot with premature grey, and her expression was weary and haggard. Sherlock Holmes ran her over with one of his quick, all-comprehensive glances.

'You must not fear,' said he soothingly, bending forward and patting her forearm. 'We shall soon set matters right, I have no doubt. You have come in by train this morning, I see.'

'You know me, then?'

'No, but I observe the second half of a return ticket in the palm of your left glove. You must have started early, and yet you had a good drive in a dog-cart, along heavy roads, before you reached the station.'

The lady gave a violent start and stared in bewilderment at my companion.

'There is no mystery, my dear madam,' said he, smiling. 'The left arm of your jacket is spattered with mud in no less than seven places. The marks are perfectly fresh. There is no vehicle save a dog-cart which throws up mud in that way, and then only when you sit on the left-hand side of the driver.'

'Whatever your reasons may be, you are perfectly correct,' said she. 'I started from home before six, reached Leatherhead at twenty past, and came in by the first train to Waterloo. Sir, I can stand this strain no longer; I shall go mad if it continues. I have no one to turn to—none, save only one, who cares for me, and he, poor fellow, can be of little aid. I have heard of you, Mr Holmes; I have heard of you from Mrs Farintosh, whom you helped in the hour of her sore need. It was from her that I had your address. Oh, sir, do you not think that you could help me, too, and at least throw a little light through the dense darkness which surrounds me? At present it is out of my power to reward you for your services, but in a month or six weeks I shall be married, with the control of my own income, and then at least you shall not find me ungrateful.'

Holmes turned to his desk and, unlocking it, drew out a small case-book, which he consulted.

'Farintosh,' said he. 'Ah yes, I recall the case; it was concerned with an opal tiara. I think it was before your time, Watson. I can only say, madam, that I shall be happy to devote the same care to your case as I did to that of your friend. As to reward, my profession is its own reward; but you are at liberty to defray whatever expenses I may be put to, at the time which suits you best. And now I beg that you will lay before us everything that may help us in forming an opinion upon the matter.'

'Alas!' replied our visitor, 'the very horror of my situation lies in the fact that my fears are so vague, and my suspicions depend so entirely upon small points, which might seem trivial to another, that even he to whom of all others I have a right to look for help and advice looks upon all that I tell him about it as the fancies of a nervous woman. He does not say so, but I can read it from his soothing answers and averted eyes. But I have heard, Mr Holmes, that you can see deeply into the manifold wickedness of the human heart. You may advise me how to walk amid the dangers which encompass me.'

'I am all attention, madam.'

'My name is Helen Stoner, and I am living with my stepfather, who is the last survivor of one of the oldest Saxon families in England, the Roylotts of Stoke Moran, on the western border of Surrey.'

Holmes nodded his head. 'The name is familiar to me,' said he.

'The family was at one time among the richest in England, and the estates extended over the borders into Berkshire in the north, and Hampshire in the west. In the last century, however, four successive heirs were of a dissolute and wasteful disposition, and the family ruin was eventually completed by a gambler in the days of the Regency. Nothing was left save a few acres of ground, and the two-hundred-year-old house, which is itself crushed under a heavy mortgage. The last squire dragged out his existence there, living the horrible life of an aristocratic pauper; but his only son, my stepfather, seeing that he must adapt himself to the new conditions, obtained an advance from a relative, which enabled him to take a medical degree and went out to Calcutta, where, by his professional skill and his force of character, he established a large practice. In a fit of anger, however, caused by some robberies which had been perpetrated in the house, he beat his native butler to death and narrowly escaped a capital sentence. As it was, he suffered a long term of imprisonment and afterwards returned to England a morose and disappointed man.

'When Dr Roylott was in India he married my mother, Mrs Stoner, the young widow of Major-General Stoner, of the Bengal Artillery. My sister Julia and I were twins, and we were only two years old at the time of my mother's re-marriage. She had a considerable sum of money—not less than £1000 a year—and this she bequeathed to Dr Roylott entirely while we resided with him, with a provision that a certain annual sum should be allowed to each of us in the event of our marriage. Shortly after our return to England my mother died—she was killed eight years ago in a railway accident near Crewe. Dr Roylott then abandoned his attempts to establish himself in practice in London and took us to live with him in the old ancestral house at Stoke Moran. The money which my mother had left was enough for all our wants, and there seemed to be no obstacle to our happiness.

'But a terrible change came over our stepfather about this time. Instead of making friends and exchanging visits with our neighbours, who had at first been overjoyed to see a Roylott of Stoke Moran back in the old family seat, he shut himself up in his house and seldom came out save to indulge in ferocious quarrels with whoever might cross his path. Violence of temper approaching to mania has been hereditary in the men of the family, and in my stepfather's case it had, I believe, been intensified by his long residence in the tropics. A series of disgraceful brawls took place, two of which ended in the police-court, until at last he became the terror of the village, and the folks would fly at his approach, for he is a man of immense strength, and absolutely uncontrollable in his anger.

'Last week he hurled the local blacksmith over a parapet into a stream, and it was only by paying over all the money which I could gather together that I was able to avert another public exposure. He had no friends at all save the wandering gipsies, and he would give these vagabonds leave to encamp upon the few acres of bramble-covered land which represent the family estate, and would accept in return the hospitality of their tents, wandering away with them sometimes for weeks on end. He has a passion also for Indian animals, which are sent over to him by a correspondent, and he has at this moment a cheetah and a baboon, which wander freely over his grounds and are feared by the villagers almost as much as their master.

'You can imagine from what I say that my poor sister Julia and I had no great pleasure in our lives. No servant would stay with us, and for a long time we did all the work of the house. She was but thirty at the time of her death, and yet her hair had already begun to whiten, even as mine has.'

'Your sister is dead, then?'

'She died just two years ago, and it is of her death that I wish to speak to you. You can understand that, living the life which I have described, we were little likely to see anyone of our own age and position. We had, however, an aunt, my mother's maiden sister, Miss Honoria Westphail, who lives near Harrow, and we were occasionally allowed to pay short visits at this lady's house. Julia went there at Christmas two years ago, and met there a half-pay major of marines, to whom she became engaged. My stepfather learned of the engagement when my sister returned and offered no objection to the marriage; but within a fortnight of the day which had been fixed for the wedding, the terrible event occurred which has deprived me of my only companion.'

Sherlock Holmes had been leaning back in his chair with his eyes closed and his head sunk in a cushion, but he half opened his lids now and glanced across at his visitor.

'Pray be precise as to details,' said he.

'It is easy for me to be so, for every event of that dreadful time is seared into my memory. The manor-house is, as I have already said, very old, and only one wing is now inhabited. The bedrooms in this wing are on the ground floor, the sitting-rooms being in the central block of the buildings. Of these bedrooms the first is Dr Roylott's, the second my sister's, and the third my own. There is no communication between them, but they all open out into the same corridor. Do I make myself plain?'

'Perfectly so.'

'The windows of the three rooms open out upon the lawn. That fatal night Dr Roylott had gone to his room early, though we knew that he had not retired to rest, for my sister was troubled by the smell of the strong Indian cigars which it was his custom to smoke. She left her room, therefore, and came into mine, where she sat for some time, chatting about her approaching wedding. At eleven o'clock she rose to leave me, but she paused at the door and looked back.

'"Tell me, Helen," said she, "have you ever heard anyone whistle in the dead of the night?"

'"Never," said I.

'"I suppose that you could not possibly whistle, yourself, in your sleep?"

'"Certainly not. But why?"

'"Because during the last few nights I have always, about three in the morning, heard a low, clear whistle. I am a light sleeper, and it has awakened me. I cannot tell where it came from—perhaps from the next room, perhaps from the lawn. I thought that I would just ask you whether you had heard it."

'"No, I have not. It must be those wretched gipsies in the plantation."

'"Very likely. And yet if it were on the lawn, I wonder that you did not hear it also."

'"Ah, but I sleep more heavily than you."

'"Well, it is of no great consequence, at any rate." She smiled back at me, closed my door, and a few moments later I heard her key turn in the lock.'

'Indeed,' said Holmes. 'Was it your custom always to lock yourselves in at night?'

'Always.'

'And why?'

'I think that I mentioned to you that the Doctor kept a cheetah and a baboon. We had no feeling of security unless our doors were locked.'

'Quite so. Pray proceed with your statement.'

'I could not sleep that night. A vague feeling of impending misfortune impressed me. My sister and I, you will recollect, were twins, and you know how subtle are the links which bind two souls which are so closely allied. It was a wild night. The wind was howling outside, and the rain was beating and splashing against the windows. Suddenly, amid all the hubbub of the gale, there burst forth the wild scream of a terrified woman. I knew that it was my sister's voice. I sprang from my bed, wrapped a shawl round me, and rushed into the corridor. As I opened my door I seemed to hear a low whistle, such as my sister described, and a few moments later a clanging sound, as if a mass of metal had fallen. As I ran down the passage, my sister's door was unlocked, and revolved slowly upon its hinges. I stared at it horror-stricken, not knowing what was about to issue from it. By the light of the corridor-lamp I saw my sister appear at the opening, her face blanched with terror, her hands groping for help, her whole figure swaying to and fro like that of a drunkard. I ran to her and threw my arms round her, but at that moment her knees seemed to give way and she fell to the ground. She writhed as one who is in terrible pain, and her limbs were dreadfully convulsed. At first I thought that she had not recognized me, but as I bent over her she suddenly shrieked out in a voice which I shall never forget, 'Oh, my God! Helen! It was the band! The speckled band!' There was something else which she would fain have said, and she stabbed with her finger into the air in the direction of the Doctor's room, but a fresh convulsion seized her and choked her words. I rushed out, calling loudly for my stepfather, and I met him hastening from his room in his dressing-gown. When he reached my sister's side she was unconscious, and though he poured brandy down her throat and sent for medical aid from the village, all efforts were in vain, for she slowly sank and died without having recovered her consciousness. Such was the dreadful end of my beloved sister.'

'One moment,' said Holmes, 'are you sure about this whistle and metallic sound? Could you swear to it?'

'That was what the county coroner asked me at the inquiry. It is my strong impression that I heard it, and yet, among the crash of the gale and the creaking of an old house, I may possibly have been deceived.'

'Was your sister dressed?'

'No, she was in her night-dress. In her right hand was found the charred stump of a match, and in her left a match-box.'

'Showing that she had struck a light and looked about her when the alarm took place. That is important. And what conclusions did the coroner come to?'

'He investigated the case with great care, for Dr Roylott's conduct had long been notorious in the county, but he was unable to find any satisfactory cause of death. My evidence showed that the door had been fastened upon the inner side, and the windows were blocked by old-fashioned shutters with broad iron bars, which were secured every night. The walls were carefully sounded, and were shown to be quite solid all round, and the flooring was also thoroughly examined, with the same result. The chimney is wide, but is barred up by four large staples. It is certain, therefore, that my sister was quite alone when she met her end. Besides, there were no marks of any violence upon her.'

'How about poison?'

'The doctors examined her for it, but without success.'

'What do you think that this unfortunate lady died of, then?'

'It is my belief that she died of pure fear and nervous shock, though what it was that frightened her I cannot imagine.'

'Were there gipsies in the plantation at the time?'

'Yes, there are nearly always some there.'

'Ah, and what did you gather from this allusion to a band—a speckled band?'

'Sometimes I have thought that it was merely the wild talk of delirium, sometimes that it may have referred to some band of people, perhaps to these very gipsies in the plantation. I do not know whether the spotted handkerchiefs which so many of them wear over their heads might have suggested the strange adjective which she used.'

Holmes shook his head like a man who is far from being satisfied. 'These are very deep waters,' said he; 'pray go on with your narrative.'

'Two years have passed since then, and my life has been until lately lonelier than ever. A month ago, however, a dear friend, whom I have known for many years, has done me the honour to ask my hand in marriage. His name is Armitage—Percy Armitage—the second son of Mr Armitage, of Crane Water, near Reading. My stepfather has offered no opposition to the match, and we are to be married in the course of the spring. Two days ago some repairs were started in the west wing of the building, and my bedroom wall has been pierced, so that I have had to move into the chamber in which my sister died, and to sleep in the very bed in which she slept. Imagine, then, my thrill of terror when last night, as I lay awake, thinking over her terrible fate, I suddenly heard in the silence of the night the low whistle which had been the herald of her own death. I sprang up and lit the lamp, but nothing was to be seen in the room. I was too shaken to go to bed again, however, so I dressed, and as soon as it was daylight I slipped down, got a dog-cart at the Crown Inn, which is opposite, and drove to Leatherhead, from whence I have come on this morning with the one object of seeing you and asking your advice.'

'You have done wisely,' said my friend. 'But have you told me all?'

'Yes, all.'

'Miss Roylott, you have not. You are screening your stepfather.'

'Why, what do you mean?'

For answer Holmes pushed back the frill of black lace which fringed the hand that lay upon our visitor's knee. Five little livid spots, the marks of four fingers and a thumb, were printed upon the white wrist.

'You have been cruelly used,' said Holmes.

The lady coloured deeply and covered over her injured wrist. 'He is a hard man,' she said, 'and perhaps he hardly knows his own strength.'

There was a long silence, during which Holmes leaned his chin upon his hands and stared into the crackling fire.

'This is a very deep business,' he said at last. 'There are a thousand details which I should desire to know before I decide upon our course of action. Yet we have not a moment to lose. If we were to come to Stoke Moran to-day, would it be possible for us to see over these rooms without the knowledge of your stepfather?'

'As it happens, he spoke of coming into town to-day upon some most important business. It is probable that he will be away all day, and that there would be nothing to disturb you. We have a housekeeper now, but she is old and foolish, and I could easily get her out of the way.'

'Excellent. You are not averse to this trip, Watson?'

'By no means.'

'Then we shall both come. What are you going to do yourself?'

'I have one or two things which I would wish to do now that I am in town. But I shall return by the twelve o'clock train, so as to be there in time for your coming.'

'And you may expect us early in the afternoon. I have myself some small business matters to attend to. Will you not wait and breakfast?'

'No, I must go. My heart is lightened already since I have confided my trouble to you. I shall look forward to seeing you again this afternoon.' She dropped her thick black veil over her face and glided from the room.

'And what do you think of it all, Watson?' asked Sherlock Holmes, leaning back in his chair.

'It seems to me to be a most dark and sinister business.'

'Dark enough and sinister enough.'

'Yet if the lady is correct in saying that the flooring and walls are sound, and that the door, window, and chimney are impassable, then her sister must have been undoubtedly alone when she met her mysterious end.'

'What becomes, then, of these nocturnal whistles, and what of the very peculiar words of the dying woman?'

'I cannot think.'

'When you combine the ideas of whistles at night, the presence of a band of gipsies who are on intimate terms with this old doctor, the fact that we have every reason to believe that the doctor has an interest in preventing his stepdaughter's marriage, the dying allusion to a band, and, finally, the fact that Miss Helen Stoner heard a metallic clang, which might have been caused by one of those metal bars that secured the shutters falling back into its place, I think that there is good ground to think that the mystery may be cleared along those lines.'

'But what, then, did the gipsies do?'

'I cannot imagine.'

'I see many objections to any such theory.'

'And so do I. It is precisely for that reason that we are going to Stoke Moran this day. I want to see whether the objections are fatal, or if they may be explained away. But what in the name of the devil!'

The ejaculation had been drawn from my companion by the fact that our door had been suddenly dashed open, and that a huge man had framed himself in the aperture. His costume was a peculiar mixture of the professional and of the agricultural, having a black top-hat, a long frock-coat, and a pair of high gaiters, with a hunting-crop swinging in his hand. So tall was he that his hat actually brushed the cross bar of the doorway, and his breadth seemed to span it across from side to side. A large face, seared with a thousand wrinkles, burned yellow with the sun, and marked with every evil passion, was turned from one to the other of us, while his deep-set, bile-shot eyes, and his high, thin, fleshless nose, gave him somewhat the resemblance to a fierce old bird of prey.

'Which of you is Holmes?' asked this apparition.

'My name, sir; but you have the advantage of me,' said my companion quietly.

'I am Dr Grimesby Roylott, of Stoke Moran.'

'Indeed, Doctor,' said Holmes blandly. 'Pray take a seat.'

'I will do nothing of the kind. My stepdaughter has been here. I have traced her. What has she been saying to you?'

'It is a little cold for the time of the year,' said Holmes.

'What has she been saying to you?' screamed the old man furiously.

'But I have heard that the crocuses promise well,' continued my companion imperturbably.

'Ha! You put me off, do you?' said our new visitor, taking a step forward and shaking his hunting-crop. 'I know you, you scoundrel! I have heard of you before. You are Holmes, the meddler.'

My friend smiled.

'Holmes, the busybody!'

His smile broadened.

'Holmes, the Scotland Yard Jack-in-office!'

Holmes chuckled heartily. 'Your conversation is most entertaining,' said he. 'When you go out close the door, for there is a decided draught.'

'I will go when I have had my say. Don't you dare to meddle with my affairs. I know that Miss Stoner has been here. I traced her! I am a dangerous man to fall foul of! See here.' He stepped swiftly forward, seized the poker, and bent it into a curve with his huge brown hands.

'See that you keep yourself out of my grip,' he snarled, and hurling the twisted poker into the fireplace he strode out of the room.

'He seems a very amiable person,' said Holmes, laughing. 'I am not quite so bulky, but if he had remained I might have shown him that my grip was not much more feeble than his own.' As he spoke he picked up the steel poker and, with a sudden effort, straightened it out again.

'Fancy his having the insolence to confound me with the official detective force! This incident gives zest to our investigation, however, and I only trust that our little friend will not suffer from her imprudence in allowing this brute to trace her. And now, Watson, we shall order breakfast, and afterwards I shall walk down to Doctors' Commons, where I hope to get some data which may help us in this matter.'

It was nearly one o'clock when Sherlock Holmes returned from his excursion. He held in his hand a sheet of blue paper, scrawled over with notes and figures.

'I have seen the will of the deceased wife,' said he. 'To determine its exact meaning I have been obliged to work out the present prices of the investments with which it is concerned. The total income, which at the time of the wife's death was little short of £1,100, is now, through the fall in agricultural prices, not more than £750. Each daughter can claim an income of £250, in case of marriage. It is evident, therefore, that if both girls had married, this beauty would have had a mere pittance, while even one of them would cripple him to a very serious extent. My morning's work has not been wasted, since it has proved that he has the very strongest motives for standing in the way of anything of the sort. And now, Watson, this is too serious for dawdling, especially as the old man is aware that we are interesting ourselves in his affairs; so if you are ready, we shall call a cab and drive to Waterloo. I should be very much obliged if you would slip your revolver into your pocket. An Eley's No. 2 is an excellent argument with gentlemen who can twist steel pokers into knots. That and a tooth-brush are, I think, all that we need.'

At Waterloo we were fortunate in catching a train for Leatherhead, where we hired a trap at the station inn and drove for four or five miles through the lovely Surrey lanes. It was a perfect day, with a bright sun and a few fleecy clouds in the heavens. The trees and wayside hedges were just throwing out their first green shoots, and the air was full of the pleasant smell of the moist earth. To me at least there was a strange contrast between the sweet promise of the spring and this sinister quest upon which we were engaged. My companion sat in the front of the trap, his arms folded, his hat pulled down over his eyes, and his chin sunk upon his breast, buried in the deepest thought. Suddenly, however, he started, tapped me on the shoulder, and pointed over the meadows.

'Look there!' said he.

A heavily timbered park stretched up in a gentle slope, thickening into a grove at the highest point. From amid the branches there jutted out the grey gables and high roof-tree of a very old mansion.

'Stoke Moran?' said he.

'Yes, sir, that be the house of Dr Grimesby Roylott,' remarked the driver.

'There is some building going on there,' said Holmes; 'that is where we are going.'

'There's the village,' said the driver, pointing to a cluster of roofs some distance to the left; 'but if you want to get to the house, you'll find it shorter to get over this stile, and so by the footpath over the fields. There it is, where the lady is walking.'

'And the lady, I fancy, is Miss Stoner,' observed Holmes, shading his eyes. 'Yes, I think we had better do as you suggest.'

We got off, paid our fare, and the trap rattled back on its way to Leatherhead.

'I thought it as well,' said Holmes as we climbed the stile, 'that this fellow should think we had come here as architects, or on some definite business. It may stop his gossip. Good-afternoon, Miss Stoner. You see that we have been as good as our word.'

Our client of the morning had hurried forward to meet us with a face which spoke her joy. 'I have been waiting so eagerly for you,' she cried, shaking hands with us warmly. 'All has turned out splendidly. Dr Roylott has gone to town, and it is unlikely that he will be back before evening.'

'We have had the pleasure of making the Doctor's acquaintance,' said Holmes, and in a few words he sketched out what had occurred. Miss Stoner turned white to the lips as she listened.

'Good heavens!' she cried, 'he has followed me, then.'

'So it appears.'

'He is so cunning that I never know when I am safe from him. What will he say when he returns?'

'He must guard himself, for he may find that there is someone more cunning than himself upon his track. You must lock yourself up from him to-night. If he is violent, we shall take you away to your aunt's at Harrow. Now, we must make the best use of our time, so kindly take us at once to the rooms which we are to examine.'

The building was of grey, lichen-blotched stone, with a high central portion and two curving wings, like the claws of a crab, thrown out on each side. In one of these wings the windows were broken and blocked with wooden boards, while the roof was partly caved in, a picture of ruin. The central portion was in little better repair, but the right-hand block was comparatively modern, and the blinds in the windows, with the blue smoke curling up from the chimneys, showed that this was where the family resided. Some scaffolding had been erected against the end wall, and the stone-work had been broken into, but there were no signs of any workmen at the moment of our visit. Holmes walked slowly up and down the ill-trimmed lawn and examined with deep attention the outsides of the windows.

'This, I take it, belongs to the room in which you used to sleep, the centre one to your sister's, and the one next to the main building to Dr Roylott's chamber?'

'Exactly so. But I am now sleeping in the middle one.'

'Pending the alterations, as I understand. By the way, there does not seem to be any very pressing need for repairs at that end wall.'

'There were none. I believe that it was an excuse to move me from my room.'

'Ah! that is suggestive. Now, on the other side of this narrow wing runs the corridor from which these three rooms open. There are windows in it, of course?'

'Yes, but very small ones. Too narrow for anyone to pass through.'

'As you both locked your doors at night, your rooms were unapproachable from that side. Now, would you have the kindness to go into your room and bar your shutters?'

Miss Stoner did so, and Holmes, after a careful examination through the open window, endeavoured in every way to force the shutter open, but without success. There was no slit through which a knife could be passed to raise the bar. Then with his lens he tested the hinges, but they were of solid iron, built firmly into the massive masonry. 'Hum!' said he, scratching his chin in some perplexity, 'my theory certainly presents some difficulties. No one could pass these shutters if they were bolted. Well, we shall see if the inside throws any light upon the matter.'

A small side door led into the whitewashed corridor from which the three bedrooms opened. Holmes refused to examine the third chamber, so we passed at once to the second, that in which Miss Stoner was now sleeping, and in which her sister had met with her fate. It was a homely little room, with a low ceiling and a gaping fireplace, after the fashion of old country-houses. A brown chest of drawers stood in one corner, a narrow white-counterpaned bed in another, and a dressing-table on the left-hand side of the window. These articles, with two small wicker-work chairs, made up all the furniture in the room save for a square of Wilton carpet in the centre. The boards round and the panelling of the walls were of brown, worm-eaten oak, so old and discoloured that it may have dated from the original building of the house. Holmes drew one of the chairs into a corner and sat silent, while his eyes travelled round and round and up and down, taking in every detail of the apartment.

'Where does that bell communicate with?' he asked at last pointing to a thick bell-rope which hung down beside the bed, the tassel actually lying upon the pillow.

'It goes to the housekeeper's room.'

'It looks newer than the other things?'

'Yes, it was only put there a couple of years ago.'

'Your sister asked for it, I suppose?'

'No, I never heard of her using it. We used always to get what we wanted for ourselves.'

'Indeed, it seemed unnecessary to put so nice a bell-pull there. You will excuse me for a few minutes while I satisfy myself as to this floor.' He threw himself down upon his face with his lens in his hand and crawled swiftly backward and forward, examining minutely the cracks between the boards. Then he did the same with the wood-work with which the chamber was panelled. Finally he walked over to the bed and spent some time in staring at it and in running his eye up and down the wall. Finally he took the bell-rope in his hand and gave it a brisk tug.

'Why, it's a dummy,' said he.

'Won't it ring?'

'No, it is not even attached to a wire. This is very interesting. You can see now that it is fastened to a hook just above where the little opening for the ventilator is.'

'How very absurd! I never noticed that before.'

'Very strange!' muttered Holmes, pulling at the rope. 'There are one or two very singular points about this room. For example, what a fool a builder must be to open a ventilator into another room, when, with the same trouble, he might have communicated with the outside air!'

'That is also quite modern,' said the lady.

'Done about the same time as the bell-rope?' remarked Holmes.

'Yes, there were several little changes carried out about that time.'

'They seem to have been of a most interesting character—dummy bell-ropes, and ventilators which do not ventilate. With your permission, Miss Stoner, we shall now carry our researches into the inner apartment.'

Dr Grimesby Roylott's chamber was larger than that of his step-daughter, but was as plainly furnished. A camp-bed, a small wooden shelf full of books, mostly of a technical character, an armchair beside the bed, a plain wooden chair against the wall, a round table, and a large iron safe were the principal things which met the eye. Holmes walked slowly round and examined each and all of them with the keenest interest.

'What's in here?' he asked, tapping the safe.

'My stepfather's business papers.'

'Oh! you have seen inside, then?'

'Only once, some years ago. I remember that it was full of papers.'

'There isn't a cat in it, for example?'

'No. What a strange idea!'

'Well, look at this!' He took up a small saucer of milk which stood on the top of it.

'No; we don't keep a cat. But there is a cheetah and a baboon.'

'Ah, yes, of course! Well, a cheetah is just a big cat, and yet a saucer of milk does not go very far in satisfying its wants, I daresay. There is one point which I should wish to determine.' He squatted down in front of the wooden chair and examined the seat of it with the greatest attention.

'Thank you. That is quite settled,' said he, rising and putting his lens in his pocket. 'Hullo! Here is something interesting!'

The object which had caught his eye was a small dog lash hung on one corner of the bed. The lash, however, was curled upon itself and tied so as to make a loop of whipcord.

'What do you make of that, Watson?'

'It's a common enough lash. But I don't know why it should be tied.'

'That is not quite so common, is it? Ah, me! it's a wicked world, and when a clever man turns his brains to crime it is the worst of all. I think that I have seen enough now, Miss Stoner, and with your permission we shall walk out upon the lawn.'

I had never seen my friend's face so grim or his brow so dark as it was when we turned from the scene of this investigation. We had walked several times up and down the lawn, neither Miss Stoner nor myself liking to break in upon his thoughts before he roused himself from his reverie.

'It is very essential, Miss Stoner,' said he, 'that you should absolutely follow my advice in every respect.'

'I shall most certainly do so.'

'The matter is too serious for any hesitation. Your life may depend upon your compliance.'

'I assure you that I am in your hands.'

'In the first place, both my friend and I must spend the night in your room.'

Both Miss Stoner and I gazed at him in astonishment.

'Yes, it must be so. Let me explain. I believe that that is the village inn over there?'

'Yes, that is the Crown.'

'Very good. Your windows would be visible from there?'

'Certainly.'

'You must confine yourself to your room, on pretence of a headache, when your stepfather comes back. Then when you hear him retire for the night, you must open the shutters of your window, undo the hasp, put your lamp there as a signal to us, and then withdraw quietly with everything which you are likely to want into the room which you used to occupy. I have no doubt that, in spite of the repairs, you could manage there for one night.'

'Oh, yes, easily.'

'The rest you will leave in our hands.'

'But what will you do?'

'We shall spend the night in your room, and we shall investigate the cause of this noise which has disturbed you.'

'I believe, Mr Holmes, that you have already made up your mind,' said Miss Stoner, laying her hand upon my companion's sleeve.

'Perhaps I have.'

'Then, for pity's sake, tell me what was the cause of my sister's death.'

'I should prefer to have clearer proofs before I speak.'

'You can at least tell me whether my own thought is correct, and if she died from some sudden fright.'

'No, I do not think so. I think that there was probably some more tangible cause. And now, Miss Stoner, we must leave you for if Dr Roylott returned and saw us our journey would be in vain. Good-bye, and be brave, for if you will do what I have told you, you may rest assured that we shall soon drive away the dangers that threaten you.'

Sherlock Holmes and I had no difficulty in engaging a bedroom and sitting-room at the Crown Inn. They were on the upper floor, and from our window we could command a view of the avenue gate, and of the inhabited wing of Stoke Moran Manor House. At dusk we saw Dr Grimesby Roylott drive past, his huge form looming up beside the little figure of the lad who drove him. The boy had some slight difficulty in undoing the heavy iron gates, and we heard the hoarse roar of the Doctor's voice and saw the fury with which he shook his clinched fists at him. The trap drove on, and a few minutes later we saw a sudden light spring up among the trees as the lamp was lit in one of the sitting-rooms.

'Do you know, Watson,' said Holmes as we sat together in the gathering darkness, 'I have really some scruples as to taking you to-night. There is a distinct element of danger.'

'Can I be of assistance?'

'Your presence might be invaluable.'

'Then I shall certainly come.'

'It is very kind of you.'

'You speak of danger. You have evidently seen more in these rooms than was visible to me.'

'No, but I fancy that I may have deduced a little more. I imagine that you saw all that I did.'

'I saw nothing remarkable save the bell-rope, and what purpose that could answer I confess is more than I can imagine.'

'You saw the ventilator, too?'

'Yes, but I do not think that it is such a very unusual thing to have a small opening between two rooms. It was so small that a rat could hardly pass through.'

'I knew that we should find a ventilator before ever we came to Stoke Moran.'

'My dear Holmes!'

'Oh, yes, I did. You remember in her statement she said that her sister could smell Dr Roylott's cigar. Now, of course that suggested at once that there must be a communication between the two rooms. It could only be a small one, or it would have been remarked upon at the coroner's inquiry. I deduced a ventilator.'

'But what harm can there be in that?'

'Well, there is at least a curious coincidence of dates. A ventilator is made, a cord is hung, and a lady who sleeps in the bed dies. Does not that strike you?'

'I cannot as yet see any connection.'

'Did you observe anything very peculiar about that bed?'

'No.'

'It was clamped to the floor. Did you ever see a bed fastened like that before?'

'I cannot say that I have.'

'The lady could not move her bed. It must always be in the same relative position to the ventilator and to the rope—or so we may call it, since it was clearly never meant for a bell-pull.'

'Holmes,' I cried, 'I seem to see dimly what you are hinting at. We are only just in time to prevent some subtle and horrible crime.'

'Subtle enough and horrible enough. When a doctor does go wrong he is the first of criminals. He has nerve and he has knowledge. Palmer and Pritchard were among the heads of their profession. This man strikes even deeper, but I think, Watson, that we shall be able to strike deeper still. But we shall have horrors enough before the night is over; for goodness' sake let us have a quiet pipe and turn our minds for a few hours to something more cheerful.'

About nine o'clock the light among the trees was extinguished, and all was dark in the direction of the Manor House. Two hours passed slowly away, and then, suddenly, just at the stroke of eleven, a single bright light shone out right in front of us.

'That is our signal,' said Holmes, springing to his feet; 'it comes from the middle window.'

As we passed out he exchanged a few words with the landlord, explaining that we were going on a late visit to an acquaintance, and that it was possible that we might spend the night there. A moment later we were out on the dark road, a chill wind blowing in our faces, and one yellow light twinkling in front of us through the gloom to guide us on our sombre errand.

There was little difficulty in entering the grounds, for unrepaired breaches gaped in the old park wall. Making our way among the trees, we reached the lawn, crossed it, and were about to enter through the window when out from a clump of laurel bushes there darted what seemed to be a hideous and distorted child, who threw itself upon the grass with writhing limbs and then ran swiftly across the lawn into the darkness.

'My God!' I whispered; 'did you see it?'

Holmes was for the moment as startled as I. His hand closed like a vice upon my wrist in his agitation. Then he broke into a low laugh and put his lips to my ear.

'It is a nice household,' he murmured. 'That is the baboon.'

I had forgotten the strange pets which the Doctor affected. There was a cheetah, too; perhaps we might find it upon our shoulders at any moment. I confess that I felt easier in my mind when, after following Holmes' example and slipping off my shoes, I found myself inside the bedroom. My companion noiselessly closed the shutters, moved the lamp onto the table, and cast his eyes round the room. All was as we had seen it in the daytime. Then creeping up to me and making a trumpet of his hand, he whispered into my ear again so gently that it was all that I could do to distinguish the words:

'The least sound would be fatal to our plans.'

I nodded to show that I had heard.

'We must sit without light. He would see it through the ventilator.'

I nodded again.

'Do not go asleep; your very life may depend upon it. Have your pistol ready in case we should need it. I will sit on the side of the bed, and you in that chair.'

I took out my revolver and laid it on the corner of the table.

Holmes had brought up a long thin cane, and this he placed upon the bed beside him. By it he laid the box of matches and the stump of a candle. Then he turned down the lamp, and we were left in darkness.

How shall I ever forget that dreadful vigil? I could not hear a sound, not even the drawing of a breath, and yet I knew that my companion sat open-eyed, within a few feet of me, in the same state of nervous tension in which I was myself. The shutters cut off the least ray of light, and we waited in absolute darkness.

From outside came the occasional cry of a night-bird, and once at our very window a long drawn catlike whine, which told us that the cheetah was indeed at liberty. Far away we could hear the deep tones of the parish clock, which boomed out every quarter of an hour. How long they seemed, those quarters! Twelve struck, and one and two and three, and still we sat waiting silently for whatever might befall.

Suddenly there was the momentary gleam of a light up in the direction of the ventilator, which vanished immediately, but was succeeded by a strong smell of burning oil and heated metal. Someone in the next room had lit a dark-lantern. I heard a gentle sound of movement, and then all was silent once more, though the smell grew stronger. For half an hour I sat with straining ears. Then suddenly another sound became audible—a very gentle, soothing sound, like that of a small jet of steam escaping continually from a kettle. The instant that we heard it, Holmes sprang from the bed, struck a match, and lashed furiously with his cane at the bell-pull.

'You see it, Watson?' he yelled. 'You see it?'

But I saw nothing. At the moment when Holmes struck the light I heard a low, clear whistle, but the sudden glare flashing into my weary eyes made it impossible for me to tell what it was at which my friend lashed so savagely. I could, however, see that his face was deadly pale and filled with horror and loathing. He had ceased to strike and was gazing up at the ventilator when suddenly there broke from the silence of the night the most horrible cry to which I have ever listened. It swelled up louder and louder, a hoarse yell of pain and fear and anger all mingled in the one dreadful shriek. They say that away down in the village, and even in the distant parsonage, that cry raised the sleepers from their beds. It struck cold to our hearts, and I stood gazing at Holmes, and he at me, until the last echoes of it had died away into the silence from which it rose.

'What can it mean?' I gasped.

'It means that it is all over,' Holmes answered. 'And perhaps, after all, it is for the best. Take your pistol, and we will enter Dr Roylott's room.'

With a grave face he lit the lamp and led the way down the corridor. Twice he struck at the chamber door without any reply from within. Then he turned the handle and entered, I at his heels, with the cocked pistol in my hand.

It was a singular sight which met our eyes. On the table stood a dark-lantern with the shutter half open, throwing a brilliant beam of light upon the iron safe, the door of which was ajar. Beside this table, on the wooden chair, sat Dr Grimesby Roylott clad in a long grey dressing-gown, his bare ankles protruding beneath, and his feet thrust into red heelless Turkish slippers. Across his lap lay the short stock with the long lash which we had noticed during the day. His chin was cocked upward and his eyes were fixed in a dreadful, rigid stare at the corner of the ceiling. Round his brow he had a peculiar yellow band, with brownish speckles, which seemed to be bound tightly round his head. As we entered he made neither sound nor motion.

'The band! the speckled band!' whispered Holmes.

I took a step forward. In an instant his strange headgear began to move, and there reared itself from among his hair the squat diamond-shaped head and puffed neck of a loathsome serpent.

'It is a swamp adder!' cried Holmes; 'the deadliest snake in India. He has died within ten seconds of being bitten. Violence does, in truth, recoil upon the violent, and the schemer falls into the pit which he digs for another. Let us thrust this creature back into its den, and we can then remove Miss Stoner to some place of shelter and let the county police know what has happened.'

As he spoke he drew the dog-whip swiftly from the dead man's lap, and throwing the noose round the reptile's neck he drew it from its horrid perch and, carrying it at arm's length, threw it into the iron safe, which he closed upon it.

Such are the true facts of the death of Dr Grimesby Roylott, of Stoke Moran. It is not necessary that I should prolong a narrative which has already run to too great a length by telling how we broke the sad news to the terrified girl, how we conveyed her by the morning train to the care of her good aunt at Harrow, of how the slow process of official inquiry came to the conclusion that the doctor met his fate while indiscreetly playing with a dangerous pet. The little which I had yet to learn of the case was told me by Sherlock Holmes as we travelled back next day.

'I had,' said he, 'come to an entirely erroneous conclusion which shows, my dear Watson, how dangerous it always is to reason from insufficient data. The presence of the gipsies, and the use of the word "band," which was used by the poor girl, no doubt, to explain the appearance which she had caught a hurried glimpse of by the light of her match, were sufficient to put me upon an entirely wrong scent. I can only claim the merit that I instantly reconsidered my position when, however, it became clear to me that whatever danger threatened an occupant of the room could not come either from the window or the door. My attention was speedily drawn, as I have already remarked to you, to this ventilator, and to the bell-rope which hung down to the bed. The discovery that this was a dummy, and that the bed was clamped to the floor, instantly gave rise to the suspicion that the rope was there as a bridge for something passing through the hole and coming to the bed. The idea of a snake instantly occurred to me, and when I coupled it with my knowledge that the doctor was furnished with a supply of creatures from India, I felt that I was probably on the right track. The idea of using a form of poison which could not possibly be discovered by any chemical test was just such a one as would occur to a clever and ruthless man who had had an Eastern training. The rapidity with which such a poison would take effect would also, from his point of view, be an advantage. It would be a sharp-eyed coroner, indeed, who could distinguish the two little dark punctures which would show where the poison fangs had done their work. Then I thought of the whistle. Of course he must recall the snake before the morning light revealed it to the victim. He had trained it, probably by the use of the milk which we saw, to return to him when summoned. He would put it through this ventilator at the hour that he thought best, with the certainty that it would crawl down the rope and land on the bed. It might or might not bite the occupant, perhaps she might escape every night for a week, but sooner or later she must fall a victim.

'I had come to these conclusions before ever I had entered his room. An inspection of his chair showed me that he had been in the habit of standing on it, which of course would be necessary in order that he should reach the ventilator. The sight of the safe, the saucer of milk, and the loop of whipcord were enough to finally dispel any doubts which may have remained. The metallic clang heard by Miss Stoner was obviously caused by her stepfather hastily closing the door of his safe upon its terrible occupant. Having once made up my mind, you know the steps which I took in order to put the matter to the proof. I heard the creature hiss as I have no doubt that you did also, and I instantly lit the light and attacked it.'

'With the result of driving it through the ventilator.'

'And also with the result of causing it to turn upon its master at the other side. Some of the blows of my cane came home and roused its snakish temper, so that it flew upon the first person it saw. In this way I am no doubt indirectly responsible for Dr Grimesby Roylott's death, and I cannot say that it is likely to weigh very heavily upon my conscience.'

BEHIND THE SHADE

Arthur Morrison

The street was the common East End street—two parallels of brick pierced with windows and doors. But at the end of one, where the builder had found a remnant of land too small for another six-roomer, there stood an odd box of a cottage, with three rooms and a wash-house. It had a green door with a well-blacked knocker round the corner; and in the lower window in front stood a 'shade of fruit'—a cone of waxen grapes and apples under a glass cover.

Although the house was smaller than the others, and was built upon a remnant, it was always a house of some consideration. In a street like this mere independence of pattern gives distinction. And a house inhabited by one sole family makes a figure among houses inhabited by two or more, even though it be the smallest of all. And here the seal of respectability was set by the shade of fruit—a sign accepted in those parts. Now, when people keep a house to themselves, and keep it clean; when they neither stand at the doors nor gossip across back-fences; when, moreover, they have a well-dusted shade of fruit in the front window; and, especially, when they are two women who tell nobody their business: they are known at once for well-to-do, and are regarded with the admixture of spite and respect that is proper to the circumstances. They are also watched.

Still, the neighbours knew the history of the Perkinses, mother and daughter, in its main features, with little disagreement: having told it to each other, filling in the details when occasion seemed to serve. Perkins, ere he died, had been a shipwright; and this was when the shipwrights were the aristocracy of the work-shops, and he that worked more than three or four days a week was counted a mean slave: it was long (in fact) before depression, strikes, iron plates, and collective blindness had driven shipbuilding to the Clyde. Perkins had laboured no harder than his fellows, had married a tradesman's daughter, and had spent his money with freedom; and some while after his death his widow and daughter came to live in the small house, and kept a school for tradesmen's little girls in a back room over the wash-house. But as the School Board waxed in power, and the tradesmen's pride in regard thereunto waned, the attendance, never large, came down to twos and threes. Then Mrs Perkins met with her accident. A dweller in Stidder's Rents overtook her one night, and, having vigorously punched her in the face and the breast, kicked her and jumped on her for five minutes as she lay on the pavement. (In the dark, it afterwards appeared, he had mistaken her for his mother.) The one distinct opinion the adventure bred in the street was Mrs Webster's, the Little Bethelite, who considered it a judgment for sinful pride—for Mrs Perkins had been a Church-goer. But the neighbours never saw Mrs Perkins again. The doctor left his patient 'as well as she ever would be,' but bed-ridden and helpless. Her daughter was a scraggy, sharp-faced woman of thirty or so, whose black dress hung from her hips as from a wooden frame; and some people got into the way of calling her Mrs Perkins, seeing no other thus to honour. And meantime, the school had ceased, although Miss Perkins essayed a revival, and joined a Dissenting chapel to that end.

Then, one day, a card appeared in the window, over the shade of fruit, with the legend 'Pianoforte Lessons'. It was not approved by the street. It was a standing advertisement of the fact that the Perkinses had a piano, which others had not. It also revealed a grasping spirit on the part of people able to keep a house to themselves, with red curtains and a shade of fruit in the parlour window; who, moreover, had been able to give up keeping a school because of ill-health. The pianoforte lessons were eight-and-sixpence a quarter, two a week. Nobody was ever known to take them but the relieving officer's daughter, and she paid sixpence a lesson, to see how she got on, and left off in three weeks. The card stayed in the window a fortnight longer, and none of the neighbours saw the cart that came in the night and took away the old cabinet piano with the channelled keys, that had been fourth-hand when Perkins bought it twenty years ago. Mrs Clark, the widow who sewed far into the night, may possibly have heard a noise and looked; but she said nothing if she did. There was no card in the window next morning, but the shade of fruit stood primly respectable as ever. The curtains were drawn a little closer across, for some of the children playing in the street were used to flatten their faces against the lower panes, and to discuss the piano, the stuff-bottomed chairs, the antimacassars, the mantelpiece ornaments, and the loo table with the family Bible and the album on it.

It was soon after this that the Perkinses altogether ceased from shopping—ceased, at any rate, in that neighbourhood. Trade with them had already been dwindling, and it was said that Miss Perkins was getting stingier than her mother—who had been stingy enough herself. Indeed, the Perkins demeanour began to change for the worse, to be significant of a miserly retirement and an offensive alienation from the rest of the street. One day the deacon called, as was his practice now and then; but, being invited no further than the doorstep, he went away in dudgeon, and did not return. Nor, indeed, was Miss Perkins seen again at chapel.

Then there was a discovery. The spare figure of Miss Perkins was seldom seen in the streets, and then almost always at night; but on these occasions she was observed to carry parcels, of varying wrappings and shapes. Once, in broad daylight, with a package in newspaper, she made such haste past a shop-window where stood Mrs Webster and Mrs Jones, that she tripped on the broken sole of one shoe, and fell headlong. The newspaper broke away from its pins, and although the woman reached and recovered her parcel before she rose, it was plain to see that it was made up of cheap shirts, cut out ready for the stitching. The street had the news the same hour, and it was generally held that such a taking of the bread out of the mouths of them that wanted it by them that had plenty was a scandal and a shame, and ought to be put a stop to. And Mrs Webster, foremost in the setting right of things, undertook to find out whence the work came, and to say a few plain words in the right quarter.

All this while nobody watched closely enough to note that the parcels brought in were fewer than the parcels taken out. Even a hand-truck, late one evening, went unremarked: the door being round the corner, and most people within. One morning, though, Miss Perkins, her best foot foremost, was venturing along a near street with an outgoing parcel—large and triangular and wrapped in white drugget—when the relieving officer turned the corner across the way.

The relieving officer was a man in whose system of etiquette the Perkinses had caused some little disturbance. His ordinary female acquaintances (not, of course, professional) he was in the habit of recognizing by a gracious nod. When he met the minister's wife he lifted his hat, instantly assuming an intense frown, in the event of irreverent observation. Now he quite felt that the Perkinses were entitled to some advance upon the nod, although it would be absurd to raise them to a level with the minister's wife. So he had long since established a compromise: he closed his finger and thumb upon the brim of his hat, and let his hand fall forthwith. Preparing now to accomplish this salute, he was astounded to see that Miss Perkins, as soon as she was aware of his approach, turned her face, which was rather flushed, away from him, and went hurrying onward, looking at the wall on her side of the street. The relieving officer, checking his hand on its way to his hat, stopped and looked after her as she turned the corner, hugging her parcel on the side next the wall. Then he shouldered his umbrella and pursued his way, holding his head high, and staring fiercely straight before him; for a relieving officer is not used to being cut.

It was a little after this that Mr Crouch, the landlord, called. He had not been calling regularly, because of late Miss Perkins had left her five shillings of rent with Mrs Crouch every Saturday evening. He noted with satisfaction the whitened sills and the shade of fruit, behind which the curtains were now drawn close and pinned together. He turned the corner and lifted the bright knocker. Miss Perkins half opened the door, stood in the opening, and began to speak.

His jaw dropped. 'Beg pardon—forgot something. Won't wait—call next week—do just as well'; and he hurried round the corner and down the street, puffing and blowing and staring. 'Why, the woman frightened me,' he afterward explained to Mrs Crouch. 'There's something wrong with her eyes, and she looked like a corpse. The rent wasn't ready—I could see that before she spoke; so I cleared out.'

'P'r'aps something's happened to the old lady,' suggested Mrs Crouch. 'Anyhow, I should think the rent 'ud be all right.' And he thought it would.

Nobody saw the Perkinses that week. The shade of fruit stood in its old place, but was thought not to have been dusted after Tuesday. Certainly the sills and the doorstep were neglected. Friday, Saturday and Sunday were swallowed up in a choking brown fog, wherein men lost their bearings, and fell into docks, and stepped over embankment edges. It was as though a great blot had fallen, and had obliterated three days from the calendar. It cleared on Monday morning, and, just as the women in the street were sweeping their steps, Mr Crouch was seen at the green door. He lifted the knocker, dull and sticky now with the foul vapour, and knocked a gentle rat-tat. There was no answer. He knocked again, a little louder, and waited, listening. But there was neither voice nor movement within. He gave three heavy knocks, and then came round to the front window. There was the shade of fruit, the glass a little duller on the top, the curtains pinned close about it, and nothing to see beyond them. He tapped at the window with his knuckles, and backed into the roadway to look at the one above. This was a window with a striped holland blind and a short net curtain; but never a face was there.

The sweepers stopped to look, and one from opposite came and reported that she had seen nothing of Miss Perkins for a week, and that certainly nobody had left the house that morning. And Mr Crouch grew excited, and bellowed through the keyhole.

In the end they opened the sash-fastening with a knife, moved the shade of fruit, and got in. The room was bare and empty, and their steps and voices resounded as those of people in an unfurnished house. The wash-house was vacant, but it was clean, and there was a little net curtain in the window. The short passage and the stairs were bare boards. In the back room by the stair-head was a drawn window-blind, and that was all. In the front room with the striped blind and the short curtain there was a bed of rags and old newspapers; also a wooden box; and on each of these was a dead woman.

Both deaths, the doctor found, were from syncope, the result of inanition; and the better-nourished woman—she on the bed—had died the sooner; perhaps by a day or two. The other case was rather curious; it exhibited a degree of shrinkage in the digestive organs unprecedented in his experience. After the inquest the street had an evening's fame: for the papers printed coarse drawings of the house, and in leaderettes demanded the abolition of something. Then it became its wonted self. And it was doubted if the waxen apples and the curtains fetched enough to pay Mr Crouch his fortnight's rent.

THE LIBRARY WINDOW

Margaret Oliphant

I

I was not aware at first of the many discussions which had gone on about that window. It was almost opposite one of the windows of the large old-fashioned drawing-room of the house in which I spent that summer, which was of so much importance in my life. Our house and the library were on opposite sides of the broad High Street of St Rule's, which is a fine street, wide and ample, and very quiet, as strangers think who come from noisier places; but in a summer evening there is much coming and going, and the stillness is full of sound—the sound of footsteps and pleasant voices, softened by the summer air. There are even exceptional moments when it is noisy: the time of the fair, and on Saturday nights sometimes, and when there are excursion trains. Then even the softest sunny air of the evening will not smooth the harsh tones and the stumbling steps; but at these unlovely moments we shut the windows, and even I, who am so fond of that deep recess where I can take refuge from all that is going on inside, and make myself a spectator of all the varied story out of doors, withdraw from my watch-tower. To tell the truth, there never was very much going on inside. The house belonged to my aunt, to whom (she says, Thank God!) nothing ever happens. I believe that many things have happened to her in her time; but that was all over at the period of which I am speaking, and she was old, and very quiet. Her life went on in a routine never broken. She got up at the same hour every day, and did the same things in the same rotation, day by day the same. She said that this was the greatest support in the world, and that routine is a kind of salvation. It may be so; but it is a very dull salvation, and I used to feel that I would rather have incident, whatever kind of incident it might be. But then at that time I was not old, which makes all the difference.

At the time of which I speak the deep recess of the drawing-room window was a great comfort to me. Though she was an old lady (perhaps because she was so old) she was very tolerant, and had a kind of feeling for me. She never said a word, but often gave me a smile when she saw how I had built myself up, with my books and my basket of work. I did very little work, I fear—now and then a few stitches when the spirit moved me, or when I had got well afloat in a dream, and was more tempted to follow it out than to read my book, as sometimes happened. At other times, and if the book were interesting, I used to get through volume after volume sitting there, paying no attention to anybody. And yet I did pay a kind of attention. Aunt Mary's old ladies came in to call, and I heard them talk, though I very seldom listened; but for all that, if they had anything to say that was interesting, it is curious how I found it in my mind afterwards, as if the air had blown it to me. They came and went, and I had the sensation of their old bonnets gliding out and in, and their dresses rustling; and now and then had to jump up and shake hands with some one who knew me, and asked after my papa and mamma. Then Aunt Mary would give me a little smile again, and I slipped back to my window. She never seemed to mind. My mother would not have let me do it, I know. She would have remembered dozens of things there were to do. She would have sent me up-stairs to fetch something which I was quite sure she did not want, or down-stairs to carry some quite unnecessary message to the housemaid. She liked to keep me running about. Perhaps that was one reason why I was so fond of Aunt Mary's drawing-room, and the deep recess of the window, and the curtain that fell half over it, and the broad window-seat where one could collect so many things without being found fault with for untidiness. Whenever we had anything the matter with us in these days, we were sent to St Rule's to get up our strength. And this was my case at the time of which I am going to speak.

Everybody had said, since ever I learned to speak, that I was fantastic and fanciful and dreamy, and all the other words with which a girl who may happen to like poetry, and to be fond of thinking, is so often made uncomfortable. People don't know what they mean when they say fantastic. It sounds like Madge Wildfire or something of that sort. My mother thought I should always be busy, to keep nonsense out of my head. But really I was not at all fond of nonsense. I was rather serious than otherwise. I would have been no trouble to anybody if I had been left to myself. It was only that I had a sort of second-sight, and was conscious of things to which I paid no attention. Even when reading the most interesting book, the things that were being talked about blew in to me; and I heard what the people were saying in the streets as they passed under the window. Aunt Mary always said I could do two or indeed three things at once—both read and listen, and see. I am sure that I did not listen much, and seldom looked out, of set purpose—as some people do who notice what bonnets the ladies in the street have on; but I did hear what I couldn't help hearing, even when I was reading my book, and I did see all sorts of things, though often for a whole half-hour I might never lift my eyes.

This does not explain what I said at the beginning, that there were many discussions about that window. It was, and still is, the last window in the row, of the College Library, which is opposite my aunt's house in the High Street. Yet it is not exactly opposite, but a little to the west, so that I could see it best from the left side of my recess. I took it calmly for granted that it was a window like any other till I first heard the talk about it which was going on in the drawing-room. 'Have you never made up your mind, Mrs Balcarres,' said old Mr Pitmilly, 'whether that window opposite is a window or no?' He said Mistress Balcarres—and he was always called Mr Pitmilly, Morton: which was the name of his place.

'I am never sure of it, to tell the truth,' said Aunt Mary, 'all these years.'

'Bless me!' said one of the old ladies, 'and what window may that be?'

Mr Pitmilly had a way of laughing as he spoke, which did not please me; but it was true that he was not perhaps desirous of pleasing me. He said, 'Oh, just the window opposite,' with his laugh running through his words; 'our friend can never make up her mind about it, though she has been living opposite it since—'

'You need never mind the date,' said another; 'the Leebrary window! Dear me, what should it be but a window? up at that height it could not be a door.'

'The question is,' said my aunt, 'if it is a real window with glass in it, or if it is merely painted, or if it once was a window, and has been built up. And the oftener people look at it, the less they are able to say.'

'Let me see this window,' said old Lady Carnbee, who was very active and strong-minded; and then they all came crowding upon me—three or four old ladies, very eager, and Mr Pitmilly's white hair appearing over their heads, and my aunt sitting quiet and smiling behind.

'I mind the window very well,' said Lady Carnbee; 'ay: and so do more than me. But in its present appearance it is just like any other window; but has not been cleaned, I should say, in the memory of man.'

'I see what ye mean,' said one of the others. 'It is just a very dead thing without any reflection in it; but I've seen as bad before.'

'Ay, it's dead enough,' said another, 'but that's no rule; for these hizzies of women-servants in this ill age—'

'Nay, the women are well enough,' said the softest voice of all, which was Aunt Mary's. 'I will never let them risk their lives cleaning the outside of mine. And there are no women-servants in the Old Library: there is maybe something more in it than that.'

They were all pressing into my recess, pressing upon me, a row of old faces, peering into something they could not understand. I had a sense in my mind how curious it was, the wall of old ladies in their old satin gowns all glazed with age, Lady Carnbee with her lace about her head. Nobody was looking at me or thinking of me; but I felt unconsciously the contrast of my youngness to their oldness, and stared at them as they stared over my head at the Library window. I had given it no attention up to this time. I was more taken up with the old ladies than with the thing they were looking at.

'The framework is all right at least, I can see that, and pented black—'

'And the panes are pented black too. It's no window, Mrs Balcarres. It has been filled in, in the days of the window duties: you will mind, Leddy Carnbee.'

'Mind!' said that oldest lady. 'I mind when your mother was marriet, Jeanie: and that's neither the day nor yesterday. But as for the window, it's just a delusion: and that is my opinion of the matter, if you ask me.'

'There's a great want of light in that muckle room at the college,' said another. 'If it was a window, the Leebrary would have more light.'

'One thing is clear,' said one of the younger ones, 'it cannot be a window to see through. It may be filled in or it may be built up, but it is not a window to give light.'

'And who ever heard of a window that was no to see through?' Lady Carnbee said. I was fascinated by the look on her face, which was a curious scornful look as of one who knew more than she chose to say: and then my wandering fancy was caught by her hand as she held it up, throwing back the lace that dropped over it. Lady Carnbee's lace was the chief thing about her—heavy black Spanish lace with large flowers. Everything she wore was trimmed with it. A large veil of it hung over her old bonnet. But her hand coming out of this heavy lace was a curious thing to see. She had very long fingers, very taper, which had been much admired in her youth; and her hand was very white, or rather more than white, pale, bleached, and bloodless, with large blue veins standing up upon the back; and she wore some fine rings, among others a big diamond in an ugly old claw setting. They were too big for her, and were wound round and round with yellow silk to make them keep on: and this little cushion of silk, turned brown with long wearing, had twisted round so that it was more conspicuous than the jewels; while the big diamond blazed underneath in the hollow of her hand, like some dangerous thing hiding and sending out darts of light. The hand, which seemed to come almost to a point, with this strange ornament underneath, clutched at my half-terrified imagination. It too seemed to mean far more than was said. I felt as if it might clutch me with sharp claws, and the lurking, dazzling creature bite—with a sting that would go to the heart.

Presently, however, the circle of the old faces broke up, the old ladies returned to their seats, and Mr Pitmilly, small but very erect, stood up in the midst of them, talking with mild authority like a little oracle among the ladies. Only Lady Carnbee always contradicted the neat, little, old gentleman. She gesticulated, when she talked, like a Frenchwoman, and darted forth that hand of hers with the lace hanging over it, so that I always caught a glimpse of the lurking diamond. I thought she looked like a witch among the comfortable little group which gave such attention to everything Mr Pitmilly said.

'For my part, it is my opinion there is no window there at all,' he said. 'It's very like the thing that's called in scientific language an optical illusion. It arises generally, if I may use such a word in the presence of ladies, from a liver that is not just in the perfitt order and balance that organ demands—and then you will see things—a blue dog, I remember, was the thing in one case, and in another—'

'The man has gane gyte,' said Lady Carnbee; 'I mind the windows in the Auld Leebrary as long as I mind anything. Is the Leebrary itself an optical illusion too?'

'Na, na,' and 'No, no,' said the old ladies; 'a blue dogue would be a strange vagary: but the Library we have all kent from our youth,' said one. 'And I mind when the Assemblies were held there one year when the Town Hall was building,' another said.

'It is just a great divert to me,' said Aunt Mary: but what was strange was that she paused there, and said in a low tone, 'now': and then went on again, 'for whoever comes to my house, there are aye discussions about that window. I have never just made up my mind about it myself. Sometimes I think it's a case of these wicked window duties, as you said, Miss Jeanie, when half the windows in our houses were blocked up to save the tax. And then, I think, it may be due to that blank kind of building like the great new buildings on the Earthen Mound in Edinburgh, where the windows are just ornaments. And then whiles I am sure I can see the glass shining when the sun catches it in the afternoon.'

'You could so easily satisfy yourself, Mrs Balcarres, if you were to—'

'Give a laddie a penny to cast a stone, and see what happens,' said Lady Carnbee.

'But I am not sure that I have any desire to satisfy myself,' Aunt Mary said. And then there was a stir in the room, and I had to come out from my recess and open the door for the old ladies and see them down-stairs, as they all went away following one another. Mr Pitmilly gave his arm to Lady Carnbee, though she was always contradicting him; and so the tea-party dispersed. Aunt Mary came to the head of the stairs with her guests in an old-fashioned gracious way, while I went down with them to see that the maid was ready at the door. When I came back Aunt Mary was still standing in the recess looking out. Returning to my seat she said, with a kind of wistful look, 'Well, honey: and what is your opinion?'

'I have no opinion. I was reading my book all the time,' I said.

'And so you were, honey, and no' very civil; but all the same I ken well you heard every word we said.'

II

It was a night in June; dinner was long over, and had it been winter the maids would have been shutting up the house, and my Aunt Mary preparing to go up-stairs to her room. But it was still clear daylight, that daylight out of which the sun has been long gone, and which has no longer any rose reflections, but all has sunk into a pearly neutral tint—a light which is daylight yet is not day. We had taken a turn in the garden after dinner, and now we had returned to what we called our usual occupations. My aunt was reading. The English post had come in, and she had got her *Times*, which was her great diversion. The *Scotsman* was her morning reading, but she liked her *Times* at night.

As for me, I too was at my usual occupation, which at that time was doing nothing. I had a book as usual, and was absorbed in it: but I was conscious of all that was going on all the same. The people strolled along the broad pavement, making remarks as they passed under the open window which came up into my story or my dream, and sometimes made me laugh. The tone and the faint sing-song, or rather chant, of the accent, which was 'a wee Fifish', was novel to me, and associated with holiday, and pleasant; and sometimes they said to each other something that was amusing, and often something that suggested a whole story; but presently they began to drop off, the footsteps slackened, the voices died away. It was getting late, though the clear soft daylight went on and on. All through the lingering evening, which seemed to consist of interminable hours, long but not weary, drawn out as if the spell of the light and the outdoor life might never end, I had now and then, quite unawares, cast a glance at the mysterious window which my aunt and her friends had discussed, as I felt, though I dared not say it even to myself, rather foolishly. It caught my eye without any intention on my part, as I paused, as it were, to take breath, in the flowing and current of undistinguishable thoughts and things from without and within which carried me along. First it occurred to me, with a little sensation of discovery, how absurd to say it was not a window, a living window, one to see through! Why, then, had they never *seen* it, these old folk? I saw as I looked up suddenly the faint greyness as of visible space within—a room behind, certainly dim, as it was natural a room should be on the other side of the street—quite indefinite: yet so clear that if some one were to come to the window there would be nothing surprising in it. For certainly there was a feeling of space behind the panes which these old half-blind ladies had disputed about whether they were glass or only fictitious panes marked on the wall. How silly! when eyes that could see could make it out in a minute. It was only a greyness at present, but it was unmistakable, a space that went back into gloom, as every room does when you look into it across a street. There were no curtains to show whether it was inhabited or not; but a room—oh, as distinctly as ever room was! I was pleased with myself, but said nothing, while Aunt Mary rustled her paper, waiting for a favourable moment to announce a discovery which settled her problem at once. Then I was carried away upon the stream again, and forgot the window, till somebody threw unawares a word from the outer world, 'I'm goin' hame; it'll soon be dark.' Dark! what was the fool thinking of? it never would be dark if one waited out, wandering in the soft air for hours longer; and then my eyes, acquiring easily that new habit, looked across the way again.

Ah, now! nobody indeed had come to the window; and no light had been lighted, seeing it was still beautiful to read by—a still, clear, colourless light; but the room inside had certainly widened. I could see the grey space and air a little deeper, and a sort of vision, very dim, of a wall, and something against it; something dark, with the blackness that a solid article, however indistinctly seen, takes in the lighter darkness that is only space—a large, black, dark thing coming out into the grey. I looked more intently, and made sure it was a piece of furniture, either a writing-table or perhaps a large book-case. No doubt it must be the last, since this was part of the old library. I never visited the old College Library, but I had seen such places before, and I could well imagine it to myself. How curious that for all the time these old people had looked at it, they had never seen this before!

It was more silent now, and my eyes, I suppose, had grown dim with gazing, doing my best to make it out, when suddenly Aunt Mary said, 'Will you ring the bell, my dear? I must have my lamp.'

'Your lamp?' I cried, 'when it is still daylight.' But then I gave another look at my window, and perceived with a start that the light had indeed changed: for now I saw nothing. It was still light, but there was so much change in the light that my room, with the grey space and the large shadowy bookcase, had gone out, and I saw them no more: for even a Scotch night in June, though it looks as if it would never end, does darken at the last. I had almost cried out, but checked myself, and rang the bell for Aunt Mary, and made up my mind I would say nothing till next morning, when to be sure naturally it would be more clear.

Next morning I rather think I forgot all about it—or was busy: or was more idle than usual: the two things meant nearly the same. At all events I thought no more of the window, though I still sat in my own, opposite to it, but occupied with some other fancy. Aunt Mary's visitors came as usual in the afternoon; but their talk was of other things, and for a day or two nothing at all happened to bring back my thoughts into this channel. It might be nearly a week before the subject came back, and once more it was old Lady Carnbee who set me thinking; not that she said anything upon that particular theme. But she was the last of my aunt's afternoon guests to go away, and when she rose to leave she threw up her hands, with those lively gesticulations which so many old Scotch ladies have. 'My faith!' said she, 'there is that bairn there still like a dream. Is the creature bewitched, Mary Balcarres? and is she bound to sit there by night and by day for the rest of her days? You should mind that there's things about, uncanny for women of our blood.'

I was too much startled at first to recognize that it was of me she was speaking. She was like a figure in a picture, with her pale face the colour of ashes, and the big pattern of the Spanish lace hanging half over it, and her hand held up, with the big diamond blazing at me from the inside of her uplifted palm. It was held up in surprise, but it looked as if it were raised in malediction; and the diamond threw out darts of light and glared and twinkled at me. If it had been in its right place it would not have mattered; but there, in the open of the hand! I started up, half in terror, half in wrath. And then the old lady laughed, and her hand dropped. 'I've wakened you to life, and broke the spell,' she said, nodding her old head at me, while the large black silk flowers of the lace waved and threatened. And she took my arm to go down-stairs, laughing and bidding me be steady, and no' tremble and shake like a broken reed. 'You should be as steady as a rock at your age. I was like a young tree,' she said, leaning so heavily that my willowy girlish frame quivered—'I was a support to virtue, like Pamela, in my time.'

'Aunt Mary, Lady Carnbee is a witch!' I cried, when I came back.

'Is that what you think, honey? well: maybe she once was,' said Aunt Mary, whom nothing surprised.

And it was that night once more after dinner, and after the post came in, and the *Times*, that I suddenly saw the Library window again. I had seen it every day and noticed nothing; but to-night, still in a little tumult of mind over Lady Carnbee and her wicked diamond which wished me harm, and her lace which waved threats and warnings at me, I looked across the street, and there I saw quite plainly the room opposite, far more clear than before. I saw dimly that it must be a large room, and that the big piece of furniture against the wall was a writing-desk. That in a moment, when first my eyes rested upon it, was quite clear: a large old-fashioned escritoire, standing out into the room: and I knew by the shape of it that it had a great many pigeon-holes and little drawers in the back, and a large table for writing. There was one just like it in my father's library at home. It was such a surprise to see it all so clearly that I closed my eyes, for the moment almost giddy, wondering how papa's desk could have come here—and then when I reminded myself that this was nonsense, and that there were many such writing-tables besides papa's, and looked again—lo! it had all become quite vague and indistinct as it was at first; and I saw nothing but the blank window, of which the old ladies could never be certain whether it was filled up to avoid the window-tax, or whether it had ever been a window at all.

This occupied my mind very much, and yet I did not say anything to Aunt Mary. For one thing, I rarely saw anything at all in the early part of the day; but then that is natural: you can never see into a place from outside, whether it is an empty room or a looking-glass, or people's eyes, or anything else that is mysterious, in the day. It has, I suppose, something to do with the light. But in the evening in June in Scotland—then is the time to see. For it is daylight, yet it is not day, and there is a quality in it which I cannot describe, it is so clear, as if every object was a reflection of itself.

I used to see more and more of the room as the days went on. The large escritoire stood out more and more into the space: with sometimes white glimmering things, which looked like papers, lying on it: and once or twice I was sure I saw a pile of books on the floor close to the writing-table, as if they had gilding upon them in broken specks, like old books. It was always about the time when the lads in the street began to call to each other that they were going home, and sometimes a shriller voice would come from one of the doors, bidding somebody to 'cry upon the laddies' to come back to their suppers. That was always the time I saw best, though it was close upon the moment when the veil seemed to fall and the clear radiance became less living, and all the sounds died out of the street, and Aunt Mary said in her soft voice, 'Honey! will you ring for the lamp?' She said honey as people say darling: and I think it is a prettier word.

Then finally, while I sat one evening with my book in my hand, looking straight across the street, not distracted by anything, I saw a little movement within. It was not any one visible—but everybody must know what it is to see the stir in the air, the little disturbance—you cannot tell what it is, but that it indicates some one there, even though you can see no one. Perhaps it is a shadow making just one flicker in the still place. You may look at an empty room and the furniture in it for hours, and then suddenly there will be the flicker, and you know that something has come into it. It might only be a dog or a cat; it might be, if that were possible, a bird flying across; but it is some one, something living, which is so different, so completely different, in a moment from the things that are not living. It seemed to strike quite through me, and I gave a little cry. Then Aunt Mary stirred a little, and put down the huge newspaper that almost covered her from sight, and said, 'What is it, honey?' I cried 'Nothing,' with a little gasp, quickly, for I did not want to be disturbed just at this moment when somebody was coming! But I suppose she was not satisfied, for she got up and stood behind to see what it was, putting her hand on my shoulder. It was the softest touch in the world, but I could have flung it off angrily: for that moment everything was still again, and the place grew grey and I saw no more.

'Nothing,' I repeated, but I was so vexed I could have cried. 'I told you it was nothing, Aunt Mary. Don't you believe me, that you come to look—and spoil it all!'

I did not mean of course to say these last words; they were forced out of me. I was so much annoyed to see it all melt away like a dream: for it was no dream, but as real as—as real as—myself or anything I ever saw.

She gave my shoulder a little pat with her hand. 'Honey,' she said, 'were you looking at something? Is't that? is't that?' 'Is it what?' I wanted to say, shaking off her hand, but something in me stopped me: for I said nothing at all, and she went quietly back to her place. I suppose she must have rung the bell herself, for immediately I felt the soft flood of the light behind me, and the evening outside dimmed down, as it did every night, and I saw nothing more.

It was next day, I think, in the afternoon that I spoke. It was brought on by something she said about her fine work. 'I get a mist before my eyes,' she said; 'you will have to learn my old lace stitches, honey—for I soon will not see to draw the threads.'

'Oh, I hope you will keep your sight,' I cried, without thinking what I was saying. I was then young and very matter-of-fact. I had not found out that one may mean something, yet not half or a hundredth part of what one seems to mean: and even then probably hoping to be contradicted if it is anyhow against one's self.

'My sight!' she said, looking up at me with a look that was almost angry; 'there is no question of losing my sight—on the contrary, my eyes are very strong. I may not see to draw fine threads, but I see at a distance as well as ever I did—as well as you do.'

'I did not mean any harm, Aunt Mary,' I said. 'I thought you said—But how can your sight be as good as ever when you are in doubt about that window? I can see into the room as clear as—' My voice wavered, for I had just looked up and across the street, and I could have sworn that there was no window at all, but only a false image of one painted on the wall.

'Ah!' she said, with a little tone of keenness and of surprise: and she half rose up, throwing down her work hastily, as if she meant to come to me: then, perhaps seeing the bewildered look on my face, she paused and hesitated—'Ay, honey!' she said, 'have you got so far ben as that?'

What did she mean? Of course I knew all the old Scotch phrases as well as I knew myself; but it is a comfort to take refuge in a little ignorance, and I know I pretended not to understand whenever I was put out. 'I don't know what you mean by "far ben",' I cried out, very impatient. I don't know what might have followed, but some one just then came to call, and she could only give me a look before she went forward, putting out her hand to her visitor. It was a very soft look, but anxious, and as if she did not know what to do: and she shook her head a very little, and I thought, though there was a smile on her face, there was something wet about her eyes. I retired into my recess, and nothing more was said.

But it was very tantalizing that it should fluctuate so; for sometimes I saw that room quite plain and clear—quite as clear as I could see papa's library, for example, when I shut my eyes. I compared it naturally to my father's study, because of the shape of the writing-table, which, as I tell you, was the same as his. At times I saw the papers on the table quite plain, just as I had seen his papers many a day. And the little pile of books on the floor at the foot—not ranged regularly in order, but put down one above the other, with all their angles going different ways, and a speck of the old gilding shining here and there. And then again at other times I saw nothing, absolutely nothing, and was no better than the old ladies who had peered over my head, drawing their eyelids together, and arguing that the window had been shut up because of the old long-abolished window tax, or else that it had never been a window at all. It annoyed me very much at those dull moments to feel that I too puckered up my eyelids and saw no better than they.

Aunt Mary's old ladies came and went day after day while June went on. I was to go back in July, and I felt that I should be very unwilling indeed to leave until I had quite cleared up—as I was indeed in the way of doing—the mystery of that window which changed so strangely and appeared quite a different thing, not only to different people, but to the same eyes at different times. Of course I said to myself it must simply be an effect of the light.

And yet I did not quite like that explanation either, but would have been better pleased to make out to myself that it was some superiority in me which made it so clear to me, if it were only the great superiority of young eyes over old—though that was not quite enough to satisfy me, seeing it was a superiority which I shared with every little lass and lad in the street. I rather wanted, I believe, to think that there was some particular insight in me which gave clearness to my sight—which was a most impertinent assumption, but really did not mean half the harm it seems to mean when it is put down here in black and white. I had several times again, however, seen the room quite plain, and made out that it was a large room, with a great picture in a dim gilded frame hanging on the farther wall, and many other pieces of solid furniture making a blackness here and there, besides the great escritoire against the wall, which had evidently been placed near the window for the sake of the light. One thing became visible to me after another, till I almost thought I should end by being able to read the old lettering on one of the big volumes which projected from the others and caught the light; but this was all preliminary to the great event which happened about Midsummer Day—the day of St John, which was once so much thought of as a festival, but now means nothing at all in Scotland any more than any other of the saints' days: which I shall always think a great pity and loss to Scotland, whatever Aunt Mary may say.

III

It was about midsummer, I cannot say exactly to a day when, but near that time, when the great event happened. I had grown very well acquainted by this time with that large dim room. Not only the escritoire, which was very plain to me now, with the papers upon it, and the books at its foot, but the great picture that hung against the farther wall, and various other shadowy pieces of furniture, especially a chair which one evening I saw had been moved into the space before the escritoire,—a little change which made my heart beat, for it spoke so distinctly of some one who must have been there, the some one who had already made me start, two or three times before, by some vague shadow of him or thrill of him which made a sort of movement in the silent space: a movement which made me sure that next minute I must see something or hear something which would explain the whole—if it were not that something always happened outside to stop it, at the very moment of its accomplishment. I had no warning this time of movement or shadow. I had been looking into the room very attentively a little while before, and had made out everything almost clearer than ever; and then had bent my attention again on my book, and read a chapter or two at a most exciting period of the story: and consequently had quite left St Rule's, and the High Street, and the College Library, and was really in a South American forest, almost throttled by the flowery creepers, and treading softly lest I should put my foot on a scorpion or a dangerous snake. At this moment something suddenly calling my attention to the outside, I looked across, and then, with a start, sprang up, for I could not contain myself. I don't know what I said, but enough to startle the people in the room, one of whom was old Mr Pitmilly. They all looked round upon me to ask what was the matter. And when I gave my usual answer of 'Nothing', sitting down again shamefaced but very much excited, Mr Pitmilly got up and came forward, and looked out, apparently to see what was the cause. He saw nothing, for he went back again, and I could hear him telling Aunt Mary not to be alarmed, for Missy had fallen into a doze with the heat, and had startled herself waking up, at which they all laughed: another time I could have killed him for his impertinence, but my mind was too much taken up now to pay any attention. My head was throbbing and my heart beating. I was in such high excitement, however, that to restrain myself completely, to be perfectly silent, was more easy to me then than at any other time of my life. I waited until the old gentleman had taken his seat again, and then I looked back. Yes, there he was! I had not been deceived. I knew then, when I looked across, that this was what I had been looking for all the time—that I had known he was there, and had been waiting for him, every time there was that flicker of movement in the room—him and no one else. And there at last, just as I had expected, he was. I don't know that in reality I ever had expected him, or any one: but this was what I felt when, suddenly looking into that curious dim room, I saw him there.

He was sitting in the chair, which he must have placed for himself, or which some one else in the dead of night when nobody was looking must have set for him, in front of the escritoire—with the back of his head towards me, writing. The light fell upon him from the left hand, and therefore upon his shoulders and the side of his head, which, however, was too much turned away to show anything of his face. Oh, how strange that there should be some one staring at him as I was doing, and he never to turn his head, to make a movement! If any one stood and looked at me, were I in the soundest sleep that ever was, I would wake, I would jump up, I would feel it through everything. But there he sat and never moved. You are not to suppose, though I said the light fell upon him from the left hand, that there was very much light. There never is in a room you are looking into like that across the street; but there was enough to see him by—the outline of his figure dark and solid, seated in the chair, and the fairness of his head visible faintly, a clear spot against the dimness. I saw this outline against the dim gilding of the frame of the large picture which hung on the farther wall.

I sat all the time the visitors were there, in a sort of rapture, gazing at this figure. I knew no reason why I should be so much moved. In an ordinary way, to see a student at an opposite window quietly doing his work might have interested me a little, but certainly it would not have moved me in any such way. It is always interesting to have a glimpse like this of an unknown life—to see so much and yet know so little, and to wonder, perhaps, what the man is doing, and why he never turns his head. One would go to the window—but not too close, lest he should see you and think you were spying upon him—and one would ask, Is he still there? is he writing, writing always? I wonder what he is writing! And it would be a great amusement: but no more. This was not my feeling at all in the present case. It was a sort of breathless watch, an absorption. I did not feel that I had eyes for anything else, or any room in my mind for another thought. I no longer heard, as I generally did, the stories and the wise remarks (or foolish) of Aunt Mary's old ladies or Mr Pitmilly. I heard only a murmur behind me, the interchange of voices, one softer, one sharper; but it was not as in the time when I sat reading and heard every word, till the story in my book, and the stories they were telling (what they said almost always shaped into stories), were all mingled into each other, and the hero in the novel became somehow the hero (or more likely heroine) of them all. But I took no notice of what they were saying now. And it was not that there was anything very interesting to look at, except the fact that he was there. He did nothing to keep up the absorption of my thoughts. He moved just so much as a man will do when he is very busily writing, thinking of nothing else. There was a faint turn of his head as he went from one side to another of the page he was writing; but it appeared to be a long long page which never wanted turning. Just a little inclination when he was at the end of the line, outward, and then a little inclination inward when he began the next. That was little enough to keep one gazing. But I suppose it was the gradual course of events leading up to this, the finding out of one thing after another as the eyes got accustomed to the vague light: first the room itself, and then the writing-table, and then the other furniture, and last of all the human inhabitant who gave it all meaning. This was all so interesting that it was like a country which one had discovered. And then the extraordinary blindness of the other people who disputed among themselves whether it was a window at all! I did not, I am sure, wish to be disrespectful, and I was very fond of my Aunt Mary, and I liked Mr Pitmilly well enough, and I was afraid of Lady Carnbee. But yet to think of the—I know I ought not to say stupidity—the blindness of them, the foolishness, the insensibility! discussing it as if a thing that your eyes could see was a thing to discuss! It would have been unkind to think it was because they were old and their faculties dimmed. It is so sad to think that the faculties grow dim, that such a woman as my Aunt Mary should fail in seeing, or hearing, or feeling, that I would not have dwelt on it for a moment, it would have seemed so cruel! And then such a clever old lady as Lady Carnbee, who could see through a millstone, people said—and Mr Pitmilly, such an old man of the world. It did indeed bring tears to my eyes to think that all those clever people, solely by reason of being no longer young as I was, should have the simplest things shut out from them; and for all their wisdom and their knowledge be unable to see what a girl like me could see so easily. I was too much grieved for them to dwell upon that thought, and half ashamed, though perhaps half proud too, to be so much better off than they.

All those thoughts flitted through my mind as I sat and gazed across the street. And I felt there was so much going on in that room across the street! He was so absorbed in his writing, never looked up, never paused for a word, never turned round in his chair, or got up and walked about the room as my father did. Papa is a great writer, everybody says: but he would have come to the window and looked out, he would have drummed with his fingers on the pane, he would have watched a fly and helped it over a difficulty, and played with the fringe of the curtain, and done a dozen other nice, pleasant, foolish things, till the next sentence took shape. 'My dear, I am waiting for a word,' he would say to my mother when she looked at him, with a question why he was so idle, in her eyes; and then he would laugh, and go back again to his writing-table. But He over there never stopped at all. It was like a fascination. I could not take my eyes from him and that little scarcely perceptible movement he made, turning his head. I trembled with impatience to see him turn the page, or perhaps throw down his finished sheet on the floor, as somebody looking into a window like me once saw Sir Walter do, sheet after sheet. I should have cried out if this Unknown had done that. I should not have been able to help myself, whoever had been present; and gradually I got into such a state of suspense waiting for it to be done that my head grew hot and my hands cold. And then, just when there was a little movement of his elbow, as if he were about to do this, to be called away by Aunt Mary to see Lady Carnbee to the door! I believe I did not hear her till she had called me three times, and then I stumbled up, all flushed and hot, and nearly crying. When I came out from the recess to give the old lady my arm (Mr Pitmilly had gone away some time before), she put up her hand and stroked my cheek. 'What ails the bairn?' she said; 'she's fevered. You must not let her sit her lane in the window, Mary Balcarres. You and me know what comes of that.' Her old fingers had a strange touch, cold like something not living, and I felt that dreadful diamond sting me on the cheek.

I do not say that this was not just a part of my excitement and suspense; and I know it is enough to make any one laugh when the excitement was all about an unknown man writing in a room on the other side of the way, and my impatience because he never came to an end of the page. If you think I was not quite as well aware of this as any one could be! but the worst was that this dreadful old lady felt my heart beating against her arm that was within mine. 'You are just in a dream,' she said to me, with her old voice close at my ear as we went down-stairs. 'I don't know who it is about, but it's bound to be some man that is not worth it. If you were wise you would think of him no more.'

'I am thinking of no man!' I said, half crying. 'It is very unkind and dreadful of you to say so, Lady Carnbee. I never thought of—any man, in all my life!' I cried in a passion of indignation. The old lady clung tighter to my arm, and pressed it to her, not unkindly.

'Poor little bird,' she said, 'how it's strugglin' and flutterin'! I'm not saying but what it's more dangerous when it's all for a dream.'

She was not at all unkind; but I was very angry and excited, and would scarcely shake that old pale hand which she put out to me from her carriage window when I had helped her in. I was angry with her, and I was afraid of the diamond, which looked up from under her finger as if it saw through and through me; and whether you believe me or not, I am certain that it stung me again—a sharp malignant prick, oh full of meaning! She never wore gloves, but only black lace mittens, through which that horrible diamond gleamed.

I ran up-stairs—she had been the last to go and Aunt Mary too had gone to get ready for dinner, for it was late. I hurried to my place, and looked across, with my heart beating more than ever. I made quite sure I should see the finished sheet lying white upon the floor. But what I gazed at was only the dim blank of that window which they said was no window. The light had changed in some wonderful way during that five minutes I had been gone, and there was nothing, nothing, not a reflection, not a glimmer. It looked exactly as they all said, the blank form of a window painted on the wall. It was too much: I sat down in my excitement and cried as if my heart would break. I felt that they had done something to it, that it was not natural, that I could not bear their unkindness—even Aunt Mary. They thought it not good for me! not good for me! and they had done something—even Aunt Mary herself—and that wicked diamond that hid itself in Lady Carnbee's hand. Of course I knew all this was ridiculous as well as you could tell me; but I was exasperated by the disappointment and the sudden stop to all my excited feelings, and I could not bear it. It was more strong than I.

I was late for dinner, and naturally there were some traces in my eyes that I had been crying when I came into the full light in the dining-room, where Aunt Mary could look at me at her pleasure, and I could not run away. She said, 'Honey, you have been shedding tears. I'm loth, loth that a bairn of your mother's should be made to shed tears in my house.'

'I have not been made to shed tears,' cried I; and then, to save myself another fit of crying, I burst out laughing and said, 'I am afraid of that dreadful diamond on old Lady Carnbee's hand. It bites—I am sure it bites! Aunt Mary, look here.'

'You foolish lassie,' Aunt Mary said; but she looked at my cheek under the light of the lamp, and then she gave it a little pat with her soft hand. 'Go away with you, you silly bairn. There is no bite; but a flushed cheek, my honey, and a wet eye. You must just read out my paper to me after dinner when the post is in: and we'll have no more thinking and no more dreaming for tonight.'

'Yes, Aunt Mary,' said I. But I knew what would happen; for when she opens up her *Times*, all full of the news of the world, and the speeches and things which she takes an interest in, though I cannot tell why—she forgets. And as I kept very quiet and made not a sound, she forgot to-night what she had said, and the curtain hung a little more over me than usual, and I sat down in my recess as if I had been a hundred miles away. And my heart gave a great jump, as if it would have come out of my breast; for he was there. But not as he had been in the morning—I suppose the light, perhaps, was not good enough to go on with his work without a lamp or candles—for he had turned away from the table and was fronting the window, sitting leaning back in his chair, and turning his head to me. Not to me—he knew nothing about me. I thought he was not looking at anything; but with his face turned my way. My heart was in my mouth: it was so unexpected, so strange! though why it should have seemed strange I know not, for there was no communication between him and me that it should have moved me; and what could be more natural than that a man, wearied of his work, and feeling the want perhaps of more light, and yet that it was not dark enough to light a lamp, should turn round in his own chair, and rest a little, and think—perhaps of nothing at all? Papa always says he is thinking of nothing at all. He says things blow through his mind as if the doors were open, and he has no responsibility. What sort of things were blowing through this man's mind? or was he thinking, still thinking, of what he had been writing and going on with it still? The thing that troubled me most was that I could not make out his face. It is very difficult to do so when you see a person only through two windows, your own and his. I wanted very much to recognize him afterwards if I should chance to meet him in the street. If he had only stood up and moved about the room, I should have made out the rest of his figure, and then I should have known him again; or if he had only come to the window (as papa always did), then I should have seen his face clearly enough to have recognized him. But, to be sure, he did not see any need to do anything in order that I might recognize him, for he did not know I existed; and probably if he had known I was watching him, he would have been annoyed and gone away.

But he was as immovable there facing the window as he had been seated at the desk. Sometimes he made a little faint stir with a hand or a foot, and I held my breath, hoping he was about to rise from his chair—but he never did it. And with all the efforts I made I could not be sure of his face. I puckered my eyelids together as old Miss Jeanie did who was shortsighted, and I put my hands on each side of my face to concentrate the light on him: but it was all in vain. Either the face changed as I sat staring, or else it was the light that was not good enough, or I don't know what it was. His hair seemed to me light—certainly there was no dark line about his head, as there would have been had it been very dark—and I saw, where it came across the old gilt frame on the wall behind, that it must be fair: and I am almost sure he had no beard. Indeed I am sure that he had no beard, for the outline of his face was distinct enough; and the daylight was still quite clear out of doors, so that I recognized perfectly a baker's boy who was on the pavement opposite, and whom I should have known again whenever I had met him: as if it was of the least importance to recognize a baker's boy!

There was one thing, however, rather curious about this boy. He had been throwing stones at something or somebody. In St Rule's they have a great way of throwing stones at each other, and I suppose there had been a battle. I suppose also that he had one stone in his hand left over from the battle, and his roving eye took in all the incidents of the street to judge where he could throw it with most effect and mischief. But apparently he found nothing worthy of it in the street, for he suddenly turned round with a flick under his leg to show his cleverness, and aimed it straight at the window. I remarked without remarking that it struck with a hard sound and without any breaking of glass, and fell straight down on the pavement. But I took no notice of this even in my mind, so intently was I watching the figure within, which moved not nor took the slightest notice, and remained just as dimly clear, as perfectly seen, yet as indistinguishable, as before. And then the light began to fail a little, not diminishing the prospect within, but making it still less distinct than it had been.

Then I jumped up, feeling Aunt Mary's hand upon my shoulder. 'Honey,' she said, 'I asked you twice to ring the bell; but you did not hear me.'

'Oh, Aunt Mary!' I cried in great penitence, but turning again to the window in spite of myself.

'You must come away from there: you must come away from there,' she said, almost as if she were angry: and then her soft voice grew softer, and she gave me a kiss: 'never mind about the lamp, honey; I have rung myself, and it is coming; but, silly bairn, you must not aye be dreaming—your little head will turn.'

All the answer I made, for I could scarcely speak, was to give a little wave with my hand to the window on the other side of the street.

She stood there patting me softly on the shoulder for a whole minute or more, murmuring something that sounded like, 'She must go away, she must go away.' Then she said, always with her hand soft on my shoulder, 'Like a dream when one awaketh.' And when I looked again, I saw the blank of an opaque surface and nothing more.

Aunt Mary asked me no more questions. She made me come into the room and sit in the light and read something to her. But I did not know what I was reading, for there suddenly came into my mind and took possession of it, the thud of the stone upon the window, and its descent straight down, as if from some hard substance that threw it off: though I had myself seen it strike upon the glass of the panes across the way.

IV

I am afraid I continued in a state of great exaltation and commotion of mind for some time. I used to hurry through the day till the evening came, when I could watch my neighbour through the window opposite. I did not talk much to any one, and I never said a word about my own questions and wonderings. I wondered who he was, what he was doing, and why he never came till the evening (or very rarely); and I also wondered much to what house the room belonged in which he sat. It seemed to form a portion of the old College Library, as I have often said. The window was one of the line of windows which I understood lighted the large hall; but whether this room belonged to the library itself, or how its occupant gained access to it, I could not tell. I made up my mind that it must open out of the hall, and that the gentleman must be the Librarian or one of his assistants, perhaps kept busy all the day in his official duties, and only able to get to his desk and do his own private work in the evening. One has heard of so many things like that—a man who had to take up some other kind of work for his living, and then when his leisure-time came, gave it all up to something he really loved—some study or some book he was writing. My father himself at one time had been like that. He had been in the Treasury all day, and then in the evening wrote his books, which made him famous. His daughter, however little she might know of other things, could not but know that! But it discouraged me very much when somebody pointed out to me one day in the street an old gentleman who wore a wig and took a great deal of snuff, and said, That's the Librarian of the old College. It gave me a great shock for a moment; but then I remembered that an old gentleman has generally assistants, and that it must be one of them.

Gradually I became quite sure of this. There was another small window above, which twinkled very much when the sun shone, and looked a very kindly bright little window, above that dullness of the other which hid so much. I made up my mind this was the window of his other room, and that these two chambers at the end of the beautiful hall were really beautiful for him to live in, so near all the books, and so retired and quiet, that nobody knew of them. What a fine thing for him! and you could see what use he made of his good fortune as he sat there, so constant at his writing for hours together. Was it a book he was writing, or could it be perhaps Poems? This was a thought which made my heart beat; but I concluded with much regret that it could not be Poems, because no one could possibly write Poems like that, straight off, without pausing for a word or a rhyme. Had they been Poems he must have risen up, he must have paced about the room or come to the window as papa did—not that papa wrote Poems: he always said, 'I am not worthy even to speak of such prevailing mysteries,' shaking his head—which gave me a wonderful admiration and almost awe of a Poet, who was thus much greater even than papa. But I could not believe that a poet could have kept still for hours and hours like that. What could it be then? perhaps it was history; that is a great thing to work at, but you would not perhaps need to move nor to stride up and down, or look out upon the sky and the wonderful light.

He did move now and then, however, though he never came to the window. Sometimes, as I have said, he would turn round in his chair and turn his face towards it, and sit there for a long time musing when the light had begun to fail, and the world was full of that strange day which was night, that light without colour, in which everything was so clearly visible, and there were no shadows. 'It was between the night and the day, when the fairy folk have power.' This was the after-light of the wonderful, long, long summer evening, the light without shadows. It had a spell in it, and sometimes it made me afraid: and all manner of strange thoughts seemed to come in, and I always felt that if only we had a little more vision in our eyes we might see beautiful folk walking about in it, who were not of our world. I thought most likely he saw them, from the way he sat there looking out: and this made my heart expand with the most curious sensation, as if of pride that, though I could not see, he did, and did not even require to come to the window, as I did, sitting close in the depth of the recess, with my eyes upon him, and almost seeing things through his eyes.

I was so much absorbed in these thoughts and in watching him every evening—for now he never missed an evening, but was always there—that people began to remark that I was looking pale and that I could not be well, for I paid no attention when they talked to me, and did not care to go out, nor to join the other girls for their tennis, nor to do anything that others did; and some said to Aunt Mary that I was quickly losing all the ground I had gained, and that she could never send me back to my mother with a white face like that. Aunt Mary had begun to look at me anxiously for some time before that, and, I am sure, held secret consultations over me, sometimes with the doctor, and sometimes with her old ladies, who thought they knew more about young girls than even the doctors. And I could hear them saying to her that I wanted diversion, that I must be diverted, and that she must take me out more, and give a party, and that when the summer visitors began to come there would perhaps be a ball or two, or Lady Carnbee would get up a picnic. 'And there's my young lord coming home,' said the old lady whom they called Miss Jeanie, 'and I never knew the young lassie yet that would not cock up her bonnet at the sight of a young lord.'

But Aunt Mary shook her head. 'I would not lippen much to the young lord,' she said. 'His mother is sore set upon siller for him; and my poor bit honey has no fortune to speak of. No, we must not fly so high as the young lord; but I will gladly take her about the country to see the old castles and towers. It will perhaps rouse her up a little.'

'And if that does not answer we must think of something else,' the old lady said.

I heard them perhaps that day because they were talking of me, which is always so effective a way of making you hear—for latterly I had not been paying any attention to what they were saying; and I thought to myself how little they knew, and how little I cared about even the old castles and curious houses, having something else in my mind. But just about that time Mr Pitmilly came in, who was always a friend to me, and, when he heard them talking, he managed to stop them and turn the conversation into another channel. And after a while, when the ladies were gone away, he came up to my recess, and gave a glance right over my head. And then he asked my Aunt Mary if ever she had settled her question about the window opposite, 'that you thought was a window sometimes, and then not a window, and many curious things,' the old gentleman said.

My Aunt Mary gave me another very wistful look; and then she said, 'Indeed, Mr Pitmilly, we are just where we were, and I am quite as unsettled as ever; and I think my niece she has taken up my views, for I see her many a time looking across and wondering, and I am not clear now what her opinion is.'

'My opinion!' I said, 'Aunt Mary.' I could not help being a little scornful, as one is when one is very young. 'I have no opinion. There is not only a window but there is a room, and I could show you' I was going to say, 'show you the gentleman who sits and writes in it,' but I stopped, not knowing what they might say, and looked from one to another. 'I could tell you—all the furniture that is in it,' I said. And then I felt something like a flame that went over my face, and that all at once my cheeks were burning. I thought they gave a little glance at each other, but that may have been folly. 'There is a great picture, in a big dim frame,' I said, feeling a little breathless, 'on the wall opposite the window—'

'Is there so?' said Mr Pitmilly, with a little laugh. And he said, 'Now I will tell you what we'll do. You know that there is a conversation party, or whatever they call it, in the big room to-night, and it will be all open and lighted up. And it is a handsome room, and two-three things well worth looking at. I will just step along after we have all got our dinner, and take you over to the pairty, madam—Missy and you—'

'Dear me!' said Aunt Mary. 'I have not gone to a pairty for more years than I would like to say—and never once to the Library Hall.' Then she gave a little shiver, and said quite low, 'I could not go there.'

'Then you will just begin again to-night, madam,' said Mr Pitmilly, taking no notice of this, 'and a proud man will I be leading in Mistress Balcarres that was once the pride of the ball!'

'Ah, once!' said Aunt Mary, with a low little laugh and then a sigh. 'And we'll not say how long ago;' and after that she made a pause, looking always at me: and then she said, 'I accept your offer, and we'll put on our braws; and I hope you will have no occasion to think shame of us. But why not take your dinner here?'

That was how it was settled, and the old gentleman went away to dress, looking quite pleased. But I came to Aunt Mary as soon as he was gone, and besought her not to make me go. 'I like the long bonnie night and the light that lasts so long. And I cannot bear to dress up and go out, wasting it all in a stupid party. I hate parties, Aunt Mary!' I cried, 'and I would far rather stay here.'

'My honey,' she said, taking both my hands, 'I know it will maybe be a blow to you, but it's better so.'

'How could it be a blow to me?' I cried; 'but I would far rather not go.'

'You'll just go with me, honey, just this once: it is not often I go out. You will go with me this one night, just this one night, my honey sweet.'

I am sure there were tears in Aunt Mary's eyes, and she kissed me between the words. There was nothing more that I could say; but how I grudged the evening! A mere party, a conversazione (when all the College was away, too, and nobody to make conversation!), instead of my enchanted hour at my window and the soft strange light, and the dim face looking out, which kept me wondering and wondering what was he thinking of, what was he looking for, who was he? all one wonder and mystery and question, through the long, long, slowly fading night!

It occurred to me, however, when I was dressing—though I was so sure that he would prefer his solitude to everything—that he might perhaps, it was just possible, be there. And when I thought of that, I took out my white frock though Janet had laid out my blue one—and my little pearl necklace which I had thought was too good to wear. They were not very large pearls, but they were real pearls, and very even and lustrous though they were small; and though I did not think much of my appearance then, there must have been something about me—pale as I was but apt to colour in a moment, with my dress so white, and my pearls so white, and my hair all shadowy perhaps, that was pleasant to look at: for even old Mr Pitmilly had a strange look in his eyes, as if he was not only pleased but sorry too, perhaps thinking me a creature that would have troubles in this life, though I was so young and knew them not. And when Aunt Mary looked at me, there was a little quiver about her mouth. She herself had on her pretty lace and her white hair very nicely done, and looking her best. As for Mr Pitmilly, he had a beautiful fine French cambrie frill to his shirt, plaited in the most minute plaits, and with a diamond pin in it which sparkled as much as Lady Carnbee's ring; but this was a fine frank kindly stone, that looked you straight in the face and sparkled, with the light dancing in it as if it were pleased to see you, and to be shining on that old gentleman's honest and faithful breast: for he had been one of Aunt Mary's lovers in their early days, and still thought there was nobody like her in the world.

I had got into quite a happy commotion of mind by the time we set out across the street in the soft light of the evening to the Library Hall. Perhaps, after all, I should see him, and see the room which I was so well acquainted with, and find out why he sat there so constantly and never was seen abroad. I thought I might even hear what he was working at, which would be such a pleasant thing to tell papa when I went home. A friend of mine at St Rule's—oh, far, far more busy than you ever were, papa! —and then my father would laugh as he always did, and say he was but an idler and never busy at all.

The room was all light and bright, flowers wherever flowers could be, and the long lines of the books that went along the walls on each side, lighting up wherever there was a line of gilding or an ornament, with a little response. It dazzled me at first all that light: but I was very eager, though I kept very quiet, looking round to see if perhaps in any corner, in the middle of any group, he would be there. I did not expect to see him among the ladies. He would not be with them,—he was too studious, too silent: but, perhaps among that circle of grey heads at the upper end of the room—perhaps—

No: I am not sure that it was not half a pleasure to me to make quite sure that there was not one whom I could take for him, who was at all like my vague image of him. No: it was absurd to think that he would be here, amid all that sound of voices, under the glare of that light. I felt a little proud to think that he was in his room as usual, doing his work, or thinking so deeply over it, as when he turned round in his chair with his face to the light.

I was thus getting a little composed and quiet in my mind, for now that the expectation of seeing him was over, though it was a disappointment, it was a satisfaction too—when Mr Pitmilly came up to me, holding out his arm. 'Now,' he said, 'I am going to take you to see the curiosities.' I thought to myself that after I had seen them and spoken to everybody I knew, Aunt Mary would let me go home, so I went very willingly, though I did not care for the curiosities. Something, however, struck me strangely as we walked up the room. It was the air, rather fresh and strong, from an open window at the east end of the hall. How should there be a window there? I hardly saw what it meant for the first moment, but it blew in my face as if there was some meaning in it, and I felt very uneasy without seeing why.

Then there was another thing that startled me. On that side of the wall which was to the street there seemed no windows at all. A long line of bookcases filled it from end to end. I could not see what that meant either, but it confused me. I was altogether confused. I felt as if I was in a strange country, not knowing where I was going, not knowing what I might find out next. If there were no windows on the wall to the street, where was my window? My heart, which had been jumping up and calming down again all this time, gave a great leap at this, as if it would have come out of me—but I did not know what it could mean.

Then we stopped before a glass case, and Mr Pitmilly showed me some things in it. I could not pay much attention to them. My head was going round and round. I heard his voice going on, and then myself speaking with a queer sound that was hollow in my ears; but I did not know what I was saying or what he was saying. Then he took me to the very end of the room, the east end, saying something that I caught—that I was pale, that the air would do me good. The air was blowing full on me, lifting the lace of my dress, lifting my hair, almost chilly. The window opened into the pale daylight, into the little lane that ran by the end of the building. Mr Pitmilly went on talking, but I could not make out a word he said. Then I heard my own voice, speaking through it, though I did not seem to be aware that I was speaking. 'Where is my window?—where, then, is my window?' I seemed to be saying, and I turned right round, dragging him with me, still holding his arm. As I did this my eye fell upon something at last which I knew. It was a large picture in a broad frame, hanging against the farther wall.

What did it mean? Oh, what did it mean? I turned round again to the open window at the east end, and to the daylight, the strange light without any shadow, that was all round about this lighted hall, holding it like a bubble that would burst, like something that was not real. The real place was the room I knew, in which that picture was hanging, where the writing-table was, and where he sat with his face to the light. But where was the light and the window through which it came? I think my senses must have left me. I went up to the picture which I knew, and then I walked straight across the room, always dragging Mr Pitmilly, whose face was pale, but who did not struggle but allowed me to lead him, straight across to where the window was—where the window was not;—where there was no sign of it. 'Where is my window?—where is my window?' I said. And all the time I was sure that I was in a dream, and these lights were all some theatrical illusion, and the people talking; and nothing real but the pale, pale, watching, lingering day standing by to wait until that foolish bubble should burst.

'My dear,' said Mr Pitmilly, 'my dear! Mind that you are in public. Mind where you are. You must not make an outcry and frighten your Aunt Mary. Come away with me. Come away, my dear young lady! and you'll take a seat for a minute or two and compose yourself; and I'll get you an ice or a little wine.' He kept patting my hand, which was on his arm, and looking at me very anxiously. 'Bless me! bless me! I never thought it would have this effect,' he said.

But I would not allow him to take me away in that direction. I went to the picture again and looked at it without seeing it: and then I went across the room again, with some kind of wild thought that if I insisted I should find it. 'My window—my window!' I said.

There was one of the professors standing there, and he heard me. 'The window!' said he. 'Ah, you've been taken in with what appears outside. It was put there to be in uniformity with the window on the stair. But it never was a real window. It is just behind that bookcase. Many people are taken in by it,' he said.

His voice seemed to sound from somewhere far away, and as if it would go on for ever; and the hall swam in a dazzle of shining and of noises round me; and the daylight through the open window grew greyer, waiting till it should be over, and the bubble burst.

V

It was Mr Pitmilly who took me home; or rather it was I who took him, pushing him on a little in front of me, holding fast by his arm, not waiting for Aunt Mary or any one. We came out into the daylight again outside, I, without even a cloak or a shawl, with my bare arms, and uncovered head, and the pearls round my neck. There was a rush of the people about, and a baker's boy, that baker's boy, stood right in my way and cried, 'Here's a braw ane!' shouting to the others: the words struck me somehow, as his stone had struck the window, without any reason. But I did not mind the people staring, and hurried across the street, with Mr Pitmilly half a step in advance. The door was open, and Janet standing at it, looking out to see what she could see of the ladies in their grand dresses. She gave a shriek when she saw me hurrying across the street; but I brushed past her, and pushed Mr Pitmilly up the stairs, and took him breathless to the recess, where I threw myself down on the seat, feeling as if I could not have gone another step farther, and waved my hand across to the window. 'There! there!' I cried. Ah! there it was—not that senseless mob—not the theatre and the gas, and the people all in a murmur and clang of talking. Never in all these days had I seen that room so clearly. There was a faint tone of light behind, as if it might have been a reflection from some of those vulgar lights in the hall, and he sat against it, calm, wrapped in his thoughts, with his face turned to the window. Nobody but must have seen him. Janet could have seen him had I called her up-stairs. It was like a picture, all the things I knew, and the same attitude, and the atmosphere, full of quietness, not disturbed by anything. I pulled Mr Pitmilly's arm before I let him go,—'You see, you see!' I cried. He gave me the most bewildered look, as if he would have liked to cry. He saw nothing! I was sure of that from his eyes. He was an old man, and there was no vision in him. If I had called up Janet, she would have seen it all. 'My dear!' he said. 'My dear!' waving his hands in a helpless way. 'He has been there all these nights,' I cried, 'and I thought you could tell me who he was and what he was doing; and that he might have taken me in to that room, and showed me, that I might tell papa. Papa would understand, he would like to hear. Oh, can't you tell me what work he is doing, Mr Pitmilly? He never lifts his head as long as the light throws a shadow, and then when it is like this he turns round and thinks, and takes a rest!'

Mr Pitmilly was trembling, whether it was with cold or I know not what. He said, with a shake in his voice, 'My dear young lady—my dear—' and then stopped and looked at me as if he were going to cry. 'It's peetiful, it's peetiful,' he said; and then in another voice, 'I am going across there again to bring your Aunt Mary home; do you understand, my poor little thing, my—I am going to bring her home—you will be better when she is here.' I was glad when he went away, as he could not see anything: and I sat alone in the dark which was not dark, but quite clear light—a light like nothing I ever saw. How clear it was in that room! not glaring like the gas and the voices, but so quiet, everything so visible, as if it were in another world. I heard a little rustle behind me, and there was Janet, standing staring at me with two big eyes wide open. She was only a little older than I was. I called to her, 'Janet, come here, come here, and you will see him,—come here and see him!' impatient that she should be so shy and keep behind. 'Oh, my bonnie young leddy!' she said, and burst out crying. I stamped my foot at her, in my indignation that she would not come, and she fled before me with a rustle and swing of haste, as if she were afraid. None of them, none of them! not even a girl like myself, with the sight in her eyes, would understand. I turned back again, and held out my hands to him sitting there, who was the only one that knew. 'Oh,' I said, 'say something to me! I don't know who you are, or what you are: but you're lonely and so am I; and I only—feel for you. Say something to me!' I neither hoped that he would hear, nor expected any answer. How could he hear, with the street between us, and his window shut, and all the murmuring of the voices and the people standing about? But for one moment it seemed to me that there was only him and me in the whole world.

But I gasped with my breath, that had almost gone from me, when I saw him move in his chair! He had heard me, though I knew not how. He rose up, and I rose too, speechless, incapable of anything but this mechanical movement. He seemed to draw me as if I were a puppet moved by his will. He came forward to the window, and stood looking across at me. I was sure that he looked at me. At last he had seen me: at last he had found out that somebody, though only a girl, was watching him, looking for him, believing in him. I was in such trouble and commotion of mind and trembling, that I could not keep on my feet, but dropped kneeling on the window-seat, supporting myself against the window, feeling as if my heart were being drawn out of me. I cannot describe his face. It was all dim, yet there was a light on it: I think it must have been a smile; and as closely as I looked at him he looked at me. His hair was fair, and there was a little quiver about his lips. Then he put his hands upon the window to open it. It was stiff and hard to move; but at last he forced it open with a sound that echoed all along the street. I saw that the people heard it, and several looked up. As for me, I put my hands together, leaning with my face against the glass, drawn to him as if I could have gone out of myself, my heart out of my bosom, my eyes out of my head. He opened the window with a noise that was heard from the West Port to the Abbey. Could any one doubt that?

And then he leaned forward out of the window, looking out. There was not one in the street but must have seen him. He looked at me first, with a little wave of his hand, as if it were a salutation—yet not exactly that either, for I thought he waved me away; and then he looked up and down in the dim shining of the ending day, first to the east, to the old Abbey towers, and then to the west, along the broad line of the street where so many people were coming and going, but so little noise, all like enchanted folk in an enchanted place. I watched him with such a melting heart, with such a deep satisfaction as words could not say; for nobody could tell me now that he was not there,—nobody could say I was dreaming any more. I watched him as if I could not breathe—my heart in my throat, my eyes upon him. He looked up and down, and then he looked back to me. I was the first, and I was the last, though it was not for long: he did know, he did see, who it was that had recognized him and sympathized with him all the time. I was in a kind of rapture, yet stupor too; my look went with his look, following it as if I were his shadow; and then suddenly he was gone, and I saw him no more.

I dropped back again upon my seat, seeking something to support me, something to lean upon. He had lifted his hand and waved it once again to me. How he went I cannot tell, nor where he went I cannot tell; but in a moment he was away, and the window standing open, and the room fading into stillness and dimness, yet so clear, with all its space, and the great picture in its gilded frame upon the wall. It gave me no pain to see him go away. My heart was so content, and I was so worn out and satisfied—for what doubt or question could there be about him now? As I was lying back as weak as water, Aunt Mary came in behind me, and flew to me with a little rustle as if she had come on wings, and put her arms round me, and drew my head on to her breast. I had begun to cry a little, with sobs like a child. 'You saw him, you saw him!' I said. To lean upon her, and feel her so soft, so kind, gave me a pleasure I cannot describe, and her arms round me, and her voice saying 'Honey, my honey!'—as if she were nearly crying too. Lying there I came back to myself, quite sweetly, glad of everything. But I wanted some assurance from them that they had seen him too. I waved my hand to the window that was still standing open, and the room that was stealing away into the faint dark. 'This time you saw it all?' I said, getting more eager. 'My honey!' said Aunt Mary, giving me a kiss: and Mr Pitmilly began to walk about the room with short little steps behind, as if he were out of patience. I sat straight up and put away Aunt Mary's arms. 'You cannot be so blind, so blind!' I cried. 'Oh, not to-night, at least not to-night!' But neither the one nor the other made any reply. I shook myself quite free, and raised myself up. And there, in the middle of the street, stood the baker's boy like a statue, staring up at the open window, with his mouth open and his face full of wonder—breathless, as if he could not believe what he saw. I darted forward, calling to him, and beckoned him to come to me. 'Oh, bring him up! bring him, bring him to me!' I cried.

Mr Pitmilly went out directly, and got the boy by the shoulder. He did not want to come. It was strange to see the little old gentleman, with his beautiful frill and his diamond pin, standing out in the street, with his hand upon the boy's shoulder, and the other boys round, all in a little crowd. And presently they came towards the house, the others all following, gaping and wondering. He came in unwilling, almost resisting, looking as if we meant him some harm. 'Come away, my laddie, come and speak to the young lady,' Mr Pitmilly was saying. And Aunt Mary took my hands to keep me back. But I would not be kept back.

'Boy,' I cried, 'you saw it too: you saw it: tell them you saw it! It is that I want, and no more.'

He looked at me as they all did, as if he thought I was mad. 'What's she wantin' wi' me?' he said; and then, 'I did nae harm, even if I did throw a bit stane at it—and it's nae sin to throw a stane.'

'You rascal!' said Mr Pitmilly, giving him a shake; 'have you been throwing stones? You'll kill somebody some of these days with your stones.' The old gentleman was confused and troubled, for he did not understand what I wanted, nor anything that had happened. And then Aunt Mary, holding my hands and drawing me close to her, spoke. 'Laddie,' she said, 'answer the young lady, like a good lad. There's no intention of finding fault with you. Answer her, my man, and then Janet will give ye your supper before you go.'

'Oh speak, speak!' I cried; 'answer them and tell them! you saw that window opened, and the gentleman look out and wave his hand?'

'I saw nae gentleman,' he said, with his head down, 'except this wee gentleman here.'

'Listen, laddie,' said Aunt Mary. 'I saw ye standing in the middle of the street staring. What were ye looking at?'

'It was naething to make a wark about. It was just yon windy yonder in the library that is nae windy. And it was open as sure's death. You may laugh if you like. Is that a' she's wantin' wi' me?'

'You are telling a pack of lies, laddie,' Mr Pitmilly said.

'I'm tellin' nae lees—it was standin' open just like ony ither windy. It's as sure's death. I couldna believe it mysel'; but it's true.'

'And there it is,' I cried, turning round and pointing it out to them with great triumph in my heart. But the light was all grey, it had faded, it had changed. The window was just as it had always been, a sombre break upon the wall.

I was treated like an invalid all that evening, and taken up-stairs to bed, and Aunt Mary sat up in my room the whole night through. Whenever I opened my eyes she was always sitting there close to me, watching. And there never was in all my life so strange a night. When I would talk in my excitement, she kissed me and hushed me like a child. 'Oh, honey, you are not the only one!' she said. 'Oh whisht, whisht, bairn! I should never have let you be there!'

'Aunt Mary, Aunt Mary, you have seen him too?'

'Oh whisht, whisht, honey!' Aunt Mary said: her eyes were shining—there were tears in them. 'Oh whisht, whisht! Put it out of your mind, and try to sleep. I will not speak another word,' she cried.

But I had my arms round her, and my mouth at her ear. 'Who is he there?—tell me that and I will ask no more—'

'Oh honey, rest, and try to sleep! It is just—how can I tell you?—a dream, a dream! Did you not hear what Lady Carnbee said?—the women of our blood—'

'What? what? Aunt Mary, oh Aunt Mary—'

'I canna tell you,' she cried in her agitation, 'I canna tell you! How can I tell you, when I know just what you know and no more? It is a longing all your life after—it is a looking—for what never comes.'

'He will come,' I cried. 'I shall see him to-morrow—that I know, I know!'

She kissed me and cried over me, her cheek hot and wet like mine. 'My honey, try if you can sleep—try if you can sleep: and we'll wait to see what to-morrow brings.'

'I have no fear,' said I; and then I suppose, though it is strange to think of, I must have fallen asleep—I was so worn-out, and young, and not used to lying in my bed awake. From time to time I opened my eyes, and sometimes jumped up remembering everything: but Aunt Mary was always there to soothe me, and I lay down again in her shelter like a bird in its nest.

But I would not let them keep me in bed next day. I was in a kind of fever, not knowing what I did. The window was quite opaque, without the least glimmer in it, flat and blank like a piece of wood. Never from the first day had I seen it so little like a window. 'It cannot be wondered at,' I said to myself, 'that seeing it like that, and with eyes that are old, not so clear as mine, they should think what they do.' And then I smiled to myself to think of the evening and the long light, and whether he would look out again, or only give me a signal with his hand. I decided I would like that best: not that he should take the trouble to come forward and open it again, but just a turn of his head and a wave of his hand. It would be more friendly and show more confidence,—not as if I wanted that kind of demonstration every night.

I did not come down in the afternoon, but kept at my own window up-stairs alone, till the tea-party should be over. I could hear them making a great talk; and I was sure they were all in the recess staring at the window, and laughing at the silly lassie. Let them laugh! I felt above all that now. At dinner I was very restless, hurrying to get it over; and I think Aunt Mary was restless too. I doubt whether she read her *Times* when it came; she opened it up so as to shield her, and watched from a corner. And I settled myself in the recess, with my heart full of expectation. I wanted nothing more than to see him writing at his table, and to turn his head and give me a little wave of his hand, just to show that he knew I was there. I sat from half-past seven o'clock to ten o'clock: and the daylight grew softer and softer, till at last it was as if it was shining through a pearl, and not a shadow to be seen. But the window all the time was as black as night, and there was nothing, nothing there.

Well: but other nights it had been like that: he would not be there every night only to please me. There are other things in a man's life, a great learned man like that. I said to myself I was not disappointed. Why should I be disappointed? There had been other nights when he was not there. Aunt Mary watched me, every movement I made, her eyes shining, often wet, with a pity in them that almost made me cry: but I felt as if I were more sorry for her than for myself. And then I flung myself upon her, and asked her, again and again, what it was, and who it was, imploring her to tell me if she knew? and when she had seen him, and what had happened? and what it meant about the women of our blood? She told me that how it was she could not tell, nor when: it was just at the time it had to be; and that we all saw him in our time—'that is,' she said, 'the ones that are like you and me.' What was it that made her and me different from the rest? but she only shook her head and would not tell me. 'They say,' she said, and then stopped short. 'Oh, honey, try and forget all about it—if I had but known you were of that kind! They say—that once there was one that was a Scholar, and liked his books more than any lady's love. Honey, do not look at me like that. To think I should have brought all this on you!'

'He was a Scholar?' I cried.

'And one of us, that must have been a light woman, not like you and me—But maybe it was just in innocence; for who can tell? She waved to him and waved to him to come over: and yon ring was the token: but he would not come. But still she sat at her window and waved and waved—till at last her brothers heard of it, that were stirring men; and then—oh, my honey, let us speak of it no more!'

'They killed him!' I cried, carried away. And then I grasped her with my hands, and gave her a shake, and flung away from her. 'You tell me that to throw dust in my eyes—when I saw him only last night: and he as living as I am, and as young!'

'My honey, my honey!' Aunt Mary said.

After that I would not speak to her for a long time; but she kept close to me, never leaving me when she could help it, and always with that pity in her eyes. For the next night it was the same; and the third night. That third night I thought I could not bear it any longer. I would have to do something if only I knew what to do! If it would ever get dark, quite dark, there might be something to be done. I had wild dreams of stealing out of the house and getting a ladder, and mounting up to try if I could not open that window, in the middle of the night—if perhaps I could get the baker's boy to help me; and then my mind got into a whirl, and it was as if I had done it; and I could almost see the boy put the ladder to the window, and hear him cry out that there was nothing there. Oh, how slow it was, the night! and how light it was, and everything so clear—no darkness to cover you, no shadow, whether on one side of the street or on the other side! I could not sleep, though I was forced to go to bed. And in the deep midnight, when it is dark dark in every other place, I slipped very softly down-stairs, though there was one board on the landing-place that creaked—and opened the door and stepped out. There was not a soul to be seen, up or down, from the Abbey to the West Port: and the trees stood like ghosts, and the silence was terrible, and everything as clear as day. You don't know what silence is till you find it in the light like that, not morning but night, no sunrising, no shadow, but everything as clear as the day.

It did not make any difference as the slow minutes went on: one o'clock, two o'clock. How strange it was to hear the clocks striking in that dead light when there was nobody to hear them! But it made no difference. The window was quite blank; even the marking of the panes seemed to have melted away. I stole up again after a long time, through the silent house, in the clear light, cold and trembling, with despair in my heart.

I am sure Aunt Mary must have watched and seen me coming back, for after a while I heard faint sounds in the house; and very early, when there had come a little sunshine into the air, she came to my bedside with a cup of tea in her hand; and she, too, was looking like a ghost. 'Are you warm, honey—are you comfortable?' she said. 'It doesn't matter,' said I. I did not feel as if anything mattered; unless if one could get into the dark somewhere—the soft, deep dark that would cover you over and hide you—but I could not tell from what. The dreadful thing was that there was nothing, nothing to look for, nothing to hide from—only the silence and the light.

That day my mother came and took me home. I had not heard she was coming; she arrived quite unexpectedly, and said she had no time to stay, but must start the same evening so as to be in London next day, papa having settled to go abroad. At first I had a wild thought I would not go. But how can a girl say I will not, when her mother has come for her, and there is no reason, no reason in the world, to resist, and no right! I had to go, whatever I might wish or any one might say. Aunt Mary's dear eyes were wet; she went about the house drying them quietly with her handkerchief, but she always said, 'It is the best thing for you, honey—the best thing for you!' Oh, how I hated to hear it said that it was the best thing, as if anything mattered, one more than another! The old ladies were all there in the afternoon, Lady Carnbee looking at me from under her black lace, and the diamond lurking, sending out darts from under her finger. She patted me on the shoulder, and told me to be a good bairn. 'And never lippen to what you see from the window,' she said. 'The eye is deceitful as well as the heart.' She kept patting me on the shoulder, and I felt again as if that sharp wicked stone stung me. Was that what Aunt Mary meant when she said yon ring was the token? I thought afterwards I saw the mark on my shoulder. You will say why? How can I tell why? If I had known, I should have been contented, and it would not have mattered any more.

I never went back to St Rule's, and for years of my life I never again looked out of a window when any other window was in sight. You ask me did I ever see him again? I cannot tell: the imagination is a great deceiver, as Lady Carnbee said: and if he stayed there so long, only to punish the race that had wronged him, why should I ever have seen him again? for I had received my share. But who can tell what happens in a heart that often, often, and so long as that, comes back to do its errand? If it was he whom I have seen again, the anger is gone from him, and he means good and no longer harm to the house of the woman that loved him. I have seen his face looking at me from a crowd. There was one time when I came home a widow from India, very sad, with my little children: I am certain I saw him there among all the people coming to welcome their friends. There was nobody to welcome me,—for I was not expected: and very sad was I, without a face I knew: when all at once I saw him, and he waved his hand to me. My heart leaped up again: I had forgotten who he was, but only that it was a face I knew, and I landed almost cheerfully, thinking here was some one who would help me. But he had disappeared, as he did from the window, with that one wave of his hand.

And again I was reminded of it all when old Lady Carnbee died—an old, old woman—and it was found in her will that she had left me that diamond ring. I am afraid of it still. It is locked up in an old sandal-wood box in the lumber-room in the little old country-house which belongs to me, but where I never live. If any one would steal it, it would be a relief to my mind. Yet I never knew what Aunt Mary meant when she said, 'Yon ring was the token,' nor what it could have to do with that strange window in the old College Library of St Rule's.

IN DULL BROWN

Evelyn Sharp

'All the same,' said Nancy, who was lazily sipping her coffee in bed, 'brown doesn't suit you a bit.'

'No,' said Jean sadly, 'and I should not be wearing it at all if my other skirt did not want brushing. Nevertheless, a russet-brown frock demands adventures. The girls in novels always wear russet-brown, whatever their complexion is, and they always have adventures. Now—'

'Isn't it time you started?' asked the gentle voice of her sister. Jean glanced at the clock and said something in English that was not classical.

'I shall have to take an omnibus. Bother!' she said, and the heroine of the russet-brown frock made an abrupt and undignified exit.

It was a fine warm morning in November, the sort of day that follows a week of stormy wet weather as though to cheat the unwary into imagining that the spring instead of the winter is on its way. The pavements were still wet from yesterday's rain, the trees in the park stood stripped by yesterday's gale; only the sun and the sparrows kept up the illusion that it was never going to rain any more. But the caprices of the atmosphere made no impression on the people who cannot help being out; and Jean, as she made the fourteenth passenger on the top of an omnibus, had a vague feeling of contempt for the other thirteen who were engrossed in their morning papers.

'Just imagine missing that glorious effect,' she thought to herself, as they rumbled along the edge of the Green Park where the mist was slowly yielding to the warmth of the sun and allowing itself to be coaxed out of growing into a fog. And almost simultaneously she became as material as the rest, in her annoyance with her neighbour for taking more than his share of the seat.

'Nice morning!' he said at that moment, and folded up his *Telegraph*.

'Yes,' said Jean, in a tone that was not encouraging. That the morning was 'nice' would never have occurred to her; and it seemed unfair to sacrifice the effect over the Green Park, even for conversational purposes. Then she caught sight of his face, which was a harmless one, and in an ordinary way good-looking, and she accused herself of priggishness, and stared at the unconscious passenger in front, preparatory to cultivating the one at her side.

'We deserve some compensation for yesterday,' she continued, more graciously.

'Yesterday? Oh, it was beastly wet, wasn't it? I suppose you don't like wet weather, eh?' said the man, with a suspicion of familiarity in his tone. Jean frowned a little.

'That comes of the simple russet gown,' she thought; 'of course he thinks I am a little shop-girl.' But the sun was shining, and life had been very dull lately, and she would be getting down at Piccadilly Circus. Besides, he was little more than a boy, and she liked boys, and there would be no harm in having five minutes' conversation with this one.

'I suppose no one does. I wasn't trying to be particularly original,' she replied carelessly.

He smiled and glanced at her with more interest. Her identity was beginning to puzzle him.

'Going to business?' he asked tentatively.

'Well, yes, I suppose so. At least, I am going to teach three children all sorts of things they don't want to learn a bit.'

'How awfully clever of you!'

The little obvious remark made her laugh. In spite of the humble brown dress that did not suit her, she looked very pretty when she threw back her head and laughed.

'That is because you have never taught,' she said; 'to be a really good teacher you must systematically forget quite half of what you do know. For instance, I can teach German better than anything else in the world, because I know less about it. Perhaps that is why I always won the German prizes at school,' she added reflectively.

'You are very paradoxical—or very cynical, which is it?' asked her neighbour, smiling.

'Oh, I don't know. Am I? But did you ever try to teach?'

'Not I. Gives one the hump, doesn't it? I should just whack the little beasts when they didn't work. Don't you feel like that sometimes?'

'Clearly you never tried to teach,' she said, and laughed again.

'Those are lucky pupils of yours,' he observed.

'Why?' she asked abruptly, and flashed a stern look at him sideways. 'Oh, because you—seem right on it, don't you know,' he answered hastily. The adroitness of his answer pleased her, and she put him down as a gentleman, and felt justified in going a little further.

'I like teaching, yes,' she went on gravely. 'But all the same I am glad that I only teach for my living and can draw for my pleasure. Now whatever made me tell you that I wonder?'

'It was awfully decent of you to tell me,' he said; 'I suppose you thought I should be interested, eh?'

'I suppose I did,' she assented, and this time she laughed for no reason whatever.

'Will you let me say something very personal?' he asked, waxing bolder. But his tone was still humble, and she felt more kindly towards him now that he evidently knew she was not to be patronized. Besides, she was curious. So she said nothing to dissuade him, and he went on.

'Why do you look so beastly happy, and all that, don't you know? Is it because you work so hard?'

'I look happy!' she exclaimed. 'I suppose it is the sun, then, or the jolly day, or—or the *feel* of everything after the rain. Yes, I suppose it must be that.'

'I don't, then. Lots of girls might feel all that and not look as you do. I think it is because you have such a bally lot to do.'

'I should stop thinking that, if I were you,' said Jean a little bitterly; 'I know that is the usual idea about women who work—among those who don't. They should try it for a time, and see.'

'I believe you are cynical after all,' observed her companion. 'Don't you like being called happy?'

'Oh, yes, I like it. But I hate humbug, and it is all nonsense to pretend that working hard for one's living is rather an amusing thing to do. Because it isn't, and if it has never been so for a man, why should it be for a woman? If anything, it is worse for women. For one happy hour it gives us two sad ones; it makes us hard—what you call cynical. It builds up our characters at the expense of our hearts. It makes heroines of us and spoils the woman in us. We learn to look the world in the face, and it teaches us to be prigs. We probe into its realities for the first time, and the disclosure is too much for us. Working hard to get enough bread and butter to eat is a sordid, demoralizing thing, and the people who talk cant about it never had to do it themselves. *You* don't like the kind of woman who works, you know you don't!'

The omnibus was slowing at the Circus. Jean stopped suddenly and glanced up at her companion with an amused, half shamefaced look.

'I am so sorry. You see how objectionable it has made *me*. Aren't you glad you will never see me again?'

And before he had time to speak she had slipped away, and the omnibus was turning ruthlessly down Waterloo Place.

'What deuced odd things women are,' he reflected, by way of deluding himself into the belief that amusement and not interest was the predominant sensation in his mind. But the next morning saw him waiting carefully in West Kensington for the same City omnibus as before; and when it rumbled on its way to Piccadilly Circus and no one in russet-brown got up to relieve the monotony of black coats and umbrellas round him, he was quite unreasonably disappointed, though he told himself savagely at the same time that of course he had never expected to see her at all.

'And if I had, she would have avoided me at once. Women are always like that,' he thought, and just as the reflection shaped itself in his mind he caught a glimpse of Air Street that sent his usual composure to the winds and brought him down the steps at a pace that upset the descent of all the other passengers who had no similar desire to rush in the direction of Air Street.

'Did yer expect us to take yer to Timbuctoo?' scoffed the conductor, with the usual contempt of his kind for the passenger who gets into the wrong omnibus. But the victim of his scorn was as regardless of it as of the pink ticket he was grinding into pulp in his hand; and he stood on the pavement with his underlip drawn tightly inwards, until he had regained his customary air of gentlemanly indifference. Then he turned up into Regent Street and made a cross cut through the slums that lie on the borders of Soho.

And as Jean was hastening along Oxford Street, ten minutes later, she met him coming towards her with a superb expression of pleased surprise on his face, which deceived her so completely that she bowed at once and held out her hand to him, although, as she said afterwards to Nancy, 'he was being most dreadfully unconventional, and I couldn't help wondering if he would have spoken to me again, if I had worn my new tailor-made gown and looked ordinary.' At the time she only felt that Oxford Street, even on a damp and muggy morning, was quite a nice place for a walk.

'Beastly day for you to be out,' he began, taking away her umbrella and holding his own over her head. To be looked after was a novel experience to Jean, and she found herself half resenting his air of protection.

'Oh, it's all right. You get used to it when you have to,' she said with a short laugh. It was not at all what she wanted to say to him, but the perversity of her nature was uppermost and she had to say it.

'All the same, it is beastly rough on you,' he persisted. 'Why? Some one must do the work,' she said defiantly.

'Is it so important, then?' he asked with a smile that was half a sneer. Jean blushed hotly.

'It means my living to me,' she said; and he winced at her unpleasant frankness.

'You were quite different yesterday, weren't you?' he complained gently.

'You speak as though my being one thing or another ought to depend on your pleasure,' she retorted; 'of course, you think like everybody else that a woman is only to be tolerated as long as she is cheerful. How can you be cheerful when the weather is dreary, and you are tired out with yesterday's work? You don't know what it is like. You should keep to the women who don't work; they will always look pretty, and smile sweetly and behave in a domesticated manner.'

'I don't think I said anything to provoke all that, did I?'

'Yes, you did,' she answered unreasonably. 'I said—I mean *you* said, oh never mind! But you do like domesticated women best, don't you? On your honour now?'

There was no doubt that he did, especially at that moment. But he lied, smilingly, and well.

'I like all women. But most of all, women like you. Didn't I tell you yesterday how happy you looked? You are such a rum little girl—oh hang, please forgive me. But without any rotting, I wish you'd tell me what you do want me to say. When I said how jolly you looked, you were offended; and now I pity you for being out in the rain, you don't like that any better. What am I to do?'

'I don't see why you should do anything,' she said curtly. They had reached the corner of Berners Street, and she came to a standstill. 'I am glad I met you again,' she added very quickly, without meeting his eyes. And then she ran down the street, and disappeared inside a doorway.

Tom Unwin stepped into a hansom with two umbrellas and an unsatisfactory impression of the last quarter of an hour. And for the next two mornings he went to the City by train. But the third saw him again in Oxford Street shortly before nine o'clock, and he held a small and elegant umbrella in his hand, although it was a cloudless day, and there was hoar frost beneath the gravel on the wood pavement.

'How very odd that we should meet again,' she exclaimed, blushing in spite of the self-possession on which she prided herself.

'Not so very odd,' he replied; 'I believe I am responsible for this meeting.'

'I feel sure there is a suitable reply to that, but you mustn't expect me to make it. I am never any good at making suitable replies,' said Jean; and she laughed as she had done the first time they met.

'I don't want suitable replies from you,' he rejoined, just as lightly; 'tell me what you really think instead.'

'That it was quite charming of you to come this particular way to the City on this particular morning,' said Jean demurely. 'Now, do you know, I should have thought it was ever so much quicker to go along the Strand.'

'On the contrary, I find it very much quicker when I come along Oxford Street.'

'At all events, *you* know how to make suitable replies.'

'Then you thought that was a suitable reply? Got you there, didn't I?' and he laughed, which pleased her immensely, although she pretended to be hurt.

'Isn't it queer how one can live two perfectly different lives at the same time?' she said irrelevantly.

'Two? I live half a dozen. But let's hear yours first.'

'I was only thinking,' continued Jean, 'that if the mother of my pupils knew I was walking along Oxford Street with some one I had never been introduced to—'

'Well?' he said, as she paused.

'Oh, well, it isn't exactly an ordinary thing to do, is it?'

'Why not?'

'Well, it isn't, is it?'

'But must one be ordinary?'

'People won't forgive you for being anything else, unless you are in a history book, where you can't do any harm.'

'People be hanged! When shall I see you again?'

'Next time you take a short cut to the City, I suppose. Good-bye.'

'Stop!' he cried. And when she did stop, with an air of innocent inquiry on her face, he found he had nothing whatever to say.

'You—you haven't told me your name,' he stammered lamely.

'Is that all? You needn't make me any later just for *that*,' she exclaimed, turning away again. 'Besides, you haven't told me yours,' she added, over her shoulder.

'Do you want to know it?'

'Why, no; it doesn't matter to me. But I thought you wanted to make some more conversation. Good-bye, again.'

'Well, I'm hanged! Look here, if I tell you mine, will you tell me yours?'

'But I don't mind a bit if you *don't* tell me yours.'

'Will you, though?'

'Oh, make haste, or else I can't wait to hear it.'

'Here you are, then. It is—Tom.'

She faced him sternly.

'Why don't you go on?'

'Unwin,' he added, hastily. 'Now yours, please.'

But the only answer he got was a mocking smile; and he was again left at the corner of Berners Street with a lady's umbrella in his hand.

The next morning there was a dull yellow fog, and Jean was in a perverse mood.

'I think you are very mistaken to walk to business on a day like this, when you might go by train,' she said, as she reluctantly gave up her books to be carried by him. The fog was making her eyes smart, and she felt cross.

'But I shall get my reward,' he said, with elaborate courtesy.

'Oh, please don't. The fog is bad enough without allusions to the hymn-book. Besides, I can't stand being used as a means for somebody else to get into heaven. It is very selfish of me, I suppose, but I don't like it.'

'I am afraid you mistake me. I never for a moment associated you with my chances of salvation.'

'Then why didn't you?' she cried indignantly. 'I should like to know why you come and bother me every morning like this if you think I am as hopelessly bad as all that! I didn't ask you to come, did I? Please give me my books and let me go.'

'I think you hopelessly bad? Why, I assure you—'

'Give me my books. Can't you see how late I am?' she said, stamping her foot impetuously. And she seized Bright's English History and Cornwall's Geography out of his hand, and left him precipitately, without another word.

'You are a most unreasonable little girl,' he exclaimed hotly; and the policeman to whom he said it smiled patiently.

He started with the intention of going by train on the following morning; then he changed his mind, and ran back to take an omnibus. After that he found it was getting late, so he took a cab to Oxford Circus, and then strolled on towards Holborn as though nothing but chance or necessity had brought him there. But, although he walked as far as Berners Street and back again to the Circus, he met no one in a dull brown frock. And he was just as unsuccessful the next morning, and the one after, and at the end of a week he found himself the sad possessor of a slender silk umbrella, a regretful remembrance, and a fresh store of cynicism.

'She is like all the others,' he told himself, with a shrug of his shoulders; 'they play the very devil with you until they begin to get frightened of the consequences, and then they fight shy. And I'm hanged if I even know her name!'

And the days wore on, and the autumn grew into winter, and Oxford Street no longer saw the playing of a comedy at nine o'clock in the morning. And Tom Unwin found other interests in life, and if a chance occurrence reminded him of a determined little figure in russet brown, the passing thought brought nothing but an amused smile to his lips.

Then the spring came, suddenly and completely, on the heels of a six weeks' frost; and chance took him down Piccadilly one morning in March, where the budding freshness of the trees drew him into the Green Park. The impression of spring met him everywhere, in the fragrance of the almond-trees, and the quarrelling of the sparrows, and the transparency of the blue haze over Westminster; and, indifferent though he was to such things, there was a note of familiarity in it all that affected him strangely, and left him with a lazy sensation of pleasure. What that something was he did not realize until his eyes fell on one of the chairs under the trees, and then, as he stood quite still and wondered whether she would know him again, he discovered what there was in the air that had seemed to him so familiar and so pleasant.

'I was just thinking about you,' he said deliberately, when she had shown very decidedly that she did mean to know him. He spoke with an easy indifference that she showed no signs of sharing.

'Oh, I have been wondering—' she began, in a voice that trembled with eagerness.

'Yes? Supposing we sit down. That's better. You have been wondering—?'

She leaned back in her chair, and looked up through the branches at the pale blue sky beyond. There was an odd little look of defiance on her face.

'So, after all, you did find that the Strand was the quickest way,' she said abruptly.

'Possibly. And you?' he asked, with his customary smile.

'How often did you go down Oxford Street after—the last time I saw you?'

'As far as I can remember, the measure of my endurance was a week. And how much longer did you take the precaution of avoiding such a dangerous person as myself?'

She turned round and stared at him with great wondering eyes, into which a look of comprehension was slowly creeping.

'You actually thought I did that? And all the time I was ill, I was having visions of you—'

'Ill? You never told me you had been ill,' he interrupted.

'You didn't exactly give me the chance, did you? It was the fog, I suppose. I am all right now. They thought I should never go down Oxford Street again. But I take a good deal of killing, and so here I am again.' She ended with a cynical smile. He was making holes in the soft turf with his walking-stick. She went on speaking to the pale blue sky and the network of branches above her.

'And the odd part is that I did not mind the illness so much as—' And she paused again.

'Yes?' he said, in a voice that had lost some of its jauntiness.

'I think it won't interest you.'

'How can you say that unless you tell me?'

'I am sure it won't,' she said decidedly. 'And I couldn't possibly tell you, really.'

'Go on, please,' he said, looking round at her; and she went on meekly.

'The thing that bothered me was my having been cross the last time we met. You see, it was not the being cross that I minded exactly; *that* wouldn't have mattered a bit if I had seen you again the next day, but—'

'I quite understand. Bad temper is a luxury we keep for our most familiar friends. I am honoured by the distinction,' he said, and his smile was not a sneer.

'I wish you wouldn't laugh at me,' she said, a little wistfully.

'I am not laughing at you, child,' he hastened to assure her, and he took one of her hands in his. 'I have missed you, too,' he went on, in a low tone that he strove to make natural.

'Did you *really*? I thought you would at first, perhaps, and then I thought you would just laugh, and forget. And you really did think of me sometimes? I am so glad.'

He had a twinge of conscience. But a reputation once acquired is a tender thing, and must be handled with delicacy.

'I have not forgotten,' he said, and tried to change the conversation. 'And you never even told me your name, you perverse little person,' he added playfully.

'You told me yours,' she said, and laughed triumphantly.

'And yours, please?'

'It will quite spoil it all,' she objected.

'Is it so bad as that, then? Never mind, I can bear a good deal. What is it—Susan, Jemima, Emmelina?'

There was a little pause, and then she nodded at the pale blue sky above and said 'Jean' in a hurried whisper. And he was less exigent than she had been, for he did not ask for any more.

When he left her on her own doorstep she lingered for a moment in the sunlight before she went in to Nancy.

'And he really is coming to see me to-morrow,' she said out loud with a joyous laugh; 'I wonder, shall I tell Nancy or not?' After mature consideration she decided not to tell Nancy, though if Nancy had been less unsuspicious she would certainly have noticed something unusual in the manner of her practical little eldest sister, when she started for Berners Street on the following morning, and twice repeated that she would be back to tea should any one call and ask for her.

'Nobody is likely to ask for you,' said Nancy with sisterly frankness, 'nobody ever does. You needn't bother to be back to tea unless you like,' she added with a self-conscious smile. 'Jimmy said he might look in.'

'So much the better,' thought Jean; 'I can bring in a cake without exciting suspicion.' And she started gaily on her way, and wondered ingenuously why all the people in the street seemed so indifferent to her happiness. At Berners Street, a shock was awaiting her. Would Miss Moreen kindly stay till five to-day as the children's mother was obliged to go out, and nurse had a holiday? And as the children's mother had already gone out and nurse's holiday had begun before breakfast, there was no appeal left to poor Jean, and she settled down to her day's work with a sense of injustice in her mind and a queer feeling in her throat that had to be overcome during an arithmetic lesson. But as the day wore on her spirits rose to an unnatural pitch; she spent the afternoon in romping furiously with her pupils; and when five o'clock came, she was standing outside in the street counting the coins in her little purse.

'I can just do it, and I shall!' she cried, and a passing cabby pulled up in answer to her graphic appeal and carried her away westwards. He whistled when she paid him an extravagant fare, and watched her with a chuckle as she flew up the steps and fumbled nervously at the keyhole before she was able to unlock the door. He would have wondered more, or perhaps less, had he seen her standing on the mat outside the front room on the first floor, giving her hat and hair certain touches which did not affect their appearance in the least, and listening breathlessly to the sound of voices that came from within. Then she turned the handle suddenly and went in.

The lamp was not yet lighted and the daylight was waning. The room was in partial darkness, but the fire was burning brightly, and it shone on the face of a man as he leaned forward in a low chair, and talked to the beautiful girl who lay on the sofa, smiling up at him in a gentle deprecating manner, as if his homage were new and overwhelming to her.

The man was not the expected Jimmy, and Jean took two swift little steps into the room. The spell was broken and they looked round with a start.

'Oh, here you are,' cried Nancy, gliding off the sofa and putting her arms round her in her pretty affectionate manner. 'Poor Mr Unwin has been waiting quite an hour for you. Whatever made you so late?'

Jean disengaged herself a little roughly, and held out her hand to Tom.

'Have you been very bored?' she asked him with a slight curl of her lip.

'That could hardly be the case in Miss Nancy's company,' he replied in his best manner; 'but if she had not been so kind to me your tardiness in coming would certainly have been harder to bear.'

The carefully picked words did not come naturally from the boyish fellow who had talked slang to her on the top of the omnibus, but Tom Unwin never talked slang when there was a situation of any kind. Jean was bitterly conscious of being the only one of the three who was not behaving in a picturesque manner. The other two vied with each other in showing her little attentions, a fact that entirely failed to deceive her.

'Do they think I am a fool?' she thought scornfully. 'Why should they suppose that I need propitiating?'

And she insisted curtly on pouring out her own cup of tea, and sat down obstinately on a high chair, without noticing the low one he was pulling forward for her.

'Don't let me disturb you,' she said calmly; 'you made such a charming picture when I came in.'

They only seemed to her to be making a ridiculous picture now. She was conscious of nothing but the satirical view of the situation, and she had a mad desire to point at them and scream with laughter at their fatuity in supposing that she did not see through their discomfiture.

'We thought you were never coming,' began Nancy in her gentle tired voice; 'I was afraid you had been taken ill or something.'

'Yes, indeed,' added Tom with strained jocularity; 'it was all I could do to restrain Miss Nancy from sending a telegram to somebody about you. She only gave up the idea when I got her to acknowledge that she didn't even know where to send it.'

'Now, that is really too bad of you,' exclaimed Nancy with a carefully studied pout; 'you know quite well—'

'Indeed, I appeal to you, Miss Moreen—'

'Don't listen to him, Jean.'

'It doesn't seem to me to matter very much,' said Jean with much composure; 'I am very glad that I gave you so much to talk about.'

They made another attempt to conciliate her.

'Do have some cake. It isn't bad,' said Nancy invitingly.

'Or some more tea?' added Tom anxiously. 'You must be so played out with your long day's work. Have the little brats been very trying?'

'Oh, you needn't worry about the little brats, thanks,' said Jean, eating bread and butter voraciously for the sake of an occupation.

'Come nearer the fire,' said Nancy coaxingly; 'Mr Unwin will move up that other chair.'

'Of course,' said Mr Unwin with alacrity, glad of any excuse that removed him for a moment from the unpleasant scrutiny of her large cold eyes.

'You are both very kind to bother about me like this. I am really not used to it,' said Jean with a hard little laugh. 'Won't you go on with your conversation while I write a postcard?'

She made a place for her cup on the tea-tray, strolled across the room to the bureau, and sat down to look vacantly at a blank postcard. The other two seated themselves stiffly at opposite ends of the hearthrug, and manufactured stilted phrases for the ears of Jean.

'Your sister draws, I believe?'

'Oh, yes. Jean is fearfully clever, you know. She used to win prizes and things. I never won a prize in my life. Oh, yes; Jean is certainly very clever indeed.'

'I am sure of it. It must be charming to be so clever.'

'Yes. Nothing else matters if you are as clever as all that. It doesn't affect Jean in the least if things happen to go wrong, because she always has her cleverness to console her, don't you see.'

'Brains are a perennial consolation,' said Tom solemnly; 'I always knew, Miss Nancy, that your sister was very exceptional.'

'Exceptional! Yes, I suppose I am that,' thought Jean with a curious feeling of dissatisfaction. The burden of her own cleverness was almost too much for her, and she would have given worlds, just then, to have been as ordinary as Nancy—and as beautiful.

'Will you forgive me if I go upstairs and finish a drawing?' she said, coming forward into the firelight again. They uttered some conventional regrets, and Tom held the door open for her. 'Good-bye,' she said, smiling, 'I am sorry my drawing won't wait. It has to go in to-morrow morning.'

'I envy you your charming talent,' he said with a sigh that was a little overdone.

'Do you? It prevents me from being domesticated, you know, and that is always a pity, isn't it?' she said, and drew her hand away quickly.

Upstairs with her head on an old brown cloak she lay and listened to the hum of voices below.

'Why wasn't I born a fool with a pretty face?' she murmured. 'Fools are the only really happy people in the world, for they are the only people the rest of us have the capacity to understand. And to be understood by the majority of people is the whole secret of happiness. No one would take the trouble to understand *me*. Of course, it is unbearably conceited to say so, but there is no one to hear.'

When Nancy came up to bed, she found her sister working away steadily at her drawing.

'It was very mean of you to leave me so long with that man, Jean; he stayed quite an hour after you left,' she said, suppressing a yawn.

'Oh, I thought you wouldn't mind; I don't get on with him half so well as you do. Stand out of the light, will you?'

'He thinks you're immensely clever,' said Nancy; 'he says he never met any one so determined and plucky in his life. Of course you will get on, he says.'

'Yes,' said Jean with a strange smile, as she nibbled the top of her pencil; 'I suppose I shall get on. And to the end of my days people will admire me from a distance, and talk about my talent and my determination, just as they talk about your beauty and your womanly ways. That is so like the world; it always associates us with a certain atmosphere and never admits the possibility of any other.'

Nancy was perched on the end of the bed in her white peignoir, with her knees up to her chin and a puzzled expression on her face.

'How queer you are to-night, Jean,' she said; 'I don't think I understand.'

'My atmosphere,' continued Jean in the same passionless tone, 'is the clever and capable one. It is the one that is always reserved for the unattractive people who have understanding, the sort of people who know all there is to know, from observation, and never get the chance of experiencing one jot of it. They are the people who learn about life from the outside, and remain half alive themselves to the end of time. Nobody would think of falling in love with them, and they don't even know how to be lovable. It is a very clinging atmosphere,' she added sadly; 'I shall never shake it off.'

Nancy stopped making a becoming wreck of her coils of hair, and looked more bewildered than before.

'I don't understand, Jean,' she said again.

Jean looked at her for a moment with eyes full of admiration.

'Don't worry about it, child,' she said slowly; 'you will never have to understand.'

THE OMNIBUS

Arthur Quiller-Couch

It was not so much a day as a burning, fiery furnace. The roar of London's traffic reverberated under a sky of coppery blue; the pavements threw out waves of heat, thickened with the reek of restaurants and perfumery shops; and dust became cinders, and the wearing of flesh a weariness. Streams of sweat ran from the bellies of 'bus-horses when they halted. Men went up and down with unbuttoned waistcoats, turned into drinking-bars, and were no sooner inside than they longed to be out again, and baking in an ampler oven. Other men, who had given up drinking because of the expense, hung about the fountains in Trafalgar Square and listened to the splash of running water. It was the time when London is supposed to be empty; and when those who remain in town feel there is not room for a soul more.

We were eleven inside the omnibus when it pulled up at Charing Cross, so that legally there was room for just one more. I had travelled enough in omnibuses to know my fellow-passengers by heart—a governess with some sheets of music in her satchel; a minor actress going to rehearsal; a woman carrying her incurable complaint for the hundredth time to the hospital; three middle-aged city clerks; a couple of reporters with weak eyes and low collars; an old loose-cheeked woman exhaling patchouli; a bald-headed man with hairy hands, a violent breast-pin, and the indescribable air of a matrimonial agent. Not a word passed. We were all failures in life, and could not trouble to dissemble it, in that heat. Moreover, we were used to each other, as types if not as persons, and had lost curiosity. So we sat listless, dispirited, drawing difficult breath and staring vacuously. The hope we shared in common—that nobody would claim the vacant seat—was too obvious to be discussed.

But at Charing Cross the twelfth passenger got in—a boy with a stick, and a bundle in a blue handkerchief. He was about thirteen; bound for the docks, we could tell at a glance, to sail on his first voyage; and, by the way he looked about, we could tell as easily that in stepping outside Charing Cross Station he had set foot on London stones for the first time. When we pulled up, he was standing on the opposite pavement with dazed eyes like a hare's, wondering at the new world—the hansoms, the yelling news-boys, the flower-women, the crowd pushing him this way and that, the ugly shop-fronts, the hurry and stink and din of it all. Then, hailing our 'bus, he started to run across—faltered—almost dropped his bundle—was snatched by our conductor out of the path of a running hansom, and hauled on board. His eyelids were pink and swollen; but he was not crying, though he wanted to. Instead, he took a great gulp, as he pushed between our knees to his seat, and tried to look brave as a lion.

The passengers turned an incurious, half-resentful stare upon him, and then repented. I think that more than one of us wanted to speak, but dared not.

It was not so much the little chap's look. But to the knot of his sea-kit there was tied a bunch of cottage-flowers—sweet williams, boy's love, love-lies-bleeding, a few common striped carnations, and a rose or two—and the sight and smell of them in that frowsy 'bus were like tears on thirsty eyelids. We had ceased to pity what we were, but the heart is far withered that cannot pity what it has been; and it made us shudder to look on the young face set towards the road along which we had travelled so far. Only the minor actress dropped a tear; but she was used to expressing emotion, and half-way down the Strand the 'bus stopped and she left us.

The woman with an incurable complaint touched me on the knee.

'Speak to him,' she whispered.

But the whisper did not reach, for I was two hundred miles away, and occupied in starting off to school for the first time. I had two shillings in my pocket; and at the first town where the coach baited I was to exchange these for a coco-nut and a clasp-knife. Also, I was to break the knife in opening the nut, and the nut, when opened, would be sour. A sense of coming evil, therefore, possessed me.

'Why don't you speak to him?'

The boy glanced up, not catching her words, but suspicious: then frowned and looked defiant.

'Ah,' she went on in the same whisper, 'it's only the young that I pity. Sometimes, sir—for my illness keeps me much awake—I lie at night in my lodgings and listen, and the whole of London seems filled with the sound of children's feet running. Even by day I can hear them, at the back of the uproar—'

The matrimonial agent grunted and rose, as we halted at the top of Essex Street. I saw him slip a couple of half-crowns into the conductor's hand: and he whispered something, jerking his head back towards the interior of the 'bus. The boy was brushing his eyes, under pretence of putting his cap forward; and by the time he stole a look around to see if anyone had observed, we had started again. I pretended to stare out of the window, but marked the wet smear on his hand as he laid it on his lap.

In less than a minute it was my turn to alight. Unlike the matrimonial agent, I had not two half-crowns to spare; but, catching the sick woman's eye, forced up courage to nod and say—

'Good luck, my boy.'

'Good day, sir.'

A moment after I was in the hot crowd, whose roar rolled east and west for miles. And at the back of it, as the woman had said, in street and side-lane and blind-alley, I heard the footfall of a multitude more terrible than an army with banners, the ceaseless pelting feet of children—of Whittingtons turning and turning again.

AMY FOSTER

Joseph Conrad

Kennedy is a country doctor, and lives in Colebrook, on the shores of Eastbay. The high ground rising abruptly behind the red roofs of the little town crowds the quaint High Street against the wall which defends it from the sea. Beyond the sea-wall there curves for miles in a vast and regular sweep the barren beach of shingle, with the village of Brenzett standing out darkly across the water, a spire in a clump of trees; and still further out the perpendicular column of a lighthouse, looking in the distance no bigger than a lead pencil, marks the vanishing-point of the land. The country at the back of Brenzett is low and flat, but the bay is fairly well sheltered from the seas, and occasionally a big ship, windbound or through stress of weather, makes use of the anchoring-ground a mile and a half due north from you as you stand at the back door of the Ship Inn in Brenzett. A dilapidated windmill nearby lifting its shattered arms from a mound no loftier than a rubbish-heap, and a Martello tower squatting at the water's edge half a mile to the south of the Coast-guard cottages, are familiar to the skippers of small craft. These are the official sea-marks for the patch of trustworthy bottom represented on the Admiralty charts by an irregular oval of dots enclosing several figures six, with a tiny anchor engraved among them, and the legend 'mud and shells' over all.

The brow of the upland overtops the square tower of the Colebrook Church. The slope is green and looped by a white road. Ascending along this road, you open a valley broad and shallow, a wide green trough of pastures and hedges merging inland into a vista of purple tints and flowing lines closing the view.

In this valley down to Brenzett and Colebrook and up to Darnford, the market town fourteen miles away, lies the practice of my friend Kennedy. He had begun life as surgeon in the Navy, and afterwards had been the companion of a famous traveller, in the days when there were continents with unexplored interiors. His papers on the fauna and flora made him known to scientific societies. And now he had come to a country practice—from choice. The penetrating power of his mind, acting like a corrosive fluid, had destroyed his ambition, I fancy. His intelligence is of a scientific order, of an investigating habit, and of that unappeasable curiosity which believes that there is a particle of a general truth in every mystery.

A good many years ago now, on my return from abroad, he invited me to stay with him. I came readily enough, and as he could not neglect his patients to keep me company, he took me on his rounds—thirty miles or so of an afternoon, sometimes. I waited for him on the roads; the horse reached after the leafy twigs, and, sitting high in the dog-cart, I could hear Kennedy's laugh through the half-open door left open of some cottage. He had a big, hearty laugh that would have fitted a man twice his size, a brisk manner, a bronzed face, and a pair of grey, profoundly attentive eyes. He had the talent of making people talk to him freely, and an inexhaustible patience in listening to their tales.

One day, as we trotted out of a large village into a shady bit of road, I saw on our left hand a low brick cottage, with diamond panes in the windows, a creeper on the end wall, a roof of shingle, and some roses climbing on the rickety trellis-work of the tiny porch. Kennedy pulled up to a walk. A woman, in full sunlight, was throwing a dripping blanket over a line stretched between two old apple-trees. And as the bobtailed, long-necked chestnut, trying to get his head, jerked the left hand, covered by a thick dogskin glove, the doctor raised his voice over the hedge: 'How's your child, Amy?'

I had the time to see her dull face, red, not with a mantling blush, but as if her flat cheeks had been vigorously slapped, and to take in the squat figure, the scanty, dusty brown hair drawn into a tight knot at the back of the head. She looked quite young. With a distinct catch in her breath, her voice sounded low and timid.

'He's well, thank you.'

We trotted again. 'A young patient of yours,' I said; and the doctor, flicking the chestnut absently, muttered, 'Her husband used to be.'

'She seems a dull creature,' I remarked listlessly.

'Precisely,' said Kennedy. 'She is very passive. It's enough to look at the red hands hanging at the end of those short arms, at those slow, prominent brown eyes, to know the inertness of her mind—an inertness that one would think made it everlastingly safe from all the surprises of imagination. And yet which of us is safe? At any rate, such as you see her, she had enough imagination to fall in love. She's the daughter of one Isaac Foster, who from a small farmer has sunk into a shepherd; the beginning of his misfortunes dating from his runaway marriage with the cook of his widowed father—a well-to-do, apoplectic grazier, who passionately struck his name off his will, and had been heard to utter threats against his life. But this old affair, scandalous enough to serve as a motive for a Greek tragedy, arose from the similarity of their characters. There are other tragedies, less scandalous and of a subtler poignancy, arising from irreconcilable differences and from that fear of the Incomprehensible that hangs over all our heads—over all our heads…'

The tired chestnut dropped into a walk; and the rim of the sun, all red in a speckless sky, touched familiarly the smooth top of a ploughed rise near the road as I had seen it times innumerable touch the distant horizon of the sea. The uniform brownness of the harrowed field glowed with a rosy tinge, as though the powdered clods had sweated out in minute pearls of blood the toil of uncounted ploughmen. From the edge of a copse a waggon with two horses was rolling gently along the ridge. Raised above our heads upon the sky-line, it loomed up against the red sun, triumphantly big, enormous, like a chariot of giants drawn by two slow-stepping steeds of legendary proportions. And the clumsy figure of the man plodding at the head of the leading horse projected itself on the background of the Infinite with a heroic uncouthness. The end of his carter's whip quivered high up in the blue. Kennedy discoursed.

'She's the eldest of a large family. At the age of fifteen they put her out to service at the New Barns Farm. I attended Mrs Smith, the tenant's wife, and saw that girl there for the first time. Mrs Smith, a genteel person with a sharp nose, made her put on a black dress every afternoon. I don't know what induced me to notice her at all. There are faces that call your attention by a curious want of definiteness in their whole aspect, as, walking in a mist, you peer attentively at a vague shape which, after all, may be nothing more curious or strange than a signpost. The only peculiarity I perceived in her was a slight hesitation in her utterance, a sort of preliminary stammer which passes away with the first word. When sharply spoken to, she was apt to lose her head at once; but her heart was of the kindest. She had never been heard to express a dislike for a single human being, and she was tender to every living creature. She was devoted to Mrs Smith, to Mr Smith, to their dogs, cats, canaries; and as to Mrs Smith's grey parrot, its peculiarities exercised upon her a positive fascination. Nevertheless, when that outlandish bird, attacked by the cat, shrieked for help in human accents, she ran out into the yard stopping her ears, and did not prevent the crime. For Mrs Smith this was another evidence of her stupidity; on the other hand, her want of charm, in view of Smith's well-known frivolousness, was a great recommendation. Her short-sighted eyes would swim with pity for a poor mouse in a trap, and she had been seen once by some boys on her knees in the wet grass helping a toad in difficulties. If it's true, as some German fellow has said, that without phosphorus there is no thought, it is still more true that there is no kindness of heart without a certain amount of imagination. She had some. She had even more than is necessary to understand suffering and to be moved by pity. She fell in love under circumstances that leave no room for doubt in the matter; for you need imagination to form a notion of beauty at all, and still more to discover your ideal in an unfamiliar shape.

'How this aptitude came to her, what it did feed upon, is an inscrutable mystery. She was born in the village, and had never been further away from it than Colebrook or perhaps Darnford. She lived for four years with the Smiths. New Barns is an isolated farmhouse a mile away from the road, and she was content to look day after day at the same fields, hollows, rises; at the trees and the hedgerows; at the faces of the four men about the farm, always the same—day after day, month after month, year after year. She never showed a desire for conversation, and, as it seemed to me, she did not know how to smile. Sometimes of a fine Sunday afternoon she would put on her best dress, a pair of stout boots, a large grey hat trimmed with a black feather (I've seen her in that finery), seize an absurdly slender parasol, climb over two stiles, tramp over three fields and along two hundred yards of road—never further. There stood Foster's cottage. She would help her mother to give their tea to the younger children, wash up the crockery, kiss the little ones, and go back to the farm. That was all. All the rest, all the change, all the relaxation. She never seemed to wish for anything more. And then she fell in love. She fell in love silently, obstinately—perhaps helplessly. It came slowly, but when it came it worked like a powerful spell; it was love as the Ancients understood it: an irresistible and fateful impulse—a possession! Yes, it was in her to become haunted and possessed by a face, by a presence, fatally, as though she had been a pagan worshipper of form under a joyous sky—and to be awakened at last from that mysterious forgetfulness of self, from that enchantment, from that transport, by a fear resembling the unaccountable terror of a brute...'

With the sun hanging low on its western limit, the expanse of the grass-lands framed in the counterscarps of the rising ground took on a gorgeous and sombre aspect. A sense of penetrating sadness, like that inspired by a grave strain of music, disengaged itself from the silence of the fields. The men we met walked past slow, unsmiling, with downcast eyes, as if the melancholy of an overburdened earth had weighted their feet, bowed their shoulders, borne down their glances.

'Yes,' said the doctor to my remark, 'one would think the earth is under a curse, since of all her children these that cling to her the closest are uncouth in body and as leaden of gait as if their very hearts were loaded with chains. But here on this same road you might have seen amongst these heavy men a being lithe, supple, and long-limbed, straight like a pine with something striving upwards in his appearance as though the heart within him had been buoyant. Perhaps it was only the force of the contrast, but when he was passing one of these villagers here, the soles of his feet did not seem to me to touch the dust of the road. He vaulted over the stiles, paced these slopes with a long elastic stride that made him noticeable at a great distance, and had lustrous black eyes. He was so different from the mankind around that, with his freedom of movement, his soft—a little startled—glance, his olive complexion and graceful bearing, his humanity suggested to me the nature of a woodland creature. He came from there.'

The doctor pointed with his whip, and from the summit of the descent seen over the rolling tops of the trees in a park by the side of the road, appeared the level sea far below us, like the floor of an immense edifice inlaid with bands of dark ripple, with still trails of glitter, ending in a belt of glassy water at the foot of the sky. The light blur of smoke, from an invisible steamer, faded on the great clearness of the horizon like the mist of a breath on a mirror; and, inshore, the white sails of a coaster, with the appearance of disentangling themselves slowly from under the branches, floated clear of the foliage of the trees.

'Shipwrecked in the bay?' I said.

'Yes; he was a castaway. A poor emigrant from Central Europe bound to America and washed ashore here in a storm. And for him, who knew nothing of the earth, England was an undiscovered country. It was some time before he learned its name; and for all I know he might have expected to find wild beasts or wild men here, when, crawling in the dark over the sea-wall, he rolled down the other side into a dyke, where it was another miracle he didn't get drowned. But he struggled instinctively like an animal under a net, and this blind struggle threw him out into a field. He must have been, indeed, of a tougher fibre than he looked to withstand without expiring such buffetings, the violence of his exertions, and so much fear. Later on, in his broken English that resembled curiously the speech of a young child, he told me himself that he put his trust in God, believing he was no longer in this world. And truly—he would add—how was he to know? He fought his way against the rain and the gale on all fours, and crawled at last among some sheep huddled close under the lee of a hedge. They ran off in all directions, bleating in the darkness, and he welcomed the first familiar sound he heard on these shores. It must have been two in the morning then. And this is all we know of the manner of his landing, though he did not arrive unattended by any means. Only his grisly company did not begin to come ashore till much later in the day...'

The doctor gathered the reins, clicked his tongue; we trotted down the hill. Then turning, almost directly, a sharp corner into the High Street, we rattled over the stones and were home.

Late in the evening Kennedy, breaking a spell of moodiness that had come over him, returned to the story. Smoking his pipe, he paced the long room from end to end. A reading-lamp concentrated all its light upon the papers on his desk; and, sitting by the open window, I saw, after the windless, scorching day, the frigid splendour of a hazy sea lying motionless under the moon. Not a whisper, not a splash, not a stir of the shingle, not a footstep, not a sigh came up from the earth below—never a sign of life but the scent of climbing jasmine;

and Kennedy's voice, speaking behind me, passed through the wide casement, to vanish outside in a chill and sumptuous stillness.

'...The relations of shipwrecks in the olden time tell us of much suffering. Often the castaways were only saved from drowning to die miserably from starvation on a barren coast; others suffered violent death or else slavery, passing through years of precarious existence with people to whom their strangeness was an object of suspicion, dislike, or fear. We read about these things, and they are very pitiful. It is indeed hard upon a man to find himself a lost stranger, helpless, incomprehensible, and of a mysterious origin, in some obscure corner of the earth. Yet amongst all the adventurers shipwrecked in all the wild parts of the world, there is not one, it seems to me, that ever had to suffer a fate so simply tragic as the man I am speaking of, the most innocent of adventurers cast out by the sea in the bight of this bay, almost within sight from this very window.

'He did not know the name of his ship. Indeed, in the course of time we discovered he did not even know that ships had names—"like Christian people"; and when, one day, from the top of the Talfourd Hill, he beheld the sea lying open to his view, his eyes roamed afar, lost in an air of wild surprise, as though he had never seen such a sight before. And probably he had not. As far as I could make out, he had been hustled together with many others on board an emigrant-ship lying at the mouth of the Elbe, too bewildered to take note of his surroundings, too weary to see anything, too anxious to care. They were driven below into the 'tween-deck and battened down from the very start. It was a low timber dwelling—he would say—with wooden beams overhead, like the houses in his country, but you went into it down a ladder. It was very large, very cold, damp and sombre, with places in the manner of wooden boxes where people had to sleep, one above another, and it kept on rocking all ways at once all the time. He crept into one of these boxes and lay down there in the clothes in which he had left his home many days before, keeping his bundle and his stick by his side. People groaned, children cried, water dripped, the lights went out, the walls of the place creaked, and everything was being shaken so that in one's little box one dared not lift one's head. He had lost touch with his only companion (a young man from the same valley, he said), and all the time a great noise of wind went on outside and heavy blows fell—boom! boom! An awful sickness overcame him, even to the point of making him neglect his prayers. Besides, one could not tell whether it was morning or evening. It seemed always to be night in that place.

'Before that he had been travelling a long, long time on the iron track. He looked out of the window, which had a wonderfully clear glass in it, and the trees, the houses, the fields, and the long roads seemed to fly round and round about him till his head swam. He gave me to understand that he had on his passage beheld uncounted multitudes of people—whole nations—all dressed in such clothes as the rich wear. Once he was made to get out of the carriage, and slept through a night on a bench in a house of bricks with his bundle under his head; and once for many hours he had to sit on a floor of flat stones dozing, with his knees up and with his bundle between his feet. There was a roof over him, which seemed made of glass, and was so high that the tallest mountain-pine he had ever seen would have had room to grow under it. Steam-machines rolled in at one end and out at the other. People swarmed more than you can see on a feast-day round the miraculous Holy Image in the yard of the Carmelite Convent down in the plains where, before he left his home, he drove his mother in a wooden cart—a pious old woman who wanted to offer prayers and make a vow for his safety. He could not give me an idea of how large and lofty and full of noise and smoke and gloom, and clang of iron, the place was, but some one had told him it was called Berlin. Then they rang a bell, and another steam-machine came in, and again he was taken on and on through a land that wearied his eyes by its flatness without a single bit of a hill to be seen anywhere. One more night he spent shut up in a building like a good stable with a litter of straw on the floor, guarding his bundle amongst a lot of men, of whom not one could understand a single word he said. In the morning they were all led down to the stony shores of an extremely broad muddy river, flowing not between hills but between houses that seemed immense. There was a steam-machine that went on the water, and they all stood upon it packed tight, only now there were with them many women and children who made much noise. A cold rain fell, the wind blew in his face; he was wet through, and his teeth chattered. He and the young man from the same valley took each other by the hand.

'They thought they were being taken to America straightaway, but suddenly the steam-machine bumped against the side of a thing like a house on the water. The walls were smooth and black, and there uprose, growing from the roof as it were, bare trees in the shape of crosses, extremely high. That's how it appeared to him then, for he had never seen a ship before. This was the ship that was going to swim all the way to America. Voices shouted, everything swayed; there was a ladder dipping up and down. He went up on his hands and knees in mortal fear of falling into the water below, which made a great splashing. He got separated from his companion, and when he descended into the bottom of that ship his heart seemed to melt suddenly within him.

'It was then also, as he told me, that he lost contact for good and all with one of those three men who the summer before had been going about through all the little towns in the foothills of his country. They would arrive on market-days driving in a peasant's cart, and would set up an office in an inn or some other Jew's house. There were three of them, of whom one with a long beard looked venerable; and they had red cloth collars round their necks and gold lace on their sleeves like Government officials. They sat proudly behind a long table; and in the next room, so that the common people shouldn't hear, they kept a cunning telegraph machine, through which they could talk to the Emperor of America. The fathers hung about the door, but the young men of the mountains would crowd up to the table asking many questions, for there was work to be got all the year round at three dollars a day in America, and no military service to do.

'But the American Kaiser would not take everybody. Oh no! He himself had a great difficulty in getting accepted, and the venerable man in uniform had to go out of the room several times to work the telegraph on his behalf. The American Kaiser engaged him at last at three dollars, he being young and strong. However, many able young men backed out, afraid of the great distance; besides, only those who had some money could be taken. There were some who sold their huts and their land because it cost a lot of money to get to America; but then, once there, you had three dollars a day, and if you were clever you could find places where true gold could be picked up on the ground. His father's house was getting over-full. Two of his brothers were married and had children. He promised to send money home from America by post twice a year. His father sold an old cow, a pair of piebald mountain ponies of his own raising, and a cleared plot of fair pasture land on the sunny slope of a pine-clad pass to a Jew inn-keeper, in order to pay the people of the ship that took men to America to get rich in a short time.

'He must have been a real adventurer at heart, for how many of the greatest enterprises in the conquest of the earth had for their beginning just such a bargaining away of the paternal cow for the mirage of true gold far away! I have been telling you more or less in my own words what I learned fragmentarily in the course of two or three years, during which I seldom missed an opportunity of a friendly chat with him. He told me this story of his adventure with many flashes of white teeth and lively glances of black eyes, at first in a sort of anxious baby-talk, then, as he acquired the language, with great fluency, but always with that singing, soft, and at the same time vibrating intonation that instilled a strangely penetrating power into the sound of the most familiar English words, as if they had been the words of an unearthly language. And he always would come to an end, with many emphatic shakes of his head, upon that awful sensation of his heart melting within him directly he set foot on board that ship. Afterwards there seemed to come for him a period of blank ignorance, at any rate as to facts. No doubt he must have been abominably sea-sick and abominably unhappy—this soft and passionate adventurer, taken thus out of his knowledge, and feeling bitterly as he lay in his emigrant bunk his utter loneliness; for his was a highly sensitive nature. The next thing we know of him for certain is that he had been hiding in Hammond's pig-pound by the side of the road to Norton, six miles, as the crow flies, from the sea. Of these experiences he was unwilling to speak; they seemed to have seared into his soul a sombre sort of wonder and indignation. Through the rumours of the countryside, which lasted for a good many days after his arrival, we know that the fishermen of West Colebrook had been disturbed and started by heavy knocks against the walls of weatherboard cottages, and by a voice crying piercingly strange words in the night. Several of them turned out even, but, no doubt, he had fled in sudden alarm at their rough angry tones hailing each other in the darkness. A sort of frenzy must have helped him up the steep Norton hill. It was he, no doubt, who early the following morning had been seen lying (in a swoon, I should say) on the roadside grass by the Brenzett carrier, who actually got down to have a nearer look, but drew back, intimidated by the perfect immobility, and by something queer in the aspect of that tramp, sleeping so still under the showers. As the day advanced, some children came dashing into school at Norton in such a fright that the schoolmistress went out and spoke indignantly to a 'horrid-looking man' on the road. He edged away, hanging his head, for a few steps, and then suddenly ran off with extraordinary fleetness. The driver of Mr Bradley's milk-cart made no secret of it that he had lashed with his whip at a hairy sort of gipsy fellow who, jumping up at a turn of the road by the Vents, made a snatch at the pony's bridle. And he caught him a good one too, right over the face, he said, that made him drop down in the mud a jolly sight quicker than he had jumped up; but it was a good half a mile before he could stop the pony. Maybe that in his desperate endeavours to get help, and in his need to get in touch with some one, the poor devil had tried to stop the cart. Also three boys confessed afterwards to throwing stones at a funny tramp, knocking about all wet and muddy, and, it seemed, very drunk, in the narrow deep lane by the limekilns. All this was the talk of three villages for days; but we have Mrs Finn's (the wife of Smith's waggoner) unimpeachable testimony that she saw him get over the low wall of Hammond's pig-pound and lurch straight at her, babbling aloud in a voice that was enough to make one die of fright. Having the baby with her in a perambulator, Mrs Finn called out to him to go away, and as he persisted in coming nearer, she hit him courageously with her umbrella over the head, and, without once looking back, ran like the wind with the perambulator as far as the first house in the village. She stopped then, out of breath, and spoke to old Lewis, hammering there at a heap of stones; and the old chap, taking off his immense black wire goggles, got up on his shaky legs to look where she pointed. Together they followed with their eyes the figure of the man running over a field; they saw him fall down, pick himself up, and run on again, staggering and waving his long arms above his head, in the direction of the New Barns Farm. From that moment he is plainly in the toils of his obscure and touching destiny. There is no doubt after this of what happened to him. All is certain now: Mrs Smith's intense terror; Amy Foster's stolid conviction, held against the other's nervous attack, that the man "meant no harm"; Smith's exasperation (on his return from Darnford Market) at finding the dog barking himself into a fit, the back door locked, his wife in hysterics; and all for an unfortunate dirty tramp, supposed to be even then lurking in his stackyard. Was he? He would teach him to frighten women.

'Smith is notoriously hot-tempered, but the sight of some nondescript and miry creature sitting cross-legged amongst a lot of loose straw, and swinging itself to and fro like a bear in a cage, made him pause. Then this tramp stood up silently before him, one mass of mud and filth from head to foot. Smith, alone amongst his stacks with this apparition, in the stormy twilight ringing with the infuriated barking of the dog, felt the dread of an inexplicable strangeness. But when that being, parting with his black hands the long matted locks that hung before his face, as you part the two halves of a curtain, looked out at him with glistening, wild, black-and-white eyes, the weirdness of this silent encounter fairly staggered him. He has admitted since (for the story has been a legitimate subject of conversation about here for years) that he made more than one step backwards. Then a sudden burst of rapid, senseless speech persuaded him at once that he had to do with an escaped lunatic. In fact, that impression never wore off completely. Smith has not in his heart given up his secret conviction of the man's essential insanity to this very day.

'As the creature approached him, jabbering in a most discomposing manner, Smith (unaware that he was being addressed as "gracious lord", and adjured in God's name to afford food and shelter) kept on speaking firmly but gently to it, and retreating all the time into the other yard. At last, watching his chance, by a sudden charge he bundled him head-long into the wood-lodge, and instantly shot the bolt. Thereupon he wiped his brow, though the day was cold. He had done his duty to the community by shutting up a wandering and probably dangerous maniac. Smith isn't a hard man at all, but he had room in his brain only for that one idea of lunacy. He was not imaginative enough to ask himself whether the man might not be perishing with cold and hunger. Meantime, at first, the maniac made a great deal of noise in the lodge. Mrs Smith was screaming upstairs, where she had locked herself in her bedroom; but Amy Foster sobbed piteously at the kitchen-door, wringing her hands and muttering, "Don't! don't!" I daresay Smith had a rough time of it that evening with one noise and another, and this insane, disturbing voice crying obstinately through the door only added to his irritation. He couldn't possibly have connected this troublesome lunatic with the sinking of a ship in Eastbay, of which there had been a rumour in the Darnford market-place. And I daresay the man inside had been very near to insanity on that night. Before his excitement collapsed and he became unconscious he was throwing himself violently about in the dark, rolling on some dirty sacks, and biting his fists with rage, cold, hunger, amazement, and despair.

'He was a mountaineer of the eastern range of the Carpathians, and the vessel sunk the night before in Eastbay was the Hamburg emigrant-ship *Herzogin Sophia-Dorothea*, of appalling memory.

'A few months later we could read in the papers the accounts of the bogus "Emigration Agencies" among the Sclavonian peasantry in the more remote provinces of Austria. The object of these scoundrels was to get hold of the poor ignorant people's homesteads, and they were in league with the local usurers. They exported their victims through Hamburg mostly. As to the ship, I had watched her out of this very window, reaching close-hauled under short canvas into the bay on a dark, threatening afternoon. She came to an anchor, correctly by the chart, off the Brenzett Coastguard station. I remember before the night fell looking out again at the outlines of her spars and rigging that stood out dark and pointed on a background of ragged, slaty clouds like another and a slighter spire to the left of the Brenzett church-tower. In the evening the wind rose. At midnight I could hear in my bed the terrific gusts and the sounds of a driving deluge.

'About that time the Coastguardmen thought they saw the lights of a steamer over the anchoring-ground. In a moment they vanished; but it is clear that another vessel of some sort had tried for shelter in the bay on that awful, blind night, had rammed the German ship amidships (a breach—as one of the divers told me afterwards—"that you could sail a Thames barge through"), and then had gone out either scatheless or damaged, who shall say; but had gone out, unknown, unseen, and fatal, to perish mysteriously at sea. Of her nothing ever came to light, and yet the hue and cry that was raised all over the world would have found her out if she had been in existence anywhere on the face of the waters.

'A completeness without a clue, and a stealthy silence as of a neatly executed crime, characterize this murderous disaster, which, as you may remember, had its gruesome celebrity. The wind would have prevented the loudest outcries from reaching the shore; there had been evidently no time for signals of distress. It was death without any sort of fuss. The Hamburg ship, filling all at once, capsized as she sank, and at daylight there was not even the end of a spar to be seen above water. She was missed, of course, and at first the Coastguardmen surmised that she had either dragged her anchor or parted her cable some time during the night, and had been blown out to sea. Then, after the tide turned, the wreck must have shifted a little and released some of the bodies, because a child—a little fair-haired child in a red frock—came ashore abreast of the Martello tower. By the afternoon you could see along three miles of beach dark figures with bare legs dashing in and out of the tumbling foam, and rough-looking men, women with hard faces, children, mostly fair-haired, were being carried, stiff and dripping, on stretchers, on wattles, on ladders, in a long procession past the door of the Ship Inn, to be laid out in a row under the north wall of the Brenzett Church.

'Officially, the body of the little girl in the red frock is the first thing that came ashore from that ship. But I have patients amongst the seafaring population of West Colebrook, and, unofficially, I am informed that very early that morning two brothers, who went down to look after their cobble hauled up on the beach, found, a good way from Brenzett, an ordinary ship's hencoop lying high and dry on the shore, with eleven drowned ducks inside. Their families ate the birds, and the hencoop was split into firewood with a hatchet. It is possible that a man (supposing he happened to be on deck at the time of the accident) might have floated ashore on that hencoop. He might. I admit it is improbable, but there was the man—and for days, nay, for weeks—it didn't enter our heads that we had amongst us the only living soul that had escaped from that disaster. The man himself, even when he learned to speak intelligibly, could tell us very little. He remembered he had felt better (after the ship had anchored, I suppose), and that the darkness, the wind, and the rain took his breath away. This looks as if he had been on deck some time during that night. But we mustn't forget he had been taken out of his knowledge, that he had been sea-sick and battened down below for four days, that he had no general notion of a ship or of the sea, and therefore could have no definite idea of what was happening to him. The rain, the wind, the darkness he knew; he understood the bleating of the sheep, and he remembered the pain of his wretchedness and misery, his heartbroken astonishment that it was neither seen nor understood, his dismay at finding all the men angry and all the women fierce. He had approached them as a beggar, it is true, he said; but in his country, even if they gave nothing, they spoke gently to beggars. The children in his country were not taught to throw stones at those who asked for compassion. Smith's strategy overcame him completely. The wood-lodge presented the horrible aspect of a dungeon. What would be done to him next? ...No wonder that Amy Foster appeared to his eyes with the aureole of an angel of light. The girl had not been able to sleep for thinking of the poor man, and in the morning, before the Smiths were up, she slipped out across the back yard. Holding the door of the wood-lodge ajar, she looked in and extended to him half a loaf of white bread—"such bread as the rich eat in my country", he used to say.

'At this he got up slowly from amongst all sorts of rubbish, stiff, hungry, trembling, miserable, and doubtful. "Can you eat this?" she asked in her soft and timid voice. He must have taken her for a "gracious lady". He devoured ferociously, and tears were falling on the crust. Suddenly he dropped the bread, seized her wrist, and imprinted a kiss on her hand. She was not frightened. Through his forlorn condition she had observed that he was good-looking. She shut the door and walked back slowly to the kitchen. Much later on, she told Mrs Smith, who shuddered at the bare idea of being touched by that creature.

'Through this act of impulsive pity he was brought back again within the pale of human relations with his new surroundings. He never forgot it—never.

'That very same morning old Mr Swaffer (Smith's nearest neighbour) came over to give his advice, and ended by carrying him off. He stood, unsteady on his legs, meek, and caked over in half-dried mud, while the two men talked around him in an incomprehensible tongue. Mrs Smith had refused to come downstairs till the madman was off the premises; Amy Foster, far from within the dark kitchen, watched through the open back door; and he obeyed the signs that were made to him to the best of his ability. But Smith was full of mistrust. "Mind, sir! It may be all his cunning," he cried repeatedly in a tone of warning. When Mr Swaffer started the mare, the deplorable being sitting humbly by his side, through weakness, nearly fell out over the back of the high two-wheeled cart. Swaffer took him straight home. And it is then that I come upon the scene.

'I was called in by the simple process of the old man beckoning to me with his forefinger over the gate of his house as I happened to be driving past. I got down, of course.

'"I've got something here," he mumbled, leading the way to an outhouse at a little distance from his other farm-buildings.

'It was there that I saw him first, in a long low room taken upon the space of that sort of coach-house. It was bare and whitewashed, with a small square aperture glazed with one cracked, dusty pane at its further end. He was lying on his back upon a straw pallet; they had given him a couple of horse-blankets, and he seemed to have spent the remainder of his strength in the exertion of cleaning himself. He was almost speechless; his quick breathing under the blankets pulled up to his chin, his glittering, restless black eyes reminded me of a wild bird caught in a snare. While I was examining him, old Swaffer stood silently by the door, passing the tips of his fingers along his shaven upper lip. I gave some directions, promised to send a bottle of medicine, and naturally made some inquiries.

'"Smith caught him in the stackyard at New Barns," said the old chap in his deliberate, unmoved manner, and as if the other had been indeed a sort of wild animal. "That's how I came by him. Quite a curiosity, isn't he? Now tell me, doctor—you've been all over the world—don't you think that's a bit of a Hindoo we've got hold of here?"

'I was greatly surprised. His long black hair scattered over the straw bolster contrasted with the olive pallor of his face. It occurred to me he might be a Basque. It didn't necessarily follow that he should understand Spanish; but I tried him with the few words I know, and also with some French. The whispered sounds I caught by bending my ear to his lips puzzled me utterly. That afternoon the young ladies from the Rectory (one of them read Goethe with a dictionary, and the other had struggled with Dante for years), coming to see Miss Swaffer, tried their German and Italian on him from the doorway. They retreated, just the least bit scared by the flood of passionate speech which, turning on his pallet, he let out at them. They admitted that the sound was pleasant, soft, musical—but, in conjunction with his looks perhaps, it was startling—so excitable, so utterly unlike anything one had ever heard. The village boys climbed up the bank to have a peep through the little square aperture. Everybody was wondering what Mr Swaffer would do with him.

'He simply kept him.

'Swaffer would be called eccentric were he not so much respected. They will tell you that Mr Swaffer sits up as late as ten o'clock at night to read books, and they will tell you also that he can write a cheque for two hundred pounds without thinking twice about it. He himself would tell you that the Swaffers had owned land between this and Darnford for these three hundred years. He must be eighty-five to-day, but he does not look a bit older than when I first came here. He is a great breeder of sheep, and deals extensively in cattle. He attends market-days for miles around in every sort of weather, and drives sitting bowed low over the reins, his lank grey hair curling over the collar of his warm coat, and with a green plaid rug round his legs. The calmness of advanced age gives a solemnity to his manner. He is clean-shaved; his lips are thin and sensitive; something rigid and monarchal in the set of his features lends a certain elevation to the character of his face. He has been known to drive miles in the rain to see a new kind of rose in somebody's garden, or a monstrous cabbage grown by a cottager. He loves to hear tell of or to be shown something what he calls "outlandish". Perhaps it was just that outlandishness of the man which influenced old Swaffer. Perhaps it was only an inexplicable caprice. All I know is that at the end of three weeks I caught sight of Smith's lunatic digging in Swaffer's kitchen garden. They had found out he could use a spade. He dug barefooted.

'His black hair flowed over his shoulders. I suppose it was Swaffer who had given him the striped old cotton shirt; but he wore still the national brown cloth trousers (in which he had been washed ashore) fitting to the leg almost like tights; was belted with a broad leathern belt studded with little brass discs; and had never yet ventured into the village. The land he looked upon seemed to him kept neatly, like the grounds round a landowner's house; the size of the cart-horses struck him with astonishment; the roads resembled garden walks, and the aspect of the people, especially on Sundays, spoke of opulence. He wondered what made them so hardhearted and their children so bold.

He got his food at the back door, carried it in both hands, carefully, to his outhouse, and, sitting alone on his pallet, would make the sign of the cross before he began. Beside the same pallet, kneeling in the early darkness of the short days, he recited aloud the Lord's Prayer before he slept. Whenever he saw old Swaffer he would bow with veneration from the waist, and stand erect while the old man, with his fingers over his upper lip, surveyed him silently. He bowed also to Miss Swaffer, who kept house frugally for her father—a broad-shouldered, big-boned woman of forty-five, with the pocket of her dress full of keys, and a grey, steady eye. She was Church—as people said (while her father was one of the trustees of the Baptist Chapel)—and wore a little steel cross at her waist. She dressed severely in black, in memory of one of the innumerable Bradleys of the neighbourhood, to whom she had been engaged some twenty-five years ago—a young farmer who broke his neck out hunting on the eve of the wedding-day. She had the unmoved countenance of the deaf, spoke very seldom, and her lips, thin like her father's, astonished one sometimes by a mysteriously ironic curl.

'These were the people to whom he owed allegiance, and an overwhelming loneliness seemed to fall from the leaden sky of that winter without sunshine. All the faces were sad. He could talk to no one, and had no hope of ever understanding anybody. It was as if these had been the faces of people from the other world—dead people—he used to tell me years afterwards. Upon my word, I wonder he did not go mad. He didn't know where he was. Somewhere very far from his mountains—somewhere over the water. Was this America, he wondered?

'If it hadn't been for the steel cross at Miss Swaffer's belt he would not, he confessed, have known whether he was in a Christian country at all. He used to cast stealthy glances at it, and feel comforted. There was nothing here the same as in his country! The earth and the water were different; there were no images of the Redeemer by the roadside. The very grass was different, and the trees. All the trees but the three old Norway-pines on the bit of lawn before Swaffer's house, and these reminded him of his country. He had been detected once, after dusk, with his forehead against the trunk of one of them, sobbing, and talking to himself. They had been like brothers to him at that time, he affirmed. Everything else was strange. Conceive you the kind of an existence overshadowed, oppressed, by the everyday material appearances, as if by the visions of a nightmare. At night, when he could not sleep, he kept on thinking of the girl who gave him the first piece of bread he had eaten in this foreign land. She had been neither fierce nor angry, nor frightened. Her face he remembered as the only comprehensible face amongst all these faces that were as closed, as mysterious, and as mute as the faces of the dead who are possessed of a knowledge beyond the comprehension of the living. I wonder whether the memory of her compassion prevented him from cutting his throat. But there! I suppose I am an old sentimentalist, and forget the instinctive love of life which it takes all the strength of an uncommon despair to overcome.

'He did the work which was given him with an intelligence which surprised old Swaffer. By-and-by it was discovered that he could help at the ploughing, could milk the cows, feed the bullocks in the cattle-yard, and was of some use with the sheep. He began to pick up words, too, very fast; and suddenly, one fine morning in spring, he rescued from an untimely death a grandchild of old Swaffer.

'Swaffer's younger daughter is married to Willcox, a solicitor and the Town Clerk of Colebrook. Regularly twice a year they come to stay with the old man for a few days. Their only child, a little girl not three years old at the time, ran out of the house alone in her little white pinafore, and, toddling across the grass of a terraced garden, pitched herself over a low wall head first into the horse-pond in the yard below.

'Our man was out with the waggoner and the plough in the field nearest to the house, and as he was leading the team round to begin a fresh furrow, he saw, through the gap of a gate, what for anybody else would have been a mere flutter of something white. But he had straight-glancing, quick, far-reaching eyes, that only seemed to flinch and lose their amazing power before the immensity of the sea. He was barefooted, and looking as outlandish as the heart of Swaffer could desire. Leaving the horses on the turn, to the inexpressible disgust of the waggoner he bounded off, going over the ploughed ground in long leaps, and suddenly appeared before the mother, thrust the child into her arms, and strode away.

'The pond was not very deep; but still, if he had not had such good eyes, the child would have perished—miserably suffocated in the foot or so of sticky mud at the bottom. Old Swaffer walked out slowly into the field, waited till the plough came over to his side, had a good look at him, and without saying a word went back to the house. But from that time they laid out his meals on the kitchen table; and at first, Miss Swaffer, all in black and with an inscrutable face, would come and stand in the doorway of the living-room to see him make a big sign of the cross before he fell to. I believe that from that day, too, Swaffer began to pay him regular wages.

'I can't follow step by step his development. He cut his hair short, was seen in the village and along the road going to and fro to his work like any other man. Children ceased to shout after him. He became aware of social differences, but remained for a long time surprised at the bare poverty of the churches among so much wealth. He couldn't understand either why they were kept shut up on week-days. There was nothing to steal in them. Was it to keep people from praying too often? The rectory took much notice of him about that time, and I believe the young ladies attempted to prepare the ground for his conversion. They could not, however, break him of his habit of crossing himself, but he went so far as to take off the string with a couple of brass medals the size of a sixpence, a tiny metal cross, and a square sort of scapulary which he wore round his neck. He hung them on the wall by the side of his bed, and he was still to be heard every evening reciting the Lord's Prayer, in incomprehensible words and in a slow, fervent tone, as he had heard his old father do at the head of all the kneeling family, big and little, on every evening of his life. And though he wore corduroys at work, and a slop-made pepper-and-salt suit on Sundays, strangers would turn round to look after him on the road. His foreignness had a peculiar and indelible stamp. At last people became used to see him. But they never became used to him. His rapid, skimming walk; his swarthy complexion; his hat cocked on the left ear; his habit, on warm evenings, of wearing his coat over one shoulder, like a hussar's dolman; his manner of leaping over the stiles, not as a feat of agility, but in the ordinary course of progression—all these peculiarities were, as one may say, so many causes of scorn and offence to the inhabitants of the village. *They* wouldn't in their dinner hour lie flat on their backs on the grass to stare at the sky. Neither did they go about the fields screaming dismal tunes. Many times have I heard his high-pitched voice from behind the ridge of some sloping sheep-walk, a voice light and soaring, like a lark's, but with a melancholy human note, over our fields that hear only the song of birds. And I should be startled myself. Ah! He was different: innocent of heart, and full of good-will, which nobody wanted, this castaway, that, like a man transplanted into another planet, was separated by an immense space from his past and by an immense ignorance from his future. His quick, fervent utterance positively shocked everybody. "An excitable devil", they called him. One evening, in the tap-room of the Coach and Horses, (having drunk some whisky), he upset them all by singing a love-song of his country. They hooted him down, and he was pained; but Preble, the lame wheelwright, and Vincent, the fat blacksmith, and the other notables, too, wanted to drink their evening beer in peace. On another occasion he tried to show them how to dance. The dust rose in clouds from the sanded floor; he leaped straight up amongst the deal tables, struck his heels together, squatted on one heel in front of old Preble, shooting out the other leg, uttered wild and exulting cries, jumped up to whirl on one foot, snapping his fingers above his head—and a strange carter who was having a drink in there began to swear, and cleared out with his half-pint in his hand into the bar. But when suddenly he sprang upon a table and continued to dance among the glasses, the landlord interfered. He didn't want any "acrobat tricks in the tap-room". They laid their hands on him. Having had a glass or two, Mr Swaffer's foreigner tried to expostulate; was ejected forcibly; got a black eye.

'I believe he felt the hostility of his human surroundings. But he was tough—tough in spirit, too, as well as in body. Only the memory of the sea frightened him, with that vague terror that is left by a bad dream. His home was far away; and he did not want now to go to America. I had often explained to him that there is no place on earth where true gold can be found lying ready and to be got for the trouble of the picking up. How then, he asked, could he ever return home with empty hands when there had been sold a cow, two ponies, and a bit of land to pay for his going? His eyes would fill with tears, and, averting them from the immense shimmer of the sea, he would throw himself face down on the grass. But sometimes, cocking his hat with a little conquering air, he would defy my wisdom. He had found his bit of true gold. That was Amy Foster's heart, which was "a golden heart, and soft to people's misery", he would say in the accents of overwhelming conviction.

'He was called Yanko. He had explained that this meant Little John; but as he would also repeat very often that he was a mountaineer (some word sounding in the dialect of his country like Goorall) he got it for his surname. And this is the only trace of him that the succeeding ages may find in the marriage register of the parish. There it stands—Yanko Goorall—in the rector's handwriting. The crooked cross made by the castaway, a cross whose tracing no doubt seemed to him the most solemn part of the whole ceremony, is all that remains now to perpetuate the memory of his name.

'His courtship had lasted some time—ever since he got his precarious footing in the community. It began by his buying for Amy Foster a green satin ribbon in Darnford. This was what you did in his country. You bought a ribbon at a Jew's stall on a fair-day. I don't suppose the girl knew what to do with it, but he seemed to think that his honourable intentions could not be mistaken.

'It was only when he declared his purpose to get married that I fully understood how, for a hundred futile and inappreciable reasons, how—shall I say odious?—he was to all the countryside. Every old woman in the village was up in arms. Smith, coming upon him near the farm, promised to break his head for him if he found him about again. But he twisted his little black moustache with such a bellicose air and rolled such big, black fierce eyes at Smith that this promise came to nothing. Smith, however, told the girl that she must be mad to take up with a man who was surely wrong in his head. All the same, when she heard him in the gloaming whistle from beyond the orchard a couple of bars of a weird and mournful tune, she would drop whatever she had in her hand—she would leave Mrs Smith in the middle of a sentence—and she would run out to his call. Mrs Smith called her a shameless hussy. She answered nothing. She said nothing at all to anybody, and went on her way as if she had been deaf. She and I alone in all the land, I fancy, could see his very real beauty. He was very good-looking, and most graceful in his bearing, with that something wild as of a woodland creature in his aspect. Her mother moaned over her dismally whenever the girl came to see her on her day out. The father was surly, but pretended not to know; and Mrs Finn once told her plainly that "this man, my dear, will do you some harm some day yet." And so it went on. They could be seen on the roads, she tramping stolidly in her finery—grey dress, black feather, stout boots, prominent white cotton gloves that caught your eye a hundred yards away; and he, his coat slung picturesquely over one shoulder, pacing by her side, gallant of bearing and casting tender glances upon the girl with the golden heart. I wonder whether he saw how plain she was. Perhaps among types so different from what he had ever seen, he had not the power to judge; or perhaps he was seduced by the divine quality of her pity.

'Yanko was in great trouble meantime. In his country you get an old man for an ambassador in marriage affairs. He did not know how to proceed. However, one day in the midst of sheep in a field (he was now Swaffer's under-shepherd with Foster) he took off his hat to the father and declared himself humbly. "I daresay she's fool enough to marry you," was all Foster said. "And then," he used to relate, "he puts his hat on his head, looks black at me as if he wanted to cut my throat, whistles the dog, and off he goes, leaving me to do the work." The Fosters, of course, didn't like to lose the wages the girl earned; Amy used to give all her money to her mother. But there was in Foster a very genuine aversion to that match. He contended that the fellow was very good with sheep, but was not fit for any girl to marry. For one thing, he used to go along the hedges muttering to himself like a dam' fool; and then, these foreigners behave very queerly to women sometimes. And perhaps he would want to carry her off somewhere—or run off himself. It was not safe. He preached it to his daughter that the fellow might ill-use her in some way. She made no answer. It was, they said in the village, as if the man had done something to her. People discussed the matter. It was quite an excitement, and the two went on "walking out" together in the face of opposition. Then something unexpected happened.

'I don't know whether old Swaffer ever understood how much he was regarded in the light of a father by his foreign retainer. Anyway the relation was curiously feudal. So when Yanko asked formally for an interview—"and the Miss too" (he called the severe, deaf Miss Swaffer simply *Miss*)—it was to obtain their permission to marry. Swaffer heard him unmoved, dismissed him by a nod, and then shouted the intelligence into Miss Swaffer's best ear. She showed no surprise, and only remarked grimly, in a veiled blank voice, "He certainly won't get any other girl to marry him."

'It is Miss Swaffer who has all the credit of the munificence; but in a very few days it came out that Mr Swaffer had presented Yanko with a cottage (the cottage you've seen this morning) and something like an acre of ground—had made it over to him in absolute property. Willcox expedited the deed, and I remember him telling me he had a great pleasure in making it ready. It recited: "In consideration of saving the life of my beloved grandchild, Bertha Willcox."

'Of course, after that no power on earth could prevent them from getting married.

'Her infatuation endured. People saw her going out to meet him in the evening. She stared with unblinking, fascinated eyes up the road where he was expected to appear, walking freely, with a swing from the hip, and humming one of the love-tunes of his country. When the boy was born, he got elevated at the Coach and Horses, essayed again a song and a dance, and was again ejected. People expressed their commiseration for a woman married to that Jack-in-the-box. He didn't care. There was a man now (he told me boastfully) to whom he could sing and talk in the language of his country, and show how to dance by-and-by.

'But I don't know. To me he appeared to have grown less springy of step, heavier in body, less keen of eye. Imagination, no doubt; but it seems to me now as if the net of fate had been drawn closer round him already.

'One day I met him on the footpath over the Talfourd Hill. He told me that "women were funny". I had heard already of domestic differences. People were saying that Amy Foster was beginning to find out what sort of man she had married. He looked upon the sea with indifferent, unseeing eyes. His wife had snatched the child out of his arms one day as he sat on the doorstep crooning to it a song such as the mothers sing to babies in his mountains. She seemed to think he was doing it some harm. Women are funny. And she had objected to him praying aloud in the evening. Why? He expected the boy to repeat the prayer aloud after him by-and-by, as he used to do after his old father when he was a child—in his own country. And I discovered he longed for their boy to grow up so that he could have a man to talk with in that language that to our ears sounded so disturbing, so passionate, and so bizarre. Why his wife should dislike the idea he couldn't tell. But that would pass, he said. And tilting his head knowingly, he tapped his breastbone to indicate that she had a good heart: not hard, not fierce, open to compassion, charitable to the poor!

'I walked away thoughtfully; I wondered whether his difference, his strangeness, were not penetrating with repulsion that dull nature they had begun by irresistibly attracting. I wondered...'

The doctor came to the window and looked out at the frigid splendour of the sea, immense in the haze, as if enclosing all the earth with all the hearts lost among the passions of love and fear.

'Physiologically, now,' he said, turning away abruptly, 'it was possible. It was possible.'

He remained silent. Then went on—

'At all events, the next time I saw him he was ill—lung trouble. He was tough, but I daresay he was not acclimatized as well as I had supposed. It was a bad winter; and, of course, these mountaineers do get fits of home-sickness; and a state of depression would make him vulnerable. He was lying half-dressed on a couch downstairs.

'A table covered with a dark oilcloth took up all the middle of the little room. There was a wicker cradle on the floor, a kettle spouting steam on the hob, and some child's linen lay drying on the fender. The room was warm, but the door opens right into the garden, as you noticed perhaps.

'He was very feverish, and kept on muttering to himself. She sat on a chair and looked at him fixedly across the table with her brown, blurred eyes. "Why don't you have him upstairs?" I asked. With a start and a confused stammer she said, "Oh! ah! I couldn't sit with him upstairs, sir."

'I gave her certain directions; and going outside, I said again that he ought to be in bed upstairs. She wrung her hands. "I couldn't. I couldn't. He keeps on saying something—I don't know what." With the memory of all the talk against the man that had been dinned into her ears, I looked at her narrowly. I looked into her short-sighted eyes, at her dumb eyes that once in her life had seen an enticing shape, but seemed, staring at me, to see nothing at all now. But I saw she was uneasy.

'"What's the matter with him?" she asked in a sort of vacant trepidation. "He doesn't look very ill. I never did see anybody look like this before..."

'"Do you think," I asked indignantly, "he is shamming?"

'"I can't help it, sir," she said stolidly. And suddenly she clapped her hands and looked right and left. "And there's the baby. I am so frightened. He wanted me just now to give him the baby. I can't understand what he says to it."

'"Can't you ask a neighbour to come in to-night?" I asked.

'"Please, sir, nobody seems to care to come," she muttered, dully resigned all at once.

'I impressed upon her the necessity of the greatest care, and then had to go. There was a good deal of sickness that winter. "Oh, I hope he won't talk!" she exclaimed softly just as I was going away.

'I don't know how it is I did not see—but I didn't. And yet, turning in my trap, I saw her lingering before the door, very still, and as if meditating a flight up the miry road.

'Towards the night his fever increased.

'He tossed, moaned, and now and then muttered a complaint. And she sat with the table between her and the couch, watching every movement and every sound, with the terror, the unreasonable terror, of that man she could not understand creeping over her. She had drawn the wicker cradle close to her feet. There was nothing in her now but the maternal instinct and that unaccountable fear.

'Suddenly coming to himself, parched, he demanded a drink of water. She did not move. She had not understood, though he may have thought he was speaking in English. He waited, looking at her, burning with fever, amazed at her silence and immobility, and then he shouted impatiently, "Water! Give me water!"

'She jumped to her feet, snatched up the child, and stood still. He spoke to her, and his passionate remonstrances only increased her fear of that strange man. I believe he spoke to her for a long time, entreating, wondering, pleading, ordering, I suppose. She says she bore it as long as she could. And then a gust of rage came over him.

'He sat up and called out terribly one word—some word. Then he got up as though he hadn't been ill at all, she says. And as in fevered dismay, indignation, and wonder he tried to get to her round the table, she simply opened the door and ran out with the child in her arms. She heard him call twice after her down the road in a terrible voice—and fled… Ah! but you should have seen stirring behind the dull, blurred glance of these eyes the spectre of the fear which had haunted her on that night three miles and a half to the door of Foster's cottage! I did the next day.

'And it was I who found him lying face down and his body in a puddle, just outside the little wicket-gate.

'I had been called out that night to an urgent case in the village, and on my way home at daybreak passed by the cottage. The door stood open. My man helped me to carry him in. We laid him on the couch. The lamp smoked, the fire was out, the chill of the stormy night oozed from the cheerless yellow paper on the wall. "Amy!" I called aloud, and my voice seemed to lose itself in the emptiness of this tiny house as if I had cried in a desert. He opened his eyes. "Gone!" he said distinctly. "I had only asked for water—only for a little water…"

'He was muddy. I covered him up and stood waiting in silence, catching a painfully gasped word now and then. They were no longer in his own language. The fever had left him, taking with it the heat of life. And with his panting breast and lustrous eyes he reminded me again of a wild creature under the net; of a bird caught in a snare. She had left him. She had left him—sick—helpless—thirsty. The spear of the hunter had entered his very soul. "Why?" he cried in the penetrating and indignant voice of a man calling to a responsible Maker. A gust of wind and a swish of rain answered.

'And as I turned away to shut the door he pronounced the word "Merciful!" and expired.

'Eventually I certified heart-failure as the immediate cause of death. His heart must have indeed failed him, or else he might have stood this night of storm and exposure, too. I closed his eyes and drove away. Not very far from the cottage I met Foster walking sturdily between the dripping hedges with his collie at his heels.

'"Do you know where your daughter is?" I asked.

'"Don't I!" he cried. "I am going to talk to him a bit. Frightening a poor woman like this."

'"He won't frighten her any more," I said. "He is dead."

'He struck with his stick at the mud.

'"And there's the child."

'Then, after thinking deeply for a while—

'"I don't know that it isn't for the best."

'That's what he said. And she says nothing at all now. Not a word of him. Never. Is his image as utterly gone from her mind as his lithe and striding figure, his carolling voice are gone from our fields? He is no longer before her eyes to excite her imagination into a passion of love or fear; and his memory seems to have vanished from her dull brain as a shadow passes away upon a white screen. She lives in the cottage and works for Miss Swaffer. She is Amy Foster for everybody, and the child is "Amy Foster's boy". She calls him Johnny—which means Little John.

'It is impossible to say whether this name recalls anything to her. Does she ever think of the past? I have seen her hanging over the boy's cot in a very passion of maternal tenderness. The little fellow was lying on his back, a little frightened at me, but very still, with his big black eyes, with his fluttered air of a bird in a snare. And looking at him I seemed to see again the other one—the father, cast out mysteriously by the sea to perish in the supreme disaster of loneliness and despair.'

THE DOOR IN THE WALL

H. G. Wells

I

One confidential evening, not three months ago, Lionel Wallace told me this story of the Door in the Wall. And at the time I thought that so far as he was concerned it was a true story.

He told it me with such a direct simplicity of conviction that I could not do otherwise than believe in him. But in the morning, in my own flat, I woke to a different atmosphere, and as I lay in bed and recalled the things he had told me, stripped of the glamour of his earnest slow voice, denuded of the focussed shaded table light, the shadowy atmosphere that wrapped about him and the pleasant bright things, the dessert and glasses and napery of the dinner we had shared, making them for the time a bright little world quite cut off from every-day realities, I saw it all as frankly incredible. 'He was mystifying!' I said, and then: 'How well he did it! ...It isn't quite the thing I should have expected him, of all people, to do well.'

Afterwards, as I sat up in bed and sipped my morning tea, I found myself trying to account for the flavour of reality that perplexed me in his impossible reminiscences, by supposing they did in some way suggest, present, convey—I hardly know which word to use—experiences it was otherwise impossible to tell.

Well, I don't resort to that explanation now. I have got over my intervening doubts. I believe now, as I believed at the moment of telling, that Wallace did to the very best of his ability strip the truth of his secret for me. But whether he himself saw, or only thought he saw, whether he himself was the possessor of an inestimable privilege, or the victim of a fantastic dream, I cannot pretend to guess. Even the facts of his death, which ended my doubts forever, throw no light on that. That much the reader must judge for himself.

I forget now what chance comment or criticism of mine moved so reticent a man to confide in me. He was, I think, defending himself against an imputation of slackness and unreliability I had made in relation to a great public movement in which he had disappointed me. But he plunged suddenly. 'I have' he said, 'a preoccupation—'

'I know,' he went on, after a pause that he devoted to the study of his cigar ash, 'I have been negligent. The fact is—it isn't a case of ghosts or apparitions—but—it's an odd thing to tell of, Redmond—I am haunted. I am haunted by something—that rather takes the light out of things, that fills me with longings...'

He paused, checked by that English shyness that so often overcomes us when we would speak of moving or grave or beautiful things. 'You were at Saint Athelstan's all through,' he said, and for a moment that seemed to me quite irrelevant. 'Well'—and he paused. Then very haltingly at first, but afterwards more easily, he began to tell of the thing that was hidden in his life, the haunting memory of a beauty and a happiness that filled his heart with insatiable longings that made all the interests and spectacle of worldly life seem dull and tedious and vain to him.

Now that I have the clue to it, the thing seems written visibly in his face. I have a photograph in which that look of detachment has been caught and intensified. It reminds me of what a woman once said of him—a woman who had loved him greatly. 'Suddenly,' she said, 'the interest goes out of him. He forgets you. He doesn't care a rap for you—under his very nose...'

Yet the interest was not always out of him, and when he was holding his attention to a thing Wallace could contrive to be an extremely successful man. His career, indeed, is set with successes. He left me behind him long ago; he soared up over my head, and cut a figure in the world that I couldn't cut—anyhow. He was still a year short of forty, and they say now that he would have been in office and very probably in the new Cabinet if he had lived. At school he always beat me without effort—as it were by nature. We were at school together at Saint Athelstan's College in West Kensington for almost all our school time. He came into the school as my co-equal, but he left far above me, in a blaze of scholarships and brilliant performance. Yet I think I made a fair average running. And it was at school I heard first of the Door in the Wall—that I was to hear of a second time only a month before his death.

To him at least the Door in the Wall was a real door leading through a real wall to immortal realities. Of that I am now quite assured.

And it came into his life early, when he was a little fellow between five and six. I remember how, as he sat making his confession to me with a slow gravity, he reasoned and reckoned the date of it. 'There was,' he said, 'a crimson Virginia creeper in it—all one bright uniform crimson in a clear amber sunshine against a white wall. That came into the impression somehow, though I don't clearly remember how, and there were horse-chestnut leaves upon the clean pavement outside the green door. They were blotched yellow and green, you know, not brown nor dirty, so that they must have been new fallen. I take it that means October. I look out for horse-chestnut leaves every year, and I ought to know.

'If I'm right in that, I was about five years and four months old.'

He was, he said, rather a precocious little boy—he learned to talk at an abnormally early age, and he was so sane and 'old-fashioned,' as people say, that he was permitted an amount of initiative that most children scarcely attain by seven or eight. His mother died when he was born, and he was under the less vigilant and authoritative care of a nursery governess. His father was a stern, preoccupied lawyer, who gave him little attention, and expected great things of him. For all his brightness he found life a little grey and dull I think. And one day he wandered.

He could not recall the particular neglect that enabled him to get away, nor the course he took among the West Kensington roads. All that had faded among the incurable blurs of memory. But the white wall and the green door stood out quite distinctly.

As his memory of that remote childish experience ran, he did at the very first sight of that door experience a peculiar emotion, an attraction, a desire to get to the door and open it and walk in. And at the same time he had the clearest conviction that either it was unwise or it was wrong of him—he could not tell which—to yield to this attraction. He insisted upon it as a curious thing that he knew from the very beginning—unless memory has played him the queerest trick—that the door was unfastened, and that he could go in as he chose.

I seem to see the figure of that little boy, drawn and repelled. And it was very clear in his mind, too, though why it should be so was never explained, that his father would be very angry if he went through that door.

Wallace described all these moments of hesitation to me with the utmost particularity. He went right past the door, and then, with his hands in his pockets, and making an infantile attempt to whistle, strolled right along beyond the end of the wall. There he recalls a number of mean, dirty shops, and particularly that of a plumber and decorator, with a dusty disorder of earthenware pipes, sheet lead ball taps, pattern books of wall paper, and tins of enamel. He stood pretending to examine these things, and coveting, passionately desiring the green door.

Then, he said, he had a gust of emotion. He made a run for it, lest hesitation should grip him again, he went plump with outstretched hand through the green door and let it slam behind him. And so, in a trice, he came into the garden that has haunted all his life.

It was very difficult for Wallace to give me his full sense of that garden into which he came.

There was something in the very air of it that exhilarated, that gave one a sense of lightness and good happening and well being; there was something in the sight of it that made all its colour clean and perfect and subtly luminous. In the instant of coming into it one was exquisitely glad—as only in rare moments and when one is young and joyful one can be glad in this world. And everything was beautiful there...

Wallace mused before he went on telling me. 'You see,' he said, with the doubtful inflection of a man who pauses at incredible things, 'there were two great panthers there... Yes, spotted panthers. And I was not afraid. There was a long wide path with marble-edged flower borders on either side, and these two huge velvety beasts were playing there with a ball. One looked up and came towards me, a little curious as it seemed. It came right up to me, rubbed its soft round ear very gently against the small hand I held out and purred. It was, I tell you, an enchanted garden. I know. And the size? Oh! it stretched far and wide, this way and that. I believe there were hills far away. Heaven knows where West Kensington had suddenly got to. And somehow it was just like coming home.

'You know, in the very moment the door swung to behind me, I forgot the road with its fallen chestnut leaves, its cabs and tradesmen's carts, I forgot the sort of gravitational pull back to the discipline and obedience of home, I forgot all hesitations and fear, forgot discretion, forgot all the intimate realities of this life. I became in a moment a very glad and wonder-happy little boy—in another world. It was a world with a different quality, a warmer, more penetrating and mellower light, with a faint clear gladness in its air, and wisps of sun-touched cloud in the blueness of its sky. And before me ran this long wide path, invitingly, with weedless beds on either side, rich with untended flowers, and these two great panthers. I put my little hands fearlessly on their soft fur, and caressed their round ears and the sensitive corners under their ears, and played with them, and it was as though they welcomed me home. There was a keen sense of home-coming in my mind, and when presently a tall, fair girl appeared in the pathway and came to meet me, smiling, and said "Well?" to me, and lifted me, and kissed me, and put me down, and led me by the hand, there was no amazement, but only an impression of delightful rightness, of being reminded of happy things that had in some strange way been overlooked. There were broad steps, I remember, that came into view between spikes of delphinium, and up these we went to a great avenue between very old and shady dark trees. All down this avenue, you know, between the red chapped stems, were marble seats of honour and statuary, and very tame and friendly white doves...

'And along this avenue my girl-friend led me, looking down—I recall the pleasant lines, the finely-modelled chin of her sweet kind face—asking me questions in a soft, agreeable voice, and telling me things, pleasant things I know, though what they were I was never able to recall... And presently a little Capuchin monkey, very clean, with a fur of ruddy brown and kindly hazel eyes, came down a tree to us and ran beside me, looking up at me and grinning, and presently leapt to my shoulder. So we went on our way in great happiness...'

He paused.

'Go on,' I said.

'I remember little things. We passed an old man musing among laurels, I remember, and a place gay with paroquets, and came through a broad shaded colonnade to a spacious cool palace, full of pleasant fountains, full of beautiful things, full of the quality and promise of heart's desire. And there were many things and many people, some that still seem to stand out clearly and some that are a little vague, but all these people were beautiful and kind. In some way—I don't know how—it was conveyed to me that they all were kind to me, glad to have me there, and filling me with gladness by their gestures, by the touch of their hands, by the welcome and love in their eyes. Yes—'

He mused for awhile. 'Playmates I found there. That was very much to me, because I was a lonely little boy. They played delightful games in a grass-covered court where there was a sun-dial set about with flowers. And as one played one loved...

'But—it's odd—there's a gap in my memory. I don't remember the games we played. I never remembered. Afterwards, as a child, I spent long hours trying, even with tears, to recall the form of that happiness. I wanted to play it all over again—in my nursery—by myself. No! All I remember is the happiness and two dear playfellows who were most with me... Then presently came a sombre dark woman, with a grave, pale face and dreamy eyes, a sombre woman wearing a soft long robe of pale purple, who carried a book and beckoned and took me aside with her into a gallery above a hall—though my playmates were loth to have me go, and ceased their game and stood watching as I was carried away. "Come back to us!" they cried. "Come back to us soon!" I looked up at her face, but she heeded them not at all. Her face was very gentle and grave. She took me to a seat in the gallery, and I stood beside her, ready to look at her book as she opened it upon her knee. The pages fell open. She pointed, and I looked, marvelling, for in the living pages of that book I saw myself; it was a story about myself, and in it were all the things that had happened to me since ever I was born...

'It was wonderful to me, because the pages of that book were not pictures, you understand, but realities.'

Wallace paused gravely—looked at me doubtfully.

'Go on,' I said. 'I understand.'

'They were realities—yes, they must have been; people moved and things came and went in them; my dear mother, whom I had near forgotten; then my father, stern and upright, the servants, the nursery, all the familiar things of home. Then the front door and the busy streets, with traffic to and fro: I looked and marvelled, and looked half doubtfully again into the woman's face and turned the pages over, skipping this and that, to see more of this book, and more, and so at last I came to myself hovering and hesitating outside the green door in the long white wall, and felt again the conflict and the fear.

'"And next?" I cried, and would have turned on, but the cool hand of the grave woman delayed me.

'"Next?" I insisted, and struggled gently with her hand, pulling up her fingers with all my childish strength, and as she yielded and the page came over she bent down upon me like a shadow and kissed my brow.

'But the page did not show the enchanted garden, nor the panthers, nor the girl who had led me by the hand, nor the playfellows who had been so loth to let me go. It showed a long grey street in West Kensington, on that chill hour of afternoon before the lamps are lit, and I was there, a wretched little figure, weeping aloud, for all that I could do to restrain myself, and I was weeping because I could not return to my dear play-fellows who had called after me, "Come back to us! Come back to us soon!" I was there. This was no page in a book, but harsh reality; that enchanted place and the restraining hand of the grave mother at whose knee I stood had gone—whither have they gone?'

He halted again, and remained for a time, staring into the fire.

'Oh! the wretchedness of that return!' he murmured.

'Well?' I said after a minute or so.

'Poor little wretch I was—brought back to this grey world again! As I realized the fulness of what had happened to me, I gave way to quite ungovernable grief. And the shame and humiliation of that public weeping and my disgraceful homecoming remain with me still. I see again the benevolent-looking old gentleman in gold spectacles who stopped and spoke to me—prodding me first with his umbrella. "Poor little chap," said he; "and are you lost then?"—and me a London boy of five and more! And he must needs bring in a kindly young policeman and make a crowd of me, and so march me home. Sobbing, conspicuous and frightened, I came from the enchanted garden to the steps of my father's house.

'That is as well as I can remember my vision of that garden—the garden that haunts me still. Of course, I can convey nothing of that indescribable quality of translucent unreality, that difference from the common things of experience that hung about it all; but that—that is what happened. If it was a dream, I am sure it was a day-time and altogether extraordinary dream... H'm!—naturally there followed a terrible questioning, by my aunt, my father, the nurse, the governess—everyone...

'I tried to tell them, and my father gave me my first thrashing for telling lies. When afterwards I tried to tell my aunt, she punished me again for my wicked persistence. Then, as I said, everyone was forbidden to listen to me, to hear a word about it. Even my fairy tale books were taken away from me for a time—because I was "too imaginative." Eh? Yes, they did that! My father belonged to the old school... And my story was driven back upon myself. I whispered it to my pillow—my pillow that was often damp and salt to my whispering lips with childish tears. And I added always to my official and less fervent prayers this one heartfelt request: "Please God I may dream of the garden. Oh! take me back to my garden! Take me back to my garden!"

'I dreamt often of the garden. I may have added to it, I may have changed it; I do not know... All this you understand is an attempt to reconstruct from fragmentary memories a very early experience. Between that and the other consecutive memories of my boyhood there is a gulf. A time came when it seemed impossible I should ever speak of that wonder glimpse again.'

I asked an obvious question.

'No,' he said. 'I don't remember that I ever attempted to find my way back to the garden in those early years. This seems odd to me now, but I think that very probably a closer watch was kept on my movements after this misadventure to prevent my going astray. No, it wasn't until you knew me that I tried for the garden again. And I believe there was a period—incredible as it seems now—when I forgot the garden altogether—when I was about eight or nine it may have been. Do you remember me as a kid at Saint Athelstan's?'

'Rather!'

'I didn't show any signs did I in those days of having a secret dream?'

II

He looked up with a sudden smile.

'Did you ever play North-West Passage with me? ...No, of course you didn't come my way!'

'It was the sort of game,' he went on, 'that every imaginative child plays all day. The idea was the discovery of a North-West Passage to school. The way to school was plain enough; the game consisted in finding some way that wasn't plain, starting off ten minutes early in some almost hopeless direction, and working one's way round through unaccustomed streets to my goal. And one day I got entangled among some rather low-class streets on the other side of Campden Hill, and I began to think that for once the game would be against me and that I should get to school late. I tried rather desperately a street that seemed a cul de sac, and found a passage at the end. I hurried through that with renewed hope. "I shall do it yet," I said, and passed a row of frowsy little shops that were inexplicably familiar to me, and behold! there was my long white wall and the green door that led to the enchanted garden!

'The thing whacked upon me suddenly. Then, after all, that garden, that wonderful garden, wasn't a dream!'...

He paused.

'I suppose my second experience with the green door marks the world of difference there is between the busy life of a schoolboy and the infinite leisure of a child. Anyhow, this second time I didn't for a moment think of going in straight away. You see... For one thing my mind was full of the idea of getting to school in time—set on not breaking my record for punctuality. I must surely have felt some little desire at least to try the door—yes, I must have felt that... But I seem to remember the attraction of the door mainly as another obstacle to my overmastering determination to get to school. I was immediately interested by this discovery I had made, of course—I went on with my mind full of it—but I went on. It didn't check me. I ran past tugging out my watch, found I had ten minutes still to spare, and then I was going downhill into familiar surroundings. I got to school, breathless, it is true, and wet with perspiration, but in time. I can remember hanging up my coat and hat... Went right by it and left it behind me. Odd, eh?'

He looked at me thoughtfully. 'Of course, I didn't know then that it wouldn't always be there. School boys have limited imaginations. I suppose I thought it was an awfully jolly thing to have it there, to know my way back to it, but there was the school tugging at me. I expect I was a good deal distraught and inattentive that morning, recalling what I could of the beautiful strange people I should presently see again. Oddly enough I had no doubt in my mind that they would be glad to see me... Yes, I must have thought of the garden that morning just as a jolly sort of place to which one might resort in the interludes of a strenuous scholastic career.

'I didn't go that day at all. The next day was a half holiday, and that may have weighed with me. Perhaps, too, my state of inattention brought down impositions upon me and docked the margin of time necessary for the detour. I don't know. What I do know is that in the meantime the enchanted garden was so much upon my mind that I could not keep it to myself.

'I told—What was his name?—a ferrety-looking youngster we used to call Squiff.'

'Young Hopkins,' said I.

'Hopkins it was. I did not like telling him, I had a feeling that in some way it was against the rules to tell him, but I did. He was walking part of the way home with me; he was talkative, and if we had not talked about the enchanted garden we should have talked of something else, and it was intolerable to me to think about any other subject. So I blabbed.

'Well, he told my secret. The next day in the play interval I found myself surrounded by half a dozen bigger boys, half teasing and wholly curious to hear more of the enchanted garden. There was that big Fawcett—you remember him?—and Carnaby and Morley Reynolds. You weren't there by any chance? No, I think I should have remembered if you were...

'A boy is a creature of odd feelings. I was, I really believe, in spite of my secret self-disgust, a little flattered to have the attention of these big fellows. I remember particularly a moment of pleasure caused by the praise of Crawshaw—you remember Crawshaw major, the son of Crawshaw the composer?—who said it was the best lie he had ever heard. But at the same time there was a really painful undertow of shame at telling what I felt was indeed a sacred secret. That beast Fawcett made a joke about the girl in green—.'

Wallace's voice sank with the keen memory of that shame. 'I pretended not to hear,' he said. 'Well, then Carnaby suddenly called me a young liar and disputed with me when I said the thing was true. I said I knew where to find the green door, could lead them all there in ten minutes. Carnaby became outrageously virtuous, and said I'd have to—and bear out my words or suffer. Did you ever have Carnaby twist your arm? Then perhaps you'll understand how it went with me. I swore my story was true. There was nobody in the school then to save a chap from Carnaby though Crawshaw put in a word or so. Carnaby had got his game. I grew excited and red-eared, and a little frightened, I behaved altogether like a silly little chap, and the outcome of it all was that instead of starting alone for my enchanted garden, I led the way presently—cheeks flushed, ears hot, eyes smarting, and my soul one burning misery and shame—for a party of six mocking, curious and threatening school-fellows.

'We never found the white wall and the green door...'

'You mean?—'

'I mean I couldn't find it. I would have found it if I could.

'And afterwards when I could go alone I couldn't find it. I never found it. I seem now to have been always looking for it through my school-boy days, but I've never come upon it again.'

'Did the fellows—make it disagreeable?'

'Beastly... Carnaby held a council over me for wanton lying. I remember how I sneaked home and upstairs to hide the marks of my blubbering. But when I cried myself to sleep at last it wasn't for Carnaby, but for the garden, for the beautiful afternoon I had hoped for, for the sweet friendly women and the waiting playfellows and the game I had hoped to learn again, that beautiful forgotten game...

'I believed firmly that if I had not told—...I had bad times after that—crying at night and wool-gathering by day. For two terms I slackened and had bad reports. Do you remember? Of course you would! It was you—your beating me in mathematics that brought me back to the grind again.'

III

For a time my friend stared silently into the red heart of the fire. Then he said: 'I never saw it again until I was seventeen.

'It leapt upon me for the third time—as I was driving to Paddington on my way to Oxford and a scholarship. I had just one momentary glimpse. I was leaning over the apron of my hansom smoking a cigarette, and no doubt thinking myself no end of a man of the world, and suddenly there was the door, the wall, the dear sense of unforgettable and still attainable things.

'We clattered by—I too taken by surprise to stop my cab until we were well past and round a corner. Then I had a queer moment, a double and divergent movement of my will: I tapped the little door in the roof of the cab, and brought my arm down to pull out my watch. "Yes, sir!" said the cabman, smartly. "Er—well—it's nothing," I cried. "My mistake! We haven't much time! Go on!" and he went on...

'I got my scholarship. And the night after I was told of that I sat over my fire in my little upper room, my study, in my father's house, with his praise—his rare praise—and his sound counsels ringing in my ears, and I smoked my favourite pipe—the formidable bulldog of adolescence—and thought of that door in the long white wall. "If I had stopped," I thought, "I should have missed my scholarship, I should have missed Oxford—muddled all the fine career before me! I begin to see things better!" I fell musing deeply, but I did not doubt then this career of mine was a thing that merited sacrifice.

'Those dear friends and that clear atmosphere seemed very sweet to me, very fine, but remote. My grip was fixing now upon the world. I saw another door opening—the door of my career.'

He stared again into the fire. Its red lights picked out a stubborn strength in his face for just one flickering moment, and then it vanished again.

'Well,' he said and sighed, 'I have served that career. I have done—much work, much hard work. But I have dreamt of the enchanted garden a thousand dreams, and seen its door, or at least glimpsed its door, four times since then. Yes—four times. For a while this world was so bright and interesting, seemed so full of meaning and opportunity that the half-effaced charm of the garden was by comparison gentle and remote. Who wants to pat panthers on the way to dinner with pretty women and distinguished men? I came down to London from Oxford, a man of bold promise that I have done something to redeem. Something—and yet there have been disappointments...

'Twice I have been in love—I will not dwell on that—but once, as I went to someone who, I know, doubted whether I dared to come, I took a short cut at a venture through an unfrequented road near Earl's Court, and so happened on a white wall and a familiar green door. "Odd!" said I to myself, "but I thought this place was on Campden Hill. It's the place I never could find somehow—like counting Stonehenge—the place of that queer day dream of mine." And I went by it intent upon my purpose. It had no appeal to me that afternoon.

'I had just a moment's impulse to try the door, three steps aside were needed at the most—though I was sure enough in my heart that it would open to me—and then I thought that doing so might delay me on the way to that appointment in which I thought my honour was involved. Afterwards I was sorry for my punctuality—I might at least have peeped in I thought, and waved a hand to those panthers, but I knew enough by this time not to seek again belatedly that which is not found by seeking. Yes, that time made me very sorry...

'Years of hard work after that and never a sight of the door. It's only recently it has come back to me. With it there has come a sense as though some thin tarnish had spread itself over my world. I began to think of it as a sorrowful and bitter thing that I should never see that door again. Perhaps I was suffering a little from overwork—perhaps it was what I've heard spoken of as the feeling of forty. I don't know. But certainly the keen brightness that makes effort easy has gone out of things recently, and that just at a time with all these new political developments—when I ought to be working. Odd, isn't it? But I do begin to find life toilsome, its rewards, as I come near them, cheap. I began a little while ago to want the garden quite badly. Yes—and I've seen it three times.'

'The garden?'

'No—the door! And I haven't gone in!'

He leaned over the table to me, with an enormous sorrow in his voice as he spoke. 'Thrice I have had my chance—thrice! If ever that door offers itself to me again, I swore, I will go in out of this dust and heat, out of this dry glitter of vanity, out of these toilsome futilities. I will go and never return. This time I will stay... I swore it and when the time came—I didn't go.

'Three times in one year have I passed that door and failed to enter. Three times in the last year.

'The first time was on the night of the snatch division on the Tenants' Redemption Bill, on which the Government was saved by a majority of three. You remember? No one on our side—perhaps very few on the opposite side—expected the end that night. Then the debate collapsed like eggshells. I and Hotchkiss were dining with his cousin at Brentford, we were both unpaired, and we were called up by telephone, and set off at once in his cousin's motor. We got in barely in time, and on the way we passed my wall and door—livid in the moonlight, blotched with hot yellow as the glare of our lamps lit it, but unmistakable. "My God!" cried I. "What?" said Hotchkiss. "Nothing!" I answered, and the moment passed.

'"I've made a great sacrifice," I told the whip as I got in.

'"They all have," he said, and hurried by.

'I do not see how I could have done otherwise then. And the next occasion was as I rushed to my father's bedside to bid that stern old man farewell. Then, too, the claims of life were imperative. But the third time was different; it happened a week ago. It fills me with hot remorse to recall it. I was with Gurker and Ralphs—it's no secret now you know that I've had my talk with Gurker. We had been dining at Frobisher's, and the talk had become intimate between us. The question of my place in the reconstructed ministry lay always just over the boundary of the discussion. Yes—yes. That's all settled. It needn't be talked about yet, but there's no reason to keep a secret from you... Yes—thanks! thanks! But let me tell you my story.

'Then, on that night things were very much in the air. My position was a very delicate one. I was keenly anxious to get some definite word from Gurker, but was hampered by Ralphs' presence. I was using the best power of my brain to keep that light and careless talk not too obviously directed to the point that concerns me. I had to. Ralphs' behaviour since has more than justified my caution... Ralphs, I knew, would leave us beyond the Kensington High Street, and then I could surprise Gurker by a sudden frankness. One has sometimes to resort to these little devices... And then it was that in the margin of my field of vision I became aware once more of the white wall, the green door before us down the road.

'We passed it talking. I passed it. I can still see the shadow of Gurker's marked profile, his opera hat tilted forward over his prominent nose, the many folds of his neck wrap going before my shadow and Ralphs' as we sauntered past.

'I passed within twenty inches of the door. "If I say good-night to them, and go in," I asked myself, "what will happen?" And I was all a-tingle for that word with Gurker.

'I could not answer that question in the tangle of my other problems. "They will think me mad," I thought. "And suppose I vanish now!—Amazing disappearance of a prominent politician!" That weighed with me. A thousand inconceivably petty worldlinesses weighed with me in that crisis.'

Then he turned on me with a sorrowful smile, and, speaking slowly; 'Here I am!' he said.

'Here I am!' he repeated, 'and my chance has gone from me. Three times in one year the door has been offered me—the door that goes into peace, into delight, into a beauty beyond dreaming, a kindness no man on earth can know. And I have rejected it, Redmond, and it has gone—'

'How do you know?'

'I know. I know. I am left now to work it out, to stick to the tasks that held me so strongly when my moments came. You say, I have success—this vulgar, tawdry, irksome, envied thing. I have it.' He had a walnut in his big hand. 'If that was my success,' he said, and crushed it, and held it out for me to see.

'Let me tell you something, Redmond. This loss is destroying me. For two months, for ten weeks nearly now, I have done no work at all, except the most necessary and urgent duties. My soul is full of inappeasable regrets. At nights—when it is less likely I shall be recognized—I go out. I wander. Yes. I wonder what people would think of that if they knew. A Cabinet Minister, the responsible head of that most vital of all departments, wandering alone—grieving—sometimes near audibly lamenting—for a door, for a garden!'

IV

I can see now his rather pallid face, and the unfamiliar sombre fire that had come into his eyes. I see him very vividly to-night. I sit recalling his words, his tones, and last evening's Westminster Gazette still lies on my sofa, containing the notice of his death. At lunch to-day the club was busy with him and the strange riddle of his fate.

They found his body very early yesterday morning in a deep excavation near East Kensington Station. It is one of two shafts that have been made in connection with an extension of the railway southward. It is protected from the intrusion of the public by a hoarding upon the high road, in which a small doorway has been cut for the convenience of some of the workmen who live in that direction. The doorway was left unfastened through a misunderstanding between two gangers, and through it he made his way...

My mind is darkened with questions and riddles.

It would seem he walked all the way from the House that night—he has frequently walked home during the past Session—and so it is I figure his dark form coming along the late and empty streets, wrapped up, intent. And then did the pale electric lights near the station cheat the rough planking into a semblance of white? Did that fatal unfastened door awaken some memory?

Was there, after all, ever any green door in the wall at all?

I do not know. I have told his story as he told it to me. There are times when I believe that Wallace was no more than the victim of the coincidence between a rare but not unprecedented type of hallucination and a careless trap, but that indeed is not my profoundest belief. You may think me superstitious if you will, and foolish; but, indeed, I am more than half convinced that he had in truth, an abnormal gift, and a sense, something—I know not what—that in the guise of wall and door offered him an outlet, a secret and peculiar passage of escape into another and altogether more beautiful world. At any rate, you will say, it betrayed him in the end. But did it betray him? There you touch the inmost mystery of these dreamers, these men of vision and the imagination. We see our world fair and common, the hoarding and the pit. By our daylight standard he walked out of security into darkness, danger and death. But did he see like that?

THE STALLS OF BARCHESTER CATHEDRAL

M. R. James

This matter began, as far as I am concerned, with the reading of a notice in the obituary section of the *Gentleman's Magazine* for an early year in the nineteenth century:

> On February 26th, at his residence in the Cathedral Close of Barchester, the Venerable John Benwell Haynes, D.D., aged 57, Archdeacon of Sowerbridge and Rector of Pickhill and Candley. He was of —— College, Cambridge, and where, by talent and assiduity, he commanded the esteem of his seniors; when, at the usual time, he took his first degree, his name stood high in the list of *wranglers*. These academical honours procured for him within a short time a Fellowship of his College. In the year 1783 he received Holy Orders, and was shortly afterwards presented to the perpetual Curacy of Ranxton-sub-Ashe by his friend and patron the late truly venerable Bishop of Lichfield … His speedy preferments, first to a Prebend, and subsequently to the dignity of Precentor in the Cathedral of Barchester, form an eloquent testimony to the respect in which he was held and to his eminent qualifications. He succeeded to the Archdeaconry upon the sudden decease of Archdeacon Pulteney in 1810. His sermons, ever conformable to the principles of the religion and Church which he adorned, displayed in no ordinary degree, without the least trace of enthusiasm, the refinement of the scholar united with the graces of the Christian. Free from sectarian violence, and informed by the spirit of the truest charity, they will long dwell in the memories of his hearers. (Here a further omission.) The productions of his pen include an able defence of Episcopacy, which, though often perused by the author of this tribute to his memory, afford but one additional instance

> of the want of liberality and enterprise which is a too common characteristic of the publishers of our generation. His published works are, indeed, confined to a spirited and elegant version of the *Argonautica* of Valerius Flaccus, a volume of *Discourses upon the Several Events in the Life of Joshua*, delivered in his Cathedral, and a number of the charges which he pronounced at various visitations to the clergy of his Archdeaconry. These are distinguished by etc., etc. The urbanity and hospitality of the subject of these lines will not readily be forgotten by those who enjoyed his acquaintance. His interest in the venerable and awful pile under whose hoary vault he was so punctual an attendant, and particularly in the musical portion of its rites, might be termed filial, and formed a strong and delightful contrast to the polite indifference displayed by too many of our Cathedral dignitaries at the present time.

The final paragraph, after informing us that Dr Haynes died a bachelor, says:

> It might have been augured that an existence so placid and benevolent would have been terminated in a ripe old age by a dissolution equally gradual and calm. But how unsearchable are the workings of Providence! The peaceful and retired seclusion amid which the honoured evening of Dr Haynes' life was mellowing to its close was destined to be disturbed, nay, shattered, by a tragedy as appalling as it was unexpected. The morning of the 26th of February—

But perhaps I shall do better to keep back the remainder of the narrative until I have told the circumstances which led up to it. These, as far as they are now accessible, I have derived from another source.

I had read the obituary notice which I have been quoting, quite by chance, along with a great many others of the same period. It had excited some little speculation in my mind, but, beyond thinking that, if I ever had an opportunity of examining the local records of the period indicated, I would try to remember Dr Haynes, I made no effort to pursue his case.

Quite lately I was cataloguing the manuscripts in the library of the college to which he belonged. I had reached the end of the numbered volumes on the shelves, and I proceeded to ask the librarian whether there were any more books which he thought I ought to include in my description. 'I don't think there are,' he said, 'but we had better come and look at the manuscript class and make sure. Have you time to do that now?' I had time. We went to the library, checked off the manuscripts, and, at the end of our survey, arrived at a shelf of which I had seen nothing. Its contents consisted for the most part of sermons, bundles of fragmentary papers, college exercises, *Cyrus*, an epic poem in several cantos, the product of a country clergyman's leisure, mathematical tracts by a deceased professor, and other similar material of a kind with which I am only too familiar. I took brief notes of these. Lastly, there was a tin box, which was pulled out and dusted. Its label, much faded, was thus inscribed: 'Papers of the Ven. Archdeacon Haynes. Bequeathed in 1834 by his sister, Miss Letitia Haynes.'

I knew at once that the name was one which I had somewhere encountered, and could very soon locate it. 'That must be the Archdeacon Haynes who came to a very odd end at Barchester. I've read his obituary in the *Gentleman's Magazine*. May I take the box home? Do you know if there is anything interesting in it?'

The librarian was very willing that I should take the box and examine it at leisure. 'I never looked inside it myself,' he said, 'but I've always been meaning to. I am pretty sure that is the box which our old Master once said ought never to have been accepted by the college. He said that to Martin years ago; and he said also that as long as he had control over the library it should never be opened. Martin told me about it, and said that he wanted terribly to know what was in it; but the Master was librarian, and always kept the box in the lodge, so there was no getting at it in his time, and when he died it was taken away by mistake by his heirs, and only returned a few years ago. I can't think why I haven't opened it; but, as I have to go away from Cambridge this afternoon, you had better have first go at it. I think I can trust you not to publish anything undesirable in our catalogue.'

I took the box home and examined its contents, and thereafter consulted the librarian as to what should be done about publication, and, since I have his leave to make a story out of it, provided I disguise the identity of the people concerned, I will try what can be done.

The materials are, of course, mainly journals and letters. How much I shall quote and how much epitomize must be determined by considerations of space. The proper understanding of the situation has necessitated a little—not very arduous—research, which has been greatly facilitated by the excellent illustrations and text of the Barchester volume in Bell's *Cathedral Series*.

When you enter the choir of Barchester Cathedral now, you pass through a screen of metal and coloured marbles, designed by Sir Gilbert Scott, and find yourself in what I must call a very bare and odiously furnished place. The stalls are modern; without canopies. The places of the dignitaries and the names of the prebends have fortunately been allowed to survive, and are inscribed on small brass plates affixed to the stalls. The organ is in the triforium, and what is seen of the case is Gothic. The reredos and its surroundings are like every other.

Careful engravings of a hundred years ago show a very different state of things. The organ is on a massive classical screen. The stalls are also classical and very massive. There is a baldacchino of wood over the altar, with urns upon its corners. Farther east is a solid altar screen, classical in design, of wood, with a pediment, in which is a triangle surrounded by rays, enclosing certain Hebrew letters in gold. Cherubs contemplate these. There is a pulpit with a great sounding-board at the eastern end of the stalls on the north side, and there is a black and white marble pavement. Two ladies and a gentleman are admiring the general effect. From other sources I gather that the archdeacon's stall then, as now, was next to the bishop's throne at the south-eastern end of the stalls. His house almost faces the west front of the church, and is a fine red-brick building of William the Third's time.

Here Dr Haynes, already a mature man, took up his abode with his sister in the year 1810. The dignity had long been the object of his wishes, but his predecessor refused to depart until he had attained the age of ninety-two. About a week after he had held a modest festival in celebration of that ninety-second birthday, there came a morning, late in the year, when Dr Haynes, hurrying cheerfully into his breakfast-room, rubbing his hands and humming a tune, was greeted, and checked in his genial flow of spirits, by the sight of his sister, seated, indeed, in her usual place behind the tea-urn, but bowed forward and sobbing unrestrainedly into her handkerchief. 'What—what is the matter? What bad news?' he began. 'Oh, Johnny, you've not heard? The poor dear archdeacon!' 'The archdeacon, yes? What is it—ill, is he?' 'No, no; they found him on the staircase this morning; it is so shocking.' 'Is it possible! Dear, dear, poor Pulteney! Had there been any seizure?' 'They don't think so, and that is almost the worst thing about it. It seems to have been all the fault of that stupid maid of theirs, Jane.' Dr Haynes paused. 'I don't quite understand, Letitia. How was the maid at fault?' 'Why, as far as I can make out, there was a stair-rod missing, and she never mentioned it, and the poor archdeacon set his foot quite on the edge of the step—you know how slippery that oak is—and it seems he must have fallen almost the whole flight and broken his neck. It *is* so sad for poor Miss Pulteney. Of course, they will get rid of the girl at once. I never liked her.' Miss Haynes's grief resumed its sway, but eventually relaxed so far as to permit of her taking some breakfast. Not so her brother, who, after standing in silence before the window for some minutes, left the room, and did not appear again that morning.

I need only add that the careless maid-servant was dismissed forthwith, but that the missing stair-rod was very shortly afterwards found *under* the stair-carpet—an additional proof, if any were needed, of extreme stupidity and carelessness on her part.

For a good many years Dr Haynes had been marked out by his ability, which seems to have been really considerable, as the likely successor of Archdeacon Pulteney, and no disappointment was in store for him. He was duly installed, and entered with zeal upon the discharge of those functions which are appropriate to one in his position. A considerable space in his journals is occupied with exclamations upon the confusion in which Archdeacon Pulteney had left the business of his office and the documents appertaining to it. Dues upon Wringham and Barnswood have been uncollected for something like twelve years, and are largely irrecoverable; no visitation has been held for seven years; four chancels are almost past mending. The persons deputized by the archdeacon have been nearly as incapable as himself. It was almost a matter for thankfulness that this state of things had not been permitted to continue, and a letter from a friend confirms this view. 'σ κατέχων,' it says (in rather cruel allusion to the Second Epistle to the Thessalonians), 'is removed at last. My poor friend! Upon what a scene of confusion will you be entering! I give you my word that, on the last occasion of my crossing his threshold, there was no single paper that he could lay hands upon, no syllable of mine that he could hear, and no fact in connection with my business that he could remember. But now, thanks to a negligent maid and a loose stair-carpet, there is some prospect that necessary business will be transacted without a complete loss alike of voice and temper.' This letter was tucked into a pocket in the cover of one of the diaries.

There can be no doubt of the new archdeacon's zeal and enthusiasm. 'Give me but time to reduce to some semblance of order the innumerable errors and complications with which I am confronted, and I shall gladly and sincerely join with the aged Israelite in the canticle which too many, I fear, pronounce but with their lips.' This reflection I find, not in a diary, but a letter; the doctor's friends seem to have returned his correspondence to his surviving sister. He does not confine himself, however, to reflections. His investigation of the rights and duties of his office are very searching and business-like, and there is a calculation in one place that a period of three years will just suffice to set the business of the Archdeaconry upon a proper footing. The estimate appears to have been an exact one. For just three years he is occupied in reforms; but I look in vain at the end of that time for the promised *Nunc dimittis*. He has now found a new sphere of activity. Hitherto his duties have precluded him from more than an occasional attendance at the Cathedral services. Now he begins to take an interest in the fabric and the music. Upon his struggles with the organist, an old gentleman who had been in office since 1786, I have no time to dwell; they were not attended with any marked success. More to the purpose is his sudden growth of enthusiasm for the Cathedral itself and its furniture. There is a draft of a letter to Sylvanus Urban (which I do not think was ever sent) describing the stalls in the choir. As I have said, these were of fairly late date—of about the year 1700, in fact.

> The archdeacon's stall, situated at the south-east end, west of the episcopal throne (now so worthily occupied by the truly excellent prelate who adorns the See of Barchester), is distinguished by some curious ornamentation. In addition to the arms of Dean West, by whose efforts the whole of the internal furniture of the choir was completed, the prayer-desk is terminated at the eastern extremity by three small but remarkable statuettes in the

> grotesque manner. One is an exquisitely modelled figure of a cat, whose crouching posture suggests with admirable spirit the suppleness, vigilance, and craft of the redoubted adversary of the genus *Mus*. Opposite to this is a figure seated upon a throne and invested with the attributes of royalty; but it is no earthly monarch whom the carver has sought to portray. His feet are studiously concealed by the long robe in which he is draped; but neither the crown nor the cap which he wears suffice to hide the prick-ears and curving horns which betray his Tartarean origin; and the hand which rests upon his knee is armed with talons of horrifying length and sharpness. Between these two figures stands a shape muffled in a long mantle. This might at first sight be mistaken for a monk or 'friar of orders gray', for the head is cowled and a knotted cord depends from somewhere about the waist. A slight inspection, however, will lead to a very different conclusion. The knotted cord is quickly seen to be a halter, held by a hand all but concealed within the draperies; while the sunken features and, horrid to relate, the rent flesh upon the cheek-bones, proclaim the King of Terrors. These figures are evidently the production of no unskilled chisel; and should it chance that any of your correspondents are able to throw light upon their origin and significance, my obligations to your valuable miscellany will be largely increased.

There is more description in the paper, and, seeing that the woodwork in question has now disappeared, it has a considerable interest. A paragraph at the end is worth quoting:

> Some late researches among the Chapter accounts have shown me that the carving of the stalls was not, as was very usually reported, the work of Dutch artists, but was executed by a native of this city or district named Austin. The timber was procured from an oak copse in the vicinity, the property of the Dean and Chapter, known as Holywood. Upon a recent visit to the parish within whose boundaries it is situated, I learned from the aged and truly respectable incumbent that traditions still lingered amongst the inhabitants of the great size and age of the oaks employed to furnish the materials of the stately structure which has been, however imperfectly, described in the above lines. Of

> one in particular, which stood near the centre of the grove, it is remembered that it was known as the Hanging Oak. The propriety of that title is confirmed by the fact that a quantity of human bones was found in the soil about its roots, and that at certain times of the year it was the custom for those who wished to secure a successful issue to their affairs, whether of love or the ordinary business of life, to suspend from its boughs small images or puppets rudely fashioned of straw, twigs, or the like rustic materials.

So much for the archdeacon's archaeological investigations. To return to his career as it is to be gathered from his diaries. Those of his first three years of hard and careful work show him throughout in high spirits, and, doubtless, during this time, that reputation for hospitality and urbanity which is mentioned in his obituary notice was well deserved. After that, as time goes on, I see a shadow coming over him—destined to develop into utter blackness—which I cannot but think must have been reflected in his outward demeanour. He commits a good deal of his fears and troubles to his diary; there was no other outlet for them. He was unmarried, and his sister was not always with him. But I am much mistaken if he has told all that he might have told. A series of extracts shall be given:

> *Aug.* 30, 1816.—The days begin to draw in more perceptibly than ever. Now that the Archdeaconry papers are reduced to order, I must find some further employment for the evening hours of autumn and winter. It is a great blow that Letitia's health will not allow her to stay through these months. Why not go on with my *Defence of Episcopacy*? It may be useful.
>
> *Sept.* 15.—Letitia has left me for Brighton.
>
> *Oct.* 11.—Candles lit in the choir for the first time at evening prayers. It came as a shock: I find that I absolutely shrink from the dark season.
>
> *Nov.* 17.—Much struck by the character of the carving on my desk: I do not know that I had ever carefully noticed it before. My attention was called to it by an accident. During the *Magnificat* I was, I regret to say, almost overcome with sleep. My hand was resting on the back of the carved figure of a cat which

is the nearest to me of the three figures on the end of my stall. I was not aware of this, for I was not looking in that direction, until I was startled by what seemed a softness, a feeling as of rather rough and coarse fur, and a sudden movement, as if the creature were twisting round its head to bite me. I regained complete consciousness in an instant, and I have some idea that I must have uttered a suppressed exclamation, for I noticed that Mr Treasurer turned his head quickly in my direction. The impression of the unpleasant feeling was so strong that I found myself rubbing my hand upon my surplice. This accident led me to examine the figures after prayers more carefully than I had done before, and I realized for the first time with what skill they are executed.

Dec. 6.—I do indeed miss Letitia's company. The evenings, after I have worked as long as I can at my *Defence*, are very trying. The house is too large for a lonely man, and visitors of any kind are too rare. I get an uncomfortable impression when going to my room that there *is* company of some kind. The fact is (I may as well formulate it to myself) that I hear voices. This, I am well aware, is a common symptom of incipient decay of the brain—and I believe that I should be less disquieted than I am if I had any suspicion that this was the cause. I have none—none whatever, nor is there anything in my family history to give colour to such an idea. Work, diligent work, and a punctual attention to the duties which fall to me is my best remedy, and I have little doubt that it will prove efficacious.

Jan. 1.—My trouble is, I must confess it, increasing upon me. Last night, upon my return after midnight from the Deanery, I lit my candle to go upstairs. I was nearly at the top when something whispered to me, 'Let me wish you a happy New Year.' I could not be mistaken: it spoke distinctly and with a peculiar emphasis. Had I dropped my candle, as I all but did, I tremble to think what the consequences must have been. As it was, I managed to get up the last flight, and was quickly in my room with the door locked, and experienced no other disturbance.

Jan. 15.—I had occasion to come downstairs last night to my workroom for my watch, which I had inadvertently left on my table when I went up to bed. I think I was at the top of the last flight when I had a sudden impression of a sharp whisper in my ear '*Take care.*' I clutched the balusters and naturally looked round at once. Of course, there was nothing. After a moment I went on—it was no good turning back—but I had as nearly as possible fallen: a cat—a large one by the feel of it—slipped between my feet, but again, of course, I saw nothing. It *may* have been the kitchen cat, but I do not think it was.

Feb. 27.—A curious thing last night, which I should like to forget. Perhaps if I put it down here I may see it in its true proportion. I worked in the library from about 9 to 10. The hall and staircase seemed to be unusually full of what I can only call movement without sound: by this I mean that there seemed to be continuous going and coming, and that whenever I ceased writing to listen, or looked out into the hall, the stillness was absolutely unbroken. Nor, in going to my room at an earlier hour than usual—about half-past ten—was I conscious of anything that I could call a noise. It so happened that I had told John to come to my room for the letter to the bishop which I wished to have delivered early in the morning at the Palace. He was to sit up, therefore, and come for it when he heard me retire. This I had for the moment forgotten, though I had remembered to carry the letter with me to my room. But when, as I was winding up my watch, I heard a light tap at the door, and a low voice saying, 'May I come in?' (which I most undoubtedly did hear), I recollected the fact, and took up the letter from my dressing-table, saying, 'Certainly: come in.' No one, however, answered my summons, and it was now that, as I strongly suspect, I committed an error: for I opened the door and held the letter out. There was certainly no one at that moment in the passage, but, in the instant of my standing there, the door at the end opened and John appeared carrying a candle. I asked him whether he had come to the door earlier; but am satisfied that he had not. I do not like the situation; but although my senses were very much on the alert, and though it was some time before I could sleep, I must allow that I perceived nothing further of an untoward character.

With the return of spring, when his sister came to live with him for some months, Dr Haynes's entries become more cheerful, and, indeed, no symptom of depression is discernible until the early part of September, when he was again left alone. And now, indeed, there is evidence that he was incommoded again, and that more pressingly. To this matter I will return in a moment, but I digress to put in a document which, rightly or wrongly, I believe to have a bearing on the thread of the story.

The account-books of Dr Haynes, preserved along with his other papers, show, from a date but little later than that of his institution as archdeacon, a quarterly payment of £25 to J. L. Nothing could have been made of this, had it stood by itself. But I connect with it a very dirty and ill-written letter, which, like another that I have quoted, was in a pocket in the cover of a diary. Of date or postmark there is no vestige, and the decipherment was not easy. It appears to run:

> Dr Sr.
>
> I have bin expctin to her off you theis last wicks, and not Haveing done so must supose you have not got mine witch was saying how me and my man had met in with bad times this season all seems to go cross with us on the farm and which way to look for the rent we have no knowledge of it this been the sad case with us if you would have the great [liberality *probably, but the exact spelling defies reproduction*] to send fourty pounds otherwise steps will have to be took which I should not wish. Has you was the Means of me losing my place with Dr Pulteney I think it is only just what I am asking and you know best what I could say if I was Put to it but I do not wish anything of that unpleasant Nature being one that always wish to have everything Pleasant about me.
>
> Your obedt Servt,
> JANE LEE.

About the time at which I suppose this letter to have been written there is, in fact, a payment of £40 to J. L.

We return to the diary:

> *Oct.* 22.—At evening prayers, during the Psalms, I had that same experience which I recollect from last year. I was resting my hand

on one of the carved figures, as before (I usually avoid that of the cat now), and—I was going to have said—a change came over it, but that seems attributing too much importance to what must, after all, be due to some physical affection in myself: at any rate, the wood seemed to become chilly and soft as if made of wet linen. I can assign the moment at which I became sensible of this. The choir were singing the words (*Set thou an ungodly man to be ruler over him and*) *let Satan stand at his right hand.*

The whispering in my house was more persistent to-night. I seemed not to be rid of it in my room. I have not noticed this before. A nervous man, which I am not, and hope I am not becoming, would have been much annoyed, if not alarmed, by it. The cat was on the stairs to-night. I think it sits there always. There *is* no kitchen cat.

Nov. 15.—Here again I must note a matter I do not understand. I am much troubled in sleep. No definite image presented itself, but I was pursued by the very vivid impression that wet lips were whispering into my ear with great rapidity and emphasis for some time together. After this, I suppose, I fell asleep, but was awakened with a start by a feeling as if a hand were laid on my shoulder. To my intense alarm I found myself standing at the top of the lowest flight of the first staircase. The moon was shining brightly enough through the large window to let me see that there was a large cat on the second or third step. I can make no comment. I crept up to bed again, I do not know how. Yes, mine is a heavy burden. [Then follows a line or two which has been scratched out. I fancy I read something like 'acted for the best'.]

Not long after this it is evident to me that the archdeacon's firmness began to give way under the pressure of these phenomena. I omit as unnecessarily painful and distressing the ejaculations and prayers which, in the months of December and January, appear for the first time and become increasingly frequent. Throughout this time, however, he is obstinate in clinging to his post. Why he did not plead ill-health and take refuge at Bath or Brighton I cannot tell; my impression is that it would have done him no good; that he was a man who, if he had confessed himself beaten by the annoyances, would have succumbed at once, and that he was conscious of this. He did seek to palliate them by inviting visitors to his house. The result he has noted in this fashion:

> *Jan.* 7.—I have prevailed on my cousin Allen to give me a few days, and he is to occupy the chamber next to mine.
>
> *Jan.* 8.—A still night. Allen slept well, but complained of the wind. My own experiences were as before: still whispering and whispering: what is it that he wants to say?
>
> *Jan.* 9.—Allen thinks this a very noisy house. He thinks, too, that my cat is an unusually large and fine specimen, but very wild.
>
> *Jan.* 10.—Allen and I in the library until 11. He left me twice to see what the maids were doing in the hall: returning the second time he told me he had seen one of them passing through the door at the end of the passage, and said if his wife were here she would soon get them into better order. I asked him what coloured dress the maid wore; he said grey or white. I supposed it would be so.
>
> *Jan.* 11.—Allen left me to-day. I must be firm.

These words, *I must be firm*, occur again and again on subsequent days; sometimes they are the only entry. In these cases they are in an unusually large hand, and dug into the paper in a way which must have broken the pen that wrote them.

Apparently the archdeacon's friends did not remark any change in his behaviour, and this gives me a high idea of his courage and determination. The diary tells us nothing more than I have indicated of the last days of his life. The end of it all must be told in the polished language of the obituary notice:

> The morning of the 26th of February was cold and tempestuous. At an early hour the servants had occasion to go into the front hall of the residence occupied by the lamented subject of these lines. What was their horror upon observing the form of their beloved and respected master lying upon the landing of the principal staircase in an attitude which inspired the gravest fears. Assistance was procured, and an universal consternation was experienced upon the discovery that he had been the object

> of a brutal and a murderous attack. The vertebral column was fractured in more than one place. This might have been the result of a fall: it appeared that the stair-carpet was loosened at one point. But, in addition to this, there were injuries inflicted upon the eyes, nose and mouth, as if by the agency of some savage animal, which, dreadful to relate, rendered those features unrecognizable. The vital spark was, it is needless to add, completely extinct, and had been so, upon the testimony of respectable medical authorities, for several hours. The author or authors of this mysterious outrage are alike buried in mystery, and the most active conjecture has hitherto failed to suggest a solution of the melancholy problem afforded by this appalling occurrence.

The writer goes on to reflect upon the probability that the writings of Mr Shelley, Lord Byron, and M. Voltaire may have been instrumental in bringing about the disaster, and concludes by hoping, somewhat vaguely, that this event may 'operate as an example to the rising generation'; but this portion of his remarks need not be quoted in full.

I had already formed the conclusion that Dr Haynes was responsible for the death of Dr Pulteney. But the incident connected with the carved figure of death upon the archdeacon's stall was a very perplexing feature. The conjecture that it had been cut out of the wood of the Hanging Oak was not difficult, but seemed impossible to substantiate. However, I paid a visit to Barchester, partly with the view of finding out whether there were any relics of the woodwork to be heard of. I was introduced by one of the canons to the curator of the local museum, who was, my friend said, more likely to be able to give me information on the point than anyone else. I told this gentleman of the description of certain carved figures and arms formerly on the stalls, and asked whether any had survived. He was able to show me the arms of Dean West and some other fragments. These, he said, had been got from an old resident, who had also once owned a figure—perhaps one of those which I was inquiring for. There was a very odd thing about that figure, he said. 'The old man who had it told me that he picked it up in a woodyard, whence he had obtained the still extant pieces, and had taken it home for his children. On the way home he was fiddling about with it and it came in two in his hands, and a bit of paper dropped out. This he picked up and, just noticing that there was writing on it, put it into his pocket, and subsequently into a vase on his mantelpiece. I was at his house not very long ago, and happened to pick up the vase and turn it over to see whether there were any marks on it, and the paper fell into my hand. The old man, on my handing it to him, told me the story I have told you, and said I might keep the paper. It was crumpled and rather torn, so I have mounted it on a card, which I have here. If you can tell me what it means I shall be very glad, and also, I may say, a good deal surprised.'

He gave me the card. The paper was quite legibly inscribed in an old hand, and this is what was on it:

When I grew in the Wood
I was water'd wth Blood
Now in the Church I stand
Who that touches me with his Hand
If a Bloody hand he bear
I councell him to be ware
Lest he be fetcht away
Whether by night or day,
But chiefly when the wind blows high
In a night of February.

This I drempt, 26 Febr. Ao 1699. JOHN AUSTIN.

'I suppose it is a charm or a spell: wouldn't you call it something of that kind?' said the curator.

'Yes,' I said, 'I suppose one might. What became of the figure in which it was concealed?'

'Oh, I forgot,' said he. 'The old man told me it was so ugly and frightened his children so much that he burnt it.'

THE JAPANESE QUINCE

John Galsworthy

As Mr Nilson, well known in the City, opened the window of his dressing-room on Campden Hill, he experienced a peculiar sweetish sensation in the back of his throat, and a feeling of emptiness just under his fifth rib. Hooking the window back, he noticed that a little tree in the Square Gardens had come out in blossom, and that the thermometer stood at sixty. 'Perfect morning,' he thought; 'spring at last!'

Resuming some meditations on the price of Tintos, he took up an ivory-backed hand-glass and scrutinized his face. His firm, well-coloured cheeks, with their neat brown moustaches, and his round, well-opened, clear grey eyes, wore a reassuring appearance of good health. Putting on his black frock-coat, he went downstairs.

In the dining-room his morning paper was laid out on the sideboard. Mr Nilson had scarcely taken it in his hand when he again became aware of that queer feeling. Somewhat concerned, he went to the French window and descended the scrolled iron steps into the fresh air. A cuckoo clock struck eight.

'Half an hour to breakfast,' he thought; 'I'll take a turn in the Gardens.'

He had them to himself, and proceeded to pace the circular path with his morning paper clasped behind him. He had scarcely made two revolutions, however, when it was borne in on him that, instead of going away in the fresh air, the feeling had increased. He drew several deep breaths, having heard deep breathing recommended by his wife's doctor; but they augmented rather than diminished the sensation—as of some sweetish liquor in course within him, together with a faint aching just above his heart. Running over what he had eaten the night before, he could recollect no unusual dish, and it occurred to him that it might possibly be some smell affecting him. But he could detect nothing except a faint sweet lemony scent, rather agreeable than otherwise, which evidently emanated from the bushes budding in the sunshine. He was on the point of resuming his promenade, when a blackbird close by burst into song, and looking up, Mr Nilson saw at a distance of perhaps five yards a little tree, in the heart of whose branches the bird was perched. He stood staring curiously at this tree, recognizing it for that which he had noticed from his window. It was covered with young blossoms, pink and white, and little bright green leaves both round and spiky; and on all this blossom and these leaves the sunlight glistened. Mr Nilson smiled; the little tree was so alive and pretty! And instead of passing on, he stayed there smiling at the tree.

'Morning like this!' he thought; 'and here I am the only person in the Square who has the—to come out and—!' But he had no sooner conceived this thought than he saw quite near him a man with his hands behind him, who was also staring up and smiling at the little tree. Rather taken aback, Mr Nilson ceased to smile, and looked furtively at the stranger. It was his next-door neighbour, Mr Tandram, well known in the City, who had occupied the adjoining house for some five years. Mr Nilson perceived at once the awkwardness of his position, for, being married, they had not yet had occasion to speak to one another. Doubtful as to his proper conduct, he decided at last to murmur 'Fine morning!' and was passing on, when Mr Tandram answered: 'Beautiful, for the time of year!' Detecting a slight nervousness in his neighbour's voice, Mr Nilson was emboldened to regard him openly. He was of about Mr Nilson's own height, with firm, well-coloured cheeks, neat brown moustaches, and round, well-opened, clear grey eyes; and he was wearing a black frock-coat. Mr Nilson noticed that he had his morning paper clasped behind him as he looked up at the little tree. And visited somehow by the feeling that he had been caught out, he said abruptly:

'Er—can you give me the name of that tree?'

Mr Tandram answered:

'I was about to ask you that,' and stepped towards it. Mr Nilson also approached the tree.

'Sure to have its name on, I should think,' he said.

Mr Tandram was the first to see the little label, close to where the blackbird had been sitting. He read it out.

'Japanese quince!'

'Ah!' said Mr Nilson, 'thought so. Early flowerers.'

'Very,' assented Mr Tandram, and added: 'Quite a feelin' in the air today.'

Mr Nilson nodded.

'It was a blackbird singin',' he said.

'Blackbirds,' answered Mr Tandram. 'I prefer them to thrushes myself; more body in the note.' And he looked at Mr Nilson in an almost friendly way.

'Quite,' murmured Mr Nilson. 'These exotics, they don't bear fruit. Pretty blossom!' and he again glanced up at the blossom, thinking: 'Nice fellow, this, I rather like him.'

Mr Tandram also gazed up at the blossom. And the little tree, as if appreciating their attention, quivered and glowed. From a distance the blackbird gave a loud, clear call. Mr Nilson dropped his eyes. It struck him suddenly that Mr Tandram looked a little foolish; and, as if he had seen himself, he said: 'I must be going in. Good morning!'

A shade passed over Mr Tandram's face, as if he, too, had suddenly noticed something about Mr Nilson.

'Good morning,' he replied, and clasping their journals to their backs they separated.

Mr Nilson retraced his steps towards his garden window, walking slowly so as to avoid arriving at the same time as his neighbour. Having seen Mr Tandram mount his scrolled iron steps, he ascended his own in turn. On the top step he paused.

With the slanting spring sunlight darting and quivering into it, the Japanese quince seemed more living than a tree. The blackbird had returned to it, and was chanting out his heart.

Mr Nilson sighed; again he felt that queer sensation, that choky feeling in his throat.

The sound of a cough or sigh attracted his attention. There, in the shadow of his French window, stood Mr Tandram, also looking forth across the Gardens at the little quince tree.

Unaccountably upset, Mr Nilson turned abruptly into the house, and opened his morning paper.

THE HONOUR OF ISRAEL GOW

G. K. Chesterton

A stormy evening of olive and silver was closing in, as Father Brown, wrapped in a grey Scotch plaid, came to the end of a grey Scotch valley and beheld the strange castle of Glengyle. It stopped one end of the glen or hollow like a blind alley; and it looked like the end of the world. Rising in steep roofs and spires of seagreen slate in the manner of the old French-Scottish châteaux, it reminded an Englishman of the sinister steeple-hats of witches in fairy tales; and the pine woods that rocked round the green turrets looked, by comparison, as black as numberless flocks of ravens. This note of a dreamy, almost a sleepy devilry, was no mere fancy from the landscape. For there did rest on the place one of those clouds of pride and madness and mysterious sorrow which lie more heavily on the noble houses of Scotland than on any other of the children of men. For Scotland has a double dose of the poison called heredity; the sense of blood in the aristocrat, and the sense of doom in the Calvinist.

The priest had snatched a day from his business at Glasgow to meet his friend Flambeau, the amateur detective, who was at Glengyle Castle with another more formal officer investigating the life and death of the late Earl of Glengyle. That mysterious person was the last representative of a race whose valour, insanity, and violent cunning had made them terrible even among the sinister nobility of their nation in the sixteenth century. None were deeper in that labyrinthine ambition, in chamber within chamber of that palace of lies that was built up around Mary Queen of Scots.

The rhyme in the country-side attested the motive and the result of their machinations candidly:

As green sap to the simmer trees,
Is red gold to the Ogilvies.

For many centuries there had never been a decent lord in Glengyle Castle; and with the Victorian era one would have thought that all eccentricities were exhausted. The last Glengyle, however, satisfied his tribal tradition by doing the only thing that was left for him to do; he disappeared. I do not mean that he went abroad; by all accounts he was still in the castle, if he was anywhere. But though his name was in the church register and the big red Peerage, nobody ever saw him under the sun.

If anyone saw him it was a solitary man-servant, something between a groom and a gardener. He was so deaf that the more business-like assumed him to be dumb; while the more penetrating declared him to be half-witted. A gaunt, red-haired labourer, with a dogged jaw and chin, but quite blank blue eyes, he went by the name of Israel Gow, and was the one silent servant on that deserted estate. But the energy with which he dug potatoes, and the regularity with which he disappeared into the kitchen gave people an impression that he was providing for the meals of a superior, and that the strange earl was still concealed in the castle. If society needed any further proof that he was there, the servant persistently asserted that he was not at home. One morning the provost and the minister (for the Glengyles were Presbyterian) were summoned to the castle. There they found that the gardener, groom and cook had added to his many professions that of an undertaker, and had nailed up his noble master in a coffin. With how much or how little further inquiry this odd fact was passed, did not as yet very plainly appear; for the thing had never been legally investigated till Flambeau had gone north two or three days before. By then the body of Lord Glengyle (if it was the body) had lain for some time in the little churchyard on the hill.

As Father Brown passed through the dim garden and came under the shadow of the château, the clouds were thick and the whole air damp and thundery. Against the last stripe of the green-gold sunset he saw a black human silhouette; a man in a chimney-pot hat, with a big spade over his shoulder. The combination was queerly suggestive of a sexton; but when Brown remembered the deaf servant who dug potatoes, he thought it natural enough. He knew something of the Scotch peasant; he knew the respectability which might well feel it necessary to wear 'blacks' for an official inquiry; he knew also the economy that would not lose an hour's digging for that. Even the man's start and suspicious stare as the priest went by were consonant enough with the vigilance and jealousy of such a type.

The great door was opened by Flambeau himself, who had with him a lean man with iron-grey hair and papers in his hand: Inspector Craven from Scotland Yard. The entrance hall was mostly stripped and empty; but the pale, sneering faces of one or two of the wicked Ogilvies looked down out of the black periwigs and blackening canvas.

Following them into an inner room, Father Brown found that the allies had been seated at a long oak table, of which their end was covered with scribbled papers, flanked with whisky and cigars. Through the whole of its remaining length it was occupied by detached objects arranged at intervals; objects about as inexplicable as any objects could be. One looked like a small heap of glittering broken glass. Another looked like a high heap of brown dust. A third appeared to be a plain stick of wood.

'You seem to have a sort of geological museum here,' he said, as he sat down, jerking his head briefly in the direction of the brown dust and the crystalline fragments.

'Not a geological museum,' replied Flambeau; 'say a psychological museum.'

'Oh, for the Lord's sake,' cried the police detective, laughing, 'don't let's begin with such long words.'

'Don't you know what psychology means?' asked Flambeau with friendly surprise. 'Psychology means being off your chump.'

'Still I hardly follow,' replied the official.

'Well,' said Flambeau, with decision; 'I mean that we've only found out one thing about Lord Glengyle. He was a maniac.'

The black silhouette of Gow with his top hat and spade passed the window, dimly outlined against the darkening sky. Father Brown stared passively at it and answered:

'I can understand there must have been something odd about the man, or he wouldn't have buried himself alive—nor been in such a hurry to bury himself dead. But what makes you think it was lunacy?'

'Well,' said Flambeau; 'you just listen to the list of things Mr Craven has found in the house.'

'We must get a candle,' said Craven, suddenly. 'A storm is getting up, and it's too dark to read.'

'Have you found any candles,' asked Brown smiling, 'among your oddities?'

Flambeau raised a grave face, and fixed his dark eyes on his friend. 'That is curious, too,' he said. 'Twenty-five candles, and not a trace of a candlestick.'

In the rapidly darkening room and rapidly rising wind, Brown went along the table to where a bundle of wax candles lay among the other scrappy exhibits. As he did so he bent accidentally over the heap of red-brown dust; and a sharp sneeze cracked the silence.

'Hullo!' he said; 'snuff!'

He took one of the candles, lit it carefully, came back and stuck it in the neck of the whisky bottle. The unrestful night air, blowing through the crazy window, waved the long flame like a banner. And on every side of the castle they could hear the miles and miles of black pine wood seething like a black sea around a rock.

'I will read the inventory,' began Craven gravely, picking up one of the papers, 'the inventory of what we found loose and unexplained in the castle. You are to understand that the place generally was dismantled and neglected; but one or two rooms had plainly been inhabited in a simple but not squalid style by somebody; somebody who was not the servant Gow. The list is as follows:

'First item. A very considerable hoard of precious stones, nearly all diamonds, and all of them loose, without any setting whatever. Of course, it is natural that the Ogilvies should have family jewels; but those are exactly the jewels that are almost always set in particular articles of ornament. The Ogilvies would seem to have kept theirs loose in their pockets, like coppers.

'Second item. Heaps and heaps of loose snuff, not kept in a horn, or even a pouch, but lying in heaps on the mantelpieces, on the sideboard, on the piano, anywhere. It looks as if the old gentleman would not take the trouble to look in a pocket or lift a lid.

'Third item. Here and there about the house curious little heaps of minute pieces of metal, some like steel springs and some in the form of microscopic wheels. As if they had gutted some mechanical toy.

'Fourth item. The wax candles, which have to be stuck in bottle necks because there is nothing else to stick them in. Now I wish you to note how very much queerer all this is than anything we anticipated. For the central riddle we are prepared; we have all seen at a glance that there was something wrong about the last earl. We have come here to find out whether he really lived here, whether he really died here, whether that red-haired scarecrow who did his burying had anything to do with his dying. But suppose the worst in all this, the most lurid or melodramatic solution you like. Suppose the servant really killed the master, or suppose the master isn't really dead, or suppose the master is dressed up as the servant, or suppose the servant is buried for the master; invent what Wilkie Collins's tragedy you like, and you still have not explained a candle without a candlestick, or why an elderly gentleman of good family should habitually spill snuff on the piano. The core of the tale we could imagine; it is the fringes that are mysterious. By no stretch of fancy can the human mind connect together snuff and diamonds and wax and loose clockwork.'

'I think I see the connexion,' said the priest. 'This Glengyle was mad against the French Revolution. He was an enthusiast for the *ancien régime*, and was trying to re-enact literally the family life of the last Bourbons. He had snuff because it was the eighteenth century luxury; wax candles, because they were the eighteenth century lighting; the mechanical bits of iron represent the locksmith hobby of Louis XVI; the diamonds are for the Diamond Necklace of Marie Antoinette.'

Both the other men were staring at him with round eyes. 'What a perfectly extraordinary notion!' cried Flambeau. 'Do you really think that is the truth?'

'I am perfectly sure it isn't,' answered Father Brown, 'only you said that nobody could connect snuff and diamonds and clockwork and candles. I give you that connexion off-hand. The real truth, I am very sure, lies deeper.'

He paused a moment and listened to the wailing of the wind in the turrets. Then he said: 'The late Earl of Glengyle was a thief. He lived a second and darker life as a desperate house-breaker. He did not have any candlesticks because he only used these candles cut short in the lantern he carried. The snuff he employed as the fiercest French criminals have used pepper: to fling it suddenly in dense masses in the face of a captor or pursuer. But the final proof is in the curious coincidence of the diamonds and the small steel wheels. Surely that makes everything plain to you? Diamonds and small steel wheels are the only two instruments with which you can cut out a pane of glass.'

The bough of a broken pine tree lashed heavily in the blast against the window-pane behind them, as if in parody of a burglar, but they did not turn round. Their eyes were fastened on Father Brown.

'Diamonds and small wheels,' repeated Craven ruminating. 'Is that all that makes you think it the true explanation?'

'I don't think it the true explanation,' replied the priest placidly; 'but you said that nobody could connect the four things. The true tale, of course, is something much more humdrum. Glengyle had found, or thought he had found, precious stones on his estate. Somebody had bamboozled him with those loose brilliants, saying they were found in the castle caverns. The little wheels are some diamond-cutting affair. He had to do the thing very roughly and in a small way, with the help of a few shepherds or rude fellows on these hills. Snuff is the one great luxury of such Scotch shepherds; it's the one thing with which you can bribe them. They didn't have candlesticks because they didn't want them; they held the candles in their hands when they explored the caves.'

'Is that all?' asked Flambeau after a long pause. 'Have we got to the dull truth at last?'

'Oh, no,' said Father Brown.

As the wind died in the most distant pine woods with a long hoot as of mockery, Father Brown, with an utterly impassive face, went on:

'I only suggested that because you said one could not plausibly connect snuff with clockwork or candles with bright stones. Ten false philosophies will fit the universe; ten false theories will fit Glengyle Castle. But we want the real explanation of the castle and the universe. But are there no other exhibits?'

Craven laughed, and Flambeau rose smiling to his feet and strolled down the long table.

'Items five, six, seven, etc.,' he said, 'are certainly more varied than instructive. A curious collection, not of lead pencils, but of the lead out of lead pencils. A senseless stick of bamboo, with the top rather splintered. It might be the instrument of the crime. Only, there isn't any crime. The only other things are a few old missals and little Catholic pictures, which the Ogilvies kept, I suppose, from the Middle Ages—their family pride being stronger than their Puritanism. We only put them in the museum because they seem curiously cut about and defaced.'

The heady tempest without drove a dreadful wrack of clouds

across Glengyle and threw the long room into darkness as Father Brown picked up the little illuminated pages to examine them. He spoke before the drift of darkness had passed; but it was the voice of an utterly new man.

'Mr Craven,' said he, talking like a man ten years younger: 'you have got a legal warrant, haven't you, to go up and examine that grave? The sooner we do it the better, and get to the bottom of this horrible affair. If I were you I should start now.'

'Now,' repeated the astonished detective, 'and why now?'

'Because this is serious,' answered Brown; 'this is not spilt snuff or loose pebbles, that might be there for a hundred reasons. There is only one reason I know of for *this* being done; and the reason goes down to the roots of the world. These religious pictures are not just dirtied or torn or scrawled over, which might be done in idleness or bigotry, by children or by Protestants. These have been treated very carefully—and very queerly. In every place where the great ornamented name of God comes in the old illuminations it has been elaborately taken out. The only other thing that has been removed is the halo round the head of the Child Jesus. Therefore, I say, let us get our warrant and our spade and our hatchet, and go up and break open that coffin.'

'What *do* you mean?' demanded the London officer.

'I mean,' answered the little priest, and his voice seemed to rise slightly in the roar of the gale. 'I mean that the great devil of the universe may be sitting on the top tower of this castle at this moment, as big as a hundred elephants, and roaring like the Apocalypse. There is black magic somewhere at the bottom of this.'

'Black magic,' repeated Flambeau in a low voice, for he was too enlightened a man not to know of such things; 'but what can these other things mean?'

'Oh, something damnable, I suppose,' replied Brown impatiently. 'How should I know? How can I guess all their mazes down below? Perhaps you can make a torture out of snuff and bamboo. Perhaps lunatics lust after wax and steel filings. Perhaps there is a maddening drug made of lead pencils!

Our shortest cut to the mystery is up the hill to the grave.'

His comrades hardly knew that they had obeyed and followed him till a blast of the night wind nearly flung them on their faces in the garden.

Nevertheless they had obeyed him like automata; for Craven found a hatchet in his hand, and the warrant in his pocket; Flambeau was carrying the heavy spade of the strange gardener; Father Brown was carrying the little gilt book from which had been torn the name of God.

The path up the hill to the churchyard was crooked but short; only under the stress of wind it seemed laborious and long. Far as the eye could see, farther and farther as they mounted the slope, were seas beyond seas of pines, now all aslope one way under the wind. And that universal gesture seemed as vain as it was vast, as vain as if that wind were whistling about some unpeopled and purposeless planet. Through all that infinite growth of grey-blue forests sang, shrill and high, that ancient sorrow that is in the heart of all heathen things. One could fancy that the voices from the underworld of unfathomable foliage were cries of the lost and wandering pagan gods: gods who had gone roaming in that irrational forest, and who will never find their way back to heaven.

'You see,' said Father Brown in a low but easy tone, 'Scotch people before Scotland existed were a curious lot. In fact, they're a curious lot still. But in the prehistoric times I fancy they really worshipped demons. That,' he added genially, 'is why they jumped at the Puritan theology.'

'My friend,' said Flambeau, turning in a kind of fury, 'what does all that snuff mean?'

'My friend,' replied Brown, with equal seriousness, 'there is one mark of all genuine religions: materialism. Now, devil-worship is a perfectly genuine religion.'

They had come up on the grassy scalp of the hill, one of the few bald spots that stood clear of the crashing and roaring pine forest. A mean enclosure, partly timber and partly wire, rattled in the tempest to tell them the border of the graveyard. But by the time Inspector Craven had come to the corner of the grave, and Flambeau had planted his spade point downwards and leaned on it, they were both almost as shaken as the shaky wood and wire. At the foot of the grave grew great tall thistles, grey and silver in their decay. Once or twice, when a ball of thistledown broke under the breeze and flew past him, Craven jumped slightly as if it had been an arrow.

Flambeau drove the blade of his spade through the whistling grass into the wet clay below. Then he seemed to stop and lean on it as on a staff.

'Go on,' said the priest very gently. 'We are only trying to find the truth. What are you afraid of?'

'I am afraid of finding it,' said Flambeau.

The London detective spoke suddenly in a high crowing voice that was meant to be conversational and cheery. 'I wonder why he really did hide himself like that. Something nasty, I suppose; was he a leper?'

'Something worse than that,' said Flambeau.

'And what do you imagine,' asked the other, 'would be worse than a leper?'

'I don't imagine it,' said Flambeau.

He dug for some dreadful minutes in silence, and then said in a choked voice: 'I'm afraid of his not being the right shape.'

'Nor was that piece of paper, you know,' said Father Brown quietly, 'and we survived even that piece of paper.'

Flambeau dug on with a blind energy. But the tempest had shouldered away the choking grey clouds that clung to the hills like smoke and revealed grey fields of faint starlight before he cleared the shape of a rude timber coffin, and somehow tipped it up upon the turf. Craven stepped forward with his axe; a thistle-top touched him, and he flinched. Then he took a firmer stride, and hacked and wrenched with an energy like Flambeau's till the lid was torn off, and all that was there lay glimmering in the grey starlight.

'Bones,' said Craven; and then he added, 'but it is a man,' as if that were something unexpected.

'Is he,' asked Flambeau in a voice that went oddly up and down, 'is he all right?'

'Seems so,' said the officer huskily, bending over the obscure and decaying skeleton in the box. 'Wait a minute.'

A vast heave went over Flambeau's huge figure. 'And now I come to think of it,' he cried, 'why in the name of madness shouldn't he be all right? What is it gets hold of a man on these cursed cold mountains? I think it's the black, brainless repetition; all these forests, and over all an ancient horror of unconsciousness. It's like the dream of an atheist. Pine-trees and more pine-trees and millions more pine-trees—'

'God!' cried the man by the coffin; 'but he hasn't got a head.'

While the others stood rigid the priest, for the first time, showed a leap of startled concern.

'No head!' he repeated. '*No head?*' as if he had almost expected some other deficiency.

Half-witted visions of a headless baby born to Glengyle, of a headless youth hiding himself in the castle, of a headless man pacing those ancient halls or that gorgeous garden, passed in panorama through their minds. But even in that stiffened instant the tale took no root in them and seemed to have no reason in it. They stood listening to the loud woods and the shrieking sky quite foolishly, like exhausted animals. Thought seemed to be something enormous that had suddenly slipped out of their grasp.

'There are three headless men,' said Father Brown, 'standing round this open grave.'

The pale detective from London opened his mouth to speak, and left it open like a yokel, while a long scream of wind tore the sky; then he looked at the axe in his hands as if it did not belong to him, and dropped it.

'Father,' said Flambeau in that infantile and heavy voice he used very seldom, 'what are we to do?'

His friend's reply came with the pent promptitude of a gun going off. 'Sleep!' cried Father Brown. 'Sleep. We have come to the end of the ways. Do you know what sleep is? Do you know that every man who sleeps believes in God? It is a sacrament; for it is an act of faith and it is a food.

And we need a sacrament, if only a natural one. Something has fallen on us that falls very seldom on men; perhaps the worst thing that can fall on them.'

Craven's parted lips came together to say: 'What do you mean?' The priest turned his face to the castle as he answered:

'We have found the truth; and the truth makes no sense.'

He went down the path in front of them with a plunging and reckless step very rare with him, and when they reached the castle again he threw himself upon sleep with the simplicity of a dog.

Despite his mystic praise of slumber, Father Brown was up earlier than anyone else except the silent gardener; and was found smoking a big pipe and watching that expert at his speechless labours in the kitchen garden. Towards daybreak the rocking storm had ended in roaring rains, and the day came with a curious freshness. The gardener seemed even to have been conversing, but at sight of the detectives he planted his spade sullenly in a bed and, saying something about his breakfast, shifted along the lines of cabbages and shut himself in the kitchen. 'He's a valuable man, that,' said Father Brown. 'He does the potatoes amazingly. Still,' he added, with a dispassionate charity, 'he has his faults; which of us hasn't? He doesn't dig this bank quite regularly. There, for instance,' and he stamped suddenly on one spot. 'I'm really very doubtful about that potato.'

'And why?' asked Craven, amused with the little man's new hobby.

'I'm doubtful about it,' said the other, 'because old Gow was doubtful about it himself. He put his spade in methodically in every place but just this. There must be a mighty fine potato just there.'

Flambeau pulled up the spade and impetuously drove it into the place. He turned up, under a load of soil, something that did not look like a potato, but rather like a monstrous, over-domed mushroom. But it struck the spade with a cold click; it rolled over like a ball, and grinned up at them.

'The Earl of Glengyle,' said Brown sadly, and looked down heavily at the skull.

Then, after a momentary meditation, he plucked the spade from Flambeau, and, saying: 'We must hide it again,' clamped the skull down in the earth. Then he leaned his little body and huge head on the great handle of the spade, that stood up stiffly in the earth, and his eyes were empty and his forehead full of wrinkles. 'If one could only conceive,' he muttered, 'the meaning of this last monstrosity.' And leaning on the large spade handle, he buried his brows in his hands, as men do in church.

All the corners of the sky were brightening into blue and silver; the birds were chattering in the tiny garden trees; so loud it seemed as if the trees themselves were talking. But the three men were silent enough.

'Well, I give it all up,' said Flambeau at last boisterously. 'My brain and this world don't fit each other; and there's an end of it. Snuff, spoilt Prayer Books, and the insides of musical boxes—what—'

Brown threw up his bothered brow and rapped on the spade handle with an intolerance quite unusual with him. 'Oh, tut, tut, tut,

tut!' he cried. 'All that is as plain as a pikestaff. I understood the snuff and clockwork, and so on, when I first opened my eyes this morning. And since then I've had it out with old Gow, the gardener, who is neither so deaf nor so stupid as he pretends. There's something amiss about the loose items. I was wrong about the torn mass-book, too; there's no harm in that. But it's this last business.

Desecrating graves and stealing dead men's heads—surely there's harm in that? Surely there's black magic still in that? That doesn't fit in to the quite simple story of the snuff and the candles.' And, striding about again, he smoked moodily.

'My friend,' said Flambeau, with a grim humour, 'you must be careful with me and remember I was once a criminal. The great advantage of that estate was that I always made up the story myself, and acted it as quick as I chose. This detective business of waiting about is too much for my French impatience. All my life, for good or evil, I have done things at the instant; I always fought duels the next morning; I always paid bills on the nail; I never even put off a visit to the dentist—'

Father Brown's pipe fell out of his mouth and broke into three pieces on the gravel path. He stood rolling his eyes, the exact picture of an idiot. 'Lord, what a turnip I am!' he kept saying. 'Lord, what a turnip!' Then, in a somewhat groggy kind of way, he began to laugh.

'The dentist!' he repeated. 'Six hours in the spiritual abyss, and all because I never thought of the dentist! Such a simple, such a beautiful and peaceful thought! Friends, we have passed a night in hell; but now the sun is risen, the birds are singing, and the radiant form of the dentist consoles the world.'

'I will get some sense out of this,' cried Flambeau, striding forward, 'if I use the tortures of the Inquisition.'

Father Brown repressed what appeared to be a momentary disposition to dance on the now sunlit lawn and cried quite piteously, like a child: 'Oh, let me be silly a little. You don't know how unhappy I have been. And now I know that there has been no deep sin in this business at all. Only a little lunacy, perhaps—and who minds that?'

He spun round once, then faced them with gravity.

'This is not a story of crime,' he said; 'rather it is the story of a strange and crooked honesty. We are dealing with the one man on earth, perhaps, who has taken no more than his due. It is a study in the savage living logic that has been the religion of this race.

'That old local rhyme about the house of Glengyle—

As green sap to the simmer trees
Is red gold to the Ogilvies—

was literal as well as metaphorical. It did not merely mean that the Glengyles sought for wealth; it was also true that they literally gathered gold; they had a huge collection of ornaments and utensils in that metal. They were, in fact, misers whose mania took that turn. In the light of that fact, run through all the things we found in the castle. Diamonds without their gold rings; candles without their gold candlesticks; snuff without the gold snuff-boxes; pencil-leads without the gold pencil-cases; a walking- stick without its gold top; clockwork without the gold clocks—or rather watches. And, mad as it sounds, because the halos and the name of God in the old missals were of real gold, these also were taken away.'

The garden seemed to brighten, the grass to grow gayer in the strengthening sun, as the crazy truth was told. Flambeau lit a cigarette as his friend went on.

'Were taken away,' continued Father Brown; 'were taken away—but not stolen. Thieves would never have left this mystery. Thieves would have taken the gold snuff-boxes, snuff and all; the gold pencil-cases, lead and all. We have to deal with a man with a peculiar conscience, but certainly a conscience. I found that mad moralist this morning in the kitchen garden yonder, and I heard the whole story.

'The late Archbishop Ogilvie was the nearest approach to a good man ever born at Glengyle. But his bitter virtue took the turn of the misanthrope; he moped over the dishonesty of his ancestors, from which, somehow, he generalized a dishonesty of all men. More especially he distrusted philanthropy or free-giving; and he swore if he could find one man who took his exact rights he should have all the gold of Glengyle. Having delivered this defiance to humanity he shut himself up, without the smallest expectation of its being answered. One day, however, a deaf and seemingly senseless lad from a distant village brought him a belated telegram; and Glengyle, in his acrid pleasantry, gave him a new farthing. At least he thought he had done so, but when he turned over his change he found the new farthing still there and a sovereign gone. The accident offered him vistas of sneering speculation. Either way, the boy would show the greasy greed of the species. Either he would vanish, a thief stealing a coin; or he would sneak back with it virtuously, a snob seeking a reward. In the middle of the night Lord Glengyle was knocked up out of his bed—for he lived alone—and forced to open the door to the deaf idiot. The idiot brought with him, not the sovereign, but exactly nineteen shillings and eleven-pence three-farthings in change.

'Then the wild exactitude of this action took hold on the mad lord's brain like fire. He swore he was Diogenes, that had long sought an honest man, and at last had found one. He made a new will, which I have seen. He took the literal youth into his huge, neglected house, and trained him up as his solitary servant and—after an odd manner—his heir. And whatever that queer creature understands, he understood absolutely his lord's two fixed ideas: first, that the letter of right is everything; and second, that he himself was to have the gold of Glengyle. So far, that is all; and that is simple. He has stripped the house of gold, and taken not a grain that was not gold; not so much as a grain of snuff. He lifted the gold leaf off an old illumination, fully satisfied that he left the rest unspoilt. All that I understood; but I could not understand this skull business. I was really uneasy about that human head buried among the potatoes. It distressed me—till Flambeau said the word.

'It will be all right. He will put the skull back in the grave, when he has taken the gold out of the tooth.'

And, indeed, when Flambeau crossed the hill that morning, he saw that strange being, the just miser, digging at the desecrated grave, the plaid round his throat thrashing out in the mountain wind; the sober top hat on his head.

ENOCH SOAMES

Max Beerbohm

When a book about the literature of the eighteen-nineties was given by Mr Holbrook Jackson to the world, I looked eagerly in the index for SOAMES, ENOCH. I had feared he would not be there. He was not there. But everybody else was. Many writers whom I had quite forgotten, or remembered but faintly, lived again for me, they and their work, in Mr Holbrook Jackson's pages. The book was as thorough as it was brilliantly written. And thus the omission found by me was an all the deadlier record of poor Soames' failure to impress himself on his decade.

I daresay I am the only person who noticed the omission. Soames had failed so piteously as all that! Nor is there a counterpoise in the thought that if he had had some measure of success he might have passed, like those others, out of my mind, to return only at the historian's beck. It is true that had his gifts, such as they were, been acknowledged in his lifetime, he would never have made the bargain I saw him make—that strange bargain whose results have kept him always in the foreground of my memory. But it is from those very results that the full piteousness of him glares out.

Not my compassion, however, impels me to write of him. For his sake, poor fellow, I should be inclined to keep my pen out of the ink. It is ill to deride the dead. And how can I write about Enoch Soames without making him ridiculous? Or rather, how am I to hush up the horrid fact that he *was* ridiculous? I shall not be able to do that. Yet, sooner or later, write about him I must. You will see, in due course, that I have no option. And I may as well get the thing done now.

In the Summer Term of '93 a bolt from the blue flashed down on Oxford. It drove deep, it hurtlingly embedded itself in the soil. Dons and undergraduates stood around, rather pale, discussing nothing but it. Whence came it, this meteorite? From Paris. Its name?

Will Rothenstein. Its aim? To do a series of twenty-four portraits in lithograph. These were to be published from the Bodley Head, London. The matter was urgent. Already the Warden of A, and the Master of B, and the Regius Professor of C, had meekly 'sat'. Dignified and doddering old men, who had never consented to sit to any one, could not withstand this dynamic little stranger. He did not sue: he invited; he did not invite: he commanded. He was twenty-one years old. He wore spectacles that flashed more than any other pair ever seen. He was a wit. He was brimful of ideas. He knew Whistler. He knew Edmond de Goncourt. He knew every one in Paris. He knew them all by heart. He was Paris in Oxford. It was whispered that, so soon as he had polished off his selection of dons, he was going to include a few undergraduates. It was a proud day for me when I—I—was included. I liked Rothenstein not less than I feared him; and there arose between us a friendship that has grown ever warmer, and been more and more valued by me, with every passing year.

At the end of Term he settled in—or rather, meteoritically into—London.

It was to him I owed my first knowledge of that forever enchanting little world-in-itself, Chelsea, and my first acquaintance with Walter Sickert and other august elders who dwelt there. It was Rothenstein that took me to see, in Cambridge Street, Pimlico, a young man whose drawings were already famous among the few—Aubrey Beardsley, by name. With Rothenstein I paid my first visit to the Bodley Head. By him I was inducted into another haunt of intellect and daring, the domino room of the Café Royal.

There, on that October evening—there, in that exuberant vista of gilding and crimson velvet set amidst all those opposing mirrors and upholding caryatids, with fumes of tobacco ever rising to the painted and pagan ceiling, and with the hum of presumably cynical conversation broken into so sharply now and again by the clatter of dominoes shuffled on marble tables, I drew a deep breath, and 'This indeed,' said I to myself, 'is life!'

It was the hour before dinner. We drank vermouth. Those who knew Rothenstein were pointing him out to those who knew him only by name. Men were constantly coming in through the swing-doors and wandering slowly up and down in search of vacant tables, or of tables occupied by friends. One of these rovers interested me because

I was sure he wanted to catch Rothenstein's eye. He had twice passed our table, with a hesitating look; but Rothenstein, in the thick of a disquisition on Puvis de Chavannes, had not seen him. He was a stooping, shambling person, rather tall, very pale, with longish and brownish hair. He had a thin vague beard—or rather, he had a chin on which a large number of hairs weakly curled and clustered to cover its retreat. He was an odd-looking person; but in the nineties odd apparitions were more frequent, I think, than they are now. The young writers of that era—and I was sure this man was a writer—strove earnestly to be distinct in aspect. This man had striven unsuccessfully. He wore a soft black hat of clerical kind but of Bohemian intention, and a grey waterproof cape which, perhaps because it was waterproof, failed to be romantic. I decided that 'dim' was the *mot juste* for him. I had already essayed to write, and was immensely keen on the *mot juste*, that Holy Grail of the period.

The dim man was now again approaching our table, and this time he made up his mind to pause in front of it. 'You don't remember me,' he said in a toneless voice.

Rothenstein brightly focussed him. 'Yes, I do,' he replied after a moment, with pride rather than effusion—pride in a retentive memory. 'Edwin Soames.'

'Enoch Soames,' said Enoch.

'Enoch Soames,' repeated Rothenstein in a tone implying that it was enough to have hit on the surname. 'We met in Paris two or three times when you were living there. We met at the Café Groche.'

'And I came to your studio once.'

'Oh yes; I was sorry I was out.'

'But you were in. You showed me some of your paintings, you know… I hear you're in Chelsea now.'

'Yes.'

I almost wondered that Mr Soames did not, after this monosyllable, pass along. He stood patiently there, rather like a dumb animal, rather like a donkey looking over a gate. A sad figure, his. It occurred to me that 'hungry' was perhaps the *mot juste* for him; but—hungry for what? He looked as if he had little appetite for anything. I was sorry for him; and Rothenstein, though he had not invited him to Chelsea, did ask him to sit down and have something to drink.

Seated, he was more self-assertive. He flung back the wings of his cape with a gesture which—had not those wings been waterproof—might have seemed to hurl defiance at things in general. And he ordered an absinthe. '*Je me tiens toujours fidèle*,' he told Rothenstein, '*à la sorcière glauque*.'

'It is bad for you,' said Rothenstein drily.

'Nothing is bad for one,' answered Soames. '*Dans ce monde il n'y a ni de bien ni de mal*.'

'Nothing good and nothing bad? How do you mean?' 'I explained it all in the preface to *Negations*.'

'*Negations*?'

'Yes; I gave you a copy of it.'

'Oh yes, of course. But did you explain—for instance—that there was no such thing as bad or good grammar?'

'N-no,' said Soames. 'Of course in Art there is the good and the evil. But in Life—no.' He was rolling a cigarette. He had weak white hands, not well washed, and with finger-tips much stained by nicotine. 'In Life there are illusions of good and evil, but'—his voice trailed away to a murmur in which the words 'vieux jeu' and 'rococo' were faintly audible. I think he felt he was not doing himself justice, and feared that Rothenstein was going to point out fallacies. Anyway, he cleared his throat and said '*Parlons d'autre chose*.'

It occurs to you that he was a fool? It didn't to me. I was young, and had not the clarity of judgment that Rothenstein already had. Soames was quite five or six years older than either of us. Also, he had written a book.

It was wonderful to have written a book.

If Rothenstein had not been there, I should have revered Soames. Even as it was, I respected him. And I was very near indeed to reverence when he said he had another book coming out soon. I asked if I might ask what kind of book it was to be.

'My poems,' he answered. Rothenstein asked if this was to be the title of the book. The poet meditated on this suggestion, but said he rather thought of giving the book no title at all. 'If a book is good in itself—' he murmured, waving his cigarette.

Rothenstein objected that absence of title might be bad for the sale of a book. 'If,' he urged, 'I went into a bookseller's and said simply 'Have you got?' or 'Have you a copy of?' how would they know what I wanted?'

'Oh, of course I should have my name on the cover,' Soames answered earnestly. 'And I rather want,' he added, looking hard at Rothenstein, 'to have a drawing of myself as frontispiece.' Rothenstein admitted that this was a capital idea, and mentioned that he was going into the country and would be there for some time. He then looked at his watch, exclaimed at the hour, paid the waiter, and went away with me to dinner. Soames remained at his post of fidelity to the glaucous witch.

'Why were you so determined not to draw him?' I asked.

'Draw him? Him? How can one draw a man who doesn't exist?'

'He is dim,' I admitted. But my *mot juste* fell flat. Rothenstein repeated that Soames was non-existent.

Still, Soames had written a book. I asked if Rothenstein had read *Negations*. He said he had looked into it, 'but,' he added crisply, 'I don't profess to know anything about writing.' A reservation very characteristic of the period! Painters would not then allow that any one outside their own order had a right to any opinion about painting. This law (graven on the tablets brought down by Whistler from the summit of Fujiyama) imposed certain limitations. If other arts than painting were not utterly unintelligible to all but the men who practised them, the law tottered—the Monroe Doctrine, as it were, did not hold good. Therefore no painter would offer an opinion of a book without warning you at any rate that his opinion was worthless. No one is a better judge of literature than Rothenstein; but it wouldn't have done to tell him so in those days; and I knew that I must form an unaided judgment on *Negations*.

Not to buy a book of which I had met the author face to face would have been for me in those days an impossible act of self-denial. When I returned to Oxford for the Christmas Term I had duly secured *Negations*. I used to keep it lying carelessly on the table in my room, and whenever a friend took it up and asked what it was about I would say 'Oh, it's rather a remarkable book. It's by a man whom I know.' Just 'what it was about' I never was able to say. Head or tail was just what I hadn't made of that slim green volume. I found in the preface no clue to the exiguous labyrinth of contents, and in that labyrinth nothing to explain the preface.

> Lean near to life. Lean very near—nearer.
>
> Life is web, and therein nor warp nor woof is, but web only.

> It is for this I am Catholick in church and in thought, yet do let swift Mood weave there what the shuttle of Mood wills.

These were the opening phrases of the preface, but those which followed were less easy to understand. Then came 'Stark: A *Conte*', about a midinette who, so far as I could gather, murdered, or was about to murder, a mannequin. It seemed to me like a story by Catulle Mendès in which the translator had either skipped or cut out every alternate sentence. Next, a dialogue between Pan and St Ursula—lacking, I rather felt, in 'snap'. Next, some aphorisms (entitled ἀφορίσματα). Throughout, in fact, there was a great variety of form; and the forms had evidently been wrought with much care. It was rather the substance that eluded me. Was there, I wondered, any substance at all? It did now occur to me: suppose Enoch Soames was a fool! Up cropped a rival hypothesis: suppose *I* was! I inclined to give Soames the benefit of the doubt. I had read 'L'Après-midi d'un Faune' without extracting a glimmer of meaning. Yet Mallarmé—of course—was a Master. How was I to know that Soames wasn't another? There was a sort of music in his prose, not indeed arresting, but perhaps, I thought, haunting, and laden perhaps with meanings as deep as Mallarmé's own. I awaited his poems with an open mind.

And I looked forward to them with positive impatience after I had had a second meeting with him. This was on an evening in January. Going into the aforesaid domino room, I passed a table at which sat a pale man with an open book before him. He looked from his book to me, and I looked back over my shoulder with a vague sense that I ought to have recognized him. I returned to pay my respects. After exchanging a few words, I said with a glance to the open book, 'I see I am interrupting you,' and was about to pass on, but 'I prefer,' Soames replied in his toneless voice, 'to be interrupted,' and I obeyed his gesture that I should sit down.

I asked him if he often read here. 'Yes; things of this kind I read here,' he answered, indicating the title of his book—*The Poems of Shelley*.

'Anything that you really'—and I was going to say 'admire?' But I cautiously left my sentence unfinished, and was glad that I had done so, for he said, with unwonted emphasis, 'Anything second-rate.'

I had read little of Shelley, but 'Of course,' I murmured, 'he's very uneven.'

'I should have thought evenness was just what was wrong with him. A deadly evenness. That's why I read him here. The noise of this place breaks the rhythm. He's tolerable here.' Soames took up the book and glanced through the pages. He laughed. Soames' laugh was a short, single and mirthless sound from the throat, unaccompanied by any movement of the face or brightening of the eyes. 'What a period!' he uttered, laying the book down. And 'What a country!' he added.

I asked rather nervously if he didn't think Keats had more or less held his own against the drawbacks of time and place. He admitted that there were 'passages in Keats', but did not specify them. Of 'the older men', as he called them, he seemed to like only Milton. 'Milton,' he said, 'wasn't sentimental.' Also, 'Milton had a dark insight.' And again, 'I can always read Milton in the reading-room.'

'The reading-room?'

'Of the British Museum. I go there every day.'

'You do? I've only been there once. I'm afraid I found it rather a depressing place. It—it seemed to sap one's vitality.'

'It does. That's why I go there. The lower one's vitality, the more sensitive one is to great art. I live near the Museum. I have rooms in Dyott Street.'

'And you go round to the reading-room to read Milton?'

'Usually Milton.' He looked at me. 'It was Milton,' he certificatively added, 'who converted me to Diabolism.'

'Diabolism? Oh yes? Really?' said I, with that vague discomfort and that intense desire to be polite which one feels when a man speaks of his own religion. 'You—worship the Devil?'

Soames shook his head. 'It's not exactly worship,' he qualified, sipping his absinthe. 'It's more a matter of trusting and encouraging.'

'Ah, yes... But I had rather gathered from the preface to *Negations* that you were a—a Catholic.'

'*Je l'étais à cette époque.* Perhaps I still am. Yes, I'm a Catholic Diabolist.'

This profession he made in an almost cursory tone. I could see that what was upmost in his mind was the fact that I had read *Negations*. His pale eyes had for the first time gleamed. I felt as one who is about to be examined, *viva voce*, on the very subject in which he is shakiest. I hastily asked him how soon his poems were to be published. 'Next week,' he told me.

'And are they to be published without a title?'

'No. I found a title, at last. But I shan't tell you what it is,' as though I had been so impertinent as to inquire. 'I am not sure that it wholly satisfies me. But it is the best I can find. It does suggest something of the quality of the poems… Strange growths, natural and wild; yet exquisite,' he added, 'and many-hued, and full of poisons.'

I asked him what he thought of Baudelaire. He uttered the snort that was his laugh, and 'Baudelaire,' he said, 'was a *bourgeois malgré lui*'. France had had only one poet: Villon; 'and two-thirds of Villon were sheer journalism.' Verlaine was 'an *épicier malgré lui*'. Altogether, rather to my surprise, he rated French literature lower than English. There were 'passages' in Villiers de l'Isle-Adam. But 'I,' he summed up, 'owe nothing to France.' He nodded at me. 'You'll see,' he predicted.

I did not, when the time came, quite see that. I thought the author of *Fungoids* did—unconsciously, no doubt—owe something to the young Parisian décadents, or to the young English ones who owed something to *them*. I still think so. The little book—bought by me in Oxford—lies before me as I write. Its pale grey buckram cover and silver lettering have not worn well. Nor have its contents. Through these, with a melancholy interest, I have again been looking. They are not much. But at the time of their publication I had a vague suspicion that they *might* be. I suppose it is my capacity for faith, not poor Soames' work, that is weaker than it once was…

TO A YOUNG WOMAN

Thou art, who hast not been!
Pale tunes irresolute
And traceries of old sounds
Blown from a rotted flute
Mingle with noise of cymbals rouged with rust,
Nor not strange forms and epicene
Lie bleeding in the dust,
Being wounded with wounds.
For this it is
That is thy counterpart
Of age-long mockeries
Thou hast not been nor art!

There seemed to me a certain inconsistency as between the first and last lines of this. I tried, with bent brows, to resolve the discord. But I did not take my failure as wholly incompatible with a meaning in Soames' mind. Might it not rather indicate the depth of his meaning? As for the craftsmanship, 'rouged with rust' seemed to me a fine stroke, and 'nor not' instead of 'and' had a curious felicity. I wondered who the Young Woman was, and what she had made of it all. I sadly suspect that Soames could not have made more of it than she. Yet, even now, if one doesn't try to make any sense at all of the poem, and reads it just for the sound, there is a certain grace of cadence. Soames was an artist—in so far as he was anything, poor fellow!

It seemed to me, when first I read *Fungoids,* that, oddly enough, the Diabolistic side of him was the best. Diabolism seemed to be a cheerful, even a wholesome, influence in his life.

NOCTURNE

Round and round the shutter'd Square
I stroll'd with the Devil's arm in mine.
No sound but the scrape of his hoofs was there
And the ring of his laughter and mine.
We had drunk black wine.

I scream'd 'I will race you, Master!'
'What matter,' he shriek'd, 'to-night
Which of us runs the faster?
There is nothing to fear to-night
In the foul moon's light!'

Then I look'd him in the eyes,
And I laugh'd full shrill at the lie he told
And the gnawing fear he would fain disguise.
It was true, what I'd time and again been told:
He was old—old.

There was, I felt, quite a swing about that first stanza—a joyous and rollicking note of comradeship. The second was slightly hysterical perhaps. But I liked the third: it was so bracingly unorthodox, even according to the tenets of Soames' peculiar sect in the faith. Not much 'trusting and encouraging' here! Soames triumphantly exposing the Devil as a liar, and laughing 'full shrill', cut a quite heartening figure,

I thought—then! Now, in the light of what befell, none of his poems depresses me so much as 'Nocturne'.

I looked out for what the metropolitan reviewers would have to say. They seemed to fall into two classes: those who had little to say and those who had nothing. The second class was the larger, and the words of the first were cold; insomuch that

> Strikes a note of modernity … These tripping numbers.
> —*Preston Telegraph*

was the sole lure offered in advertisements by Soames' publisher. I had hoped that when next I met the poet I could congratulate him on having made a stir; for I fancied he was not so sure of his intrinsic greatness as he seemed. I was but able to say, rather coarsely, when next I did see him, that I hoped *Fungoids* was 'selling splendidly.' He looked at me across his glass of absinthe and asked if I had bought a copy. His publisher had told him that three had been sold. I laughed, as at a jest.

'You don't suppose I *care*, do you?' he said, with something like a snarl. I disclaimed the notion. He added that he was not a tradesman. I said mildly that I wasn't, either, and murmured that an artist who gave truly new and great things to the world had always to wait long for recognition. He said he cared not a sou for recognition. I agreed that the act of creation was its own reward.

His moroseness might have alienated me if I had regarded myself as a nobody. But ah! hadn't both John Lane and Aubrey Beardsley suggested that I should write an essay for the great new venture that was afoot—*The Yellow Book?* And hadn't Henry Harland, as editor, accepted my essay? And wasn't it to be in the very first number? At Oxford I was still *in statu pupillari*. In London I regarded myself as very much indeed a graduate now—one whom no Soames could ruffle. Partly to show off, partly in sheer good-will, I told Soames he ought to contribute to *The Yellow Book*. He uttered from the throat a sound of scorn for that publication.

Nevertheless, I did, a day or two later, tentatively ask Harland if he knew anything of the work of a man called Enoch Soames. Harland paused in the midst of his characteristic stride around the room, threw up his hands towards the ceiling, and groaned aloud: he had often met 'that absurd creature' in Paris, and this very morning had received some poems in manuscript from him.

'Has he *no* talent?' he asked.

'He has an income. He's all right.' Harland was the most joyous of men and most generous of critics, and he hated to talk of anything about which he couldn't be enthusiastic. So I dropped the subject of Soames. The news that Soames had an income did take the edge off solicitude. I learned afterwards that he was the son of an unsuccessful and deceased bookseller in Preston, but had inherited an annuity of £300 from a married aunt, and had no surviving relatives of any kind. Materially, then, he was 'all right.' But there was still a spiritual pathos about him, sharpened for me now by the possibility that even the praises of *The Preston Telegraph* might not have been forthcoming had he not been the son of a Preston man. He had a sort of weak doggedness which I could not but admire. Neither he nor his work received the slightest encouragement; but he persisted in behaving as a personage: always he kept his dingy little flag flying. Wherever congregated the *jeunes féroces* of the arts, in whatever Soho restaurant they had just discovered, in whatever music-hall they were most frequenting, there was Soames in the midst of them, or rather on the fringe of them, a dim but inevitable figure. He never sought to propitiate his fellow-writers, never bated a jot of his arrogance about his own work or of his contempt for theirs. To the painters he was respectful, even humble; but for the poets and prosaists of *The Yellow Book*, and later of *The Savoy*, he had never a word but of scorn. He wasn't resented. It didn't occur to anybody that he or his Catholic Diabolism mattered. When, in the autumn of '96, he brought out (at his own expense, this time) a third book, his last book, nobody said a word for or against it. I meant, but forgot, to buy it. I never saw it, and am ashamed to say I don't even remember what it was called. But I did, at the time of its publication, say to Rothenstein that I thought poor old Soames was really a rather tragic figure, and that I believed he would literally die for want of recognition. Rothenstein scoffed. He said I was trying to get credit for a kind heart which I didn't possess; and perhaps this was so. But at the private view of the New English Art Club, a few weeks later, I beheld a pastel portrait of 'Enoch Soames, Esq.' It was very like him, and very like Rothenstein to have done it. Soames was standing near it, in his soft hat and his waterproof cape, all through the afternoon. Anybody who knew him would have recognized the portrait at a glance, but nobody who didn't know him would have recognized the portrait from its bystander: it 'existed' so much more than he; it was bound to. Also, it had not that expression of faint happiness which on this day was discernible, yes, in Soames' countenance. Fame had breathed on him. Twice again in the course of the month I went to the New English, and on both occasions Soames himself was on view there. Looking back, I regard the close of that exhibition as having been virtually the close of his career. He had felt the breath of Fame against his cheek—so late, for such a little while; and at its withdrawal he gave in, gave up, gave out. He, who had never looked strong or well, looked ghastly now—a shadow of the shade he had once been. He still frequented the domino room, but, having lost all wish to excite curiosity, he no longer read books there. 'You read only at the Museum now?' asked I, with attempted cheerfulness. He said he never went there now. 'No absinthe there,' he muttered. It was the sort of thing that in the old days he would have said for effect; but it carried conviction now. Absinthe, erst but a point in the 'personality' he had striven so hard to build up, was solace and necessity now. He no longer called it 'la sorcière glauque'. He had shed away all his French phrases. He had become a plain, unvarnished, Preston man.

Failure, if it be a plain, unvarnished, complete failure, and even though it be a squalid failure, has always a certain dignity. I avoided Soames because he made me feel rather vulgar. John Lane had published, by this time, two little books of mine, and they had had a pleasant little success of esteem. I was a—slight but definite—'personality'. Frank Harris had engaged me to kick up my heels in the *Saturday Review*, Alfred Harmsworth was letting me do likewise in the *Daily Mail*. I was just what Soames wasn't. And he shamed my gloss. Had I known that he really and firmly believed in the greatness of what he as an artist had achieved, I might not have shunned him. No man who hasn't lost his vanity can be held to have altogether failed. Soames' dignity was an illusion of mine. One day in the first week of June, 1897, that illusion went. But on the evening of that day Soames went too.

I had been out most of the morning, and, as it was too late to reach home in time for luncheon, I sought 'the Vingtième'. This little place—Restaurant du Vingtième Siècle, to give it its full title—had been discovered in '96 by the poets and prosaists, but had now been more or less abandoned in favour of some later find. I don't think it lived long enough to justify its name; but at that time there it still was, in Greek Street, a few doors from Soho Square, and almost opposite to that house where, in the first years of the century, a little girl, and with her a boy named De Quincey, made nightly encampment in darkness and hunger among dust and rats and old legal parchments. The Vingtième was but a small whitewashed room, leading out into the street at one end and into a kitchen at the other. The proprietor and cook was a Frenchman, known to us as Monsieur Vingtième; the waiters were his two daughters, Rose and Berthe; and the food, according to faith, was good. The tables were so narrow, and were set so close together, that there was space for twelve of them, six jutting from either wall.

Only the two nearest to the door, as I went in, were occupied. On one side sat a tall, flashy, rather Mephistophelian man whom I had seen from time to time in the domino room and elsewhere. On the other side sat Soames. They made a queer contrast in that sunlit room—Soames sitting haggard in that hat and cape which nowhere at any season had I seen him doff, and this other, this keenly vital man, at sight of whom I more than ever wondered whether he were a diamond merchant, a conjurer, or the head of a private detective agency. I was sure Soames didn't want my company; but I asked, as it would have seemed brutal not to, whether I might join him, and took the chair opposite to his. He was smoking a cigarette, with an untasted salmi of something on his plate and a half-empty bottle of Sauterne before him; and he was quite silent. I said that the preparations for the Jubilee made London impossible. (I rather liked them, really.) I professed a wish to go right away till the whole thing was over. In vain did I attune myself to his gloom. He seemed not to hear me nor even to see me. I felt that his behaviour made me ridiculous in the eyes of the other man. The gangway between the two rows of tables at the Vingtième was hardly more than two feet wide (Rose and Berthe, in their ministrations, had always to edge past each other, quarrelling in whispers as they did so), and any one at the table abreast of yours was practically at yours. I thought our neighbour was amused at my failure to interest Soames, and so, as I could not explain to him that my insistence was merely charitable, I became silent. Without turning my head, I had him well within my range of vision. I hoped

I looked less vulgar than he in contrast with Soames. I was sure he was not an Englishman, but what *was* his nationality? Though his jet-black hair was *en brosse*, I did not think he was French. To Berthe, who waited on him, he spoke French fluently, but with a hardly native idiom and accent. I gathered that this was his first visit to the Vingtième; but Berthe was off-hand in her manner to him: he had not made a good impression. His eyes were handsome, but—like the Vingtième's tables—too narrow and set too close together. His nose was predatory, and the points of his moustache, waxed up beyond his nostrils, gave a fixity to his smile. Decidedly, he was sinister. And my sense of discomfort in his presence was intensified by the scarlet waistcoat which tightly, and so unseasonably in June, sheathed his ample chest. This waistcoat wasn't wrong merely because of the heat, either. It was somehow all wrong in itself. It wouldn't have done on Christmas morning. It would have struck a jarring note at the first night of 'Hernani'. I was trying to account for its wrongness when Soames suddenly and strangely broke silence. 'A hundred years hence!' he murmured, as in a trance.

'We shall not be here!' I briskly but fatuously added.

'We shall not be here. No,' he droned, 'but the Museum will still be just where it is. And the reading-room, just where it is. And people will be able to go and read there.' He inhaled sharply, and a spasm as of actual pain contorted his features.

I wondered what train of thought poor Soames had been following. He did not enlighten me when he said, after a long pause, 'You think I haven't minded.'

'Minded what, Soames?'

'Neglect. Failure.'

'*Failure?*' I said heartily. 'Failure?' I repeated vaguely. 'Neglect—yes, perhaps; but that's quite another matter. Of course you haven't been—appreciated. But what then? Any artist who—who gives—' What I wanted to say was, 'Any artist who gives truly new and great things to the world has always to wait long for recognition'; but the flattery would not out: in the face of his misery, a misery so genuine and so unmasked, my lips would not say the words.

And then—he said them for me. I flushed. 'That's what you were going to say, isn't it?' he asked.

'How did you know?'

'It's what you said to me three years ago, when *Fungoids* was published.' I flushed the more. I need not have done so at all, for 'It's the only important thing I ever heard you say,' he continued. 'And I've never forgotten it. It's a true thing. It's a horrible truth. But—d'you remember what I answered? I said 'I don't care a sou for recognition.' And you believed me. You've gone on believing I'm above that sort of thing. You're shallow. What should *you* know of the feelings of a man like me? You imagine that a great artist's faith in himself and in the verdict of posterity is enough to keep him happy… You've never guessed at the bitterness and loneliness, the'—his voice broke; but presently he resumed, speaking with a force that I had never known in him. 'Posterity! What use is it to *me*? A dead man doesn't know that people are visiting his grave—visiting his birthplace—putting up tablets to him—unveiling statues of him. A dead man can't read the books that are written about him. A hundred years hence! Think of it! If I could come back to life *then*—just for a few hours—and go to the reading-room, and *read*! Or better still: if I could be projected, now, at this moment, into that future, into that reading-room, just for this one afternoon! I'd sell myself body and soul to the devil, for that! Think of the pages and pages in the catalogue: 'SOAMES, ENOCH' endlessly—endless editions, commentaries, prolegomena, biographies'—but here he was interrupted by a sudden loud creak of the chair at the next table. Our neighbour had half risen from his place. He was leaning towards us, apologetically intrusive.

'Excuse—permit me,' he said softly. 'I have been unable not to hear. Might I take a liberty? In this little restaurant-sans-façon'—he spread wide his hands—'might I, as the phrase is, 'cut in'?'

I could but signify our acquiescence. Berthe had appeared at the kitchen door, thinking the stranger wanted his bill. He waved her away with his cigar, and in another moment had seated himself beside me, commanding a full view of Soames.

'Though not an Englishman,' he explained, 'I know my London well, Mr Soames. Your name and fame—Mr Beerbohm's too—very known to me. Your point is: who am *I*?' He glanced quickly over his shoulder, and in a lowered voice said 'I am the Devil.'

I couldn't help it: I laughed. I tried not to, I knew there was nothing to laugh at, my rudeness shamed me, but—I laughed with increasing volume. The Devil's quiet dignity, the surprise and disgust of his raised eyebrows, did but the more dissolve me. I rocked to and fro, I lay back aching. I behaved deplorably.

'I am a gentleman, and,' he said with intense emphasis, 'I thought I was in the company of *gentlemen*.'

'Don't!' I gasped faintly. 'Oh, don't!'

'Curious, *nicht wahr?* I heard him say to Soames. 'There is a type of person to whom the very mention of my name is—oh-so-awfully-funny! In your theatres the dullest comédien needs only to say "The Devil!" and right away they give him "the loud laugh that speaks the vacant mind". Is it not so?'

I had now just breath enough to offer my apologies. He accepted them, but coldly, and readdressed himself to Soames.

'I am a man of business,' he said, 'and always I would put things through "right now", as they say in the States. You are a poet. *Les affaires*—you detest them. So be it. But with me you will deal, eh? What you have said just now gives me furiously to hope.'

Soames had not moved, except to light a fresh cigarette. He sat crouched forward, with his elbows squared on the table, and his head just above the level of his hands, staring up at the Devil. 'Go on,' he nodded. I had no remnant of laughter in me now.

'It will be the more pleasant, our little deal,' the Devil went on, 'because you are—I mistake not?—a Diabolist.'

'A Catholic Diabolist,' said Soames.

The Devil accepted the reservation genially. 'You wish,' he resumed, 'to visit now—this afternoon as-ever-is—the reading-room of the British Museum, yes? but of a hundred years hence, yes? *Parfaitement*. Time—an illusion. Past and future—they are as ever-present as the present, or at any rate only what you call "just-round-the-corner". I switch you on to any date. I project you—pouf! You wish to be in the reading-room just as it will be on the afternoon of June 3rd, 1997? You wish to find yourself standing in that room, just past the swing-doors, this very minute, yes? and to stay there till closing time? Am I right?'

Soames nodded.

The Devil looked at his watch. 'Ten past two,' he said. 'Closing time in summer same then as now: seven o'clock. That will give you almost five hours. At seven o'clock—pouf!—you find yourself again here, sitting at this table. I am dining to-night *dans le monde—dans le higlif*. That concludes my present visit to your great city. I come and fetch you here, Mr Soames, on my way home.'

'Home?' I echoed.

'Be it never so humble!' said the Devil lightly.

'All right,' said Soames.

'Soames!' I entreated. But my friend moved not a muscle.

The Devil had made as though to stretch forth his hand across the table and touch Soames' forearm; but he paused in his gesture.

'A hundred years hence, as now,' he smiled, 'no smoking allowed in the reading-room. You would better therefore—'

Soames removed the cigarette from his mouth and dropped it into his glass of Sauterne.

'Soames!' again I cried. 'Can't you'—but the Devil had now stretched forth his hand across the table. He brought it slowly down on the table-cloth. Soames' chair was empty. His cigarette floated sodden in his wine-glass. There was no other trace of him.

For a few moments the Devil let his hand rest where it lay, gazing at me out of the corners of his eyes, vulgarly triumphant.

A shudder shook me. With an effort I controlled myself and rose from my chair. 'Very clever,' I said condescendingly. 'But—*The Time Machine* is a delightful book, don't you think? So entirely original!'

'You are pleased to sneer,' said the Devil, who had also risen, 'but it is one thing to write about a not possible machine; it is a quite other thing to be a Supernatural Power.' All the same, I had scored.

Berthe had come forth at the sound of our rising. I explained to her that Mr Soames had been called away, and that both he and I would be dining here. It was not until I was out in the open air that I began to feel giddy. I have but the haziest recollection of what I did, where I wandered, in the glaring sunshine of that endless afternoon. I remember the sound of carpenters' hammers all along Piccadilly, and the bare chaotic look of the half-erected 'stands'. Was it in the Green Park, or in Kensington Gardens, or *where* was it that I sat on a chair beneath a tree, trying to read an evening paper? There was a phrase in the leading article that went on repeating itself in my fagged mind—'Little is hidden from this august Lady full of the garnered wisdom of sixty years of Sovereignty.' I remember wildly conceiving a letter (to reach Windsor by express messenger told to await answer):

'

> MADAM,—Well knowing that your Majesty is full of the garnered wisdom of sixty years of Sovereignty, I venture to ask your advice in the following delicate matter. Mr Enoch Soames, whose poems you may or may not know, …

Was there *no* way of helping him—saving him? A bargain was a bargain, and I was the last man to aid or abet any one in wriggling out of a reasonable obligation. I wouldn't have lifted a little finger to save Faust. But poor Soames!—doomed to pay without respite an eternal price for nothing but a fruitless search and a bitter disillusioning…

Odd and uncanny it seemed to me that he, Soames, in the flesh, in the waterproof cape, was at this moment living in the last decade of the next century, poring over books not yet written, and seeing and seen by men not yet born. Uncannier and odder still, that to-night and evermore he would be in Hell. Assuredly, truth was stranger than fiction.

Endless that afternoon was. Almost I wished I had gone with Soames—not indeed to stay in the reading-room, but to sally forth for a brisk sight-seeing walk around a new London. I wandered restlessly out of the Park I had sat in. Vainly I tried to imagine myself an ardent tourist from the eighteenth century. Intolerable was the strain of the slow-passing and empty minutes. Long before seven o'clock I was back at the Vingtième.

I sat there just where I had sat for luncheon. Air came in listlessly through the open door behind me. Now and again Rose or Berthe appeared for a moment. I had told them I would not order any dinner till Mr Soames came. A hurdy-gurdy began to play, abruptly drowning the noise of a quarrel between some Frenchmen further up the street. Whenever the tune was changed I heard the quarrel still raging. I had bought another evening paper on my way. I unfolded it. My eyes gazed ever away from it to the clock over the kitchen door…

Five minutes, now, to the hour! I remembered that clocks in restaurants are kept five minutes fast. I concentrated my eyes on the paper. I vowed I would not look away from it again. I held it upright, at its full width, close to my face, so that I had no view of anything but it… Rather a tremulous sheet? Only because of the draught, I told myself.

My arms gradually became stiff; they ached; but I could not drop them—now. I had a suspicion, I had a certainty. Well, what then?

...What else had I come for? Yet I held tight that barrier of newspaper. Only the sound of Berthe's brisk footstep from the kitchen enabled me, forced me, to drop it, and to utter:

'What shall we have to eat, Soames?'

'*Il est souffrant, ce pauvre Monsieur Soames?*' asked Berthe. 'He's only—tired.' I asked her to get some wine—Burgundy—and whatever food might be ready. Soames sat crouched forward against the table, exactly as when last I had seen him. It was as though he had never moved—he who had moved so unimaginably far. Once or twice in the afternoon it had for an instant occurred to me that perhaps his journey was not to be fruitless—that perhaps we had all been wrong in our estimate of the works of Enoch Soames. That we had been horribly right was horribly clear from the look of him. But 'Don't be discouraged,' I falteringly said. 'Perhaps it's only that you—didn't leave enough time. Two, three centuries hence, perhaps—'

'Yes,' his voice came. 'I've thought of that.'

'And now—now for the more immediate future! Where are you going to hide? How would it be if you caught the Paris express from Charing Cross? Almost an hour to spare. Don't go on to Paris. Stop at Calais. Live in Calais. He'd never think of looking for you in Calais.'

'It's like my luck,' he said, 'to spend my last hours on earth with an ass.' But I was not offended. 'And a treacherous ass,' he strangely added, tossing across to me a crumpled bit of paper which he had been holding in his hand. I glanced at the writing on it—some sort of gibberish, apparently. I laid it impatiently aside.

'Come, Soames! pull yourself together! This isn't a mere matter of life and death. It's a question of eternal torment, mind you! You don't mean to say you're going to wait limply here till the Devil comes to fetch you?'

'I can't do anything else. I've no choice.'

'Come! This is "trusting and encouraging" with a vengeance! This is Diabolism run mad!' I filled his glass with wine. 'Surely, now that you've *seen* the brute—'

'It's no good abusing him.'

'You must admit there's nothing Miltonic about him, Soames.'

'I don't say he's not rather different from what I expected.'

'He's a vulgarian, he's a swell-mobsman, he's the sort of man who hangs about the corridors of trains going to the Riviera and steals ladies' jewel-cases. Imagine eternal torment presided over by *him*!'

'You don't suppose I look forward to it, do you?'

'Then why not slip quietly out of the way?'

Again and again I filled his glass, and always, mechanically, he emptied it; but the wine kindled no spark of enterprise in him. He did not eat, and I myself ate hardly at all. I did not in my heart believe that any dash for freedom could save him. The chase would be swift, the capture certain. But better anything than this passive, meek, miserable waiting. I told Soames that for the honour of the human race he ought to make some show of resistance. He asked what the human race had ever done for him. 'Besides,' he said, 'can't you understand that I'm in his power? You saw him touch me, didn't you? There's an end of it. I've no will. I'm sealed.'

I made a gesture of despair. He went on repeating the word 'sealed'. I began to realize that the wine had clouded his brain. No wonder! Foodless he had gone into futurity, foodless he still was. I urged him to eat at any rate some bread. It was maddening to think that he, who had so much to tell, might tell nothing. 'How was it all,' I asked, 'yonder? Come! Tell me your adventures.'

'They'd make first-rate "copy", wouldn't they?'

'I'm awfully sorry for you, Soames, and I make all possible allowances; but what earthly right have you to insinuate that I should make "copy", as you call it, out of you?'

The poor fellow pressed his hands to his forehead. 'I don't know,' he said. 'I had some reason, I'm sure… I'll try to remember.'

'That's right. Try to remember everything. Eat a little more bread. What did the reading-room look like?'

'Much as usual,' he at length muttered.

'Many people there?'

'Usual sort of number.'

'What did they look like?'

Soames tried to visualize them. 'They all,' he presently remembered, 'looked very like one another.'

My mind took a fearsome leap. 'All dressed in Jaeger?'

'Yes. I think so. Greyish-yellowish stuff.'

'A sort of uniform?' He nodded. 'With a number on it, perhaps?—a number on a large disc of metal sewn on to the left sleeve? DKF 78,910—that sort of thing?' It was even so. 'And all of them—men and women alike—looking very well-cared-for? very Utopian? and smelling rather strongly of carbolic? and all of them quite hairless?' I was right every time. Soames was only not sure whether the men and women were hairless or shorn. 'I hadn't time to look at them very closely,' he explained.

'No, of course not. But—'

'They stared at *me*, I can tell you. I attracted a great deal of attention.' At last he had done that! 'I think I rather scared them. They moved away whenever I came near. They followed me about at a distance, wherever I went. The men at the round desk in the middle seemed to have a sort of panic whenever I went to make inquiries.'

'What did you do when you arrived?'

Well, he had gone straight to the catalogue, of course—to the S volumes, and had stood long before SN–SOF, unable to take this volume out of the shelf, because his heart was beating so... At first, he said, he wasn't disappointed—he only thought there was some new arrangement. He went to the middle desk and asked where the catalogue of twentieth-century books was kept. He gathered that there was still only one catalogue. Again he looked up his name, stared at the three little pasted slips he had known so well. Then he went and sat down for a long time...

'And then,' he droned, 'I looked up the *Dictionary of National Biography* and some encyclopaedias... I went back to the middle desk and asked what was the best modern book on late nineteenth-century literature. They told me Mr T. K. Nupton's book was considered the best. I looked it up in the catalogue and filled in a form for it. It was brought to me. My name wasn't in the index, but—Yes!' he said with a sudden change of tone. 'That's what I'd forgotten. Where's that bit of paper? Give it me back.'

I, too, had forgotten that cryptic screed. I found it fallen on the floor, and handed it to him.

He smoothed it out, nodding and smiling at me disagreeably. 'I found myself glancing through Nupton's book,' he resumed. 'Not very easy reading. Some sort of phonetic spelling... All the modern books I saw were phonetic.'

'Then I don't want to hear any more, Soames, please.'

'The proper names seemed all to be spelt in the old way. But for that, I mightn't have noticed my own name.'

'Your own name? Really? Soames, I'm *very* glad.'

'And yours.'

'No!'

'I thought I should find you waiting here to-night. So I took the trouble to copy out the passage. Read it.'

I snatched the paper. Soames' handwriting was characteristically dim. It, and the noisome spelling, and my excitement, made me all the slower to grasp what T. K. Nupton was driving at.

The document lies before me at this moment. Strange that the words I here copy out for you were copied out for me by poor Soames just seventy-eight years hence...

> From p. 234 of 'Inglish Littracher 1890–1900,' bi T. K. Nupton, published bi th Stait, 1992:
>
> Fr. egzarmpl, a riter ov th time, naimd Max Beerbohm, hoo woz stil alive in th twentieth senchri, rote a stauri in wich e pautraid an immajnari karrakter kauld 'Enoch Soames'—a thurd-rait poit hoo beleevz imself a grate jeneus an maix a bargin with th Devvl in auder ter no wot posterriti thinx ov im! It iz a sumwot labud sattire but not without vallu az showing hou seriusli the yung men ov th aiteen-ninetiz took themselvz. Nou that the littreri profeshn haz bin auganized az a department of publik servis, our riters hav found their levvl an hav lernt ter doo their duti without thort ov th morro. 'Th laibrer iz werthi ov hiz hire,' an that iz aul. Thank hevvn we hav no Enoch Soameses amung us to-dai!

I found that by murmuring the words aloud (a device which I commend to my reader) I was able to master them, little by little. The clearer they became, the greater was my bewilderment, my distress and horror. The whole thing was a nightmare. Afar, the great grisly background of what was in store for the poor dear art of letters; here, at the table, fixing on me a gaze that made me hot all over, the poor fellow whom—whom evidently... but no: whatever down-grade my character might take in coming years, I should never be such a brute as to—

Again I examined the screed. 'Immajnari'—but here Soames was, no more imaginary, alas! than I. And 'labud'—what on earth was that? (To this day, I have never made out that word.) 'It's all very—baffling,' I at length stammered.

Soames said nothing, but cruelly did not cease to look at me.

'Are you sure,' I temporized, 'quite sure you copied the thing out correctly?'

'Quite.'

'Well, then it's this wretched Nupton who must have made—must be going to make—some idiotic mistake... Look here, Soames! you know me better than to suppose that I... After all, the name "Max Beerbohm" is not at all an uncommon one, and there must be several Enoch Soameses running around—or rather, "Enoch Soames" is a name that might occur to any one writing a story. And I don't write stories: I'm an essayist, an observer, a recorder... I admit that it's an extraordinary coincidence. But you must see—'

'I see the whole thing,' said Soames quietly. And he added, with a touch of his old manner, but with more dignity than I had ever known in him, '*Parlons d'autre chose.*'

I accepted that suggestion very promptly. I returned straight to the more immediate future. I spent most of the long evening in renewed appeals to Soames to slip away and seek refuge somewhere. I remember saying at last that if indeed I was destined to write about him, the supposed 'stauri' had better have at least a happy ending. Soames repeated those last three words in a tone of intense scorn. 'In Life and in Art,' he said, 'all that matters is an *inevitable* ending.'

'But,' I urged, more hopefully than I felt, 'an ending that can be avoided *isn't* inevitable.'

'You aren't an artist,' he rasped. 'And you're so hopelessly not an artist that, so far from being able to imagine a thing and make it seem true, you're going to make even a true thing seem as if you'd made it up. You're a miserable bungler. And it's like my luck.'

I protested that the miserable bungler was not I—was not going to be I—but T. K. Nupton; and we had a rather heated argument, in the thick of which it suddenly seemed to me that Soames saw he was in the wrong: he had quite physically cowered. But I wondered why—and now I guessed with a cold throb just why—he stared so, past me. The bringer of that 'inevitable ending' filled the doorway.

I managed to turn in my chair and to say, not without a semblance of lightness, 'Aha, come in!' Dread was indeed rather blunted in me by his looking so absurdly like a villain in a melodrama. The sheen of his tilted hat and of his shirtfront, the repeated twists he was giving to his moustache, and most of all the magnificence of his sneer, gave token that he was there only to be foiled.

He was at our table in a stride. 'I am sorry,' he sneered witheringly, 'to break up your pleasant party, but—'

'You don't: you complete it,' I assured him. 'Mr Soames and I want to have a little talk with you. Won't you sit? Mr Soames got nothing—frankly nothing—by his journey this afternoon. We don't wish to say that the whole thing was a swindle—a common swindle. On the contrary, we believe you meant well. But of course the bargain, such as it was, is off.'

The Devil gave no verbal answer. He merely looked at Soames and pointed with rigid forefinger to the door. Soames was wretchedly rising from his chair when, with a desperate quick gesture, I swept together two dinner-knives that were on the table, and laid their blades across each other. The Devil stepped sharp back against the table behind him, averting his face and shuddering.

'You are not superstitious!' he hissed.

'Not at all,' I smiled.

'Soames!' he said as to an underling, but without turning his face, 'put those knives straight!'

With an inhibitive gesture to my friend, 'Mr Soames,' I said emphatically to the Devil, 'is a *Catholic* Diabolist'; but my poor friend did the Devil's bidding, not mine; and now, with his master's eyes again fixed on him, he arose, he shuffled past me. I tried to speak. It was he that spoke. 'Try,' was the prayer he threw back at me as the Devil pushed him roughly out through the door, '*try* to make them know that I did exist!'

In another instant I too was through that door. I stood staring all ways—up the street, across it, down it. There was moonlight and lamplight, but there was not Soames nor that other.

Dazed, I stood there. Dazed, I turned back, at length, into the little room; and I suppose I paid Berthe or Rose for my dinner and luncheon, and for Soames': I hope so, for I never went to the Vingtième again. Ever since that night I have avoided Greek Street altogether. And for years I did not set foot even in Soho Square, because on that same night it was there that I paced and loitered, long and long, with some such dull sense of hope as a man has in not straying far from the place where he has lost something… 'Round and round the shutter'd Square'—that line came back to me on my lonely beat, and with it the whole stanza, ringing in my brain and bearing in on me how tragically different from the happy scene imagined by him was the poet's actual experience of that prince in whom of all princes we should put not our trust.

But—strange how the mind of an essayist, be it never so stricken, roves and ranges!—I remember pausing before a wide doorstep and wondering if perchance it was on this very one that the young De Quincey lay ill and faint while poor Ann flew as fast as her feet would carry her to Oxford Street, the 'stony-hearted stepmother' of them both, and came back bearing that 'glass of port wine and spices' but for which he might, so he thought, actually have died. Was this the very doorstep that the old De Quincey used to revisit in homage? I pondered Ann's fate, the cause of her sudden vanishing from the ken of her boy-friend; and presently I blamed myself for letting the past over-ride the present. Poor vanished Soames!

And for myself, too, I began to be troubled. What had I better do? Would there be a hue and cry—Mysterious Disappearance of an Author, and all that? He had last been seen lunching and dining in my company. Hadn't I better get a hansom and drive straight to Scotland Yard? …They would think I was a lunatic. After all, I reassured myself, London was a very large place, and one very dim figure might easily drop out of it unobserved—now especially, in the blinding glare of the near Jubilee. Better say nothing at all, I thought.

And I was right. Soames' disappearance made no stir at all. He was utterly forgotten before any one, so far as I am aware, noticed that he was no longer hanging around. Now and again some poet or prosaist may have said to another, 'What has become of that man Soames?' but I never heard any such question asked. The solicitor through whom he was paid his annuity may be presumed to have made inquiries, but no echo of these resounded. There was something rather ghastly to me in the general unconsciousness that Soames had existed, and more than once I caught myself wondering whether Nupton, that babe unborn, were going to be right in thinking him a figment of my brain.

In that extract from Nupton's repulsive book there is one point which perhaps puzzles you. How is it that the author, though I have here mentioned him by name and have quoted the exact words he is going to write, is not going to grasp the obvious corollary that I have invented nothing? The answer can but be this: Nupton will not have read the later passages of this memoir. Such lack of thoroughness is a serious fault in any one who undertakes to do scholar's work. And I hope these words will meet the eye of some contemporary rival to Nupton and be the undoing of Nupton.

I like to think that some time between 1992 and 1997 somebody will have looked up this memoir, and will have forced on the world his inevitable and startling conclusions. And I have reasons for believing that this will be so. You realize that the reading-room into which Soames was projected by the Devil was in all respects precisely as it will be on the afternoon of June 3rd, 1997. You realize, therefore, that on that afternoon, when it comes round, there the self-same crowd will be, and there Soames too will be, punctually, he and they doing precisely what they did before. Recall now Soames' account of the sensation he made. You may say that the mere difference of his costume was enough to make him sensational in that uniformed crowd. You wouldn't say so if you had ever seen him. I assure you that in no period could Soames be anything but dim. The fact that people are going to stare at him, and follow him around, and seem afraid of him, can be explained only on the hypothesis that they will somehow have been prepared for his ghostly visitation. They will have been awfully waiting to see whether he really would come. And when he does come the effect will of course be—awful.

An authentic, guaranteed, proven ghost, but—only a ghost, alas! Only that. In his first visit, Soames was a creature of flesh and blood, whereas the creatures into whose midst he was projected were but ghosts, I take it—solid, palpable, vocal, but unconscious and automatic ghosts, in a building that was itself an illusion. Next time, that building and those creatures will be real. It is of Soames that there will be but the semblance. I wish I could think him destined to revisit the world actually, physically, consciously. I wish he had this one brief escape, this one small treat, to look forward to. I never forget him for long. He is where he is, and forever. The more rigid moralists among you may say he has only himself to blame. For my part, I think he has been very hardly used. It is well that vanity should be chastened; and Enoch Soames' vanity was, I admit, above the average, and called for special treatment. But there was no need for vindictiveness. You say he contracted to pay the price he is paying; yes; but I maintain that he was induced to do so by fraud. Well-informed in all things, the Devil must have known that my friend would gain nothing by his visit to futurity. The whole thing was a very shabby trick. The more I think of it, the more detestable the Devil seems to me.

Of him I have caught sight several times, here and there, since that day at the Vingtième. Only once, however, have I seen him at close quarters. This was in Paris. I was walking, one afternoon, along the Rue d'Antin, when I saw him advancing from the opposite direction—over-dressed as ever, and swinging an ebony cane, and altogether behaving as though the whole pavement belonged to him. At thought of Enoch Soames and the myriads of other sufferers eternally in this brute's dominion, a great cold wrath filled me, and I drew myself up to my full height. But—well, one is so used to nodding and smiling in the street to anybody whom one knows, that the action becomes almost independent of oneself: to prevent it requires a very sharp effort and great presence of mind. I was miserably aware, as I passed the Devil, that I nodded and smiled to him. And my shame was the deeper and hotter because he, if you please, stared straight at me with the utmost haughtiness.

To be cut—deliberately cut—by *him*! I was, I still am, furious at having had that happen to me.

THE MARK ON THE WALL

Virginia Woolf

Perhaps it was the middle of January in the present year that I first looked up and saw the mark on the wall. In order to fix a date it is necessary to remember what one saw. So now I think of the fire; the steady film of yellow light upon the page of my book; the three chrysanthemums in the round glass bowl on the mantelpiece. Yes, it must have been the winter time, and we had just finished our tea, for I remember that I was smoking a cigarette when I looked up and saw the mark on the wall for the first time. I looked up through the smoke of my cigarette and my eye lodged for a moment upon the burning coals, and that old fancy of the crimson flag flapping from the castle tower came into my mind, and I thought of the cavalcade of red knights riding up the side of the black rock. Rather to my relief the sight of the mark interrupted the fancy, for it is an old fancy, an automatic fancy, made as a child perhaps. The mark was a small round mark, black upon the white wall, about six or seven inches above the mantelpiece.

How readily our thoughts swarm upon a new object, lifting it a little way, as ants carry a blade of straw so feverishly, and then leave it... If that mark was made by a nail, it can't have been for a picture, it must have been for a miniature—the miniature of a lady with white powdered curls, powder-dusted cheeks, and lips like red carnations. A fraud of course, for the people who had this house before us would have chosen pictures in that way—an old picture for an old room. That is the sort of people they were—very interesting people, and I think of them so often, in such queer places, because one will never see them again, never know what happened next. They wanted to leave this house because they wanted to change their style of furniture, so he said, and he was in process of saying that in his opinion art should have ideas behind it when we were torn asunder, as one is torn from the old lady about to pour out tea and the young man about to hit the tennis ball in the back garden of the suburban villa as one rushes past in the train.

But as for that mark, I'm not sure about it; I don't believe it was made by a nail after all; it's too big, too round, for that. I might get up, but if I got up and looked at it, ten to one I shouldn't be able to say for certain; because once a thing's done, no one ever knows how it happened. Oh! Dear me, the mystery of life; The inaccuracy of thought! The ignorance of humanity! To show how very little control of our possessions we have—what an accidental affair this living is after all our civilization—let me just count over a few of the things lost in one lifetime, beginning, for that seems always the most mysterious of losses—what cat would gnaw, what rat would nibble—three pale blue canisters of book-binding tools? Then there were the bird cages, the iron hoops, the steel skates, the Queen Anne coal-scuttle, the bagatelle board, the hand organ—all gone, and jewels, too. Opals and emeralds, they lie about the roots of turnips. What a scraping paring affair it is to be sure! The wonder is that I've any clothes on my back, that I sit surrounded by solid furniture at this moment. Why, if one wants to compare life to anything, one must liken it to being blown through the Tube at fifty miles an hour—landing at the other end without a single hairpin in one's hair! Shot out at the feet of God entirely naked! Tumbling head over heels in the asphodel meadows like brown paper parcels pitched down a shoot in the post office! With one's hair flying back like the tail of a race-horse. Yes, that seems to express the rapidity of life, the perpetual waste and repair; all so casual, all so haphazard...

But after life. The slow pulling down of thick green stalks so that the cup of the flower, as it turns over, deluges one with purple and red light. Why, after all, should one not be born there as one is born here, helpless, speechless, unable to focus one's eyesight, groping at the roots of the grass, at the toes of the Giants? As for saying which are trees, and which are men and women, or whether there are such things, that one won't be in a condition to do for fifty years or so. There will be nothing but spaces of light and dark, intersected by thick stalks, and rather higher up perhaps, rose-shaped blots of an indistinct colour—dim pinks and blues—which will, as time goes on, become more definite, become—I don't know what...

And yet that mark on the wall is not a hole at all. It may even be caused by some round black substance, such as a small rose leaf, left over from the summer, and I, not being a very vigilant housekeeper—look at the dust on the mantelpiece, for example, the dust which, so they say, buried Troy three times over, only fragments of pots utterly refusing annihilation, as one can believe.

The tree outside the window taps very gently on the pane... I want to think quietly, calmly, spaciously, never to be interrupted, never to have to rise from my chair, to slip easily from one thing to another, without any sense of hostility, or obstacle. I want to sink deeper and deeper, away from the surface, with its hard separate facts. To steady myself, let me catch hold of the first idea that passes... Shakespeare... Well, he will do as well as another. A man who sat himself solidly in an arm-chair, and looked into the fire, so—A shower of ideas fell perpetually from some very high Heaven down through his mind. He leant his forehead on his hand, and people, looking in through the open door,—for this scene is supposed to take place on a summer's evening—But how dull this is, this historical fiction! It doesn't interest me at all. I wish I could hit upon a pleasant track of thought, a track indirectly reflecting credit upon myself, for those are the pleasantest thoughts, and very frequent even in the minds of modest mouse-coloured people, who believe genuinely that they dislike to hear their own praises. They are not thoughts directly praising oneself; that is the beauty of them; they are thoughts like this:

'And then I came into the room. They were discussing botany. I said how I'd seen a flower growing on a dust heap on the site of an old house in Kingsway. The seed, I said, must have been sown in the reign of Charles the First. What flowers grew in the reign of Charles the First? I asked—(but I don't remember the answer). Tall flowers with purple tassels to them perhaps. And so it goes on. All the time I'm dressing up the figure of myself in my own mind, lovingly, stealthily, not openly adoring it, for if I did that, I should catch myself out, and stretch my hand at once for a book in self-protection. Indeed, it is curious how instinctively one protects the image of oneself from idolatry or any other handling that could make it ridiculous, or too unlike the original to be believed in any longer. Or is it not so very curious after all? It is a matter of great importance. Suppose the looking glass smashes, the image disappears, and the romantic figure with the green of forest depths all about it is there no longer, but only that shell of a person which is seen by other people—what an airless, shallow, bald, prominent world it becomes! A world not to be lived in. As we face each other in omnibuses and underground railways we are looking into the mirror; that accounts for the vagueness, the gleam of glassiness, in our eyes. And the novelists in future will realize more and more the importance of these reflections, for of course there is not one reflection but an almost infinite number; those are the depths they will explore, those the phantoms they will pursue, leaving the description of reality more and more out of their stories, taking a knowledge of it for granted, as the Greeks did and Shakespeare perhaps—but these generalizations are very worthless. The military sound of the word is enough. It recalls leading articles, cabinet ministers—a whole class of things indeed which as a child one thought the thing itself, the standard thing, the real thing, from which one could not depart save at the risk of nameless damnation. Generalizations bring back somehow Sunday in London, Sunday afternoon walks, Sunday luncheons, and also ways of speaking of the dead, clothes, and habits—like the habit of sitting all together in one room until a certain hour, although nobody liked it. There was a rule for everything. The rule for tablecloths at that particular period was that they should be made of tapestry with little yellow compartments marked upon them, such as you may see in photographs of the carpets in the corridors of the royal palaces. Tablecloths of a different kind were not real tablecloths. How shocking, and yet how wonderful it was to discover that these real things, Sunday luncheons, Sunday walks, country houses, and tablecloths were not entirely real, were indeed half phantoms, and the damnation which visited the disbeliever in them was only a sense of illegitimate freedom. What now takes the place of those things I wonder, those real standard things? Men perhaps, should you be a woman; the masculine point of view which governs our lives, which sets the standard, which establishes Whitaker's Table of Precedency, which has become, I suppose, since the war half a phantom to many men and women, which soon, one may hope, will be laughed into the dustbin where the phantoms go, the mahogany sideboards and the Landseer prints, Gods and Devils, Hell and so forth, leaving us all with an intoxicating sense of illegitimate freedom—if freedom exists...

In certain lights that mark on the wall seems actually to project from the wall. Nor is it entirely circular. I cannot be sure, but it seems to cast a perceptible shadow, suggesting that if I ran my finger down that strip of the wall it would, at a certain point, mount and descend a small tumulus, a smooth tumulus like those barrows on the South Downs which are, they say, either tombs or camps. Of the two I should prefer them to be tombs, desiring melancholy like most English people, and finding it natural at the end of a walk to think of the bones stretched beneath the turf... There must be some book about it. Some antiquary must have dug up those bones and given them a name... What sort of a man is an antiquary, I wonder? Retired Colonels for the most part, I daresay, leading parties of aged labourers to the top here, examining clods of earth and stone, and getting into correspondence with the neighbouring clergy, which, being opened at breakfast time, gives them a feeling of importance, and the comparison of arrow-heads necessitates cross-country journeys to the county towns, an agreeable necessity both to them and to their elderly wives, who wish to make plum jam or to clean out the study, and have every reason for keeping that great question of the camp or the tomb in perpetual suspension, while the Colonel himself feels agreeably philosophic in accumulating evidence on both sides of the question. It is true that he does finally incline to believe in the camp; and, being opposed, indites a pamphlet which he is about to read at the quarterly meeting of the local society when a stroke lays him low, and his last conscious thoughts are not of wife or child, but of the camp and that arrowhead there, which is now in the case at the local museum, together with the foot of a Chinese murderess, a handful of Elizabethan nails, a great many Tudor clay pipes, a piece of Roman pottery, and the wine-glass that Nelson drank out of—proving I really don't know what.

No, no, nothing is proved, nothing is known. And if I were to get up at this very moment and ascertain that the mark on the wall is really—what shall we say?—the head of a gigantic old nail, driven in two hundred years ago, which has now, owing to the patient attrition of many generations of housemaids, revealed its head above the coat of paint, and is taking its first view of modern life in the sight of a white-walled fire-lit room, what should I gain?—Knowledge? Matter for further speculation? I can think sitting still as well as standing up. And what is knowledge? What are our learned men save the descendants of witches and hermits who crouched in caves and in woods brewing herbs, interrogating shrew-mice and writing down the language of the stars? And the less we honour them as our superstitions dwindle and our respect for beauty and health of mind increases... Yes, one could imagine a very pleasant world. A quiet, spacious world, with the flowers so red and blue in the open fields. A world without professors or specialists or house-keepers with the profiles of policemen, a world which one could slice with one's thought as a fish slices the water with his fin, grazing the stems of the water-lilies, hanging suspended over nests of white sea eggs... How peaceful it is down here, rooted in the centre of the world and gazing up through the grey waters, with their sudden gleams of light, and their reflections—if it were not for Whitaker's Almanack—if it were not for the Table of Precedency!

I must jump up and see for myself what that mark on the wall really is—a nail, a rose-leaf, a crack in the wood?

Here is nature once more at her old game of self-preservation. This train of thought, she perceives, is threatening mere waste of energy, even some collision with reality, for who will ever be able to lift a finger against Whitaker's Table of Precedency? The Archbishop of Canterbury is followed by the Lord High Chancellor; the Lord High Chancellor is followed by the Archbishop of York. Everybody follows somebody, such is the philosophy of Whitaker; and the great thing is to know who follows whom. Whitaker knows, and let that, so Nature counsels, comfort you, instead of enraging you; and if you can't be comforted, if you must shatter this hour of peace, think of the mark on the wall.

I understand Nature's game—her prompting to take action as a way of ending any thought that threatens to excite or to pain. Hence, I suppose, comes our slight contempt for men of action—men, we assume, who don't think. Still, there's no harm in putting a full stop to one's disagreeable thoughts by looking at a mark on the wall.

Indeed, now that I have fixed my eyes upon it, I feel that I have grasped a plank in the sea; I feel a satisfying sense of reality which at once turns the two Archbishops and the Lord High Chancellor to the shadows of shades. Here is something definite, something real. Thus, waking from a midnight dream of horror, one hastily turns on the light and lies quiescent, worshipping the chest of drawers, worshipping solidity, worshipping reality, worshipping the impersonal world which is a proof of some existence other than ours. That is what one wants to be sure of... Wood is a pleasant thing to think about. It comes from a tree; and trees grow, and we don't know how they grow. For years and years they grow, without paying any attention to us, in meadows, in forests, and by the side of rivers—all things one likes to think about. The cows swish their tails beneath them on hot afternoons; they paint rivers so green that when a moorhen dives one expects to see its feathers all green when it comes up again. I like to think of the fish balanced against the stream like flags blown out; and of water-beetles slowly raising domes of mud upon the bed of the river. I like to think of the tree itself: first the close dry sensation of being wood; then the grinding of the storm; then the slow, delicious ooze of sap. I like to think of it, too, on winter's nights standing in the empty field with all leaves close-furled, nothing tender exposed to the iron bullets of the moon, a naked mast upon an earth that goes tumbling, tumbling, all night long. The song of birds must sound very loud and strange in June; and how cold the feet of insects must feel upon it, as they make laborious progresses up the creases of the bark, or sun themselves upon the thin green awning of the leaves, and look straight in front of them with diamond-cut red eyes... One by one the fibres snap beneath the immense cold pressure of the earth, then the last storm comes and, falling, the highest branches drive deep into the ground again. Even so, life isn't done with; there are a million patient, watchful lives still for a tree, all over the world, in bedrooms, in ships, on the pavement, lining rooms, where men and women sit after tea, smoking cigarettes. It is full of peaceful thoughts, happy thoughts, this tree. I should like to take each one separately—but something is getting in the way... Where was I? What has it all been about? A tree? A river? The Downs? Whitaker's Almanack? The fields of asphodel? I can't remember a thing. Everything's moving, falling, slipping, vanishing... There is a vast upheaval of matter. Someone is standing over me and saying—

'I'm going out to buy a newspaper.'

'Yes?'

'Though it's no good buying newspapers... Nothing ever happens. Curse this war; God damn this war! ...All the same, I don't see why we should have a snail on our wall.'

Ah, the mark on the wall! It was a snail.

THE LETTER

Viola Meynell

There came a day when it was realized at the farm that Jessie was no longer working. It was this that brought the truth of her condition suddenly forward, as nothing else had done, into the full glare of recognition and disapproval. Until now it had been lurking in the background, half ignored, or at least postponed in the perpetually behind-hand pressure of farm life. For some time she had been slackening off; she gave no helping hand at the anxious time of harvest, and at last she stopped milking, with inconceivable inconvenience. In that work-ridden household the matter had at last become prominent and disastrous. George Troubridge evidently thought that by setting her to tasks different from those to which she was accustomed he could still draw service out of his daughter. His wife in similar circumstances always worked right up to the end. But all the same, it was his wife who now defended the girl from the necessity to perform these tasks, telling him sharply that he could see for himself that she wasn't fit for work. Never, however, was a defence more coldly put forward, purely on its merits, and without a touch of personal bias in Jessie's favour. This protection of her by her mother was like the cold intervention of the law against some popular act of mob justice.

Once made a conspicuous question, therefore, the whole matter emerged out of its silence. 'Something'll have to be done,' said George Troubridge. Repeating this several times, the necessity took a more definite form in his mind. 'She'll have to write to him and tell him,' he said doggedly. 'I don't care who he is, he's got to be told. You'll have to make her sit down and write to him,' he said to his wife in the presence of the girl; and Jessie's sudden flood of tears at that pronouncement only made him more certain that he was right.

At first it was just a blow dealt her by her father, but presently it became something gradually closing her in on every side—that she must write. No matter how often her father or mother repeated it, the effect on Jessie was the same—one stiff, frightened look and she was dissolved in tears which made her eyes swollen for hours. So that even when the subject might have been laid aside for a time—as everything but death gets laid aside for the immediate task in farm life—people were constantly being reminded of it by the sight of the girl's tear-stained face.

As she was no longer driven here and there by her work, and had strange free-time to dispose of, she began to spend hours in the fields and woods, and there at any rate she could feel a little removed from the necessity to write her letter. But how odd an inhabitant she felt of the familiar places! She was nearly eighteen, and had never lived anywhere else, and yet she felt a stranger now. Everything was new to her. There was one thing that she had never considered in the past about the roads and paths her feet used to cover so swiftly and lightly, and that was whether they were up or downhill. The country had been all flat beneath her swift, untiring feet. Now it rose and fell in so marked a way that this seemed to be the most noticeable thing about it. The slightest gradient shortened her breath and reminded her of her distress and weakness. As for all the village girls who could move quickly and lightly, she still might be their contemporary, but she was no longer of their kind; she was of an age and kind all to herself. She was more like an old man she met creeping up the lane than like those who used to be her playmates.

One day when she came down pale in the early morning her father, pressed by the excess of things to do, just found time, amidst all his preparations for market, to be fretted intolerably by the sight of her uselessness.

'Have you written that letter?' he asked.

'No.'

'Then you'll write it today! You've got plenty of time on your hands, by the look of it.' He slammed the door—all his useful work on one side of it, all her useless tears on the other.

She did what she could to help her mother through her tears; but Mrs Troubridge, busy giving the younger children their breakfast, and nursing in her arms the youngest of all, seemed to Jessie silently to repeat her father's command, if only because she had been present when it was made and had heard it and had not contradicted it. The very children by their mere complacence were of the same mind as their father. The servant-girl, because she had run so quickly to fetch his leggings when he asked for them, was obviously of his mind.

She felt alone with the impossibility that confronted her. With dismay she watched her mother. Mrs Troubridge reached down from a shelf a box that for years had contained a few pieces of best note-paper, and laid one of the sheets, almost as thick as blotting-paper, and with fretted edges, on the table for Jessie. The girl gave one helpless look at it and went out.

It had not rained, and yet when her arm touched a low branch heavy drops hung on her sleeve. No surface was exempt from the drenching wet. Even the tiny scarlet field-poppy, with petals so flimsy that they seemed to be made of nothing but light and redness, had to support a layer of moisture. The sun, wherever it was, could do nothing; it was one of those autumn days of dew and mist too heavy to lift, when midday is no lighter than dawn.

Jessie walked slowly, breathing hard. Her thin face, in which the youth and beauty should have been so full of flitting subtle things to say, had now the simplest and singlest look in the world, the look of suffering. It was not mental strain that marked her; she had not lived long enough to be marked by the kind of trouble that writes slowly on young faces. But her body's woes, with their much quicker signals, had reduced all the sparkle to languor, and she was a pale, haggard beauty instead of a fresh rosy one.

She had not walked far through the first field before each of her ankles was bound round and round with threads of moist cobweb, spun between one stalk and another. If those threads had been cords, she would have been a close prisoner, neatly caught and fastened up. But as it was she went idly through the stubble, unconscious that with each step she was bursting bonds, dragging chains, and escaping a thousand prisons. From the bonds and prisons she was conscious of there was no escape. She knew that the letter must be written, for her father was determined.

The knowledge that she must write overwhelmed her with simple, mystified dismay. What could she say to him? She had said so little to him at any time—never anything that was not timid and shy, and breathed out wildly and gently on the secret pulses of love. When her father said angrily, 'You'll write to him and tell him!' she seemed to have a hard harangue of threats and disgrace and retribution thrust upon her with which to speak to him, instead of those soft broken flowers of speech which were all that she could remember or imagine with him; and her mind and heart were powerless and refused.

She was out as long as possible that day, until clinging round each of her ankles was such a mass of the threads of cobweb that they seemed woven into soft grey fabric. The day faded away early from the light it had never really seemed to attain. When evening came she was at home getting the younger children to bed, while downstairs the evening that awaited her held nothing but her father's homecoming, and the sheet of note-paper lying on the table.

After supper her father asked the dreaded question, which her mother answered for her.

'No, she hasn't written yet.'

'She's got to do as she's told, do you hear?'

'Yes, the girl knows that.'

'Then why hasn't she done it?'

Mrs Troubridge explained.

'She says she doesn't know what to say.'

George Troubridge took this in slowly. His silence continued to listen to the words after they were spoken; it also allowed the difficulty, though without acknowledging that he was himself beaten by it. He was sitting at his ease in the cosy lamp-lit room, but his hard limbs seemed to be so stiff-shaped as to be beyond the comfortable ministrations of the arm-chair. Two of the elder children were playing cards at the table. Their Aunt Isabel, whose status in the house as Mrs Troubridge's sister gave her the privilege of doing twice as much work as any maid, came and sat down with her mending. But because the younger children were in bed, and the indoor man gone to his quarters, and the hour come when it was unlikely that George Troubridge would be interrupted again that night, a suitable degree of privacy seemed to have been achieved.

'She doesn't know what to say, doesn't she?' began Mr Troubridge. 'Oh, so she doesn't know what to say,' he repeated, gaining time. Sudden inspiration came to him. 'Well, then, let her tell him he's got her into trouble and he'll have to do something about it. Let her tell him that.'

'Yes, and she must tell him a man might be the highest in the land, but it doesn't excuse him,' said his wife, catching the inspiration herself. 'And she must say he'll never have any rest to his mind nor enjoy any of his blessings unless he does something for her and the child,' she proclaimed doubtfully.

Each time they stopped speaking Jessie made a faint movement, not a reply, but something more dutiful than absolute stillness would have been. Her downcast eyes and helpless mouth just stirred—a faint, dumb, despairing signal of obedience.

'So you don't know what to say, don't you?' said George Troubridge once more. 'Well, then tell him that what with dear labour and cheap corn, and what with the taxes, and the market flooded with imports, you might say I'm a ruined man. You tell him that. And the harder I work, the more money I lose, by the look of it,' he grumbled. 'And so it's going on, by what I can see. And it isn't likely I'm going to pay for his wrong-doing. That's what you've got to tell him.'

'And tell him,' said Mrs Troubridge, 'that you've had a bad time with it so far, shocking bad; and that you've been as good as useless in the house for some time past.'

'And you must say,' came from Mrs Troubridge's hard-worked sister, startling them all with unexpectedness, 'that a man should do everything in his power to atone for such wickedness—yes, everything, and then he could never do enough.' Her face was flushed and her eyes bright with indignation.

This outburst closed the subject; anything added at that moment would have been an anticlimax, and no further material for Jessie's letter was supplied to her that night.

But when she woke up the next morning she knew that the letter had come closer, and she did not see how she could avoid writing it that day.

That night her father asked:

'Has she written to him?'

'No, she hasn't exactly written yet,' replied her mother.

'Then why hasn't she?'

'Well, she didn't really know if that's all she has to say.'

He reflected.

'She can tell him I've always been a fair man myself, and I look for fair treatment from others. But there's no fairness in how this is! None at all! And she's got to let him know it.'

Another day went by and when evening came the sight of her immediately reminded her father.

'Has she done what she's told?' he asked.

'Not yet,' said her mother, 'but now that she knows what she's got to say, she'll be writing. I was just wondering whether that's all, or whether there's anything else she ought to add.'

They meditated, with the slightly pleasant consciousness that the execution of this disagreeable duty did at any rate provide the opportunity to distinguish oneself by the value of the ideas one contributed to the letter. It was to Mrs Troubridge that the honours fell this evening.

'I was thinking,' she said, 'that she might also put that a girl's fair name is her all, and that once she's lost that she's lost everything.'

'Yes,' said Mr Troubridge, 'she can put a piece about that if she likes.'

Jessie went out the next day to wander in her father's big fields. Today only the early morning was misty, and the dark-gold sun of autumn shone powerfully, scattering the vapours. The fields were of an unusual size; it would seem at first as if this were a wide undivided sweep of tilled land, until far away could be seen the hedges that squared-in the vast spaces and made them, after all, into fields—but such fields as required a mammoth sowing, and made large ricks and filled great barns. Passing into one of these fields with her tired distressed walk, Jessie could hardly see its limits. For one of those great fields was large enough to contain rises and falls, to hold not only the deeply coloured sunshine close around her, but also the mists of autumn in its distant parts. When afternoon came she and the red setting sun stood in the same field, at either end of it.

In the grandeur and spaciousness of the day her thoughts passed beyond her immediate preoccupation, and opened her mind to memories and to faint thrills of the future. Earlier in the day she had thought she would have done best to stay at home in the arm-chair. But as she wandered her weariness passed away for once. She entered a field that from the gate was nothing but monotonous stubble from end to end; she came out of the same field with her hands full of bright yellow and white and purple wild-flowers gathered from the profusion lurking in that colourless stubble. She passed into a little wood, and came out of it with her face bright, leaving it lingeringly as if she had never wished to leave it again. And then when she could delay no longer she turned her footsteps toward home.

Going indoors she saw the sheet of letter-paper lying where it had waited so long for her. With a leap of her heart she knew she was to write to him, and she sat at the table and took up the pen.

Do not be angry at getting these few lines from one you have perhaps forgotten now you are so far away. It is because I had such a happy day, and it seems as if I am speaking to you now. Excuse me for telling you what a joyful thing happened today. I passed through Hayter's copse where I lost the bracelet you gave me and where we searched so long. I've spent many an hour looking for it since then, but after all these months I found it today at my feet in some moss.

I went also by the lane where you sprained your ankle, and how I wish with all my heart you had never had that pain to bear and need never know what it is to suffer pain. If these few lines could bring you a hundredth part of what I wish you would be happy for always.

JESSIE

That evening her father, when he came indoors and settled himself in his arm-chair, said:

'Has the girl written that letter yet?'

'Yes,' said her mother, 'she's written.'

'She has written? Oh well, never mind. Only I was going to tell her another bit to put in if she hadn't written yet. Here I've been to market today with the pigs and the chicken and had a terrible bad trade; they didn't make much above what they cost me to rear. How's that going to pay for extra expenses? And what's the good of me going out to earn sixpence if she stops at home and spends a shilling! Just let her tell him that!'

'Yes, but the letter's written,' his wife reminded him.

'So it is. Well, then, let Tom slip along to the cross-roads and catch the postman with it.'